CHEYNEY FOX

Also by Roberta Latow

Three Rivers
Tidal Wave
Soft Warm Rain
This Stream of Dreams
White Moon Black Sea

CHEYNEY FOX

Roberta Latow

HEADLINE

First published in 1990
by HEADLINE BOOK PUBLISHING PLC

10 9 8 7 6 5 4 3 2 1

Poem on page vii reprinted from *The Collected Poems of
C.P. Cavafy* edited by George Savidis, translated by Edmund
Keeley and Philip Sherrard, by kind permission of Chatto
& Windus and The Hogarth Press Ltd and the estate of
C.P. Cavafy

British Library Cataloguing in Publication Data

Latow, Roberta
Cheyney fox.
I. Title
813.54 [F]

ISBN 0-7472-0115-3

Typeset in 11/12¾ pt Plantin
by Colset Private Limited, Singapore

Printed and bound in Great Britain by
Richard Clay Ltd, Bungay, Suffolk

HEADLINE BOOK PUBLISHING PLC
Headline House,
79 Great Titchfield Street
London W1P 7FN

For
John Mann, Ted Carey, Peter Jacobs
who were there for me then
and
Donald Munson
who is here for me now

It does not bother me if outside
winter spreads fog, clouds, and cold.
Spring is within me, true joy.
Laughter is a sun ray, all pure gold,
there is no other garden like love,
the warmth of song melts all the snows.

Cavafy

NEW YORK
AUTUMN 1988

Chapter 1

The New York law firm of Dewey, Chapin & Rosewarne was definitely prestigious, and David Rosewarne was everything a woman in distress could want in a lawyer: Jewish Ivy League from his Brooks Brothers button-down shirt to every consonant or vowel he uttered. His baldness was not unattractive, sensuous even, combined with the handsome face and the intelligent, observant manner. He wore conservatism and the law like a suit of shining armour.

The troubled woman was Cheyney Fox, mega-wealthy member of international high society and celebrated art dealer. Famous for her beauty, the power she wielded in the world's art markets, and for being the widow of Kurt Walbrook, art collector and philanthropist *extraordinaire*. An erudite, sexy lady, jetting around in a champagne world of dazzling good times on the arm of men in high places.

He was bound to look older but how very personable David still was. It took her by surprise. Faint memories of him back in the sixties became instantly vivid. That had been a crushing time in her life. It had proved to be a turning-point in his. They had had their victories as lawyer and client, but had been defeated in their attachment to one another by convention, moral and family obligations, by passion and by guilt.

They greeted each other cautiously. 'What brings you here?' he asked.

Cheyney Fox paced nervously around his office, rather obviously trying to compose herself. He sat back in his chair, eyes following her. Silent and waiting. Finally she stood squarely in front of him and, grabbing the edge of the desk, leaned forward.

'Important secrets buried long ago. Ghosts that speak the truth. Mysteries better unsolved.'

There was an edge of panic – or was it anger? – in her voice. She closed her eyes and pressed her fingers to her chest, as if trying to suppress her anxiety. She took a deep breath. Slowly she opened her eyes, stared into his, and sighed.

'Cheyney—' with a gesture he offered her a chair '– take your time. Tell me everything, from the beginning.'

A few simple words and a way of looking at her. It was enough. Her calm restored, she sat down. 'Something has happened. I have had a call from Washington. A new post is to be created by the President. He wants the country to have a Department of Fine Arts, and he has asked me if I will consent to be his first Secretary of State for Art for the United States. He wants Congress to pass funding for it and to ratify my nomination.'

'Congratulations.'

'A little premature. I have not, as yet, accepted. I am not sure I want to become a public figure, have my personal life investigated by a federal body. As you well know, my background isn't exactly Rebecca of Sunny-brook Farm. If the results of any investigation were exposed to the media
. . .'

'I've never thought of you as a Great Train Robber, a Wall Street thief. You're not into murder or drug dealing. What's so scary about standing in the limelight? You've been doing it admirably for the last few years. You're a celebrity.'

'Mini, David. And we're talking maxi here. Public office is not the same thing as private enterprise. I'm worried. I don't want to disappoint anyone.'

'Why should you? Your sponsor doesn't seem to be concerned. I can assure you, he would have had you checked out by the authorities long before he even approached you. The President of the United States thinks twice before appointing anyone to a position of power – no matter how much regard he has for them – if there's a possibility it might cause him embarrassment.'

'Maybe. But if I do accept, a more thorough vetting will follow. I could be faced with ruin on several fronts. I won't put my son at risk. Taggart's only fifteen, and he is the most important thing in my life. This could be a life or death matter for me, David.'

'Cheyney, that's a bit dramatic.'

'I think not. Though it *is* ironic. To have made it to the top of my profession at last, to have everything I've ever wanted within my grasp – only to find it poses a serious dilemma for me: whether to grab for the brass ring or gracefully decline. That's not dramatic, it's pathetic.'

The sudden calm in her voice, the sadness in her eyes, spoke volumes.

'Are you telling me you have things in your past which could cause a public furore, and threaten your credibility as a candidate for office?'

She placed her hands back in her lap and, not quite looking at him, answered. 'Without a doubt. It will be a fight every inch of the way to win through.'

'This isn't the Cheyney Fox I know. Good God, what are you afraid of?'

'I'm not quite sure. I've done nothing wrong, but that didn't prevent my being dragged through the courts once before, and having my business and

4

personal affairs twisted and turned against me. I've been there. You saw how the facts of my life were distorted to make a picture the opposition wanted to see. It would be no easy thing for me to submit to that again.

'Of course I have done nothing wrong. But nobody likes a victim, David, and you and I know that in the past I have been the victim of circumstances beyond my control. Who hasn't been? But the public tends to forget that when they're reading about someone else. And especially a someone else who doesn't keep to the middle lane in life.'

'Well, it's a simple decision. How much do you want to be the first lady of art in the United States? Enough to face whatever you must to get the job? Or would you rather pass it up?'

'Oh, I want it. Every instinct I have tells me to go for it. But although these are heady days for me, my first thought must be for my son. How the nomination and the publicity will affect him and his life. To fight is one thing. To face having some very private aspects of my life and work laid bare before Taggart is another. For fifteen years I have hidden behind a marriage, a network of galleries and corporations, before breaking out, for a second time, into the forefront of the art world. Do I want the secrets of those years, all the ruthless wheeling and dealing, revealed?'

'Cheyney, be honest with me. We're not talking about your going outside the law?'

'Absolutely not. No need to worry about that.'

'Then be specific. Tell me how I can help you.'

She looked away from him before answering. 'I want you, David, and your firm, to act on my behalf, handle complications that may arise from an investigation of my past – the demise of the gallery, and all my personal and business dealings in the early sixties. I feel strong enough to face any investigation, but I need to be prepared and advised by a top team to help me win through. I don't intend to have my chances ruined because of any malicious misrepresentation of the facts. And that is what might happen.

'During the time you and I were in and out of bankruptcy courts, I was traumatised by failure. Anguished by having to prove that I had not robbed my own gallery of its assets. I was such an innocent, so dumb. The humiliation of it! The years of being down on my luck afterwards, and just the passage of time, have blocked out memories too painful to contemplate. So how am I expected to answer questions about a past that is barely even real to me? Compared to the life I lead now, it all seems like a bad black and white B-movie, the theme-music blaring "He done her wrong". Time and emotion tend to blur things. I need you to help me focus on the truth if I am to come through this.'

David Rosewarne rubbed his chin thoughtfully as he contemplated Cheyney's words and studied her face.

She looked not so much older as more mature. And she had a son. He liked that softness he saw in her face when she spoke of the boy. Not so the determination in her voice, the hardness in her manner, when she spoke to her lawyer. What was the glint in her eye – ambition? A steely protective shield? Or could it be ruthlessness? He didn't much like that edge of world-weariness he sensed, but he could understand it. It did nothing to detract from her good looks. They could still make a man lose his head. Before he even realised what he was saying, it was out.

'You changed my life.'

She had not expected that. David Rosewarne had never been a man to give things away. She was quick with her retort: 'But not for long.'

For a few seconds they stared at one another intently and he felt the sting of an undelivered reprimand. Sufficient to snap him back to the business at hand. He could have wished for a flicker of something more. Affection? Intimacy? But it wasn't there, and he wasn't surprised.

'Your reputation as a clever art-dealer, museum director and generous patron of the art world these last few years has preceded you. You've come a long way from the naive girl I once defended.' He made no mention of love. An appointment had been made for a consultation, not a reconciliation. 'You've acquired a taste for power, that's obvious. And you know how to go for what you want, and get it. But I respect your caution, Cheyney. Am I right in assuming that if we act on your behalf you will accept the nomination?'

'Yes, but only after I've talked to Taggart and that means a trip to Eton, where he's in school. I need to discuss the situation and its implications with him.'

From her handbag she took a box of Jujues and put one of the gummy yellow drops in her mouth. She looked up at him and announced, 'I gave up cigarettes years ago.' The only personal note in her conversation that morning. Then she fixed him with a gaze that said, 'Well, I'm waiting for your answer.'

'We here at DCR could represent you. But surely you must have a team of lawyers handling your various business affairs? Wouldn't it be better for us to act as consultants to them on the years we represented you, if indeed that would be necessary?'

It was a cop-out he was going for, not a mere compromise. Determined to have him on her side, she pressed on. 'Yes, of course I have lawyers. Judd Whyatt, of Draycott, Whyatt & Fowler, has been my business and corporate lawyer since I started collecting and dealing again ten years ago.'

Cheyney watched David Rosewarne's face intently for a reaction to the name, anxious for a sign of approval. But lawyers have cornered the market in deadpan expressions.

'Look, David, I did consider what you suggest, but I feel, as does Judd, that I would be better represented if you were to handle directly any questions arising from the years when you acted on my behalf. Judd will do the same, only dealing with my affairs where your knowledge of them leaves off. The three of us will, of course, work as a team.'

He recognised the note of anxiety returning to her voice and other signs of distress: a change in the tempo of her breathing, the nervous energy returning. She needed him far more than he had realised. And she wasn't sure she was going to get him. She rose from the chair and stood in front of him. A flush to her face, she raised her chin and gave him a haughty look. Cheyney Fox was putting on a brave front.

Restless, she walked first to the bookshelves and ran her hand across the bindings, then to the window and looked out across the skyline of New York. Neither of them spoke, and the silence weighed heavy between them. With her back still to him she broke the stillness of the room. She neither pleaded nor demanded, she simply asked him in a voice devoid of emotion. 'Do this for me, David. I need you, take me on.'

At the very moment Cheyney Fox was consulting David Rosewarne, at 11.30 on that beautiful spring morning, Judd Whyatt went through the swing doors of the New York Athletic Club into the breezy warm sunshine of Fifty-Seventh Street. He was feeling on top form, having just played a hard game of squash. OK, so he had lost: but to a champion, and only just.

As Judd Whyatt walked the streets of New York towards his office at Rockefeller Center, his thoughts were on all the information and documentation concerning Cheyney Fox and her holdings being piled up on his desk. Over breakfast with her at seven o'clock that morning, he had instantly made up his mind that she was going to come out of this the first Secretary of State for Art in the United States. It was the sort of challenge that drew the best from the famous lawyer.

Draycott, Whyatt & Fowler were international lawyers who handled large corporations and a few wealthy individuals with smaller corporate holdings and businesses in their portfolio. Cheyney was one of those, and by far the most interesting. He had taken her on as a client ten years before, after they had met previously under strange and secret circumstances involving her then husband Kurt Walbrook. Hence his somewhat proprietorial pride in her rise to power and wealth in the art world. He knew things about Cheyney Fox that only a few other men did. They were the aces he could always play if needed to win the day for her. Whether he used them all depended on just how hairy the investigations became, just how much fabricated smut was scattered by her enemies and competitors. She had made more than a few of them since her exposé of Andy Warhol and Pop Art, and by her relentless rise to success as one of the top dealers of contemporary art. Judd was ready to fight to win for Cheyney; she was too valuable an asset to lose.

He saw a pretty girl give him the once-over and smile at him while he waited for a street-light to change. Young enough to be his daughter. He gave her a dazzling smile, and surprised them both by leaving her standing at the kerb.

Once in the impressive skyscraper, Judd Whyatt stepped out on the forty-fifth floor and walked down the hall and up a few stairs to one of the penthouses where his firm's offices were located. He opened the plate-glass doors and cheerfully greeted his staff as he breezed through, issuing orders to hold all calls with the exception of Cheyney Fox's. In his office he opened the safe. He placed the file marked *Cheyney Fox – Kurt Walbrook, CIA Classified Material* on his desk and flipped it open. He removed his jacket, sat down and began to read. Half an hour later the phone rang. Judd swivelled his chair around to face the glass wall behind his desk. He looked down at the people scurrying like ants through the canyons of steel and glass. Finally he spoke.

'Yes, Cheyney.'

'Judd, I'm here in David Rosewarne's office.'

'Now, do you feel more secure about making a date with destiny?' he asked teasingly.

'I never felt, and don't feel now, insecure about my destiny, Judd. I'm just lining up my generals. One thing I have learned about destiny – it's always better to be ready for it.'

Judd smiled. A few blocks away David Rosewarne smiled. Both men enjoyed the excitement in her voice, each proud of the role he had played in turning the one-time loser Cheyney Fox into a big-time winner. Businesswoman of the year? Understatement. Probably of the decade, and soon to be the most glamorous lady serving her country, if she rose to the bait that was on offer.

'And has David Rosewarne agreed to act on your behalf?'

A waspish 'Not yet' told him Cheyney was not having an easy time with Rosewarne. But the determination in her voice assured he would. 'I'll call you from England. I intend to take the afternoon Concorde. I don't dare lose any time getting to Taggart, otherwise someone there will garble my news for me.'

'Cheyney, how will you deliver your answer to the President?'

'A direct call to his office, don't you think?'

'Yes, I do, actually. Inadvisable to do anything else. No press release or anything that smacks of your campaigning for the job. Just a call to him, and let the White House make any announcement they choose to. I suggest that the gallery and your staff should give no statements, just take messages

8

until your return. It should remain business as usual. I think that's essential.'

'Thanks for everything, Judd.'

Cheyney hung up the telephone. She looked across the desk at David Rosewarne. They smiled at each other. He stood up and offered his hand. Hesitantly she took it.

'Good luck, Cheyney. It's really very thrilling all this.'

'Yes, it is, isn't it? But you still have not given me an answer. Will you take me on or not, David?'

'That is up to you, Cheyney. You go away and see your son. Make your decision about becoming the first Secretary of Art. Then make a second decision as to whether or not you are prepared to tell me everything, all the things you're holding back from me about the life you have led since we last met, the life you're so afraid to reveal publicly. If you call me, I'll know it's on those terms and I will be acting as your lawyer.'

Embarrassed by the ultimatum, and at having slipped into his clever trap – he had left her no scope to charm him on to her side, on her own terms – she slowly withdrew her hand from his. 'Thank you for seeing me, David. I am really very grateful for the time you have taken with me.'

As she turned away from him her eye rested on a silver-framed photograph. In spite of herself, a wave of jealousy came over her. She picked up the picture: it was of Mrs Rosewarne. And then the hurt surfaced. She looked at him fleetingly before turning her back and walking from the room. The hurt had shown in both their faces.

Whatever fantasy Cheyney had been conjuring up about David Rosewarne and herself, his wife's photograph had dispelled. These were not the desperate days of long ago, when Cheyney had been swept into love by David Rosewarne and all he stood for: security, respectability, his deep and abiding honesty, the care and protection he offered. Had what she had felt for him been nothing more than a desperate need for comfort and peace of mind? Of course not. There had also been the unblushing excitement of sexual attraction towards a man she trusted.

Cheyney was surprised that her emotions were still so fragile after a gap of twenty years. It had been the same family photograph of Jane and David Rosewarne with their two boys, Joshua and Calvin, that she had learned to live with, and, in the end, given him up for.

In the lift, Cheyney began to feel as if the past was pursuing her. She hurried through the lobby as if it were nipping at her heels. She burst through the doors into the street almost at a run. Heads turned for the stunningly beautiful woman dressed in a red and black suit who was dashing across the pavement, long silky black hair a web of seduction dancing on a gust of wind. As she ducked into a waiting limousine purring at the ready for her, she looked back through the rear window and into the past.

NEW YORK
AUTUMN 1959

Chapter 2

A New York City, end-of-October rain. The huge drops tap-danced on the sidewalks and over the streets. Once they had beat out their rhythm, they dissolved into instant pools of water. The puddles, skimmed by a chill wind with the scent of autumn in it, swirled over the tops of well-shod feet. The rain made no distinction between Gucci loafers, Delman high heels, McCann's hushpuppies or any other footwear for that matter. Every shoe in town was waterlogged.

High-speed wipers swooshed streams of water off windscreens. Rubber tyres navigated flooded streets. Small tidal waves of water pressed pedestrians against skyscraper walls and store fronts. Shoppers sought shelter or dashed from canopied entrance to entrance, froghopping towards their destinations. Empty taxis with their flags down swished past stranded travellers in a pipeline of water, refusing fares and drenching all within range, as they made for their garages. The grey sky turned into waterlogged daytime darkness.

The city was under siege from the elements. In fifteen minutes the streets of the world's greatest metropolis were almost deserted. Except for the occasional car, the odd umbrella blown inside out and rolling through the streets on the sodden wind, a Manhattan tumbleweed.

Cheyney stood huddled with twenty other people under an arched, dirt-smudged, yellow canopy whose flounce, flapping in the wind and dripping rivulets of rainwater, read, 'Joe Maranetti's Hero Sandwiches'. It stretched from the entrance of an old renovated brownstone building to the kerb. Every surge of wind down West Forty-Ninth Street brought with it a sheet of water that doused the refugees and drew an answering wave of protest, a gust of despair. They stood shivering, crushed against one another, giving off a mingled perfume of damp wool, after-shave, French and some not-so-French scent, body odour, and a faint whiff of Italian meat balls with oily, thick tomato sauce.

A little too close to Manhattan's human element, thought Cheyney. She stood on one foot and then the other, eyeing her chilled, wet feet. Positively the last outing for these shoes: they made watery squishing sounds as she shifted her weight. Whipped by the wind and spray of rain off the

13

pavement, even her ankles were damp and cold. She looked up from them to the office building across the way. Floor upon floor of lighted windows reaching skywards exhibited their inhabitants. The motions of 'business as usual' cast a warm yellow glow on the gloom of the day.

Cheyney liked the slick glass curtain walls of modern architecture that punctured Manhattan's pre-war cityscape and gave rein to a new kind of American art royalty – the architect. So many American princes who at first danced in the shadows of Mies Van der Rohe, Walter Gropius, Le Corbusier, were now beating their own drums and vying to be crowned king with every new and exciting building erected. The thrill of Skidmore, Owings & Merrill's 1952 Lever House as the new look in American architectural palaces immediately dictated change on Manhattan's skyline, and along with it a broader recognition for the modern arts. Even more exciting, American modern art. For seven years, ever since she had first seen the Lever House and felt the excitement of its architecture, she had been on the fringe of the American art world. In just a few days she would be right in the middle of it.

Cheyney suddenly felt ridiculous, standing on one foot, allowing herself to be stranded by a storm. She was living in the most exciting city in the world, a city she loved with passion, in a place where every sight, every scent, teased the senses and set the adrenalin flowing. New York dictated, 'Experience everything, take it all. Live and laugh and love at high speed, success is just around the corner.' And she was living up to its every demand. How silly to let a little rain put a damper on one's *joie de vivre*. She began to plot the route she would take in her race to get to the gallery in time to talk with the electricians. Time was running out before they left for the day, and before the opening of the Cheyney Fox Gallery. Just eight days to go.

Several minutes later, still standing there in the chilling rain, it was a matter of the spirit overcoming the reality of the situation. It was a bitch of a cold and windy rain storm. She pushed her way to the edge of the crowd and made an instinctive but foolish gesture. She held her arm out, palm up, from under the shelter. Rain drops beat into it and soaked the sleeve of her jacket while she contemplated her sixteen-block dash for the gallery. An accidental shove from someone in the crowd sent her stumbling into the torrential rain just as a speeding Series 60 special, hardtop black Cadillac, elaborate fish-tail fenders and all, displaced a wave of water and drenched her. Furious, she swung around to make her protest. Seeing the miserable grumbling crowd, she burst out laughing instead. No one smiled. And no one made room for her to come in out of the rain. The storm was no laughing matter to them.

Joe Maranetti's sandwich shop's extractor-fan switched on and swirled out a gust of hot air. The heat felt good, but, oh, the smell! Cheyney watched the blue-grey cloud of fumes billow out over the heads of the crowd huddled under the canopy and dust them down with its fragrance: a double dose of stale smoke, garlic and oregano-scented oil finally moved Cheyney to call out, 'That's it.'

She walked as fast as she could, darting for cover wherever she found any, sprinting in short bursts. By the time she reached Saks Fifth Avenue, the storm had drenched her spirit as well as her clothes, but not her resolve. She was determined to get to the gallery. Cold and wet through, she could hardly see the point of stopping now. She pressed on. At Best & Company, she flattened herself against the wall for a moment to catch her breath and wring out her silk kerchief before she pushed on. A gust of wind, and it was gone. She shook her head in disbelief as she watched it disappear up Fifth Avenue. Oh, well, her hair was soaked anyway. She was nearly half way to the gallery.

As she rushed past F.A.O Schwartz, a man in a clean, crisp, Burberry trench-coat and a brown felt hat came bounding out through the plate-glass doors and cannoned into her. Both of them were taken aback. Only his quick reflexes saved her from crashing on to the wet pavement when her knees buckled. He pulled her up by the elbow.

'Good God, woman, one of us doesn't know the rules of navigation.'

'Obviously not,' she snapped back, pulling her elbow away from his hand and releasing herself from his arms.

Without another word she walked somewhat shakily to the corner and had the bad luck to have the traffic light change just as she was about to cross the street. She caught a glimpse of the man as he passed to one side of her and around the corner. He slipped into the back seat of a waiting taxi. Before he even had the door firmly closed, the yellow cab rolled up the street and past her. She had no chance of avoiding the splash.

Grant Madigan placed his hand on the cab-driver's shoulder and said, 'Stop the cab, Harry.' The cabbie slammed on the brakes just as he was negotiating the corner to go up Fifth Avenue. He turned and looked at his fare. 'Back up, Harry. We're going to give that idiot woman a lift before Fifth Avenue has its first suicide by storm drowning.'

The cabbie reversed, looking back over his shoulder through the rear windows while navigating, and asked, 'You sure about this? We don't have much time to spare if you wanna make that plane of yours.'

'Time enough. She gets a lift only if she's going our way.' He pulled off his hat, shook the water from its brim and placed it on the rear window-ledge. He ran his fingers through his hair and opened the top button of his raincoat before he flung the door open squarely in front of Cheyney. Ducking down, so he could see her from inside the taxi, he shouted over the sound of the rain, 'Hop in, we'll give you a lift.'

15

Cheyney's hesitation had more to do with relief at being rescued than concern about getting into a cab with a stranger. The man in the back seat was not to know that. Impatient to get on his way, he reached out to grab her by the wrist and yank her into the cab, saying 'Don't flatter yourself. This is no abduction. Just a mercy mission.' Leaning over her, he slammed the cab door closed.

Cheyney Fox and Grant Madigan had a really good look at each other. The rain drummed on the roof of the taxi, pounded at the windows. Shivering with cold, Cheyney began to rub her hands together. 'Where to?' he finally asked, rather too sharply for a man on a mission of mercy.

Shaking with cold, dripping water everywhere, Cheyney was a sorry sight. Her teeth chattered but she managed to get out, 'Sixty-Third Street, between Fifth and Madison.'

Grant Madigan looked towards Harry, who had twisted around in the front seat to face them and was lighting a big fat cigar. Madigan asked a shade grudgingly, 'Did you get that, Harry?'

'Yeah, I got it. Sixty-Third goes the wrong way for us. So we go east on Sixty-Second, up Madison and west on Sixty-Third. So we drop her on the corner of Madison and Sixty-Third and save a few minutes?'

'What's the house number, Miss?' asked Cheyney's knight.

She stuttered, 'Thirteen, the middle of the block.'

'So we drop her on Fifth or Madison and beat it back to the Triborough Bridge. Then we don't get caught twice in cross-town traffic.'

Cheyney was beginning to find the conversation, the ride that had not yet even begun, and the state she was in, too embarrassing. She held up a hand signalling them to stop. 'Never mind, but thanks for the offer,' she managed with as much dignity as she could muster.

'Oh, do sit back and be quiet, woman, while we figure out how to get you home. We take her to the door, Harry.'

'OK, you're the boss, Mr Madigan. And the one that has to make the plane.' With that, Harry turned round, released the emergency brake and let the yellow cab roll up to the traffic light.

Grant Madigan eyed his rescue mission. She was dripping all over his portable Olivetti. He picked it up off the seat between them and placed it next to his hat. He watched her rubbing her hands together, tapping her feet, trying to get warm. He took her hands in his and was appalled at how cold they were. He rubbed first one then the other between his palms and, when he felt some warmth coming back into them, removed the yellow cashmere scarf from around his neck, dropped it over her head and vigorously towelled the water from her hair. He was too rough. She took his hands away and continued herself. He watched her. She was still trembling with cold. He began to unbutton her black wool jacket. She tried to

16

stop him. Angrily he said, 'I am only trying to help, silly lady.'

The saturated jacket was both heavy and floppy. Clumsily he removed it. Cheyney watched him wring it out and sensed the strength of his hands. She watched the stream of water flow from it to the floor. The demise of her Tregere suit jacket, as it slapped on to the plastic-covered seat, gave her a pang. Untying the belt of his Burberry, he opened his coat and pulled her close into his arms. Almost at once, the heat from his body stilled her trembling.

He removed her shoes and rubbed her feet. That particular kindness somehow felt too intimate. She flushed with embarrassment and, to hide it, murmured: 'Please, let me go. I'm all right now.'

They gazed into each other's faces. For the first time they became aware of one another as man and woman. Cheyney felt something stir within her, something more than sensual, more than a deep feeling of belonging. It was as if she had come home. Don't be fanciful, she told herself. That's an ancient stereotype. You aren't going to fall for it, are you?

'I suppose you pick up stray dogs and wandering waifs, and help old ladies across the street as well? I am very grateful for this ride.'

'No, I don't, actually. Only beautiful, misguided ladies in distress.'

'Well, I wasn't exactly in distress.'

'A moot point.'

'In a rush to make an appointment. Wet, cold, not wanting to be defeated by a rainstorm. Unwilling to have it ruin my day, yes. Distressed, no.' There was a feisty little edge to her voice that was not unattractive.

He smiled at her for the first time as he raised her foot and slipped her shoe back on. Handing her the other shoe, he said, 'You still have the arrogance of youth.'

'If you knew me, you would understand how wrong you are.' She raised her chin just a bit too high and gave him a hint of haughtiness. She had passionate violet eyes, and he knew he had got it quite right. That knowledge broadened his smile. 'Alas, that's not meant to be.'

'You could have left me there on the kerb. I dare say I would have survived.'

The taxi swung off Madison and into Sixty-Third Street. She was looking at him, waiting for some answers. And something inexplicable happened: for a few minutes she fell in love with a stranger.

'How do the numbers run? You on the right or the left side here?' asked Harry through the rear-view mirror.

She heard the cab driver but didn't answer. She was trying to hold on to her exquisite sensation of love, even as she felt it slipping away. It wasn't as if she were dreaming, she was aware of everything around her. The rugged handsomeness of the stranger next to her, his scent, his maleness, power, sexuality. The cloying heat from the noisy fan-heater, the din and rhythm of the rain on the roof of the cab, the steamed-up windows, even her own Jolie Madame scent and Harry's cigar smoke.

And then she lost it. Those few fleeting minutes of oneness and love and being in the heart of life. She knew something remarkable had happened to her and she would never forget it, ever. Humbled by her experience, rather too softly, she answered, 'On the right, the middle of the block.'

Grant Madigan and Cheyney were still engrossed in each other. Without taking his eyes from her, he repeated what she had said just loud enough for Harry to hear. He watched her slip the ruined Tregere jacket on to her shoulders, tuck her handbag under her arm. The taxi stopped. Grant Madigan wiped the mist from the window and glimpsed the number on a handsome, limestone-fronted house. Thirteen. There was a change in the pitter-patter of rain on the roof. It was barely audible. He wound the window down. In the back seat of the overheated taxi, the damp cold air was strangely invigorating. Gloomy darkness was lifting and the storm was raining itself out. Wet pavements glistened like mirrors. He slipped out of his raincoat and put his hat on. 'I'll see you to the door. Here, hold this over your head.'

'No, please. You've done enough.' She reached up to unwind his cashmere scarf, wrapped round her head like a turban. He stopped her with a hand on her wrist.

'I'll see you to the door. Leave the scarf on at least until you are out of the rain.' It was an emphatic declaration, not meant to be disobeyed.

Neither of them made a move. They kept a silent watch on each other for several seconds. Then Grant Madigan broke the passionless interval, his voice still tinged with annoyance but with a softer edge of kindness to it. 'Let a passing stranger give you a piece of advice. Learn to know when you need someone, and then, if he should drop into your lap as I have, be smart enough to accept all the help on offer.'

The sting in his voice irritated her, she wanted to say something cutting, but before she could muster the words he had opened the cab door and she was stepping into a puddle. She had his Burberry in her hands. He took it from her and held it over both their heads, his arm around her shoulders as together they ran through the rain to the door of the gallery.

Sheltered by a cornice of carved stone, they huddled under the coat together while she fumbled in her handbag for her key. Cheyney opened the door and stepped into the entrance-hall of the building. She pulled at the turban and it collapsed into his damp, much-creased cashmere scarf. She watched him slip his arms into the sleeves of his raincoat, button it, secure the belt, and turn to leave. She stopped him.

'You mean that's it? I'm not to be given the chance to say thank you? To

18

repay your kindness in some way? Can't I have your scarf cleaned and pressed and returned to you? At least have a cup of coffee – a drink even?'

He was about to tell her that all he wanted was to get to the airport when something about her, standing there in the stark white emptiness of the entrance hall, stopped him. It was something more than the woman herself: pretty, beautiful even, as she was with her mass of wet, long, black tangled hair. He was caught by her air of vulnerability. He sensed that here was a tragic figure of a woman who was unaware of her tragedy. And yet, he saw something else as well – a glimmer of a passionate, sensual beauty that promised much. He hoped so, for her sake.

Her jacket had slipped off one of her shoulders. Her still-wet, white silk blouse clung to her, outlining the pale pinkness of her flesh; the voluptuous roundness of her breasts, the nipples erect from the cold. She was unaware of how ripe she looked, how exposed she was. That was her problem, she had no real vision of herself. He was a lover of women, all kinds of women, but never got involved with complicated ones. They took up too much time.

He caught her jacket as it slipped off the other shoulder and placed it on the hall radiator, then he grasped her waist and pulled her towards him, crushing her in his arms. His face brushing against hers, he said, 'This is thanks enough for me. A hug from a beautiful lady and a promise from her to learn to take care of herself. If you don't have the good sense to come in from the rain, how much sense do you have? Ask yourself that. It's a cruel world out there. You think you're going to conquer it, that you're a survivor. I hope for your sake you are.'

He could feel anger at his words pulsating through her body. He released her and at the same time pulled the scarf from her hand. He was so quick she had no time to recover herself. For one brief moment, before he turned on his heel and walked away from her, he caressed her breasts in his large strong hands and ran his thumbs across her nipples. How lovely the weight of them, the soft yet firm roundness that filled his hands. Too bad she had not been another kind of woman: he would have made love to her then.

As Harry pulled away from the kerb, Grant Madigan caught a last glimpse of her through the rain-streaked window. She was still standing where he had left her. She had not even closed the front door. He lit a cigar and, as they turned on to Fifth Avenue, said, aloud, 'Well, good luck to us both, kid. We each of us have our war to go to.'

Chapter 3

The door was ajar. Cheyney pushed it open and stepped into the gallery. Semi-darkness, empty and silent. She flicked the light switch on the wall. Nothing happened. 'Oh, no!' she exclaimed aloud. Irritated, she played the switch several times, then a bank of switches next to it. Still nothing. Filled with frustration she called out, 'Max, Morris?' Silence. Just the disturbing echo of her own voice bouncing off the walls. 'Dora, Sebastian.' Still nothing. A puzzle that no one should be there. To have left the door ajar and the gallery unattended was utterly irresponsible. That rainstorm had a lot to answer for.

She walked to the staircase and looked up the graceful curve to the floor above. She shouted, in a voice filled with frustration, 'Max, Morris?' Nothing. A forlorn kind of emptiness, accentuated by the hissing sound from a radiator valve somewhere in the gallery.

She draped her jacket over an empty packing case, placed her handbag on the carpeted bottom stair. She stepped out of her soggy shoes and damp stockings, and slipped very carefully out of her wet skirt. No dripping on that newly-polished oak floor.

She walked barefoot across the gallery to stand in the main exhibition hall. Cheyney felt herself sliding towards despair, lonely to the very core of her being, and couldn't understand why. Because her electricians had not waited for her? Her staff had left the place unattended? Her supreme effort to get to the gallery on time had been in vain? Max and Morris had gone, without finishing the job as promised? Hardly reasons to feel herself spiralling down, down, down, as if pulled by some dark and dangerous vortex. Or was it because Christopher was not there to support her, love her?

'Goddamnit!' she said aloud, unable to hold back her frustration. 'This is definitely not my day.'

The door from the entrance-hall swung open, and the gallery lit up. 'When Max and Morris Abrams make a promise, Max and Morris Abrams keep a promise. You were already crossing us off, no? *A mistake.* Oy, a drowned rat she looks like!' said Max.

Morris gave his brother a poke in the ribs. Max pressed his lips tight together, screwed up his face and quickly added, 'Mmmm, well, maybe not a rat. That's just a phrase to be going on with, you understand. No offence meant. You shouldn't take it personal. Let's just say, it's *some* cold you're gonna catch.'

Cheyney, as if riding the golden disc of a pendulum, swung from despair to delight. For an instant, the white of the gallery walls stung her eyes. Then it receded in deference to the paintings. She caught her breath and clapped her hands together. Everything but the gallery and the paintings ceased to exist for her.

It was always that way when she looked at paintings, sculpture or architecture. At any art form that had vestiges of greatness in it. And it had always been that way for her. Often she was asked what were the first works of art she could remember – those all-important primal encounters? Several times she had told, and then she stopped telling. Art-people sought a rather more erudite and sophisticated answer than the green and white Rinso box that was on permanent display on the draining board of her mother's kitchen, mealtimes included. To Cheyney at the age of three, it had been as impressive as the Mona Lisa had been, when, at twenty-three, she had seen it in the Louvre. When other children had been running around, being cutely precocious and reciting in baby whines: 'Cat, C-A-T. Dog, D-O-G,' little Cheyney Fox was saying and spelling, 'Rinso, R-I-N-S-O.' Her very first word.

The true object of her earliest appreciation never satisfied her art-world friends. They would have found it more acceptable had she dredged up a memory of a Matisse, a Georges Braque, an Uffizi Botticelli – The Birth Of Venus, say. Surely there had been a toddler's assignation with a Marcel Duchamps, a Kandinsky? Or was it a nice, straightforward Picasso – any title or period – that had got to her first? Rinso was just no dice.

A big smile lit up Cheyney's face. 'Max, Morris, the lighting is great! Just brilliant! Exactly the way I wanted the recessed spots, and the surface-mounted fixtures are fantastic. They wash the walls with just the right degree of light. Oh, God, it works! Does it ever work!' She clapped her hands together once more and walked around the gallery, viewing the exhibition as a whole. It almost sang to her. Every painting hung in perfect harmony with the others.

'Max, Morris,' she said as she went up to them and hugged them both at the same time, 'thanks. Thanks for everything.'

The two men watched her walk barefoot over to one of the several stacks of paintings leaning against the walls, waiting to be hung. She began looking through them. So much work yet to be done, two more rooms without a painting on the walls. Max and Morris looked at each other and then decided to do something about Cheyney Fox.

'How would you like to catch pneumonia instead of opening an art gallery? 'cause that's what you're gonna do, standing barefoot in a damp blouse and your underwear,' announced Max.

She looked down in surprise at her silk-and-lace underslip. 'Oh, I got so carried away I forgot it was my lingerie you'd just illuminated.'

'Look, don't blush for us,' said Morris. 'You're decent enough. You wouldn't believe the things we've seen, the chances we've had with some of our customers.'

'The chances we've taken,' bubbled Max. A twinkle in his eye, a faint smile of remembrance on his lips.

Morris poked him in the ribs and gave him a disapproving look. Cheyney sneezed, but wanted to laugh. The brothers took charge. Each holding an arm they marched her up the stairs, picking up her discarded clothing and handbag en route.

'It always begins with a sneeze,' said Max.

'Or a cough,' Morris confirmed.

'You can't afford it. Pneumonia,' said Max.

'No, not pneumonia *and* the Abrams brothers.' That was Morris.

'So, since you got the Abrams brothers' bill to pick up, you'd better take a hot bath, a *schnapps*, and go to bed.'

'Hey, fellas, it's only four o'clock,' she managed to get in.

Morris ignored four o'clock, 'A *schnapps* and hot tea is better.'

Max didn't. 'So is there some law says you can't go to bed at four o'clock in the afternoon? I never heard of such a law. You, Morris?'

'Not, me.'

'Guys, guys, I only sneezed once. You'll be prescribing chicken soup next.'

'And why not? It's the best medicine. The other day I heard somebody say, "If I just had some Jewish penicillin, I could shake this cold in a day." "Jewish penicillin?" I asked, "Chicken soup," I got told.'

The brothers beamed. Max and Morris Abrams, master electricians, came over as a pair of vaudeville comics who took turns at playing the straight man in their act.

The upper hall was stacked with paintings. The trio walked through it to the first-floor room overlooking the garden. Max found two rheostats on the wall and turned them to maximum power. The spot and flood lights played dramatically on the stark white walls. The room was architectural perfection. A double cube, with all the impact of that classical proportion; cold, empty and vast. The thick, sunflower-yellow carpet was like the masterly stroke of an artist's brush.

Cheyney was impressed. Against all advice, she had insisted it would work, and it did. She had taken a quantum leap in choosing that colour.

But then, that was Cheyney: always aiming outward in time and space. In fact, Cheyney's 'instinctive' actions were always near-certainties. She was a young woman who did not lightly take a chance.

The room was an artistic power-house even without its paintings. It was super-charged with an ethereal energy that pricked the senses, and the memory.

Hans Hoffman, his house, his paintings . . . It had been in Provincetown, Massachusetts, several years before. Trashy, ramshackle Provincetown. A seaside village, quasi-town, of grey two-storey fishing shacks teetering over the water, only slivers of space between them along the crescent-shaped bay-side of its long, narrow main street. More weather-worn wooden houses stretched back into the narrow lanes of the town. Only Provincetown, of all of the artists' summer colonies, had that cheap, honky-tonk, seaside atmosphere, that total absence of chic. That was its charm: trash on the outside, the promise of greatness behind a few firmly closed doors.

From the moment she stepped into the small wooden house, she had the feeling she had stepped into one of Hoffman's paintings. The overall impression was of whiteness, pure white walls in every direction she looked. Almost bare of furniture, with pure and rich slashes of bright colour strategically placed: a painted chair vibrating with one colour while standing on bare boards painted another. It had made the heart sing. A door stood open – and where you could see from one room to the next, the space and everything within seemed to be used as a canvas. One painting, one chair, the sun streaming like a corn-yellow beam through the window.

Cheyney had felt instantly enriched, refreshed, and joyful. Enfolded by an atmosphere she could not define she had dissolved into its magic, yet felt rooted to the spot where she stood, listening to Hans Hoffman. He was wearing a short-sleeved, open-necked shirt of slate-grey cotton, worn over baggy, putty-coloured slacks, bare feet showing through the leather criss-crosses of his sandals. With his large round face and receding hairline fringed with thick white hair, Hoffman had looked like a wise, indulgent grandaddy cum philosophy teacher lecturing on art to the younger men in the room, the painters Rothko, Motherwell, the critic Greenberg, and Hoffman's dealer Sam Kootz.

The open discussion that had reverberated between them had astounded Cheyney. She drank in their enthusiasm, their passion and belief in abstract expressionist painting. Here was an art that was as cerebral as it was visual as it was expressive. Provocative by its insistence on forcing, pushing, always pushing, the viewer to use his brain as well as his eyes and his heart and his soul. An art that triggered its viewer to experience his own abstract expressions buried deep within. This was no-easy-on-the-

23

eyes, folksy, Norman Rockwell art. This was postwar American art, American modern art taking wing.

Cheyney had been taken to the Hoffman house by her host, Acton Pace, another abstract expressionist painter, a one-time lover, kindred spirit and close friend. Acton saw more in Cheyney than just an intelligent, sensuously beautiful young woman, passionately interested in art, who ran a fascinating gallery in the provinces. She combined in her personality both sexy lady and art-dealer. The mix appealed to the artistic mind. And not only his. It gave her entry to houses and studios like Hoffman's, and a stable of interesting lovers to choose from. But it also left Cheyney Fox with a confused picture of herself. She never knew quite how seriously she was being taken as non-woman, art-dealer, gallery owner. In the fifties to be a non-woman woman in the business world was a prerequisite for success.

Cheyney gave a sigh, less of anguish than of relief that she had done it: destroyed one life designed to make anyone but herself happy, in order to build another. She was here where she wanted to be. And if it was scary – which it was, this beginning again – that was just because for too long she had been too weak to break out and fight for what she wanted.

'So long, see you tomorrow.' Max broke into her reverie.

'Yeah, seeya,' added Morris. 'And don't forget the hot bath and the *schnapps*.'

'We'll lock the door behind us,' said Max as the pair walked away from her.

'And turn off the light,' added Morris.

They were half way down the stairs when Cheyney rushed across the upper gallery to flash them a smile and call down to them, 'Thanks again, for everything. See you tomorrow.'

Chapter 4

A tap at the door, a voice way off in the distance. Cheyney struggled out of a deep sleep. It was like swimming against a fluffy, pink tide of candy floss. Exhausted she felt herself slipping, slipping, back into a hazy mist somewhere between sleep and day-dreaming.

The grasp of a cool hand on her naked shoulder. More awake now than asleep, she heard, 'Yuh've been doin an awful lotta sleepin these mornens. What I call lazy, somethin's wrong sleepen. Are you sick'nen for somethin beside that hansum devil of a man of yours, Miss Cheyney?'

Dora's voice brought a faint smile to Cheyney's lips. It usually did. Dora Washington was Cheyney's black housekeeper, a rich presence in the background of her life. Her smile faded as Dora's words registered. Maybe her housekeeper was right. For weeks now she had had enormous difficulty not only rising in the morning but keeping awake during the day. She opened her eyes. The housekeeper had more to say.

'Well, if you is, you ain't goin' to be no longer. Look what I have.' On the bed Dora placed the antique breakfast tray of coral-coloured Japanese lacquer with its pale yellow silk organza cloth and white napkin, its Lalique glass dishes: cup and saucer, plate and glass, including a slim vase in the shape of a lily that proffered a perfect white rose. From the pocket of the black uniform dress, she wore under her crisp white apron, she took out a cablegram. Cheyney's lethargy vanished. Wide awake now, she pulled herself up against the pillows and tore open the envelope.

PLANE 8 TONIGHT STOP DON'T COME AIRPORT STOP DINNER TWOSOME YOUR PLACE SOONEST STOP LOVE CHRISTOPHER

Cheyney crushed the cable against her heart, closed her eyes and felt tears of joy brimming beneath her lids. Not like her, this lack of control over her emotions. Opening her eyes, she announced to Dora rather more calmly than she felt, 'Tonight. He'll be here tonight, Dora.' Happiness took over.

Dora gave her employer a severe glance. She shook her head disapprovingly before turning her back on Cheyney to open the draperies and then the windows. 'You are a *mess*. One word from that man and yuh're always a mess. He's *too* han'sum, Miss Cheyney,' she said, clicking her tongue against the roof of her mouth and continuing to shake her head from side to side. 'He's *too* han'sum a man, *too charmin*. A charmin man, like Mistah Christopha . . . Oh my, you better be careful. That man spells trouble, ah can feel it in mah bones. Ah should know. He's just lahk mah Bill. He's baaad people.'

Dora returned to the bed, bent down and poured a cup of fragrant Blue Mountain coffee for Cheyney. She snapped the crisp white napkin in the air and handed it to her employer unfurled.

'If he's such "bad people", Dora, then why do you make so much fuss over him the minute he walks through the door?'

'Ah tell yuh why, 'cause that man, he shore can weave a spell around a woman, even a black maid like me. There ain't a man, woman or chile is safe from Mistah Christopha when he lays on that charm o'his. An' God help yah, he's 'n *love* with yuh. He's bad people, an bad people 'n love that's mighty big danger. That ain't their natural state. Yuh gotta watch out.'

Cheyney had to smile. Dora was no fool. Cheyney hoped that she wasn't being one either.

'Well, Mr Charm himself is arriving from Paris tonight, Dora, only one day later than he promised. It's to be dinner in the Ninety-Fourth Street flat.'

Dora's eyes took on a glazed look. She glanced at her wristwatch. Cheyney knew why the handsome, slender black woman was checking the time – Dora was a drinker, and no sneak drinker either. There was nothing sneaky about Dora. She and Cheyney had an understanding about the drinking. Cheyney never checked the whisky bottle, and Dora drank no more than she could hold without its showing. There were occasional lapses on Dora's part, but both employer and housekeeper tended to ignore them. They had never been offensive enough to cause trouble between them.

'What time is it, Dora?'

'Eight-fifteen, but it feels like eleven. Lordy, lord, does it evah feel lahk eleven. Shoot, Miss Cheyney, don'ya look at me lahk that! You know I got mah drinkin rules.' Eleven was when she always claimed she took her first drink but they both knew that it was an elastic eleven: more often than not, it stretched back to ten o'clock.

Cheyney watched Dora walk to the mirror and fuss with the perfectly neat chignon she wore at the nape of her neck. Dora was a terrific housekeeper, a brilliant cook, but an even better performer.

She spoke a servant's classy affected English but liked slipping into her other accent, which Cheyney suspected was an equally affected negroid folk tongue from the deep South. She did both very well, considering she was Harlem born and bred. Dora was quick to impress on any guest who offered a compliment that she had learned her manners and her work and all about *huooomannity* from her one-time employer, Fanny Brice, whom she had clearly adored. Her style, class pretensions (which she chided her employer for not cultivating) and dress-sense came from Miss Fanny and her girlfriend, Mae West. Dora Washington was a one-off, New York character, wise without being wily, interesting because she knew how to please and at the same time command respect and affection from those she served. Dora knew how to play the game.

Cheyney watched Dora studying her in the mirror. The housekeeper spoke to her, hands on hips.

'Yuh do spoil that man too much.'

'He spoils me.'

'Big girl, you don't know what real spoilin is. What you mean is, if you don't mind my sayin so, he gives you mighty good lovin. It ain't the same as real spoilin. It's good, mindja, but it would be better if that man warn't so devilment charmin. Don't fret, I said my piece now, and I'll make dinner for you, with all them favourite things your man likes t'eat. Not for him, mindja, for you, 'cause you're so happy he's com'n home.' She paused for a moment then said, 'Lordy, but yuh do look a peaky thing this mornin. You sure you're feelin all right?'

'Me? I feel wonderful.'

Dora watched the woman she referred to as 'mah madam' spoon out her grilled grapefruit. She sat down at the end of the bed. 'A word?' she asked.

'Sure. What's on your mind, Dora?'

'I hope we're doin right, Miss Cheyney. This business of you givin up your home to make and live in this here gallery of yours. Yuh do realize in two days' time you're goin be livin here permanent-like? Don't look like much of a home to me, not after what you've been used to.'

'Well, too late to worry about it now, Dora. The gallery has demanded a great many sacrifices. Let's not go back over them now. Just pray it all works out according to plan.'

Dora abruptly changed the subject. 'Yuh better get up. Ah've got them 'lectricians here workin downstairs. Mr Sebastian's waitin on yuh, and he says, would ah come in an tell yuh we've all got a big day today? Ah'll leave yuh now. Ah got a mountain o' work ta do now Mistah Christopha's comin home.'

'Mistah Christopha's comin home.' Those words kept ringing in Cheyney's ears. So many firsts suddenly loomed – The first time he would have seen the gallery . . . Pursuing their separate careers while living together under one roof . . . Facing the world as a couple . . . For Cheyney they were monumental steps, not easily taken.

27

It meant ignoring the disapproval of friends, family, associates. She wasn't even sure she herself approved of what she was doing. So she had made one fast rule where Christopher was concerned. They would ask nothing of each other. Their being together had to be natural, easy, without artifice. Whatever they were to give to each other would have to be voluntary. She wanted nothing but love to govern what they had together. And to that end she demanded of herself that she see Christopher in real terms and without illusions, and accept him or reject him for the man he was. To stay with him for as long as their love lasted was just about all Cheyney dared to hope for in their relationship. She needed no Dora to tell her her lover was 'baad people'. She knew it deep in the very core of loving him.

It wasn't going to be easy. How would they react to each other under the pressures of the real world? They had only known the glamour of a Greek island love affair, an Athens cultural hop in the sunshine of their infatuation with each other, a romantic weekend in Paris. They had been a couple besotted by romance, sharing erotic yearnings, who fed each other oysters and drank chilled Chablis in a bistro on the Rue de Seine, as if they were the only lovers the city had ever seen. Love letters filled with passion and affection, and reminders of sexual delights, to ease their long separations, were about to be replaced by day to day living and loving in the hard reality of New York City.

Easy for them – how could it be? Their love affair was an enormous intrusion into their routine lives. Even so, to give each other up? Unthinkable!

Cheyney was no wealthy heiress with an ancient European title. Nor was she high society, or old money, or a celebrity of any kind – the types Christopher usually cultivated using his struggling expatriate-painter image, his grand manner and his charm in the search for position and security. She wasn't even a Paris, London or New York collector, top art-dealer or museum director. Cheyney Fox did not fit into Christopher Corbyn's scheme of things. She just happened.

And Christopher – an only moderately interesting American painter, in the process of divorcing a Spanish duchess, frittering his talent away on decorative collages, spoiled by women, torn between high society, the grand European life and the bohemian and artistic world – was hardly the kind of man she had expected to capture her heart. But he had.

A penniless artist living in a grand period house on a remote Greek island, with an equally grand *palazzo* in Florence and a *pied à terre* in Paris, all stuffed full of shabby possessions. He shared ownership with a cunning Greek painter who was as flamboyant a homosexual and amoral snob, pimping for the need of both, as Christopher was conservative and a

28

periodic recluse. Christopher appeared, when in the capital cities of the world, in his slightly shiny but well-presented Brooks Brothers clothes as the beautiful, even bashful, gentleman painter whose only interest was his work. Hard to equate the image he projected with the gossip that named him an accomplished lover and user of lonely, wealthy women.

Costas and Christopher: partners in houses and studios, and the people they cultivated. Close as brothers, movers and pushers for their own selfish ends – more like partners in crime, some even hinted. No, not exactly the sort of man Cheyney Fox needed. Love had set a time bomb ticking away in both their lives. Or so people said, until they saw the couple together. Then they were not so sure.

Was Christopher too handsome? A tall, broad-shouldered man with thick, dark blond hair streaked with white from the sun, he was yet fair skinned. His eyes were a seductive blue, yes, but it was his face that captivated: big with a wide forehead, and determined square chin, its masculinity countered by a finely chiselled nose, and a mouth that would have been mean but for the lips. Their shape and softness made him look sensitive, vulnerable even. There was a combination of virile masculinity shaded by an innocent boyishness in his face, that, along with his character, voice and manner, charmed on a grand scale.

Cheyney never believed – but then she never disbelieved either – the gossip, or other people's reactions to Christopher or Costas. She was living her love for him on a day-to-day basis. All she hoped for was that she could get on with her life, he with his, and they with a life together. No fantasies, no rose-tinted in glasses.

Cheyney was reminded of what Dora had said. She was giving up her home, the love-place they had hidden in the last time they were together in New York. Tonight a reunion there, tomorrow night a farewell to their secret hideaway. Christopher. Suddenly she felt only half alive without him. As if she was treading the waters of a life, and not living it at all. She laughed out loud as she hopped out of bed to bathe and dress.

In her private office on the ground floor of the gallery, she found Sebastian. He was, as usual, on the telephone. Cheyney riffled through the post. She tried not to become annoyed with him but lately Sebastian had become an irritant that she found increasingly hard to take. They would have to sort a few things out, and soon. But not today, she thought. As she heard the tail end of his conversation, she turned to face him.

'Good morning, Sebastian.'

He rose from her chair and, putting his hands on her shoulders, gave her a kiss, first on one cheek and then the other. 'Good morning, Cheyney. You look radiant this morning.'

'Every time you bestow your De Gaulle kiss on me, Sebastian, I half expect to be given the *Croix de Guerre*. What act of bravery have I unknowingly committed this morning?'

'You were a great success at my drinks party last night. Truman Capote thought you were charming. He will come to our *vernissage*. That's very important.

'Why, Sebastian? Is he a potential customer?' Cheyney was sorry the moment she said it. The last thing she wanted this morning was a confrontation. But, for weeks now, ever since he had bought into the gallery for a small share of the profits, she had been concerned that Sebastian was using the gallery, and her, more as a social entrée than a business. His contribution was supposed to have been public relations, since he claimed to be on intimate terms with everyone who was anyone in New York artistic circles.

That was turning out to be not quite true. And as for those he did know – well, Sebastian Cohen had no influence on them whatsoever. Quite the reverse, in fact. They looked on him as a well trust-funded, ineffectual, social butterfly, a well-read, much-travelled young gentleman. An inverted snob, living as close to the poverty line as society would allow him lest it label him rich Jew. The label he was looking for was intellectual-poet-Jew, with not too much emphasis on the Jew. For him, society was made up of gods. He basked in their glory, making it a part of his life.

Cheyney was learning fast that Sebastian Cohen, son of a wealthy West Virginia industrialist, with his Harvard education, New England accent and hesitant speech combined with an upper-class stutter, who dressed J. Press and Brooks Brothers, Savile Row, Lobb's and Herbert Johnson, was nothing more than an intellectual, intercontinental lounge lizard. But, like everyone else, she also saw him as a harmless creature who meant well.

So Cheyney, who needed all the capital she could raise to get the gallery off the ground, agreed to take Sebastian in as a very junior working-partner. She stood before him now, and hoped that had not been a big mistake. So far, all he had done was wine and dine every closet queen in the art and literary world who would accept his invitation, and clash with her on the artists she had chosen to represent.

Sebastian put on his hurt look, and reinforced it with a disapproving silence. He actually found it distasteful when Cheyney spoke in business terms.

'Why do you look at me that way, Sebastian? Why do you find the word "customer" crass? This is a business venture. I'm not in this to boost my own ego, or to shine in artistic circles. I have a job to do. I cannot afford not to think customers, sales, profits. We are going to need to place every painting we possibly can to stay afloat. You know that.' She said it as mildly as she could, and yet tried to make her point clear to him. Then felt foolish for adopting an apologetic manner. But it seemed to work. Sebastian's face relaxed and for one fleeting moment Cheyney thought, 'It's going to be all right, he's listening.'

'Truman might bring Auden and Chester. And I'm sure we will have two curators, one from the Metropolitan and one from the Museum of Modern Art. I'm taking an old Harvard friend out to lunch. He says if Tennessee Williams is in town, he will bring him along.' Cheyney was appalled. He hadn't listened, not one bit.

'Sebastian, we must have a talk. Not necessarily now, but we must.'

'I couldn't agree more. I am not very happy with the direction the gallery is taking.'

Cheyney seized her opportunity and pinned him down right then and there. 'Sebastian, so far your contribution to the gallery has been anything but constructive. The fact of the matter is that not one of the artists you introduced me to was available. All of them had commitments elsewhere. Embarrassingly for me, every one of them suggested that in future, if I am interested in their work, I should buy through their own dealers. I don't need you to place me in situations like that, or to find me bad deals, Sebastian. All your work was fruitless, and it cost the gallery.'

Enraged, he started to walk out of the office. Cheyney stopped him. 'Sebastian, please, we're friends, trying to work together. We have too much at stake for you to get huffy and walk out. This is an exciting time for art in New York, and we can make it. But I need you to work and not play at being in the gallery. This is not one long cocktail party, a teddy bears' picnic, you are involved in. This is a hard, creative, and tough business. And you need this job if you want to gain any measure of respect from your "friends".'

An awkward moment of silence. Then he asked facetiously, 'Who do you want to exhibit? Picasso?'

Cheyney tried to hold her temper. 'Of course. And Rothko, and Motherwell, and Barnet Newman, and Miro, and Calder, Kurt Shwitters, and Mondrian, and, and, and . . . And don't be bitchy with me, Sebastian! I spend eight to ten hours a day looking at works of art, trying to find artists who have in them that little something that is special, and who are available for me to handle. I am discovering, together I'm sure with every dealer in this city, that something new is rumbling, looming large on the art world's horizon. Something very different from the American art of the fifties we've been told to admire. I fear *it* – whatever *it* is – is going to leave the art market in a turmoil. It's almost as if American art doesn't know where to go next. And that's exciting but could be unhealthy for us as a new gallery, because collectors and art institutions don's like to buy unless the market is stable and knows where it's going.'

'You have an interesting viewpoint. Why haven't you spoken to me about this before, Cheyney?'

'I have been trying to, Sebastian, and you haven't wanted to listen. I would have thought you'd have recognised by now that I am having a difficult time of it, trying to put together an exciting and relevant gallery. I have poured everything I have into this business, changed my life for it. And if you want to be a part of it too, you have to open your eyes, forget the booze-and-chat parties, and get into this thing with me. I need *you*, not just your money. So get your brain working, and your eyes, and put your ego aside for a while.'

Cheyney and Sebastian stood looking at each other until the silence became awkward. She was embarrassed for both of them, and turned away to busy herself at her desk.

'I'm taking Jeremy Weintraub to dinner this evening. You know they think he will be made curator of drawings at the Met. It will be a big jump for him from the position he holds at the Brooklyn Museum. I went to Harvard with him. The last time I saw him was in Paris at Caresse Crosby's. Or was it Mary MacCarthy's? No, it was at Caresse's. I don't think you know Caresse, do you?'

Cheyney turned around to face Sebastian, speechless. There was just nothing more to say to the man. She had to face the fact that he was the gallery's first deficit. And they hadn't even opened the doors yet.

'He's very well placed you know, invited everywhere, very talented, and could be very helpful. I would ask you along, but it will be an old-school, all-boys-together supper. When he hears about our gallery, he will be very surprised. I'm certain I can get him to come to the opening.'

Cheyney sensed a note of bravado in his voice, a kind of one-upmanship, because he had rankled her and remained calm, cool, the perfect gentleman, steadfast in his opinion. And he had said 'our' gallery, something he had never before dared say to her face. It was the bitchy look in the eyes behind the round, slim-edged, tortoise-shell eyeglasses, worn affectedly low on the nose, that said, 'Cheyney Fox you are stuck with me. And, for better or worse, you will accept me as I am, and take my contributions more seriously.'

She was shocked. She had never seen that side of Sebastian before. She decided not to pick him up on that 'our', though it simply was not true. There were enough escape-clauses in their business agreement, inserted solely to protect Sebastian in the event of the gallery's failure, to prove it. She wanted only to be rid of him so she could get on with her day.

'As it happens I am not free. Christopher Corbyn is arriving from Paris tonight. I'm having dinner with him.'

'You didn't say!'

'I've hardly had the chance.'

'How long will he be in the States?'

'I'm not sure. A few months, anyway.'

'He never stays that long.'

'He will this time.'

Something was very wrong, and Cheyney didn't understand what it was. Sebastian had gone pale at the news of Christopher's arrival. His speech had disintegrated. It was all stutters and hesitation.

'Where is he staying and why has he come?'

'With me, Sebastian. And he's here in New York for an exhibition of his work.'

'He and Costas can't possibly stay with you. I won't have those scroungers taking advantage of your hospitality. And I certainly will never allow him to have an exhibition in this gallery, you can be certain of that!'

'Sebastian, you're out of line. Costas is not coming with Christopher, and taking advantage does not come into it. And never, ever, tell me who I can or cannot exhibit in my gallery! You don't have that right. Read your contract.'

Even that did not stem the tide of venom rising in this usually harmless, quiet man. His face changed. Twisted with anxiety, contorted more by a sick destructive will than anything evil, he gave off the scent of danger. Cheyney thought of Oscar Wilde's *Picture of Dorian Gray*. She tried to avert disaster. 'Sebastian, please, this is getting out of hand.'

'I should say it is. You deceived me, you never let me know Corbyn would be involved here. He has charmed his way into every chic salon on both sides of the Atlantic. Well, he will be banned from this one, I can promise you that. And if he thinks he can flirt his way around me, he is sadly mistaken. You have yet to see him in action. Man or woman, he doesn't care which. He's a whore, my dear, a gigolo. He danced attendance on me when I first met him at Harvard, and then again years later in Paris, but I never fell for his charm!

'They say he made love to his mother-in-law, one of the most powerful aristocrats in Spain, and only married the daughter to get a castle. And that palazzo in Florence Costas and he say they own . . . well, not quite. Stealing it away room by room from the old woman is more the real story. Give me your word he will never enter this gallery, or I will walk out now and demand my money back.'

Cheyney felt her body turn cold. She was trembling. She looked past Sebastian through the open, double doors to the ground-floor room of the gallery. His outburst had been so violent it had brought Dora, Max and Morris to stand there. She saw them, but was so upset their presence hardly registered.

'Well?' he demanded.

'Sebastian, this has nothing to do with me or the gallery, and obviously

33

everything to do with you and Christopher. I know nothing of what has happened between you, and don't care to. But you will destroy our relationship, maybe even ruin the gallery, by reneging on your contract and withdrawing your financial investment now. Are you sure you want to do that?'

'You have heard my conditions. I want an answer.'

'An answer to blackmail? Very well, you leave me with no choice. I reject your conditions. I could never live with myself if I submitted to them. I have never been exposed to blackmail before, Sebastian. It's a foul experience, and I don't believe I will ever forgive you for it.'

She turned away from him. Trembling with rage and a degree of fear for what she was about to do, she tried to steady her hand as she opened the gallery cheque-book. 'I am making out a cheque for two thousand five hundred dollars, and post-dating another for thirty days from now for the same amount.' Placing the cheques in front of her, she swivelled the chair around. She wound a sheet of blank paper into the typewriter, and hammered out:

I, Sebastian Cohen, do hereby accept the return of $5000.00 (the sum I have invested in the Cheyney Fox Gallery) paid in two cheques by Cheyney Fox on behalf of the Cheyney Fox Gallery, in cancellation of my contract with the gallery. I will make no further demands on Miss Fox or the Cheyney Fox Gallery either now or in the future.

She tore the sheet of paper from the typewriter and handed it with a pen to Sebastian. 'We can do it this way, or we can go to lawyers. I would have thought you'd rather not do that, since it'll be costly and very embarrassing for you to explain why you have decided to break your contract – in direct contravention of the procedure for dissolving it outlined in our partnership agreement. Sign here.'

Cheyney knew she was being much too generous in returning the money to Sebastian. But the possibility of his making a scandal to get every last cent back was something she simply could not cope with. She watched him read the document carefully, twice. He signed it and handed it back to her and she in turn handed him the two cheques.

'Now, get out,' she said, fighting back tears.

He actually offered her his hand, stuttering and stammering in between long pauses, 'I think we should at least shake hands and agree to be civil with each other. Maybe after a time we can become friends again.'

'Now why would we ever want to do that, Sebastian? Dora, would you please show Mr Cohen out? He is no longer working here, so there will be no reason to let him into the gallery until it is open to the public. At that time we will turn no one away.' She stood and watched in silence as he walked out.

Afterwards she collapsed in her chair, depressed over the scene which had just passed but nonetheless certain that she had done the only right and honourable thing in the circumstances.

Cheyney's deliberations were interrupted by Max and Morris. They presented her with their bill and left the gallery. Alone, she opened the envelope. The amount invoiced was correct, but it gave her a jolt. Only then did she realize how really disastrous it was to have written those two cheques. They represented ten months' rent for the gallery at a time when she was severely under-capitalised. Another pressure she hadn't expected to have to deal with.

Suddenly she felt sick. She raced up to the privacy of her bathroom, and only just made it to her knees over the WC where she retched uncontrollably. Afterwards she bathed her face and tried to calm herself. Cheyney was frightened: she was rarely sick. She lay down on her bed, trying to tell herself it was anxiety over the dreadful scene Sebastian had made, and over money. But she knew she was fooling herself. She fell into a disturbed sleep.

Chapter 5

Ten o'clock and still no word from Christopher. Cheyney went to the window, pulled the sheer silk curtains back and looked up and down the street. It was very black outside, except for the two pools of light spreading gently from the lamp posts, one a few feet from her window and another much further down on the opposite side of the street. Only the occasional lighted window among the brownstone town houses. It was eerily quiet. No sound or sight of a taxi or car shooting east across town from Fifth Avenue. No driver cruising the line of bumper-to-bumper cars on either side of the street, looking for a space to squeeze a car into. No one was even walking his dog.

She was reminded of Zazou, her Lapsa. Spoilt, faithful, her best friend and constant companion, sent home with Dora because Cheyney couldn't bear to share this reunion with even her canine Cleopatra. And now she wished her flirtatious, demanding Zazou and she were down there below in the deserted street taking their evening walk.

Cheyney made herself a promise not to look at her watch or through the window again. This was to be her final time. She was driving herself crazy with anticipation over Christopher's arrival. But, much as she willed it, she was unable to pull herself away from the window. She was certain her anxiety would pass if she could see his taxi pull up, or him walking up the street, or hear the doorbell. But for the moment, she was feeling something close to desperation.

She tried to distract herself. Still looking out of the window, she took note that there was no light on in the Segovia apartment on the first floor diagonally across from her. She wondered if Vladimir Horowitz, in his apartment almost directly opposite Segovia's, was at home playing the piano. That stirred a memory of several months earlier, when the city was in one of its torrid heatwaves. Approaching her apartment, she had heard the sound of the classical guitar. She had looked up and seen there, sitting on a chair in the window, Andres Segovia trying to catch a breath of air while he played. Several people stood in doorways listening to the maestro. When he stopped they applauded, including someone from the first-floor window above her head. She caught sight of Vladimir Horowitz sitting discreetly behind a drapery, absorbing every nuance of the Bach adaptation for the guitar.

The next day, the heat was even more oppressive. All her windows thrown open, she heard the faint sound of exquisite piano music. She leaned out of the window to listen and saw, this time, Andres Segovia sitting quietly and savouring the genius of Horowitz. She had rushed into the street, better to hear the impromptu concert. The three windows of the Horowitz flat were fully open and the sound filled that part of the street. You could see nothing of Horowitz – he was hidden behind the piano – only Segovia's blissful face opposite. It was another of New York's special vignettes that made her love that big bad city, and inspired her to push on and be a part of it.

Cheyney let the curtain slip from her hand into place. The view through the curtain was diffused by the silk, hazy, dreamlike. After a few minutes, she finally gave up and went to sit on the sofa in front of the open fire. She sat staring into the leaping flames.

Why, she wondered, do women in love, sensible, intelligent women such as she hoped she was, suffer the sorts of anguish she was going through right now while waiting for her lover? While the minutes ticked by, she could sense a closing of the physical and emotional distance between Christopher and herself. And that was both frightening and thrilling at the same time. Reunion after a long absence, based on a relationship with only free love to hold it together, is a tough scene to play. So many unasked questions, so much emotional baggage left over from other times, other loves, have to be discarded.

Here-and-now love can die an instant death from insecurity, expectations, demands of any kind on a couple as uncommitted yet in love as Christopher and Cheyney. Will he find me beautiful? Cheyney asked herself. Like my hair, me in the colour mauve, the cut of my kaftan? The scent of my skin, the feel of me in his arms? What about me? Will I still find him handsome, tremble under his touch? Was he a romantic illusion, nothing more than a European holiday fling? Questions that tore at the heart, shredded confidence, and triggered that devilish emotion, fear of loss.

Cheyney thought of their sexual life together. They had even laughed about it, labelling themselves 'the reluctant lovers'. In spite of their hesitation to let themselves go, overcome a sexual bashfulness even, theirs had been an instant attraction, where they had been helpless to hold back their passion for each other or the waves of orgasm they succumbed to during intercourse, more natural and intense than they had ever achieved with other partners.

The last time, more than three months ago, in that small, first-floor

37

hotel room on the Rue de Rivoli. The walls and French window were draped in a romantic blue and white *toile* – a pattern of a shepherdess and her lover, in eighteenth-century costume, lying together under a capacious chestnut tree, wolf-hounds by their side, sheep gambolling on a faintly etched hillside. The memory was exquisite. So vivid. The sex, the unstoppable, breathtaking orgasms of that night. It had been the first time Cheyney had ever been lost to all else in the world but lust. It had been the same for Christopher, and that night they swept each other to the outer edges of passion and erotic love.

She bowed her head and covered her face with her hands, and to herself she whispered, 'Oh, God, please give me strength never to abuse what I have with Christopher, always to do what is right for both of us.'

Cheyney felt a flush of warmth course through her body. She tried to hold back the rush of orgasm, and sensed the moistness that gave her that special pleasure like no other she experienced. She tried to ignore it, embarrassed at the joy she felt in her new-found lust. She lowered her hands from her face and was lost in the memory of one moment during another orgasm. It had been in that room, that last night, but it had been a shared orgasm with Christopher, so intense for both of them that together they cried out to the gods in thanks for their plunge into oblivion.

Cheyney rose from the sofa and went to stand by the fireplace. It came to her in that moment of remembering. The sleepiness, the sickness that afternoon after her confrontation with Sebastian . . . 'Oh, no. It can't be,' she said aloud. But in her heart she sensed that she was pregnant.

A baby! How might Christopher react? What would he say? She guessed that he would not be very gallant about it. She knew in her heart that he was not the sort of man to make a good father to a child. And there was something else: it was not in Cheyney's nature to trap a man into anything, least of all marriage and the long grind of parenthood. Disturbing thoughts. They did, however, make her face the fact that an illegitimate child with no father to help bring it up was out of the question.

Thinking in those terms, she managed to block out of her mind what she knew was possibly the most important decision in her life. To abort a baby was no easy thing. 'Strong men and stronger women have baulked at it. Oh please, please, let it not be true,' she said to the indifferent room. 'Let there be no baby, not now. I know I can't carry another huge commitment at this time in my life. Maybe there is no baby. Let me forget it, at least for tonight. Don't ruin our reunion.'

What more, she wondered, could happen to shatter her joy at Christopher's return? She was pondering the ups and downs of her see-saw day: Christopher's cable, a definite up. Sebastian and their unfortunate confrontation, a definite down. Lunch with Betty Parsons at her gallery

– a significant figure among the contemporary dealers in art, who happened to be a nice person – another up. Cheyney's simultaneous agreement to give Betty Parsons the artist her first one-man show of paintings and take her on as one of the Cheyney Fox Gallery's stable of painters – more than an up, a positive coup. A meeting with her book-keeper, Tony Caletti, to listen to a convoluted scheme for reorganising the gallery books, her industrial design company books, and her personal accounts. The predictable heat over that pair of cheques totalling $5000 dollars to Sebastian without consulting her book-keeper – the see-saw striking rock bottom.

That had left her terribly disturbed, and prompted her to make a call for an appointment to meet and consult with Bernard Reiss, a well-known patron of the arts as well as a modish and respected accountant for several top galleries in the city, and the financial adviser to many famous artists. She had to drop four names of considerable importance before she could get him on the line. In fact she found it all a bit embarrassing since she had met him half a dozen times, had twice sat next to him at dinner when he had chatted her up most of the evening. She had an uneasy premonition about that conversation.

Back at the gallery in the afternoon and early evening the highs and lows had continued. She and Sally Wichell, her part-time secretary, worked out an arrangement for Sally to work full time. With the loss of Sebastian as back-up in the gallery, that became essential. One immediate problem was solved. But another loomed: the additional cost to the gallery in wages, not included in the already tight budget. Neither was a consultation with Reiss – and he didn't come cheap. Sebastian had really dropped her in it. An aftershock of rage against him swept through her.

Then two hours of hanging the last of the paintings for the opening exhibition, assisted by Henry Stover, the gallery's odd-job man, a Columbia University art major. That was a thrill, a constructive high – to watch her choice of someone's work go up for the first time on the wall of her gallery in anticipation of what might be her first impact on art in New York.

Cheyney turned from the fireplace and looked across the room, impressive and elegant with its eighteen-foot ceiling and its bay window on to the street. The sight of the square, eighteenth-century French Provincial table standing in the bay, dressed for an intimate *dîner à deux*, made her smile. It was perfect: the crystal, the linen, the Limoges china, the silver, the white stargazer lilies in the low bowl in the centre of the table, the tall cream-coloured candles. And soon Christopher would be sitting there with her.

Cheyney looked away from the table and used her eyes like a camera.

She wanted to capture every beautiful detail of her living-room; the pair of Georgian wing chairs, covered in a plum and silver Fortuny fabric, which flanked the fireplace; the sofa, matching the one already moved into the gallery; the period tables of peach and pear wood; the soft light that filtered through cream-coloured silk lampshades over antique Chinese celadon pots; the gilded mirrors, and the walls lined with books and gilt-framed drawings. All this had been sold, given up to finance the gallery, together with all the consultancy fees from her industrial design work.

The smell of Dora's cooking was tantalising. She felt a pang of hunger, and a fearful need for Christopher. Cheyney was quick to make light of it to herself, and check the lapse. There was something in Christopher's character that she knew would make him bolt if he caught any hint of her need for him. And she couldn't bear that, not now.

In the kitchen, Cheyney opened the oven door and the sumptuous odour of roast lamb, boned and stuffed with mushrooms, apricots, prunes and sausage meat, gusted out on the escaping air. She checked the rice boiled in a chicken stock and mixed with pine nuts and tiny shrimp, cooking in a wrapped package of thin filo pastry. It was crisping nicely. She was admiring the *crème brulée* decorated with fresh-peeled lychees standing in readiness on the kitchen counter, Christopher's favourite dessert, when the doorbell rang. Her lover had come home.

There was no intercom, just a buzzer to release the downstairs entry door. She pressed it. How many times had she imagined this meeting, and where she would stand, what she would say? She had no idea but for the moment it felt like a thousand, and she was frozen behind the apartment door, trying to compose herself and to recall just one of her pre-rehearsed welcomes. She could hear Christopher taking the stairs two at a time.

Cheyney went on to automatic, and opened the apartment door. She felt unable to meet him on the landing, or to greet him over the curved balustrade winding down to the ground floor, or in the barren empty hall outside her flat. All too impersonal, frightening even. And so, leaving the door ajar, she retreated into the centre of the living-room and watched and waited for him to come to her.

He held a suitcase in one hand and carried, over his shoulder and across his back, a large and heavy roll of unstretched canvases wrapped in a waterproof sailcloth cover, more like a cross he had to bear than an artist's unmounted exhibition. He wore no hat, and his hair flopped to one side over his forehead. Christopher sported a well-worn, black wool dress-coat with a tan velvet collar. He was so very good looking and elegant in his fine coat, but there was something else about him, a cool yet dangerously sensuous air. And then there was, too, that ostentatious ambience he cocooned himself in. It did not hint so much as shout, 'I am an artist. Handle with care.'

If he saw Cheyney as he walked the length of the hall to her apartment, which he easily could have, or when he entered the vestibule and placed his things on the floor, leaning the heavy sailcloth roll against the wall, he made no sign. She watched him turn and close the door, then turn again and walk towards her, unbuttoning his coat. He entered the living-room and dropped the coat over the back of the sofa, still walking towards her, and at last they were face to face. She realised at once that they were nervous of each other.

He combed the hair back from his forehead with his fingers.

'You have no idea what it means to have you waiting here. New York is always hard for me.'

'You look exhausted.'

'I am, I seem to have been travelling forever.'

'Christopher . . .'

Before she could say another word, he interrupted her with, 'The apartment looks the same – beautiful, chic, extravagant. Smells wonderful. Lilies and Dora's cooking.'

Pleasant enough words, but the indifference, the chilling denial of love, affection even, in his voice or his manner . . . It was all so strange and banal. Not at all what she had envisaged for them; it was no kind of reunion at all. Why didn't he sweep her into his arms, acknowledge her existence with a touch of the hand, a hug, a kiss on the cheek at the very least? They were after all lovers, with a history of heat and passion between them. Was it too late for them? Had the fire of erotic love gone out for them? What then was this meaningless social chatter between them?

She watched him walk to the dining table, bury his face in the lilies to drink in their scent. He looked across the room at her and smiled for the first time. She felt ill with desire for him. From there he went to the window, looked out, and then drew the cerise damask draperies closed over the sheer white silk curtains. He gazed briefly at her once more. It was a merciless look that told her nothing but both chilled and inflamed her, banking the flames of her passion still higher.

From there he walked to the kitchen. She heard him open the oven door and close it again. 'God bless Dora. I'm famished,' he called out, walking towards a pair of decorative Lalique glass doors. He hesitated. Slowly, seductively, he slid one of the doors open to reveal the bed filling the alcove behind. Christopher looked at it, and then provocatively at her. His gaze steadied on her while he slid the door closed.

His steps now were swift and sure, not unlike some magnificent jungle cat's: a lion or tiger who has marked his place, making it his own. She watched him move closer to her, loosen his tie, unbutton the jacket of his grey flannel suit. He stood inches away from her, not exactly cold, not exactly distant. Finally, he reached out to her and took her in his arms. She slipped her hands under his jacket, around his waist, and crushed herself to him. She felt at once that his hard yearning desire for her was at least as great as hers for him. They kissed.

Hand in hand, they walked together to the sofa. 'Hello,' he said.

'Welcome home,' she answered. 'I have missed you so terribly.'

He flicked his hair off his forehead with a quick turn of his head. A gesture of his she always found touching: there was something boyish, innocent, about it. He raised her hand and placed it on the bulging erection straining his trousers. Then he brought the open palm that had caressed him to his mouth and kissed it. 'And you can see and feel how much I have missed you.' They were both smiling now. The attraction was still there and as strong as ever. Standing up, he removed his jacket, tore off his tie and threw them on to the wing chair. His shirt unbuttoned, he stood above her and between her legs, and gently took her head in his hands to press her face against what he knew she yearned for. She remained there caressing him with her face, absorbing the faint raunchy scent of her lover.

Cheyney had to restrain herself from weeping with joy, from begging him to take her. Her need for him to make love to her was enormous. To feel his lips devour her, his hands caress, to feel him inside her, dissolving with every thrust the separateness he created between them. Only then, in the toils of sexual intercourse, was he able to express his love for her, show affection and passion, a oneness with her, or expose the real depth of his feeling for her. Until he wanted her desperately enough to do that, he would tease her with his sex, torture her with his charm and promise. Cheyney could accept the teasing games of seduction he was so good at, the subtle manoeuvres to gain power and position, the little cruelties he employed with her and others who fell in love with him. All this fell away during those shattering encounters when he surrendered all of himself to Cheyney, confessed his love and the overwhelming sexual bliss he achieved with her. In gratitude, he would turn himself into her slave, shorn of all desire but to fuck her into sexual oblivion.

He pulled her up by her hands and asked, 'Are we drinking red or white? A glass now before dinner would be nice.'

How shallow his love must be for me, she thought. A shallowness that kept her on guard. It served as a constant reminder that their relationship was too flimsy to survive. A twinge of sadness, a forced smile to cover it up. She answered, 'Red, I thought.'

He placed his arm around her and they strolled together to the table. He busied himself with opening the wine. She eyed him and could understand the Sebastians of this world, and the women, all of whom had been infatuated with Christopher. What pain he must have caused them with his half-innocent nurturing of their weaknesses, their headlong course towards self-destruction. Not me, she promised herself. 'This is just for as long as it lasts. She hung on to the motto like a life line.

'How's Costas?' she asked.

'Not happy about my being here. He's afraid you're going to seduce me into staying. Never let me return to Europe.'

'I just might.'

'That's what he says. But you and I know different. You know better than to try. That's part of the power you have over me. The freedom, the lack of commitment, the sex – all given and all taken with no strings attached. He's just jealous because he's not here with us. He loves New York, and both of us, and wants us to be happy. But, at the same time, he's afraid you are going to interfere with our relationship – solitary, spiritual brothers working together for a life of creativity.'

'What did you tell him?'

'That I will return to Europe as soon as I have achieved everything I want to here. That you have your own life, and now your gallery. That I don't intend my life or its goals to change. That you and I have some special feelings for each other, and we'll see each other when we want to and when it fits in with our other plans. Nothing is going to change my resolve that my work, my art, is my life. Everything that comes my way has to serve that end.'

Christopher had never spelled it out so clearly to Cheyney before. Her blood chilled at his explicit warning to her. She was certain that little speech had been discussed between them before Christopher left Paris, and Costas been promised delivery upon arrival. There was something sinister about that. A surge of queasiness succeeded the chill.

His eyes on her were as cold as steel when he dropped that hard line. If he were waiting for Cheyney to challenge it, show a reaction, attack Costas as she had heard so many others do in the short time she had known them, he would be sorely disappointed. She showed nothing, said nothing, except to herself.

He placed a glass of wine in her hand, and toasted her with, 'You spoil me. All this—' he waved his arm – 'I know you did it all for me, for my home-coming.' The hardness in his eyes faded as he touched the rim of his glass to hers. But the look was more greedy than loving, more arrogant than humbled by her love and generosity.

With raised eyebrows, she said, 'Make no mistake, Christopher, I did it for *us*. When I spoil you, I reap untold rewards. Just as you do when you're fucking me.' She tried to make her gaze as hard as the rim of the glass over which she engaged his eye.

'That's a bit coarse, don't you think, my dear?'

'Better a coarse truth, perhaps, than a soggy denial of one's own emotions, *my dear*. Now then, I think dinner, don't you?'

Somewhat haughtily she brushed past him towards the kitchen. 'Not quite yet, I think,' he said, grabbing her by the wrist. 'I'm more hungry for you.'

'Only hungry? I'm famished for you.'

'That's the way I want you always to be. Hungry, famished, starved for me.' And he pulled her into his arms and made love to her with one ravishing kiss. His urgency made her heart race. He slid the Lalique glass screen aside and together they stood beside the bed where they disposed of their clothes, tossing them out of the way. Naked and erect, all ego and self lost to the god Eros, Christopher was hers. He placed his hand between her legs, and his fingers searched out that place where he yearned to be. She was warm and moist and it spurred his passion on. She used her hands to caress his rampant, throbbing penis, his velvety balls, her eyes never leaving the handsome face turned lustily decadent. He pulled her roughly into his arms and together they collapsed on to the bed. All love gone, sex their master now.

Chapter 6

Streaks of dawn pierced the narrow opening where the draperies did not quite meet. A misty light suffused the darkened room, just enough to shadow its shapes and forms: the elegant furnishings, the remnants of a well-savoured dinner, the candles which had recently flickered out. Christopher's unstretched canvases and collages were strewn everywhere – draped over sofas and wing chairs, hung in front of mirrors, propped against walls and mantelpiece.

In the alcove of the one-room apartment, the light just allowed Cheyney to study her sleeping lover's handsome face. She lay on her side, propped up against the pillows, leaning on one elbow. Sleep never came easily to Cheyney when she shared a bed with Christopher. She was unable to doze off until she was certain he was asleep, and was always wide awake long before he was.

Christopher was the only man she had ever shared a bed with all through the night, or washed socks for, or begun and ended days with; the only one she had ever planned to share her life with. And her feelings for him were shaking the last vestiges of her middle-class American morality. In the Fall of '58 when they had met and fallen in love, the Pill and the sexual revolution were still a few years off. Which was too bad, because she could have used the new morality of the sixties, its bid for sexual freedom, its move towards open cohabitation with whoever you happened to love. If for no other reason than to get more sleep.

She gazed lovingly at Christopher, completely absorbed by him. Asleep, his mesmerising beauty was even more apparent. And it combined with the appeal of a sleeping innocent child, for he slept with his thumb at his lips. This virile, masterly lover – who was able to admit his love for her only with slow, sure thrusts, and who taunted her with, 'This is what you want. Just this, more and more and more of this,' until he exhausted them both on a wave of shared ecstasy.

She looked away from his face only briefly but in that moment reality intruded. An interior voice asserted, 'In love with love: not a bad thing. In love with Christopher: not a bad thing either. But not to be confused.' She smiled in the darkness. So long as she could hear that still

45

small voice in her head, she knew everything between them would be all right.

She poured herself another cup of coffee and then topped up his cup. The mid-morning sun was streaming across the dining table.

Cheyney was still in her silk dressing gown, Christopher in jeans and his shirt from the night before. He appeared relaxed, completely at home, and Cheyney was happier than she could ever have imagined. They were together.

'A November New York sun may shine, but it never warms you the way a Mediterranean sun does. I'm always chilled when I'm in New York.'

He walked from the table to his open suitcase and pulled out a crew-neck, navy-blue cashmere sweater, its yarn worn thin with the years. He drew it over his head. A tight fit, his elbows perilously straining the threads. It was difficult not to feel a pang for the man. The mere sight of his pathetic, threadbare clothing spilling out of the battered suitcase, an address book, several well-worn but clean paint brushes, sable and bristle, tubes of cadmium white, black, and chrome yellow oil paint, a palette of watercolour paints and a block of 9 x 12 watercolour paper of not the best quality – it all declared: struggle, long hard road, artist.

'My paintings seem to have taken over the entire room. *I* have taken over the entire room. Seems it's mine. Does that bother you?'

'My home is your home when you're here in New York. Here, and as of tomorrow my private quarters at the gallery.'

'I'm anxious to see the gallery.'

'I'm even more anxious for you to see it.'

'Let's go after I've made some phone calls. I may use the telephone, mayn't I?'

Cheyney bristled, recognising that over-solicitous tone he switched on, the seductive smile of a Romeo, a Valentino, he adopted as he reached across the table to take her hand while asking to use the telephone. She resented his thinking he had to hustle her for telephone calls. Rising from her chair, she said, 'Christopher, for a phone call? You really don't need to use your charm on me like that. I have just told you, my house is your house. That includes the telephone.'

He stood up immediately and put his arm around her. 'You're very touchy this morning.'

'Maybe I am. I'm going to have to be, aren't I, if you lump me in with those to be conquered or used? That's not what we're about, and you would do well not to forget it.'

'Is that a threat?' he asked, a teasing tone in his voice, a smile on his lips. He kissed her and pulled her to him in a hug. Before she could answer him, he changed the subject with, 'I should go see John Snyder about my exhibition. Do you think I should arrive there for our first meeting with or without the work I plan to show?'

'Without.'

Christopher released her from his arms. 'That was a bit emphatic.'

'I didn't mean it to sound that way. It's just that there's so much for you and John to arrange. The concept of the show, the advertising, the catalogue, the *vernissage*. And most important, presentation.'

Christopher ran his fingers through his hair before he spoke. 'This exhibition has cost me years of hustling. I've been courting John by arranging introductions for him to all the right people in Europe for – oh, it seems a lifetime!' He sighed and then went on, 'I've brought a strong collection of my work, don't you think?' She nodded. 'He's seen most of it this summer when he came to visit me at the Greek house, so there will be few surprises for him.'

Cheyney saw her opportunity to talk to Christopher about the paintings and collages he intended to exhibit, and she grabbed it. 'You're the one that's going to get the surprise, darling,' she said.

'What do you mean by that?'

'There are some really sassy exhibitions going on in many of the galleries right now. How about you do the galleries before you assemble your show with John? Sort of get into the New York art scene. Get a whiff of what's going on.' She continued talking about the art world much as she had with Sebastian the day before. It was less of a waste of breath with Christopher. His questions and keen responses showed that. His calls were to fellow artists living in the city, as well as to his 'A'-list ladies, united by the bonds of high society and old money. The dowager princesses of the arts he was forever trying to wean off John Singer Sargent family portraits, Corot or Corbet landscapes, or a cross-section of French Impressionists. He reckoned they ought to cut any teeth remaining to them on contemporary art. In particular, his own work.

She was finishing yet another cup of coffee and the morning newspaper when he started on his third call. His telephone seductions embarrassed her, she wanted to leave the room. He grabbed her by the wrist as she passed by him. He could hardly miss the flush in her face. Their eyes met while he kept up the flow of honey to one of 'my Mayflower dowagers', as he called them, on the other end of the line. His gaze quickly turned from affectionate to something more steely, and he released her.

In the bath, Cheyney relaxed in the almond scent of water made smooth as satin by rich and luxurious oils. She kept working the large sponge; filling it and then squeezing it over her arms and her shoulders. Rivulets of glistening, sensuous warmth trickled over her breasts and teased her skin, caressed her nipples. A knock at the door, and then he was sitting on the edge of the deep, old-fashioned bathtub. He took the sponge from her and continued to bathe her with it just as she had been doing.

'Ten phone calls, ten invitations, ten people at least for the opening of my exhibition. Eight of them millionaires, five of them collectors. Not bad for my first morning in New York.' He looked very pleased with himself. 'Instead of flushing with embarrassment over my seductions, you should have taken notes and headed them "How To Play The Art Game". I should have thought you would have learned that lesson from Sebastian.'

'He and I dissolved our business arrangement yesterday. He's no longer involved in the gallery.'

Christopher stopped caressing her with the bath water. Simply sat there, sponge in hand, looking at her intently. Then he asked, 'What brought that about?'

'Differences of opinion.'

Christopher dipped the sponge in the bath water and resumed his bathing of her. 'Because of me, my arrival. Sebastian would feel himself threatened by my appearance on the scene. Am I right?'

There was a smugness in his tone, a glint of satisfaction in his eye. Cheyney resented his obvious enjoyment of the situation, even as she acknowledged his canny guesswork. Not wanting to feed his rampant egotism, she answered, 'There was more than one reason for breaking our contract. Now let's just drop it.'

It was the sponge that Christopher dropped in the water, as he threw his head back to laugh. He stood up and pulled off his sweater and shirt in one wrench, flicked off his shabby shoes. He dropped his jeans and stepped out of them. He was quick, so quick Cheyney hadn't the chance to say anything before he was in the bath with her, straddling and looming over her, massively virile and handsome. Cheyney reacted with a racing heart as she reached out to caress a muscular thigh, a slender hip, and confronted the bared sex of the man of her life. He placed his hands on her shoulders and lowered himself into the warm water. 'Jealousy. Sebastian is always jealous of whatever I have. Without lifting a finger, I have done you a great service, getting rid of him for you.'

He picked up the sponge and handed it to her. 'Bathe me, Cheyney. My reward for services rendered.' He smiled broadly at her and leaned over to caress her cheek, demanding, 'Smile. Be happy. You have one less thing to worry about with Sebastian gone.'

'Nice if that were true, Christopher.' She showed him a faint smile and suggested, 'Stand up.' He straddled her once more but not before he used his toes most deftly to toy with her silky warm cunt. She clasped the sponge in both hands and bathed her lover. Again and again she dipped the large sponge into the water and squeezed it out over his shoulders, across his chest, over his thighs, between his legs until he shone like a magnificent Greek statue. She was enchanted by the sight of the water cascading down his body, the way it turned his skin to shiny satin, the steam that swirled up from his flesh. She turned him slowly round while still bathing him and transformed his strong back, his sensuous buttocks, into live shiny marble. Then spreading his legs as far apart as was possible, she slipped her hand underneath him and caressed him with the hot soapy water until she could resist him no longer. She dropped the sponge and used her hands and then her lips and then her mouth until, unable to hold back any longer, he chose to collapse on top of her in the bath, displacing a huge wave of water and plunging wildly into her. In a frenzy of passion he fucked her and they flailed around in the hot, sensuous, slippery water. They came together in a thrilling explosive orgasm, and lay naked, entwined in each other's arms, in the few inches of water left in the bath. Silently each thanked the gods for giving them a glimpse of bliss, a moment of magnificent sexual oblivion.

Cheyney was driving the pale blue Alfa Romeo Sprite with her usual assurance down Park Avenue, Christopher at her side. 'Happy?' he asked.

'Very. Happier than I have ever been,' she answered, throwing the gears into third as she wove in and out of the traffic.

'Because of me?'

'Of course.'

'That's nice. I like that.'

'And me, and the gallery, and us,' she added giving him a delectably winning smile.

'But mostly because of me,' he insisted.

'Question or declaration?' she teased.

'Declaration.'

They turned into East Sixty-Third Street. Miraculously Cheyney found a parking space almost exactly in front of number thirteen. She switched off the engine and, turning to face Christopher, placed a hand on his. 'Welcome to the Cheyney Fox Gallery. I'm nearly bursting with excitement for you to see it.'

Cheyney had never wholly understood how impressive the gallery and its premises were, or what a monumental change *and* chance she had undertaken in creating it, until she saw Christopher's reaction to it.

She had called before she left the Ninety-Fourth Street flat to ask Dora to disappear for an hour. Her secretary, Sally, had been given a similar message. Cheyney opened the front door with her key. It was a far more emotional moment for her than she had expected it to be. Suddenly all the pressure of the last few months – the work, the anxieties of constant decision-making, her plunge into New York's art world, the responsibilities she had taken upon herself, her lone leap into a new and exciting life – seemed to bear down upon her shoulders. She gazed into Christopher's face as she pushed the door open for them to step into the gallery, and she watched it change almost instantaneously.

Power of place. A special energy, impossible to label. The gallery had that. Cheyney saw it take Christopher over. The way he looked at the paintings, reacted to the internal space of the gallery and its palpable relation to the works of art. The sculpture garden.

Christopher made no comment during their tour of the public gallery and her private quarters, where they would be living together from the following day. It seemed to her that he was somewhat edgy when shown the bedroom. The place that was meant to blot out the rest of the world, be their intimate haven away from their public lives. Their sexual playground where no holds were barred.

For the first time since they began their grand tour, Christopher touched her. He took her by the arm and propelled her from the bedroom into the double-cubed gallery, and gently sat her down on the Georgian sofa in the centre of the room. He circled the gallery once more, leaving a trail of footprints in the fluffy pile of the new sunflower-yellow carpet.

When he returned to stand before her, she saw something in his face that she had never seen there before. The arrogance was gone, and the soft, selfish greed. And yet, there was no humility in his face. Nor surprise. Could it be admiration? He squatted on his haunches and, gazing into her eyes, said, 'You did all this for me.'

He raised his arm and waved it to encompass the room. 'All this for *me*. Because you love *me*. I'm impressed with what you've accomplished. And so quickly! You're in with a chance in big-league art in New York with a gallery like this. And all because you love me. I told you that first night we met on the island: "Cheyney Fox, beautiful Cheyney Fox, I'm going to make love to you and change your life." Well, I certainly have.'

'All this because you love me.' Those words kept playing through her mind, ringing in her ears. Oh, the complacency of the man! It robbed Cheyney of the joy she might have had in the limelight of Christopher's admiration and respect. But worse, it frightened her.

She wanted to shout: 'It's not true. I did it for *me*. For *me*, Christopher, not for you, I changed my life, I opened this gallery.'

But how could she speak the words aloud? His blatant egotism had planted seeds of doubt within her. His instinctive assumption that she had changed her life for him stunned her. Could he be right? Was it possible that she had fallen under the Christopher Corbyn spell and, knowing his weakness for the rich and successful, actually changed her life so as not to lose him? Was she less than in control of her emotions where they involved her lover? Cheyney was appalled at the very idea that she might not be on top of her relationship with Christopher, but might, instead, be at his mercy.

Her eyes followed him for some time while he walked around the room looking at the paintings. Christopher Corbyn was not her artistic catalyst, just a man she was in love with. Once she had assured herself of that, sweet relief followed. Immediately she went to him and, raising his arm, she draped it around her shoulders. She smiled at him and said, 'They say that Gertrude Stein's last words before she kicked off to artists' heaven were, "So what was the question?" And she began to laugh.

Chapter 7

Being on the threshold of the new decade didn't mean a thing to Cheyney, any more than it did to millions of other people. Nobody then was lauding 'the sixties'. Yet for Cheyney those last weeks at the end of a dull decade were thrilling, bursting with vitality. Dramatic, unexpected things were happening. Every day was like stepping off a cliff, protected by a parachute. The free fall was sensational, the chute ride a floating kind of ecstasy like the romance in her life, the landings sometimes bumpy. It was near-impossible to plot one's actions from day to day – or reactions, for that matter – and nothing was coming out as Cheyney had planned.

She was living her life on several levels at once. Remarkably, they amalgamated, and she made huge strides as a new dealer on the New York art scene; in her relationship with Christopher; as an independent human being trying to make a success of her life. But it wasn't easy. Escalators had not replaced stairways in her life. Nothing removed the twists and turns, the sheer upward slog of existence, that accompanied the dramatic intervals of free fall.

Cheyney had no doubt that she was strong enough, determined enough, to make a success of her endeavours. It was not a matter of arrogance: she had no reason to think otherwise. And so she was able to take the downsides along with the upsides of her new life with equal aplomb.

Soon a pattern established itself in their lives, one that Cheyney could not have envisaged. She withstood its pressures.

That Christopher and she loved each other was not in doubt. What she hadn't bargained for was that they didn't like each other very much. That she could never mean enough to him for him to give up his 'Mayflower dowagers', and his flirtations with anyone, man or woman, whom he could exploit for gain. Worse, he imagined she would not only accept that flaw in him but share his relish for such exploits.

Remarkably, their love affair flourished, flaws and all, but only behind closed doors. It had not been a conscious decision by either of them to hide their love from public view. Things just emerged that way. A further mysterious facet to the romance was that each of them was an enormously positive influence on the other's life. At the end of each day, in the privacy of their love, they had glorious sex. Cheyney looked forward to those nights together, clung to the memory of them. They nourished and sustained her.

This pattern was just establishing itself by the night of the gallery's official opening. Cheyney's nerves were frayed, in spite of the fact that all was, at least for the night, under control. Even Christopher had been aware of the pressure she was under, and had surprised her with his unqualified support. She looked ravishing and every inch the intelligent avant-garde art dealer in a Russian flat black karacul fur suit. Designed by Revillon of Paris especially for the occasion, its short black jacket with wide pointed lapels and a plunging neckline was worn over a skintight fitted skirt slightly slit up the back, accentuating Cheyney's sensuous but chic look.

There were hundreds of guests, waiters in white jackets and black tie proffering Kir Royale or Pernod, and pretty black girls in white dresses with frilly black silk organza aprons serving bite-size Chinese food: dim sum, egg roll, spare ribs. That night Christopher worked the crowd hard: flirting with the art critics and collectors, the dealers and the museum curators. He had played Don Juan to the dowagers and the millionaire closet-queens. He had given a wide berth to the unknown painters, and made a bee-line for the famous artists. With his good looks and charming, courtly manners, Christopher had an unsettling effect on his victims, putting them on edge. A dozen times Cheyney watched him take out his pocket diary. To fix up a business engagement, or just some clandestine rendezvous? At other times she caught in the faces of his prey an ambivalence towards him, jealousy, anguish even, at his very presence.

The evening was made for Cheyney by the loyal support of her friends in the New York art world. Betty Parsons had been there, that grand lady of the arts, loved by every artist lucky enough to cross her path or to have her as a dealer. There was Acton Pace, supportive as always, and Mervyn Jules and Walter Kamus. Tomayo turned up; Milton Avery and his wife; the two Soyers, Moses and Raphael, separately; Saul Steinberg; Chaim Gross. They were viewing and talking art, and giving her the back-up she needed by their very presence. There were others like Richard Lindner, Adolph Gotlieb, Alexander Lieberman, Barnet Newman and Mark Rothko, who had arrived with Betty Parsons. Their words of encouragement saw Cheyney through. It had been the artists who had taken the edge of anxiety off the evening for her. The people who were fearful for her, because they knew how tough it was to make it in the New York art world. They had wished her well and had given her support with invitations to their studios. Friendship could ask no more.

Several museum curators, and critics also turned up. Some with smiles, others with raised eyebrows, and a 'We'll wait and see what she can do' attitude towards her. She was not unhappy about that. None of the really big collectors showed up, a disappointment to her only because their mere appearance at the opening would have sent a buzz through the crowd. Good for press-reviews, a boost to business. A number of small ones did, and, by the time the last supper-guest had left, red stickers were glowing in the lower right-hand corners of seven picture-frames. Seven sold the first night was no disgrace. Cheyney had been launched.

A dozen times during the evening Cheyney pinched herself. No it wasn't a dream. Cheyney Fox, that nice Jewish girl from Connecticut, was in the middle of her dream come true. Oh, how she would have liked to share this evening with family. But there had been no family there. An over-possessive mother, whose constant parade of unsuitable role models for her daughter led to their estrangement long before her father skidded off an icy road into a ravine one New Year's Eve somewhere near Great Barrington in the Berkshires, killing himself and his wife. A brother, he too died one cold winter day, in action, in Korea. Estrangement hadn't cancelled love. She still missed the three of them.

They talked for hours about the evening, its success and the artists who had turned up to fête her. Christopher had clearly been impressed. The excitement he had felt at being steeped in the New York art world left him glowing. The competition he was faced with that evening served to spur him on in his own work. In the dawn hours he confessed he was less than satisfied to show what he had brought for his own exhibition.

'It's scheduled for fifteen weeks from now,' he said. 'I'll paint a new show for it. Find a studio to borrow as soon as I return. You were so right, something new is happening in art now. By God, I'm going to be part of it.'

'Return?' Cheyney felt as if she had been hit with a wooden bat. Where was he going? Why? When? All she had been able to think while she had tried to get her breath back was, It's not possible. I've mis-heard him. I've left it too late to tell him if he's going away. But he's part of this, he has to know about the baby. The guilt, the sadness of destroying a life we created, I need him to help me get through this. She felt queasy when he took her in his arms and brought her to her knees, slipping her silver silk nightgown up over her hips and breasts, over her head and abandoning it to the room. He placed her on her back and slid very carefully on top of her saying, 'In honour of this dazzling evening and our life in the art world.'

He teased, he taunted the outer lips of her clitoris and her vagina with adept fingers, and used the tip of his now large and hard penis to caress the opening with delicate seductive strokes. He created his own special sexual dance, penetrating no deeper than the rim of her cunt. In and out, in and out, only enough each time to open her wider, make her ready and yearning, desperate even, to receive the full thrust of his masterly cock. To have it buried deep inside her, to feel that exquisite movement of the grand fuck. That was the bliss she craved. And now he was penetrating much deeper, and withdrawing, with an exquisite leisure that tortured. She could feel every nuance of his penetration, accentuated a hundredfold by her moistness. It was time. Deeper, deeper, until he filled her full of himself, and then . . .

Their intercourse was sublime. Their orgasms, like sexual tidal waves, swept away any doubts that anything but love governed what they had together.

How could she tell him in the midst of their passion? Afterwards, before either had fully recovered from their exertion, he had announced he was leaving to visit his uncle in San Francisco that afternoon. Back in three weeks.

'Can you put if off for a week?'

'Why would I?'

'Bad timing, I'm afraid. I have a problem that could complicate our lives if I don't do something about it in the next few days.'

His silence was like a reprimand in the dark, worse than a slap in the face. It said bleakly, 'You're alone.' It brought tears to her eyes.

More silence, more darkness, until he snapped on the bedside light close to where they lay. Meticulously he arranged the dishevelled bed, then sat up against the pillows. He did nothing about his own nakedness but attended to hers. He gathered a diaphanous lavender silk shawl embroidered with cream-coloured silk flowers from the floor and draped it around her shoulders. He took time to arrange the fine silk fringe over her breasts so that their round voluptuousness was not obscured. He strewed the long threads decoratively around the sensuous nipples that gave him such endless pleasure. Otherwise she remained naked down to her toes. With mock painterly solemnity he made of her a Goya, and called her 'My own naked Maja, my Duchess of Alba' in a husky whisper. Tenderly he touched the flat of her stomach, caressed the triangle of curly black hair and then the roundness of her thigh. He stroked himself erect, and, sidling tight up against her side, spoke.

'Then it's a good thing I'm leaving tomorrow. It will give you time to heal yourself and be well by the time I return. You do understand that I can't help you in this? You know I can't cope with one more complication in my life. Especially now, with a whole new show to paint. I must erase anything else from my mind: a divorce still not finalised, Costas in a fallow period in his work, the money needed for repairs on my houses, even you and your problem. Tell me you understand.'

55

'I understand,' she answered in a hallow voice. And the worst thing about it was that she did. That she expected no more than she got from Christopher. That she accepted her pregnancy as her responsibility, hers alone, just as he expected her to. But his insensitivity caused her untold pain.

'I'll call you from the coast,' he said magnanimously.

Where was her pride? she wondered, when he touched her lips with his in a passionless kiss. Then, seconds later, he slipped between her legs and fucked her with a kind of desperation. He demanded she reciprocate with a frenzy of lust so passionate as to send her into paroxysms of orgasm. And she did. Only then was he able to express his real feelings, able to say, 'I love you, Cheyney. Against everything I believe in and want, I have fallen in love with you because there is no measure in your love for me.' There had been tears on his cheeks when he had made his confession of love for her. She saw that it was true. It showed in his eyes. But there was, too, something else she recognized, a rage at her within his love, rage held in check, for having made him fall in love.

Cheyney pulled her hands from her face and wiped the tears from her eyes. She was sobbing with self-pity. She looked at her watch yet again, and imagined the wheels of the plane lifting off the tarmac at Eidelwild airport, the plane ascending dramatically into the air. And was relieved to think he was gone and out of her life for the next three weeks, so that she could confront her immediate, appalling problem: the abortion. Her mind was so fragmented she had no idea what to do first, or indeed what to do about it at all. What if his plane had not taken off? She distracted herself with that, until she worked herself up into such a state that she had to call the airport to make sure. Once the flight was confirmed, there was little choice but to get on with it. But how?

This was 1959, New York. To get a legal abortion you quitted the country for Mexico, Europe – or was it Puerto Rico? She wasn't even sure about that. Anyway, she was tied to the gallery. How could she leave it now, just as it had opened itself to the world and called for her nurturing presence? To go abroad would be impossible. She needed to have the operation done on a Saturday evening. To recuperate over Sunday and be able to be on her feet and in the gallery again on the Monday morning. She was only beginning to perceive the extent of the trouble she was in, the difficulties she was going to have to face.

Cheyney didn't have the sort of friends who knew about illegal matters, especially ones that involved life-and-death issues. Secrecy soon became all important as she realised she was about to become a criminal. Who could she turn to? The doctors she knew were out. Their licences would be in jeopardy if they so much as recommended another practitioner. Her friend Lala? Impossible. She gossiped too much. Her other friends? They would be shocked and embarrassed for her and she didn't want that. Her family? Unthinkable. That left only Dora. She called her housekeeper into her office.

'It sure is hell bein' a woman. Shit, girl, you is in trouble, an I can't help yah. I could find you somebody, but it ain't the kinda job you want done. A cheapo job is what you'll get up my end of town. And them Harlem abortionists ain't renown for their ability, nor the places for cleanliness. You gotta find a good one, Miss Cheyney, an get the job done right. You're a young woman. One day you might want babies not hysterectomies.'

Cheyney felt a chill rack her body. She had hardly thought of the actual physical side of what had to be done, the danger involved. 'I don't know anyone else to ask.'

'That's simple – your hairdresser. Those fairies know everything. All them rich ladies confidin their indiscretion on em. Your guy Roland, he's the one to ask.'

Cheyney called Roland at once. And indeed he had come through for her, Roland and another client of his, a glamorous Hungarian woman-about-town. By seven that evening, he was sitting in the upper gallery on the Georgian sofa, sipping a martini while dialling his Hungarian client's telephone number. Now Cheyney wanted it done immediately if it were possible, not to lose a day, for fear that the more she heard, and the more she thought about her condition, the less she would want to do it at all.

By nine o'clock that evening, Cheyney was sitting between a dazzling Zsa Zsa Gabor-type of indeterminate age, and a Muncie, Indiana, bleached-blond homosexual hairdresser in a Park Avenue doctor's waiting-room, trying to figure out how she could have sunk to this humiliating level.

There was a buzz and the inner office door clicked open. Nadja nudged her and whispered, 'Just go in and sit down, dawlink. Not to worry, we'll wait here for you, dawlink.' Roland squeezed her arm.

The doctor was an immaculate, white-haired man in his late sixties. Handsome, well-dressed, sitting in an expensively appointed office, he motioned her to be seated, and then asked several questions about her condition and the father of the child, whether he was a husband or a casual lover. No names, and he took no notes. Cheyney felt confused and set on guard by his cold matter-of-fact manner, and a mean glint in the steady gaze he fixed on her.

'Are these questions necessary?' she asked defensively.

'As necessary as your being here because you have been negligent and rather stupid. Now shall we get on with it?'

She felt her lower lip tremble and bit the inside of it so as not to burst into tears. She answered several more questions.

'Good,' he said, and rose from his desk and walked around it. 'Now come with me.' He took her by the elbow and ushered her through a door, flicking on a light switch. They were in a white-tiled, antiseptic-smelling, examining room. In the centre, under a large surgical light, a black, leather-covered operating-table was supported on a metal frame dominated by large and small adjusting wheels. At one end of it, a pair of shining chrome contraptions raised two feet above the table, culminating in foot-stirrups, was flung wide apart. Cabinets of chrome and glass, with shelf upon shelf of gleaming, bizarre-shaped surgical instruments, stood against its walls. A white-painted iron chair and a backless, black-leather seat on wheels, a white enamel wash basin . . . the place terrified Cheyney.

The doctor walked her to the table and said, 'There is nothing to be frightened about. I'm going to examine you, nothing more. Take off all your clothes and leave them on that chair.'

Cheyney found everything the doctor did frightening, seemingly calcu-lated to humiliate her. There was no screen to undress behind. He sat in a chair opposite her. Was he actually watching her remove her clothes? When she asked for a robe, a smock, he answered, 'No. Place your hands by your side and stand up straight.'

Never taking his eyes off hers, he stood up and removed his jacket, unbuttoned his tweed waistcoat and placed them both on the chair where he had been sitting. He had her nearly frozen with terror when he touched her breasts, pressed the flat of his hand just above her pubis, and said, 'You're a beauty and sensuous, a good body in good health. Take a sheet from that cabinet, open it and cover the table with it.' She did as she was told, and, from the corner of her eye, watched him roll up his sleeves to wash his hands.

She didn't cry when he lifted her up by the waist and sat her down on the table, nor when he examined her breasts more sensually than profes-sionally. When he had her lie down flat, and roughly pulled her down to the edge of the table by her naked hips. Nor when she asked him for a sheet to cover her nakedness and he refused, answering her by raising her legs and spreading them wide apart, adjusting her thighs on the curved braces and buckling them secure, placing her heels in the stirrups and prising her legs even further apart. Not even over having to tolerate the discomfort, the humiliation of lying thus exposed and vulnerable under the glaring light. Only when he spread her vaginal lips, examined them with gloveless fingers, found her clitoris, did she cover her face with her arm and cry.

'You like your sex, my girl. You always will. Even if you have to pay the piper for it. That's the way you're made. Over-sensitive genitalia, used to masturbation. I could, even now, unhappy as you are, bring you on.'

He adeptly propelled himself on his mobile seat away from between her legs and said, 'Hasn't anyone told you that there are few things more fascinating for a man than a woman who enjoys her sexuality? Or, for that matter, anything more uplifting for a woman? For that you don't have to cry. But you certainly should for being here. I give no lectures to women who come to me with your problem. I am only telling you what I tell the others: I will not help you again. Not to have taken precautions makes you criminally negligent.'

With that he rose from the seat and went to the wash basin. There he put on a white coat and washed his hands again. Cheyney heard the snap of the rubber gloves and sensed him sitting beside her again. 'Take your arm away and look at me. Good. Now let's make this easy for both of us. Relax. If you're tense, it will be more difficult for you.' The thrust of rubber fingers deep inside her, exploring, and then cold, cold steel. She shrank from the idea that he was looking right into the most secret, intimate place in her body.

Afterwards she dressed and felt more composed. Or as composed as she could possibly be under the circumstances. Looking across his Park Avenue desk at her, he made his prognosis. 'It's not going to be easy. You have left it dangerously late. But it will be all right, and so will you. Someone will call you.' He looked at his watch. 'I doubt whether it will be tonight. Write your telephone number down here, and see to it that you are available to take the call. You can go now.'

'I would like . . .', she started to say as she passed the scrap of paper across the desk to him.

He took it, interrupting her with, 'No questions. I thought you understood that.' He stood up and ushered her to the waiting-room door.

The first thing Nadja said as they walked out into the damp, bitter cold night air was, 'He is a pig, darlink, but safe. Come, we go for a drink to cheer you up. You have cash in the house? It's always cash. No? Oh! You must go to the bank in zee morning. Zat *cochon* iss one of zee best lovers in New York. Wheeman are maad for him. Two wheeman I know tried the suisside because he left them. Imagine, eh?'

Cheyney imagined only one thing – that she was going to be sick in the street. A block later she was. It didn't get better. In fact, it got worse and worse, like some terrible nightmare that was never-ending. At six o'clock in the morning the telephone woke her from a restless sleep. A strange voice told her, 'I believe you are waiting for this call. Eight hundred dollars in cash. I will call back to tell you where and when. It will be short notice, make sure you're ready. It's best to stay close to the telephone for the next few days.' Then a click and nothing but the dialling tone. It had been a man's voice.

The second call came at eleven that evening. 'The Dudley Court Hotel, room 1247, West Eighty-Ninth Street, just off Central Park West. You must come alone, by taxi, and be dropped off a few doors from the hotel. Only enter the Dudley Court after the taxi has driven away. Don't stop at the desk. Go right to the self-service elevator and up to the twelfth floor. Remember, these precautions are as important for you as for us. Wear something loose, and no under-garments. And leave your house now.'

Giving herself into the hands of other people was not easy for Cheyney at the best of times. What she was going through now was almost unendurable for her. The Park Avenue visit had been dreadful enough, but at least then she had the kindness of Roland and Nadja to help her through her ordeal. To think of another uncaring stranger violating her body again was enough to convulse her. For a brief moment she considered the alternative, only to realise that it was no solution.

She dressed as she had been told. Then put on her mink-lined raincoat, a matching fedora with a leopard-skin band around the crown, and leather boots to protect her from the cold sleet that had been gusting over the city for the last few hours. It would be hell to get a taxi, she thought. She planned to try to catch one at the Pierre, where she knew the doorman.

She hurried through the darkened, deserted streets, anxious to reach room 1247 and get the whole appalling mess over with. She felt dirty and cheap. She fought against the wind and the sleet for no more than two blocks before the sleet turned to snow, great, luscious flakes that fell in abundance and dissolved on the wet pavement. A taxi set down a fare. She jumped into it before the driver had a chance to protest.

The cabbie looked at her and said, 'You sure this trip is necessary, lady? Maybe you should stay in on a night like this.'

'Eighty-Ninth Street just off Central Park West,' she answered, and remembered the handsome stranger who had picked her up in the rain. Had that been only a couple of weeks ago? It seemed like years. And the warmth and love and protection she had felt in his arms for a fleeting moment? All mere illusion now for Cheyney Fox.

She had actually to press herself against a building and bite into her gloved hand to suppress an impulse to scream. She had to take deep breaths to quell her anxiety, so overwhelmed was she by the sight of the seedy Dudley Court Residential Hotel. From the broken letters of its sign, its filthy windows and torn and sagging draperies to its dimly lit lobby, shabby furniture, threadbare carpets, its pock-marked stucco walls of slime-green, the place spelled 'end of the line'. It was overheated and smelled of stale cabbage. The rattling metal elevator was scored with initials and a few choice graffiti – 'Shirley sucks cunt', 'Irving takes it up the poop' – partially obliterated. Stench of cat piss. Cheyney broke into a sweat that left her drenched and trembling. She escaped the elevator, walked the length of the deathly silent dim corridor. She knocked on the door of room 1247.

Inside was a sour-faced woman with a pock-marked face but a soothing voice. Cheyney was ushered through the dingy sitting-room to a windowless kitchenette, glaringly bright with chipped, blood-red enamel paint under a tube of fluorescent light. Up against one wall there was a small table of white formica covered with a transparent sheet of plastic.

'The money, please. It's payable in advance.'

Cheyney took the unmarked envelope from her handbag and handed it to the woman. She looked inside but didn't count the bills. 'You can take off your hat but nothing else, not even your boots.' And hoicking Cheyney's clothes up around her waist, she helped her on to the table.

'I'm so hot and so frightened,' confessed Cheyney, wiping the beads of perspiration from her face. The woman opened her coat for her and said, with a degree of sympathy, 'I know, but it can't be helped. We must be able to leave here as soon as you are able to walk. Rest assured, you are in good hands. I'm a trained operating-theatre nurse. The doctor knows his job. You will be fine in a few days, with not even an internal scar to remind you of tonight.'

'No? But the humiliation, the degradation and, I expect, the pain to come. And the guilt – oh, yeah, the guilt – what about all that? I don't expect I'll ever lose those scars,' Cheyney heard herself saying. She felt angry at how much worse the law made what was always going to be a desperate experience.

'Tell that to your congressman,' said the doctor, a young, presentable man. She sought compassion in his face. He placed a soothing hand on her forehead, and took her pulse.

61

Chapter 8

Nothing would ever be the same for Cheyney after the abortion. In the misery of that evening, any illusions she might have had about her own superiority were shed forever. Her sense of her own vulnerability magnified, she realised that everyone, no matter who they were or how protected they might think themselves, was only a hair's breadth from despair.

Nadja had been right. Unpalatable as it had been, Cheyney had had the safest illegal medical care that was available. After a few uncomfortable days, life was 'business as usual'. By day, that is. But by night, after the gallery had closed and she was alone, it was a different matter.

Cheyney was haunted. She kept re-living fragments of that night. The needle pricking her skin and sinking into a vein. Sensations of being half-clothed, half-naked, boiling hot above her waist, icy cold below. Counting back, 100, 99, 98. A searing pain. But the worst memories were of the isolation and the aura of lovelessness, her own and that of others around her.

Visions of herself struggling on wobbly legs, in a not wholly conscious state, to get out of the filth and ugliness of that hotel without being caught. Feeling weak and faint while clinging to a lamp-post for support, on a near-deserted Central Park West in the middle of the night, heavy showers of wet snow driven in gusts and swirls all around her. It all lingered in the recesses of her mind. The massive seepage of her self-esteem, as if from an open wound, during her seemingly endless, cross-town taxi journey to the gallery was the most dangerous of the losses she sustained that night. She cried, and her body healed itself, and she recovered and got on with her life. But now she didn't expect too much from it.

'Cheyney, how are you?'

'Fine, Christopher.'

'Really fine?'

'Yes, really fine,' she answered with as much gaiety as she could muster.

'I miss you. It's only been a week, and all I want is to be there with you, if you know what I mean?'

'Yes, I think I know.'

'Only think.'

'I know, Christopher, I know. In bed, inside me, making passionate love to me.' His response was a nervous boyish laugh. Hers icy silence.

'It will be all right for us when I come home, won't it? You'll be all well?' He lowered his voice almost to a whisper and added, 'I wish I could take you right now. Make you the happiest of women. I want to give you all the fucking you can take, and more. More even than that. When can we be together in that way?'

'Not for a few weeks.'

'But you do want it, as much as I do, to be together in that way?' he pleaded.

'Yes,' she whispered huskily into the telephone receiver, and despised her own weakness.

Cheyney was surprised to feel sexual stirrings. Desire for Christopher. She began to relax. She had been so worried that neither he nor any other man would be able to excite sexual passion in her again. Most especially Christopher, because of his response to her predicament.

It wasn't just his words that were seducing her. She was able to conjure up a precise vision of his seductive lips, feel again the allure of his charm. She wanted him as he wanted her, but more, she needed him to want her, to restore some of her lost self-esteem. She needed his desire for her to confirm she was not the lowly half-female she felt herself to be at this traumatic time.

'Then I'll be home two weeks from today.'

Nadja, hitherto a perfect stranger, became a friend. That was something Cheyney had to get used to. Instant, fair-weather, New Yorker friends. Strangers seeking out strangers for instant companionship. Every day you were meeting your new best friend. The common link, the climb. Up that success-ladder or die. And dead in New York while still breathing is the same as being ten feet under, marble slab and all.

In 1959 New York, the magic ingredient was not brains, although they helped. Not talent – the city was drowning in its pool of talented people. Money? Power? Both necessary, but still useless without pumping out that old magic, the success twins, energy and stamina. By God, you needed that cocktail to make it in New York City! There were no second chances, just the main chance and keep going.

Three weeks after the gallery opened Cheyney had met every type of climber: social, political, career, and a whole bunch of culture-climbers. Eight million people scampering on those rungs, and the operative word was always *up*. You simply had to be going *up* so they could go with you. There was nothing miserly about New Yorkers, or most Americans for that matter, when it came to success. They could be the most generous people on earth, they wanted everybody to make it. Hit the top, grab the brass ring, win the jackpot, be rich and famous. But you had to prove you *were* before they put their money where their mouth was.

And that was where Cheyney's real trouble lay. The sharp, sophisticated city folk in the art world were not putting their money on the line. Not buying art from her, or from anyone else for that matter, who had not been tried and tested for being in, possessing a smart eye, and declared 'Go, Go, Go,' by the art pundits: *Art News* magazine, *Vogue*, the *New York Times* and the Museum of Modern Art. And they were holding back, just like everyone else, because American art couldn't make up its mind where to go in the approaching decade. The brand new sixties.

Three weeks was all it took for Cheyney to understand that she was in deep trouble. She wasn't going to make it in New York City.

She didn't have what it took. She had the energy, the stamina, it was just luck that was missing. Time was not on her side. She could hardly close her doors after just three weeks and save herself. She had commitments. She must soldier on, try to weather the art storm, but for that she needed enough capital to sustain the gallery for a minimum of two years. Without it, she was through before she had even begun.

The financial side of the gallery had never been her strong point. She didn't understand it, was not even interested in it, so long as the books balanced and it was legal. Did that make her a bad businesswoman?

For months she had been happy to let Tony Caletti handle that side of things. Then there had been the contretemps with him over the five thousand dollar cheque she had issued to Sebastian, and her consultation with the new accounting firm. That made her suspicious and watchful of Tony as never before. A second clash occurred several days after the Sebastian incident.

'Cheyney, what's this cheque-stub made out to cash for eight hundred dollars?'

'Personal.'

'You wrote a personal cheque out of the gallery account?'

'Only because you transferred all my personal funds *into* the gallery account. And, by the way, without my authority.'

'I thought we agreed, *I* write the cheques around here. It's me handles the money, not you. You want money, OK, you ask me for it. Your job is to play the art game. I play the money game.'

He seemed cool and calm. But there had been fury in his face, his voice. He had continued, 'Now what was it for? Unless you've already spent it, hand it over at once.'

'Tony, what I do with *my* money is my business. "Personal" is quite enough for bookkeeping purposes. Why the fuss every time I write a cheque? And why have you left me with barely a cent for my own personal use? I'm not at all happy with your management of my money.'

He had not missed the tone in her voice, the lightly veiled warning that she could fire him and would if she had to. If she could have read his mind she would have been even more worried. *So that's how it is. Well, it's already too late for warnings. But too soon to let you know about it.* He did a rapid back pedal. He placed a conciliatory hand on her shoulder and said, soothingly, 'Because there is no need for you to bother yourself with financial matters. You've got too much else to do. All I want is to move money around in the way that is most beneficial to your business interests. And I can't do that if you go writing out cheques without consulting me. I thought I made it clear to you. I thought you understood we were forming three companies out of your personal holdings for that purpose.'

'I asked why then, Tony, and didn't understand the answer. But you convinced me that in time I would be grateful for the benefits. Well, I'm not. Not yet, anyway.'

'You will be. Trust me. It's early days yet. But please leave it all to me. If you have to write a cheque, talk to me about it. Try to remember the Cheyney Fox Gallery, Cheyney Fox Industrial Design Inc., the Cheyney Fine Arts Trading Company, are no longer just your one-man band to play with. Now, don't worry yourself about it. Just leave everything to me or I might have to slap your little hand.'

Condescending jerk, she thought, repelled by the way he slid his arm around her as he ushered her from her office. She had no time for this short, sloppily dressed, pudgy man. Everything about Tony Caletti was just a little bit seedy. A single glace declared him penny-pinching, mean of spirit. But then, she hadn't hired him to be chic.

He had been, for twenty years, the head book-keeper with a firm Cheyney occasionally designed for. When he had approached her for extra part-time work, he seemed perfectly suited to take over those areas of her business she was least competent in. She had known him casually for five years before she hired him. Now, two years later, she knew no more about the man that she had then. Married with two children and living in New Jersey, he had dandruff and sometimes halitosis.

Right now Cheyney wanted just to pull away, wipe his very touch from her. But good sense prevailed. Intuition had signalled red. From now on she'd be cautious.

Cheyney kept her unease to herself. Although alert to the shift in his attitude towards her and her various business interests – aggressive, seeking even greater control of her affairs than he already had – she was cunning enough to hide her growing doubts about his integrity and his manic need to control her business affairs.

Too much was already going against her for her to admit that Tony was mishandling the gallery's affairs as well. She had to believe all was in order until she had proof that it was not. So she watched, she listened, and discreetly queried cheques and documents put before her to sign. A hazy image was slowly developing into a black and white picture she did not want to focus on. Her only consolation was that Tony Caletti was not robbing her. Not yet.

She bided her time as she gathered information from him. Tony Caletti was another Sebastian: a man supposed to take some of an already heavy work-load off her who had proved to be just deadweight. The gods had something special up their immortal sleeves for Cheyney Fox and her gallery. Cheyney felt as if she were living with the threat of death every day. The death of her baby, the end of her great romantic interlude, the demise of her gallery. How could she go on?

She kept her emotional traumas to herself, and silence served her well. It honed her personality, giving it a new texture, a richness of spirit that intrigued Christopher and the passing parade of instant friends. It enhanced her with a more powerful presence, a new maturity, of which she was scarcely aware. She was too busy hiding the bruises caused by her rapidly changing life, coping with the world without the benefit of rose-tinted glasses, making her hectic run for survival in the art world.

For months, they came and they went and came back to her gallery, that cross-section of American humanity that fed on art, the excitement of creation, the passionate interpretations of life and time. Cheyney, too, was nourished by being a part of it.

Of the two hundred-odd galleries that Cheyney knew well, seventy-six of them, located above Fifty Seventh Street on the upper east side alone, were exhibiting American Contemporary Art. Men and women like Damuth, Jim Dine, Sam Francis, Kline, Gottlieb, Georgia O'Keeffe, Philip Guston, Clifford Still, Hans Hoffmann, Morris Louis, Mark Toby, Roy Lichtenstein, Agnes Martin, Robert Motherwell, Barnet Newman, Noland, Jules Olitski, Pollock, Larry Poons, Rauschenberg, James Rosenquist, Rothko, Frank Stella – some of the giants, and some of what the dealers were banking on as incipient giants, to carry them through the Sixties.

Every dealer like Cheyney was looking, searching out any young artist who might make it, who might boost their galleries with a new art-image, one that could take off as *the* new movement. And, except for those who handled exclusively the well-established master-painters and sculptors, they were all worried, jumpy about the future. Rosenquist, Jim Dine, Oldenberg, Chryssa, were giving hints of what was to come. Teasing hints, no more.

The Cheyney Fox Gallery produced some good exhibitions, and every day Cheyney sought for her own new giant, and the more she saw the more desperate she was to find that third artist, the one whose work could pack the punch to challenge the Abstract Expressionists, those still untoppled moguls of American Contemporary Art.

Rauschenberg and Johns broke away from the abstract expressionists. Everyday images and objects of a bourgeois life – a coke bottle, a light bulb, a boot – were painted but devoid of the artist's own reactions to it. Roy Lichtenstein was doing comic-strip paintings: Nancy and Sluggo and Mickey Mouse were suddenly fine art. They were emitting the message, 'Instant recognition, instant gratification, instant art. No thinking, no feeling necessary. It is what it is, and that's it, fellas. Freedom and happiness, the happiest times of one's life were on the cards. All that was needed was the ability to read them, and play. Hooray, we're all going to be children again. No wonder the American art market was in trouble, the dealers trembling with indecision.

There had been other signs in which people chose to foretell some kind of revolution. Bill Haley and the Comets rocked around the airwaves for four years and more. Elvis Presley with his steamy good looks and his electric guitars, drums, an amplified vocalist for backup helped narrow the message of liberation to that of more noise, more sex. The bumping and grinding and amplification shouted: Let yourself go, get free. And Cheyney hadn't understood until then that what the public at large wanted in art and politics, music and relationships, was instant recognition and pleasure. They had tired of works of art that made you think or qualified feeling. And there was the core of the American art scene's problem. Cheyney doubled her efforts to find the painter who could paint it away.

Chapter 9

Two young men, lovers, who collected works of art, returned often to Cheyney's gallery to see what there was new to buy. Tom and Paul did the rounds of the galleries every Saturday afternoon. They clearly found Cheyney an exciting dealer, and she, once she had been to see their store of paintings and sculpture, marked them down as important collectors with an excellent eye. But they were more than that: they were good people, intelligent and kindly. It was easy to like them. Without a great deal of money, they were assembling an interesting collection of contemporary art of the New York School.

One Saturday afternoon they brought a friend. A seemingly innocent, naive or hollow (it was difficult to tell) creature, cadaverously ugly with his fleshy Slavish nose, narrow empty dark eyes, and pustular skin. His coarse pasty face was topped by a cheap, badly fitted, grimy white wig. He seemed not quite of this earth with his old clothes and silent, vacuous air.

He appeared orphaned, a lost soul, next to the two pretty boys who emanated sweetness and love. One of society's natural aliens. He sighed pathetically when Cheyney shook his limp white hand. She instantly felt the need to be kind to him, protective even, she wanted to supply whatever might fill the emptiness he appeared to have fallen victim to.

'Nice gallery.'

'I'm pleased you like it, Mr Warhol.'

'Andy. Everybody calls me Andy.'

The three went through the gallery looking at the paintings and asked the price of several works. Tom and Paul bought a small Taunton. They were all of them excited by the purchase. Dora brought the men tiny cups of espresso, a bright yellow streak of twisted lemon rind floating on the hot black liquid.

A famous critic arrived to review the show, then the sculptor David Smith and the painter Acton Pace. They kissed her and joined the other three visitors for a coffee, eyeing the collection of ten small Henry Moores that Cheyney had purchased. Each piece, five of which were seated or reclining figures, was just big enough to fill the palm of the hand. The artists congratulated Cheyney on her clever buy and left. But not before

David Smith had put his arm around her and kissed her. 'Cheyney, you're not nearly mean or hard enough to be in this business. Take care.' He kissed her once more and was gone, a big, handsome bear of a man, strong and powerful.

Tom, Paul and Andy had stood by in silence, taking it all in. 'Wow,' gasped Andy, 'I wanna be a famous artist like them.'

'You are,' said John kindly. 'A show at the Bodley and one at Serendipity.'

Andy ignored that. 'Jasper is a star. He and Rauschenberg think I'm too commercial. I'm no more commercial than they are! All I need is a good idea and I can be a star like them, like those guys that just left, like you Cheyney Fox.'

'Andy, I'm no star, just a struggling dealer.'

'You're a star all right, you just don't know it yet, 'cause it's too new.'

A few days later he stopped in at the gallery again. Alone this time. He bought a painting and went on endlessly worrying whether it had been a good investment or not. Several days after that he was there again to ask Cheyney to lunch at Serendipity, a restaurant-cum-shop, all Tiffany lamps and palm trees, feather boas, clever gifts, large floppy felt hats trimmed with paper flowers. On sale were original Andy Warhol drawings of shoes made for I. Miller, and books he had illustrated. It was over the top, crazy fun, and suited Andy right down to the ground. Cheyney found it amusing. Introduced to the boys who ran it, she was made a great fuss of. Once their order arrived and they were left alone, she took him to task.

'You set me up, Andy. What did you tell those boys?'

'Just that you're the newest, the hottest, dealer. A star. Everybody loves a star, Cheyney. Being a star in the art world is almost as good as being a movie star.'

She shrugged her shoulders and said, 'Andy, seems like you have a problem about fame, and, I dare say, fortune. Being a star is not everything.'

He looked over the large glass *coupe* filled with an extravaganza of ice cream, cherries, chocolate fudge, whipped cream and pecans, and said, 'Now there you're wrong, Cheyney. It *is* everything. There is nothing else.'

That shocked Cheyney, actually sent a shiver through her. Walking home from Serendipity, she tried to forget Andy Warhol and that look of near-religious belief that had briefly animated his pasty face, the momentary tremor in his voice as he bleated, 'Make me a star, Cheyney.'

He was there again with two friends a few days later, asking for her autograph. She had been too embarrassed to refuse. Then the calls and the visits became a habit, as did the invitations to luncheons and parties and dinners. And always there was 'Do you want to go shopping?': endlessly he wanted her to do the shops with him.

She did, just once, on a bright sunny day with a nip of winter in the air. Tom and Paul and Andy called for Cheyney in a taxi. 'Where shall we have lunch?' asked Paul.

'Serendipity,' answered Andy.

'Not again!' exclaimed all three.

'How about Chinese, in Chinatown?' suggested Tom.

'You never meet anybody eating Chinese,' complained Andy.

'We're talking good food not people, Andy.'

'Serendipity's good food,' he answered defensively.

'Do we always have to eat in a shop?' asked Tom.

'I *love* eating in a shop. It's fun. And anyway, shopping is better than eating, and at Serendipity's we can do both. *And* I've got an account there.'

Tom jumped in with, 'And, are you telling us this lunch is on you?'

'I didn't say *that*. Dutch treat. We always go Dutch. Except we invited Cheyney, so we'll split her lunch three ways, OK? Then it's Serendipity's?'

Paul was firm. 'No, Andy. We're going Chinese. How does that suit you, Cheyney?'

'Chinese sounds great to me,' she agreed, embarrassed over the fuss being made about the cost of a lunch.

Not to be put off his shopping, Andy insisted, 'Oh, all right, but there's no rush. We can taxi-shop on the way. I saw a terrific tin tub in a camp boutique on lower Third Avenue. If it's still there I'll buy it. And there's a guy not far from there who's got a shoe fetish. His whole back room has nothing but shelves of fabulous famous people's shoes. Judy Garland's, Mae West's, a Ronald Coleman brogue, a pair of Errol Flynn's sneakers. He told me he was on to a Carmen Miranda platform shoe topped with a miniature bowl of fruit that she wore in the last number she sang with Xavier Cugat's band. You know, cherries and plums and grapes and a miniature banana all dribbling over her tiny toes. If he gets that shoe I'm going to buy it. Boy, I wish I could find the guy who's selling her hats.'

Saturday lunchtime in New York – it seemed like half of the city was out shopping. The streets appeared to be crawling with sharp, hard-nosed buyers, half of whom were professional lookers. The taxi crawled down the avenue and between Sixty-Third Street and Chinatown. Cheyney, Tom and Paul followed Andy in mad dashes in and out of sixteen shops. Andy never gave up. It was a constant. 'Stop! That's a sensational beaded curtain. Oh, look. I love that wooden pair of giant size eyeglasses. I'll have them *and* that stuffed panther. I don't know anybody that's got a stuffed panther. Stop! I'll have that and those. Those dishes, *not bad*. That's not a

70

real Tiffany lamp. I'll take it anyway. Too expensive. You've overcharging me. I haven't got my cheque book, so charge it. Call me if you can do a better price. I'll have to think about it. I want it. I have to have it. I love it. It's mine.'

They were exhausted before they got to Chinatown and then in the restaurant all he had to say was. 'There's nothing but food to buy here.'

Cheyney offered, 'There are a few shops we can go to visit after lunch, Andy.'

'Selling what – jade? I'd rather have a diamond, an emerald. The service here is too slow. The food is too hot. We should take too long over lunch. I *could* buy some jade . . . what do you think, Cheyney? If you think it's a good thing to buy, I'll buy jade. Yeah, maybe jade.'

Before they reached Oldenberg's studio he tried to convince Tom and Paul to buy a department store male dummy with all its private parts intact (a rare thing, he claimed), a white porcelain arm with two fingers of the hand broken, black leather shorts, a huge painting of the Statue of Liberty. Cheyney he pressed to consider a trashy twenties beaded hat, a penis-shaped ashtray made of pink plastic, a jade bangle, and a wheelchair with cane back and sides. Three of them were depressed and worn out by the end of the afternoon while Andy was energised because, he claimed, 'There was so much good stuff!'

Cheyney was dizzy from it all. The endless foraging through shops. The spending and spending and endless dickering over price. The constant reassurance he needed that each item was a bargain, could only be an investment. The telephone calls to his mother to accept the parcels stuffed into taxis and vans, one thing even went by motor scooter, so that everything would be at home waiting for him on his return. The greed!

At Claus Oldenberg's studio, Tom and Paul bought one of the artist's pieces, a chocolate bar, from a selection of food sculptures. The ice cream cones, and candy bars, and slices of cake and pie, cast in metal and painted in vibrant colours, had a special kind of life of their own that Andy could not understand. He kept taking Cheyney to one side and saying, 'I could have done that, and it's going to make *him* famous. Is that what I should do? A cup cake, maybe? Should I buy one? If I don't and he becomes famous? You're a dealer, would you buy one? Why don't you buy one? Why is Tom buying one?' He seemed amazingly confused and unhappy.

At another artist's studio the boys bought a stunning painting that Cheyney would herself have bought had things not been so tight financially at the gallery. It was as if real talent was more than Andy could take. Now all he wanted was to go home. Worn, frazzled, Cheyney swore never again to spend a day shopping with Andy Warhol – the greediest, stingiest, meanest buyer of them all.

The months rolled by, and the Cheyney Fox Gallery was still in there with a slim chance of making it. The gallery's reputation grew, but every day brought a financial crisis of one sort or another. The ten Henry Moores, bought as a collection for ten thousand dollars, temporarily bailed her out when she made a profit in excess of twenty thousand dollars by selling them one by one. But deals like that didn't come every day.

Christopher and she were still together but the relationship showed signs of strain whenever letters came from Costas. Christopher finally confessed that he should have returned to Europe and his life there immediately after his exhibition had finished, that soon he must leave her. More months went by, more letters, some now from Florence in lavender ink and smelling of violets. Then the phone calls began. And still Christopher put off his departure. Cheyney was happy, convinced that he was still in love with her and New York. Whatever his plans, she imagined she was by now a part of them. She felt they were, after all, a couple.

A dazzling opening night. Art stars. Hundreds of people streamed through the gallery all day and into the evening, and, before the doors closed, twenty of the Betty Parsons paintings and drawings had been sold. Betty glowed. Her quick, petite figure darted this way and that, shoulder-length bob swinging back from her usually calm, quiet, classically sophisticated good looks.

The next evening was no less exciting. A line of folding chairs followed the curtain walls of glass on the first floor of the Museum of Modern Art, above its famous sculpture garden, cleared this evening of its customary cache of treasures. Excitement hummed within the milling black-tie, long-dress crowd of invited art-people. Below under floodlights in the crisp evening air, a long hulking, sculpture of many parts, rising some ten feet or more above the ground and resembling a pile of junk from some up-market trash heap, randomly or artistically deposited, according to the eye of the beholder. It brooded in the sparkling light, against the black night and the skyscrapers of lighted windows with people pressed against them on the street beyond the garden. Like the guests within, they were hoping to catch sight of a sculpture said to be able to come alive and transform itself before your very eyes. And certainly, the pile looked capable of starting to crawl at any moment.

The spectacle was running late. A fine drizzle of rain, and the fire department dressed in full regalia, were holding things up. While the museum people and fire chiefs remained in confrontation, the artist, Jean Tinguely, raced around the mammoth piece adjusting wheels and cranks and boxes, balls and glass bottles. He even plunked a few notes on a battered upright piano, accompanying his instructions to several assistants. It was mad. It was glad. But, most of all, it was a bold challenge to the art establishment.

Good luck MOMA. I hope you do better than I did with my machine exhibition, thought Cheyney. A sudden surge of applause sent the mass of people rushing to the windows to look below. Once again, they dispersed because nothing was happening.

Cheyney saw Christopher making his way through the crush of people to her. Christopher had on his arm one of his Mayflower matrons, very Elizabeth Arden, all family emeralds, patently a museum trustee type. The Metropolitan. Cheyney steeled herself to be charming to the woman who every time they met cut her dead. Evidently this was not the day for breaking the sequence. Cheyney's charm was duly cut dead.

Christopher had come to the exhibition as the woman's guest and wore his uppity, high-society face. This irritated Cheyney even more than the woman and he conversing in French next to her as if she were wallpaper. She turned to walk away, but was stopped by Christopher's discreetly grabbing her hand and squeezing hard on it to keep her at his side. She managed to slip away when three other people joined them and he was forced to let go of her.

She wandered back to her front row seat overlooking the garden, and sat down. All the real excitement was going on just below. She wasn't going to allow Christopher to spoil the exhibition for her.

The drizzle had stopped. It had lent a kind of gloss to the scene below. The clouds parted like a theatre's velvet curtain. A sky studded with stars shimmered an all-clear. At last those in the garden – shiny, miniature tin people dressed as firemen or in tuxedos – shook hands with the artist. Everyone except Tinguely retreated to the sidelines of his garden-stage. Cheyney was loving every minute of the tension this controversial artist was creating with his work. The seats on either side of her were empty. She sat there alone, feeling quite happy, and tapped out a tune with her foot. She hummed and sang under her breath, 'Is you is, or is you ain't my baby . . . and gave a soft, throaty laugh, meant only for herself.

Someone caught her eye. He had been standing next to the window, about ten feet away from her, in a group of several very glamorous women and men Cheyney recognised as VIPs. The ones she could put a name to were the Secretary of State, a Rockefeller, a Whitney, and Aly Kahn. The women were French and Italian, radiating their own special chic.

She laughed again, openly this time, for having been caught out by him. He was a man well into middle age, not very tall, well-proportioned, well-dressed to an extreme in conservative, old-money style. He had thick white hair, and deep blue, fiercely intelligent yet decadently sensuous eyes dominating a handsome Teutonic face. A man of some charisma who emanated wealth and power. He both frightened and excited Cheyney. The way he looked at her made her restless. She felt as if he was undressing her from across the room, and as if the act was not unwelcome to her.

He surprised her by detaching himself from the woman on his arm and confronting her. He leaned forward and, raising her hand from her lap, lowered his head and just grazed his lips over the back of it. The classic continental kiss.

He smiled. 'You seem to be thoroughly enjoying yourself.'

He sounded English rather than American, with just the trace of a Viennese accent. Cheyney's immediate reaction was, 'Ladykiller'. 'Yes, I am,' she answered and, feeling herself obliged to, rose from her chair.

In her startling all-black sheath of satin, sliced at the side from floor to thigh, she was aware that she looked more like a movie star about to commence the long descent of a sweeping staircase than an art-dealer. The sheath, modest at the front, seductively backless, was the perfect vamp's dress. Cheyney was not unaware that business can be done just as easily in black satin as in Harris tweed, nor of the siren stirring in her at the sight of an attractive, important man.

She was enjoying her little flirtation. With a swish of her long black hair, she turned from the man to remove the black, transparent silk jacket, banded in slashes of satin ribbon on the wide sleeves and along the hem, from the back of the chair next to hers.

Turning to confront him once more, her face lit up. She smiled at him as if he were the only man in the world, and then she tossed her head back ever so slightly and gave him a sexy, promising laugh. His attention made her feel so alive, so female, happy with herself.

Something was on the point of beginning down in the garden that took her attention from him. She heard someone say, 'It's about to happen.' The news rippled through the by now impatient crowd.

'How exciting!'

'Ridiculous, more like.'

'So that's art, is it?'

Comments that went with sniggers or nervous laughter, and some up-state sardonic grins. People began rushing to their seats, or pressing as close as they could to the windows. Cheyney and the man saw an elegant couple approaching them. He turned a whispery sort of voice, as seductive as silk, on Cheyney to announce, 'We'll meet again, in another place. And after that –' he bent forward to speak close to her ear as his companions beckoned him in Italian not to miss anything ' – possibly one more time. And then I will marry you.' He gave her a brief but captivating glance and was gone.

Cheyney watched him walk away flanked by his friends. He did not look back. She had to smile at the man's arrogance, his plausibility and the most direct line she had ever had thrown her.

Down in the garden, a large chrome wheel began to turn. The spokes of a second, somewhat smaller, wheel spun at twice the speed of the first. A ball rolled down a plank. Jean Tinguely kept rushing around his creation, pushing a button, twitching a lever. The guests began to applaud. The sculpture was coming alive. Dozens of pieces were now in motion and the great pile of junk began to change form. In sections it sprayed itself with colour or lit bulbs. It was fantastic as it cranked and choked and sputtered into action. A riveting piece. Cheyney admired its uselessness, its clumsy beauty, the pure-fun philosophy behind it, its audacity. The drizzle began again, just as the old upright began to play its out-of-tune self. The mobile had so far transformed its shape twice. Certain sections ground to a halt while certain others were in motion. One section, near the piano – or maybe it *was* the piano, difficult to tell from her angle of vision – burst into flames. The sculpture was destroying itself.

'That's auto-eroticism for you.'

'What a mess!'

'Is it a phoenix?'

Titters from the crowd.

'It's called Assemblagism.'

'I believe you.'

'Wrong,' shouted a man with a French accent, 'Tinguely is a Nouveau Realiste.'

'Wrong again, he's a mechanic,' quipped a booming Texan voice. More titters.

The flames lapped at various inviting pieces of wood. Now it was fire that was transforming the work. Swirling smoke began to transform the garden too. Of course, the fire was part of the creation. But the firemen don't like to see a fire go unattended. This was their cue to make their entrance with hoses and extinguishers at the ready. Miss it they would not. Tinguely sprang forward to exclude them from the world of art. A hush descended once again upon the guests watching the scene below. The flames were becoming very artistic. The museum men joined the fracas. Firemen were taking their positions. No amount of assurance from the artist that the fire was contained within the sculpture could hold them back. The poor man appeared distraught, but kept working transformations on his piece. It was still alive with motion, flames and smoke. Rain seemed to be stealing some of the firemen's thunder. Now you could only see the sculpture through thick white smoke, like the white ground on a canvas awaiting paint. Art did battle with flames against the rain and the fire service.

The great art-extravaganza ended in fiasco, the waiting firemen only too willing to take hose and axe to the disintegrating sculpture. Earth to earth, and junk to junk. The last thing Cheyney saw before she pushed through the crowd to leave the museum was a dejected Tinguely slumped on the steaming ground, his head between his hands.

These were the best of times. But they were the calm before the storm.

Chapter 10

A few days after the Betty Parsons *Vernissage*, Cheyney stopped by her office one evening to get some money for taxi-fare, and found Tony Caletti working late.

'Hi, Tony.'

'Don't you look all glamorous! Another big night in the art world with those phoneys. How much did that dress set the gallery back?'

'This one was on me, like all my clothes – as you well know. Why not cut the bitching? You're out of line. What's bothering you?'

'Not true.'

'What's not true?'

'The books say the gallery has been paying your personal bills. And Uncle Sam may not like that.'

'Then why, for God's sake, did you pay them through the gallery account?'

'Because if there is a nil balance in one, the office uses another. And there is always the temptation to try for tax-deductibles.'

'Is that legal?'

'Maybe yes, maybe no. It all depends how I present it in your next tax-return. So now you know who to be nice to.'

Cheyney's patience ran out. For months she had strung him along, given him plenty of rope. Tonight she decided he could hang himself.

'I'm always nice to you, Tony. But not nice enough, it seems. I think you've taken on too much, so I'm lifting some of the burden off you. You won't have to do the tax-returns, or any more financial tap dancing, just book-keeping, which I suspect is how we should have left it in the first instance. Just pull out the relevant documents and we'll send them over to Bernard Reiss. He's our new accounting consultant. Anything else you have to say can wait 'til morning. I must dash. You know how it is when you're late . . .'

He was visibly upset, but held his ground. 'I wouldn't want you to do that.'

'I'm afraid you don't have a choice.'

'I think I do.'

'Oh?'

'I haven't worked this hard to set things up so you could eventually become a rich lady without thinking of myself too. I won't have you hand it all over to some slick, artsy-fartsy accountants. Now we can do this the hard way or the easy way. Which is it to be?'

'Tony, that's a pretty silly question.'

'Is it?'

He opened his shabby briefcase and drew from it a manilla folder. And from that he withdrew a cheque. Rising from his chair, he leaned across the desk and placed it squarely in front of Cheyney.

'This is the easy way. Sign it.' The cheque was made out to him for the sum of ten thousand dollars. He placed a cheap ballpoint pen at an angle across the cheque, and sat down again.

Stunned, Cheyney tried to play for time. She picked up the cheque, and studiously read it aloud. Turning the cheque over, she saw typed across the narrow end, 'Please pay bearer cash', a space for her signature and then her name.

'Now why would I sign this?'

Tony Caletti bent forward to shuffle through his briefcase once again. He pulled out a wadge of envelopes. 'Because if you don't I'll post these. This one will be the first, because it's the most dangerous: something for the Internal Revenue Service.' Then, one by one he pulled other envelopes from the pile. 'The landlords, the Morgan Guarantee Bank, your most lucrative client, each and every one of your creditors. Inside each envelope is a simple statement suggesting that the recipients demand payment by return post of the monies owed them. Otherwise, it suggests, they might get as little as ten cents on the dollar. Or nothing at all. So they had better rush to get in on this first come, first served situation. I stuck stamps on the envelopes. If you are stupid enough not to sign that cheque, then I walk out this door and put them in the nearest post box. That will bankrupt your three companies and you personally within a week. Ten days at the most.'

Pure and simple blackmail. In a voice barely audible, she asked: 'Why? Why are you doing this to me?'

'Money.'

'You would destroy me and everything I've worked for, for money? Why didn't you ask me for it?'

'Ask you for it? That's a joke, you sanctimonious bitch! Because you wouldn't give it to me, that's why. You like to think that that you're generous, a lady bountiful who would give me a hand-out if I came begging to you. What a lotta bull! Oh, yeah, you're generous – to some snotty, gigolo artist-type who thinks himself too good even to speak to the likes of me. To a drinking nigger, 'cause she cleans up and yes-mam's you all the time. To a bunch of phoneys, fags and fairies – people who really matter! And you think you're generous to me? Well, you're not. I don't call the few

78

bucks you pay me generous. The Christmas bonus, fifty dollars, generous? Chicken shit. You don't actually think I put in all this work just to be treated like some Victorian book-keeper kept in a dark corner, head down over the ledgers under some dim light bulb, and nothing more?'

Devastated by his words, the violence in his voice, the crude vulgarity of the man, she stammered, 'I never knew you wanted more. You never said.'

'Never said! What the fuck did you think I was saying with all that overtime when I was re-structuring your business? You're either naive, or stupid, or both, if you think anybody works the way I did for you without expecting a piece of the action. Turn my books over to Bernard Reiss, see you pay him what I deserve? Not on your life. Sign the fucking cheque, *Miss Fox*, and cut all the squealing. Or you get what you deserve.'

'I can't do that.' Cheyney picked up the cheque and tore it in half. They both watched the scraps flutter to the desk. 'Now get out. And I mean it, Tony. If you're not out of here in ten seconds, I'll call the police.'

'I don't think so.'

'Don't gamble on it. You're nothing to me. Just a thief, a blackmailer, scum. I must have been blind not to read the evil in you.'

'I need that money, Cheyney. I'm desperate for it, and you're gonna give it to me.' Tony Caletti was visibly sweating.

'Not on your life. Out, I said, and out I mean.' She picked up the telephone.

'If I go down, bitch, you're doing down too. That's the way you want it, that's the way you'll get it. You'll die more than one death over this story. And, if I get my way, you'll get a conviction for fraud.'

He mopped his face with the sleeve of his jacket. He was white with rage. He raised his arm to hit her. Through her fear and fury, she saw herself grab her handbag and swing it across his face. She was appalled, yet could not stop herself from continually beating him across his shoulders and head. One lens of his glasses smashed. He fled, cradling his briefcase to himself for protection. Cheyney chased him from the darkened gallery. Obscenities mingled with the obscure sounds of struggle as she propelled the book-keeper out of the door.

Christopher found her barely an hour after the rumpus had subsided. She spared him the most unsavoury details of the confrontation, but was in such a traumatised state he knew things were far worse than she had described. Her fear that Tony was going to return, assault her, burn the place down or at least vandalise it, made him summon help from friends. Roberto Fadagatti, an Italian count, and his mistress of many years, Lala de Ganza, arrived at once to offer their support.

Christopher could not calm Cheyney, but when Roberto walked into the room she was miraculously restored. His arm around her seemed to enfold her in reassurance. His kiss to her hand suddenly eased her erratic breathing. 'My dear girl, you are too sensible and clever to be broken by such a petty thief. He will do his worst, and you – well, you must do your best, no matter what. Or he wins.'

It was simple, it was clear. It was delivered with a trace of Italian accent, enough to give it a momentary flavour of the ancient wisdom of the Mediterranean, older than feuds and vendettas. The mild flattery worked, too. Cheyney began to emerge from her shocked, hyper-anxious state.

She sat with Roberto in silence for several minutes, Christopher and Lala anxiously looking on. Cheyney felt herself coming alive again in the mere presence of the gaunt and craggy-faced Roberto, handsome in his nobility, calm as a Giacometti sculpture. He wore his kindness and unquestioned integrity like a modest prince of the realm, which some said he most definitely was and which he denied.

Exiled counts abounded in Europe after 1945. Roberto Fadagatti's truest claim to nobility lay in his obvious integrity. Beyond that were titles renounced amid the violence and anarchy of Italian Fascism, and an impeccable record of resistance to Nazi tyranny.

He and Lala lived from hand to mouth on the outer edges of international high society. As art-dealers, they had eked out a living in Rome. In New York they were trying to establish themselves in a small gallery where they would represent Italian and French painters, but it was hopeless. They were the least likely pair to be in business. Roberto gave away more than he ever sold. Any sob-story opened his lean purse. Any favour was granted, no matter the cost. Lala tried, and tried hard, for them both. She was better at it, but only slightly. She worked in their gallery between hair appointments at Bergdorf's, shoe buying at Ferragamo, dress fittings at Saks Fifth Avenue, visits to her jeweller. She was forever redesigning old family bits of rose-cut diamond brooches, aquamarine necklaces, ruby rings, emerald bracelets, that miraculously popped up from nowhere. Cheyney had never seen her outdone in elegance, even by the Duchess of Windsor herself, one of Lala's role models.

Lala was young, dark and slender – more the contessa than the beautiful society lady. She could, and did when it suited her, play the helpless little female, and make it work. She was at her most clever when needing to get out of a scrape of some sort. In and out of the pawn shop with her pearls, the questionable family silver or her diamond earrings, using the place more as bank than shop, trading in desperation.

No one in the New York art world took them seriously, but no one took against them either. The one thing they did very well was enjoy themselves and amuse at the same time, wherever they went, whatever the circumstances. That and the exercise of perfect courtly manners made them ideally qualified for up-market New York party lists even if Lala had to pawn a wristwatch for money to send three dozen white roses to some ambassadress as a thank-you. They were genuine eccentrics.

The couple survived by the generosity of the wealthy Italian nobility and industrialists who respected Roberto's goodness and supported it when they had a chance to. The occasional purchase, a public relations job that was low on work, high on salary, all designed to help without offending his easygoing pride.

By local standards, Roberto and Lala were no more making it in New York than they had in Rome. Cheyney knew that and had to admire how philosophical they were about it.

To her, Roberto seemed all that was good, just as Tony Caletti and his schemes seemed the embodiment of all that was perfidious.

'Roberto has the knack of taking the sting out of adversity,' said Lala, handing Cheyney a champagne glass, and Roberto a chilled bottle of Dom Perignon to be opened. 'So tell him everything that happened. Maybe he can help you find a way out. At least you'll get a bit of good advice.'

Thumb on the wire cage around the cork, Roberto said, 'Helping is trickier than getting a bottle open. But perhaps I have already given you my best advice, "Do your best, no matter what." That means *whatever* he does. *If* he does anything.'

A lively pop, as Roberto twisted the cork from the bottle. A steam of vapour swirled out like the bottle's own genie. He poured champagne while Cheyney disgorged more lucidly than to Christopher the details of her slanging-match with her book-keeper.

'Call the police, have him arrested,' advised Lala, 'and don't think another thing about it. What a louse.'

'I'm more worried that he is going to have me arrested for assault and battery. I can't believe I was so violent.'

'Stop thinking about that, Cheyney. No police,' said Christopher. 'You do that, and the scandal will leak out. You don't want that, do you?'

Cheyney could see more annoyance than concern in his face. It sobered her, leaving her feeling vulnerable again. Lala dispensed more calm.

'Have another glass of champagne, Cheyney. Everything will come all right, you'll see. Now that you're over the initial shock, you're looking much better. Let's all go out to dinner. Roberto will treat us, won't you, darling?'

Typical of Lala to turn a disaster into a celebration. Cheyney watched her slip her arm through Christopher's and cajole him into supporting her. Roberto's generosity was instantly forthcoming, as usual. Still, Cheyney wished that Lala could understand that Cheyney was hardly more than the ghost of her usual self. Maybe the decade was only just starting to borrow the word 'trauma' from medical jargon. But a girl still knew when she was trau-matised. It was asking a lot of Cheyney to play 'Let's pretend' right now.

But then, how could Lala understand? Her whole life was lived in 'Let's pretend'. Lala was an orphan. Her wealthy foster parents had doted on her. Her childhood fantasy world made her the illegitimate daughter of a Spanish prince and a German princess. The foster parents, amused by her fantasies, and seeing no harm in a child's game of make-believe, strung along. By the time she was eight, Lala had a collection of Spanish royal memorabilia. In her fantasy, they were simply relics of her royal past. Her quixotic foster-parents, the Rafaels, nurtured a fantasy of their own: their little girl's fascination with European royalty meant she loved history. Clearly, they were raising a future luminary of the academic world. They eagerly scoured the antique shops. Everybody's fantasy grew fat on the scourings. The house was crammed with regal junk.

For her twelfth birthday, Lala got her own coat of arms. By the time she entered an exclusive finishing school in Switzerland, she had expanded a childhood fantasy into a life (brilliantly contrived and executed, with an extraordinary amount of false documentation, and a collection of crested, cartouched or emblazoned heirlooms). It was now too late not to believe in that life. Nearly everyone had been dragged into it. When the Rafaels finally realised how lost she was in her dream, there was nothing they could do about it. Have her committed indefinitely to some exclusive mental clinic? They could not bear to consign their harmless, straight-forward, happily deranged child to that.

Of course, Lala flowered in Europe: it suited the life she had designed for herself. For her eighteenth birthday and graduation from finishing school the Rafaels, now octogenarians, and already banned for several years from appearing in public with her – there was no role for them in her fantasy – gave her a trip around the world. With it, a trust fund to support her in the style to which she had become accustomed, to last until her twenty-first birthday. After that their princess was on her own. The elderly couple retreated to their estate in upper-state New York. When she visited them, which was once every few years, she had somehow contrived to weave them into her story, as the old friends of her grandmother.

Nearly everyone gossiped that Lala de Ganza was not who she said she was. But no one was ever able to prove it.

'But it's impossible. I can't leave the gallery tonight,' Cheyney protested.

'Nothing's impossible. Don't be a party-pooper. And, besides, you have to come – if only because it will get you out of yourself and back to reality,' insisted Lala.

'Why can't you leave?' asked Christopher. 'If he hasn't come back by now, he won't be back.'

'But he might. And then what?'

'Does he have a key?' asked Christopher.

'No, though he was always after me to get one cut for him.'

'Well, that's settled then,' said Roberto, relieved.

'But he knows where the spare keys hang. How do I know that he hasn't removed them for a few hours and had copies made? If he's an extortionist, stealing and duplicating a set of keys certainly wouldn't faze him.'

'Far-fetched.'

'She has a point.'

Roberto looked worried again, Christopher merely annoyed.

'A locksmith. I must have the locks changed, before I dare go anywhere.'

'No problem,' beamed Lala. 'I've got the best emergency service in the city. Plaza 87101. I know the guys, sweeties. I lose my keys so often, I've even got an account with them.'

She was already dialling the number to call them out. 'We can celebrate the changing of the locks with another bottle. *Encore du bubbly*! And you can take a hot bath and squeeze into a gorgeous dress. I'll keep you company and try to spruce myself up. Maybe borrow something amusing from your wardrobe, just for tonight. After dinner, we'll all go to Ariadne's party.'

'I forgot all about that,' sighed Cheyney.

'We'll have to go. All the top art-dealers and collectors will be there. They wouldn't dare refuse that Greek drama-queen genius. It will look odd if we don't put in an appearance. It's no secret that you and I have been helping her all week to arrange her work and clean the coach house. And what about Dora? She's been there all day cooking.'

'I don't really feel up to all this,' said an obviously distressed Cheyney.

'Well, up to all this is what you're going to have to be. It's happened, and we just have to get on with tonight,' said Christopher, putting his arm round her. Kissing her gently on the lips, he walked her to their bedroom.

She wanted to shout 'The hell I do!' but didn't have a chance because Lala burst into their room.

'Of course she feels up to it, and she wants to go out. Don't you, Cheyney? Now shoo, Christopher. Go talk to Roberto and let her get dressed.'

Putting the finishing touches to her make-up, Cheyney saw Lala reflected in the mirror. She was sitting on the edge of her bed, looking unusually thoughtful.

'You're very quiet suddenly.'

'I was thinking of Christopher. Wondering about that magic formula he has for making women fall in love with him. Even I go under, temporarily, every time I see your guy. You're the envy and the heartbreak of a lot of silly women, Cheyney.'

Surprised, she turned to face Lala as she toyed with a pile of scarves she had pulled from Cheyney's chest of drawers. One at a time she draped them around her shoulders and discarded them on the bed. Her voice, too, seemed to fondle the ideas it chanced upon.

'Who exactly are you thinking, of Lala?'

'That poor old girl with the palazzo in Florence who's still so besotted by him. He just can't let his victims go. For years I've seen him take up with women and, well, not so much dump them – he never really does that – more just file them away for another day. One day soon, you too could be popped back in the file.'

'Lala, stop. Are you trying to tell me something?'

'Yes, I guess I am. Something I heard when I was having lunch at the Plaza today with a girlfriend. She had just flown in from Italy. When she was in Florence, she had lunch with the old woman who lives in the Palazzo Faviani with Christopher and Costas.'

'The elderly Contessa with the purple ink? Christopher has told me all about her, Lala. For her, he's just the son she never had.'

'More than that, I suspect,' said a serious-faced Lala. 'My friend Gina says the Contessa is so passionately in love with Christopher, that it's gone beyond obsession. She is quite desperate, Cheyney. Enough to make her indiscreet about their intimate life together. To anyone who'll listen.'

'They don't have any life together for her to be indiscreet about.'

'That's not what she's claiming. And the details are pretty torrid. He will have to go to her, Cheyney, and soon. Or he might lose the palazzo. And I know Christopher will never give up the Palazzo Faviani. Crumbling it may be, but it's still one of the most romantically beautiful palazzos in the city. I can assure you, Christopher will do whatever he has to to keep it. Even make love to a seventy-seven-year-old woman.

'Anyway, we're not talking of just any old hag. She was once Italy's greatest, most talked-about beauty, the best-loved mistress of a king and of the country's favourite poet. She may be old and faded and on the edge of destitution, but she still has friends in high places. Gina says, even in the state she's in, she remains a seductive romantic creature. She can still glide through Italian bureaucracy and red tape. Now that's influence, my girl.'

This was the most Cheyney had ever been able to find out about the Contessa and the palazzo Christopher had spoken of. She was fascinated to know more. For weeks now, since the crested envelopes had begun arriving regularly from Florence, she had been sceptical of Christopher's version of his relationship with 'the woman who lives in our house'. Now curiosity got the better of her.

'Tell me.'

'First they were just renting two rooms. Now it's twenty-two rooms, plus the gardens. The dotty old dear is holed up in one wing of the place with what's left of her treasures, which is hardly anything. That's where Gina spent the afternoon with her. When Gina asked to see the rest of the palazzo, the Contessa told her that she, the Contessa, was not allowed in that part of the house until Christopher got back. Then she might be invited.

'When Costas arrived, the old dear went for her siesta and he took her around, showing the place off. Gina says it is unimaginably beautiful – and Gina has great taste. Costas claims that eighty per cent of what is there is original stuff. He and Christopher are supposed to have been buying pieces from the Contessa. For a pittance, obviously. It seems that the two men live in princely splendour on pennies, while the Contessa is incarcerated in a few tumbledown rooms in a property worth possibly a million dollars. Gina feels responsible for the situation – after all, she introduced them. So she asked the Contessa if she could help. "Yes," she was told, "find a way to tell him that every day that we are not lying naked in each other's arms, my heart is filled with sorrow and pain. I have only to think of my beautiful love, his lips upon mine, to remember a kiss, and I am restored." '

Cheyney's face was ashen. The two women saw tears in each other's eyes, tears for a stranger in a Florentine palazzo who had lived the whole of her life for great and passionate love, and now was dying of it.

The door opened and Christopher entered the room. Cheyney stood up, Lala shook out another scarf. Neither woman spoke.

'Now what have you two been up to?' he asked, a mischievous glint in his eye, one of his sensual smiles on his lips. 'Don't tell me I've missed some good gossip?'

'No,' said Cheyney, 'just a horror story.'

Chapter 11

The nineteenth-century coach house on West Fourth Street was aglow with light and sparkling people. Everyone who was anyone in the art world and high society mingled with the painters and writers, sculptors and musicians, who contributed to the great New York buzz. Dazzlingly delectable New York women in Tregere, Dior and Balmain dresses vied for attention with Italian Contessas, French actresses and English beauties dressed in Chanel and Hardy Amies. The strobe lighting flashed a rainbow of colours on the zaniest girls in New York. Poor art students and groupies, full of enthusiasm and crazy fun, had dressed in skintight fitted jeans and feather boas, floppy hats, purple and pink and yellow hair, to outshine the other women by the sheer power of their youth and imagination, their overt sexual promiscuity. It hung around them like a strong perfume.

The men were turned out like fairytale princes, nine to five slaves, or looked like beggars on the make. The scent of musk, incense and Gauloise cigarettes mingled with the aroma of oil paints and turpentine and candle wax. A thousand fat white candles were burning and their wavering lights broke the darkness of the two-storey studio with its iron spiral staircase and narrow gallery chock-a-block with guests. The room churned with fun and sex and booze and the promise of more of all of them.

Ariadne's party vibrated to the raunchy sounds of rock and roll. Cheyney realised how far she had travelled from the mainstream of conventional life. She hardened her heart against self-pity, knowing that, by morning, when her doors opened, she would have to take hold and do the best she could, efficiently and speedily, with the minimum of scandal, to wind up the gallery. She resolved to accomplish it all with dignity. No matter how many times Lala suggested the book-keeper would not carry out his threats, Cheyney instinctively knew Tony Caletti was certain to deliver every last one of his promises.

Cheyney absorbed each nuance of all she saw, heard and experienced at the party, wanting to remember the fun part, the being in the steam of things, on the way up, in the New York art world. With every embrace, every smile or handshake exchanged, she was warmed, enriched for the last time by this world she loved too much. She had no illusions about her immediate future. It did not include fun or success. Survival would be the name of her game now. Failure would surely strike her off the art-circuit guest-lists. She made the most of the evening.

Andy Warhol pushed his way through the crush of people. 'You look wonderful. A real art-star. How does it feel?'

She laughed, 'Terrific, Andy. I have to admit, terrific.'

'But what's it *like*?'

Thinking of what was to come in the morning, she laughed a little too hilariously. 'Like being Queen for a day.'

He beamed with pleasure. 'That wonderful? Oh, you're such a star.'

Christopher was suddenly there, and with an arm around her shoulders. He greeted Andy with the kind of flirtatious look that Christopher knew rattled the young man. Andy squirmed and begged, 'And what's it like, Cheyney. to have a handsome, sexy lover. Do you two do it a lot?'

Unsubtle. But Cheyney and Christopher had grown used to Andy's curiosity about their intimate life. His voyeuristic probing had been much worse when they had agreed to let his pencil immortalise their feet for a book he was planning entitled *Famous People's Feet*.

Cheyney heard herself repeating, 'Like being Queen for a day.' Her long, intense look at Christopher as she said it quite took him by surprise. It promoted the remark beyond flippancy.

Unbidden, a tear glinted in her eye. She slipped away from the two men and into the crowd, before either of them could say anything more. She felt a wrench of pain, but bit the inside of her lip: she would not cry out. Emotionally she had let Christopher go. They had both realised that the moment she had spoken.

They never discussed it. Not once in the weeks that followed. Nor did they mention Tony Caletti, or what was happening as a result of her last encounter with the book-keeper. Christopher never again asked about her plans for the gallery. They never even spoke of his departure, although it was implicit in everything he was doing. They distanced themselves from each other in public. In private their sexual life became more intense. A new kind of wildness surfaced in their lovemaking. Every fuck was as if it had to last them for a lifetime. They behaved like strangers, cautious of each other all the time, until they slipped together beneath the sheets. Then they were everything and everyone to each other, and Christopher branded her with every fuck, marked her for his own, told her, 'No man, ever, will be able to fuck you as I do, give you what I give you.' And sadly she believed him.

The first thing to go was her jewellery. Then the furs. The last thing of value was the car. The stock of paintings owned by the gallery went up for sale at whatever price she could get. Cheyney didn't have to be a genius to realise she had to liquidate her assets as quickly as possible, to raise cash and stave off bankruptcy, keep the gallery doors open.

Tony Caletti had not given her a single day's reprieve. The letters he had threatened Cheyney with had been delivered for the most part by hand. The telephone started ringing by nine-thirty. It was all bad news. Cheyney was still telling Dora and Sally what had happened, and asking them to stay with her.

'Everything must carry on as normal in the gallery. The panic must be kept behind the scenes. Out front there is no problem. My aim is to carry on as long as we can. Certainly until the last scheduled exhibition closes. It's not going to be easy. You will both have to fend off people, maybe writs, if it comes to what Tony has promised.

'You and I, Sally, will have to go over the ledgers right now, to find out what difficulties we are in. I can't be sure that wretched man has not manipulated them to put me in an incriminating position. I feel we can cope with everything but a criminal prosecution.'

She handed out the new sets of keys to Dora and Sally, who agreed to stay on. Then a somewhat embarrassed Cheyney asked them not to allow her problems to become public knowledge. They were not to be discussed with anyone – including Christopher.

'There is no fooling you two. You know what he means to me. But I don't want my problems laid upon him. I got myself into this mess. Oh, and there is another thing. He'll be leaving me soon. I have no idea when, but I want no sad atmosphere around here because of it. Just remember, if you want to help me: everything as normal for as long as we can.'

Cheyney took the rush of telephone calls and made appointments to see the callers. She managed to put them all off until the following day. Of course, by then there were as many new ones again to deal with.

It was all so simple, the way Tony Caletti had helped Cheyney Fox to her ruin. He formed three limited companies, one for the gallery, one for her design work, and the third, a trading company, for the sole purpose of purchasing works of art. He then proceeded systematically to strip the three companies of their assets. Money was freely moved from one to the other, to provide balance sheets healthy enough to merit bank loans. All this, although masterminded by Caletti, was apparently endorsed by Cheyney: by the very fact that only her signature was to be found on the records, not his.

The statements submitted to the bank and the IRS were unquestionably false. It was impossible for Sally and Cheyney, despite poring over the company ledgers for hours, to tell which assets and which debts truly belonged to which company. All three companies had bank loans due or overdue for payment.

Scariest for Cheyney was the fact that the books now indicated she had drawn cheques from all three companies and deposited them in her own personal account. It looked as if she was the one stripping the assets. There was nothing in the ledgers to show what she had done with the funds received. Every injection of capital into the companies was recorded not as company profits re-invested, but as personal loans from Cheyney Fox. It was impossible for Sally and Cheyney to untangle the Tony Caletti legacy.

Sebastian! It all harked back to him, and his five thousand dollar investment. When he pulled out, the gallery's working capital vanished with him. Cheyney had always known that was the beginning of the end. She had fought from that day until now for the right at least to close the gallery with some honour. Now she was in deeper trouble than she could ever have imagined. Her resolve was still the same. But with what she had learned in the last twenty-four hours, what hope had she? Only one. Selling paintings.

Cheyney kept at bay one writ after another, working night and day to keep up the payments she was committed to. She extended herself unremittingly to make any deal, and did indeed bring off some art-dealing, several design contracts. The result was a modicum of profit for each of her companies. But it added up only to dimes when hundred-dollar bills were what she needed. To the casual eye she was presiding over a struggling art gallery, doing a little business and still weathering a minor storm – but not for long.

As soon as the first of the gallery's stock paintings were sold at a knock-down price, the rumours began. After a second and a third sale, the artists with paintings on loan to the Cheyney Fox Gallery started calling them in.

Cheyney appeared at few parties and gallery openings now. Every minute she was not fighting to stay afloat she remained at home, replenishing her nervous energy. Christopher: she watched him day by day buying things, masses of things, for the houses in Greece and Florence, the flat in Paris, with the money he made on his successful sales. A new Brooks Brothers coat, a button-down shirt. Every night, before he climbed into bed with her to make love, he rearranged the open suitcases in the bottom of her cupboard. She waited for weeks for him to say, 'There's always a place for you in my house. You will never be homeless. Come to me when your mess is over.' In vain.

The time came. He was finally ready to leave. 'Cheyney, I'm going on Wednesday, three days from now. You have too many problems. I can't help you. When they're resolved, let me know and I'll come back. I'm sure you will make it all come right. Don't despair, we'll write.'

It hurt more than she thought it could, but she refused to let it show. At some point he volunteered, 'This is as difficult for me as it is for you.' She didn't believe him.

'No sad farewells, promise me that.'

'I couldn't agree more,' she said. 'All emotions in check at the airport, is that to be the form? I think I can manage that.'

'You're not coming to the airport, Cheyney. It will be easier on both of us.'

'How will you get there if I don't borrow Della's car and take you?

A sheepish look. 'I'll be travelling with Marie Waldren. She happens to be on the same flight. Her chauffeur will take us to the airport.'

That was a blow. Only she was to be left alone in this love story. *He*, not for a minute. Why hadn't she figured that out?

It was the first warning signal that, no matter how she tried to control the hurt of his departure, it wouldn't be possible. The hurt might still be fatal. She covered up the pain with the shifting business of the day, the continuing fight for survival, and distanced herself from Christopher even further than she had done since the night of Ariadne's party. As a practised seducer, he was quick to recognise what Cheyney was doing. He was having none of it.

Especially so on the eve of his departure. Christopher's ego demanded that he leave Cheyney still loving and longing for him and no other. Whatever ploy she used as an emotional escape, Christopher was able to block. At first, arriving back from one of his dowager duchesses' cocktail parties, with tentative kisses. During their somewhat tense *dîner à deux* with steamy looks and sensual innuendo. At last, in front of the open log fire burning in the bedroom, Christopher was at his most ruthless. Demanding from Cheyney every morsel of love she was so desperately trying to withhold. He yanked her back to him with his sexual prowess. He confirmed again his power to deliver her into streams of sexual ecstasy. He transported her from the nightmare of her problems into moments of pure pleasure. Oblivion, that quiescence beyond pain.

Cheyney had dressed very carefully. She wore a short, burgundy satin quilted jacket with long puffed sleeves over a slinky black silk jersey dress. The halter top clung seductively to her body and the skirt finished just below her ankle to reveal high-heeled satin sandals. Naked under the sensual fabric, the breasts round and firm, the hint of nipple, the luscious roundness of thigh and bottom, tempted and teased with every move she made.

Cheyney had dressed with great care. She wanted to be more beautiful, more seductive and in control of herself than she had ever been with Christopher. She wanted their last night of sex to be something he would remember and miss for the rest of his life. Cheyney's pride dictated that if he saw fit to leave her at this time when she needed him most, he should go away remembering how sexually good they were together and what he was throwing away by his callous departure.

Her resolve to maintain a cool, calm, unemotional façade began to crack with his first tentative kiss. She struggled valiantly not to let him see her love for him, the pain she felt over his departure. As his tentative kisses changed to parted lips, deeper, richer, emotional needs surfaced and swept them both away into that special erotic passion they felt for each.

He removed her earrings and whispered in her ear, 'I've wanted you all evening, from the moment I walked in the door. You are so beautiful, too beautiful, too sexy to be had by anyone else but me. You're mine and don't ever forget it. Don't for one minute think I don't know what you're trying to do. A waste of time. You can't throw me out of your heart because I'll never let you go. I'll yank you back to me with my cock.' She trembled with fear that he might be right.

A kiss on the neck, another more passionate under the chin, and a tease of the tongue in the hollow of her throat. A light tantalising kiss on her still closed and resisting lips. Another, and another. He nibbled their soft flesh, and traced the shape of them with the tip of his tongue. Then he licked them, until slowly, reluctantly, her lips parted. She was helpless to do anything but take and return his kisses with fiery and passionate ones of her own. It no longer mattered to her that she was bursting with desire and need for more of him, and that he knew it.

It was Cheyney's ability to let go, give herself up totally to him, that always excited Christopher and spurred him on to unbridled lust. Until he went to bed with her he never realised how sexually starved he had been. He both loved and hated Cheyney for his carnal appetite for her. She could feel his passion and his anger as he unfastened the halter at the back of her neck. She felt the silk jersey slide down over her breasts to her waist. It sent a shiver through her. Her naked breasts yearned for his hands, his mouth sucking ravenously on her nipples. He lowered his head. The moist, warm pull of his mouth, the teasing teeth on the tender erect nipple. She closed her eyes and sighed and felt the core of her very being dissolve into a light sweet orgasm.

He teased the zipper open and she felt the dress glide smoothly off her hips and drop to the floor. His caresses were like tongues of fire scorching her skin. She backed away from him against the wall and, all resolve lost, she whimpered.

'I love you. I always want you. Every minute of every day I always want what's happening to me now. And tomorrow you will be gone and I will be so alone.'

He silenced her by kissing her eyes, nibbling fiercely at her lips. His passionate kisses trailed over her breasts. He bit hard into her nipples and she writhed between alternate pain and pleasure. Hands on her hips he pressed her hard against the wall, and dropping to his knees he buried his face in the triangle of her soft black pubic hair. He had her now, with searching fingers and his tongue teasing her clitoris, licking the inside of her satiny smooth, lusciously female slit.

Slowly she slid down the wall and on to the floor, taking him down with her. So lost in the moment, and her own lasciviousness, even her mind stopped crying 'Don't leave me.' He dragged her, naked except for the burgundy satin bolero jacket and high-heeled sandals, across the carpet to lie in front of the hearth. He placed a pillow under her head and beneath her. And she lay as he arranged her, legs bent at the knee and spread wide apart so that her most raunchy, vulnerable sex shone by the light of the fire.

He stood between her legs, looking down at her. She saw it in his face. He, too, was lost to all else except sex and the blissful escape it provided. He was dominated now only by passion, an overwhelming desire for her and where their coupling could take them. In that and that alone was Cheyney victorious. Awareness of her victory over him brought out the animal in Christopher. He tore off his clothes. Naked and rampant, wild with desire for her, without ceremony he plunged himself deep inside her, calling out her name again and again, ecstatic with the pleasure he felt fucking her. Unable to contain her own pleasure, with every exquisite thrust he delivered she answered him with the sound that sexual thrills can produce. He filled not only her yearning cunt but the void in her life and she knew a few hours' bliss.

When she woke up the next morning she was just in time to see the door to the flat close behind him. She felt excruciating heartbreak, an instantaneous aloneness. For several minutes she struggled to still her acute anxiety. Then, still dazed, Cheyney ran to the window and looked down into the street. Just in time to see a liveried chauffeur loading rolled-up canvases and luggage into the boot, and Christopher slip into the back seat of a cream Rolls-Royce. His goodbye to her? To flee without even a word of love and farewell.

Cheyney found the crumpled letter next to the waste paperbasket. She recognised the distinctive colour of the ink and the penmanship as that of the Contessa. Without a qualm she carefully straightened out the pages and read, 'My life, my love, my Christopher'. Cheyney was shocked by the tone of the letter. She was numbed by the Contessa's passionate outpourings – but because they confirmed what Cheyney had most feared: Christopher loved her no more than he loved the Contessa.

92

The Contessa had written, 'When I read your words, Christopher,' and then quoted him: 'You must forgive me, my one and only true love, this small distraction of the last few months. I promise you it does not affect my life with you. I will prove it to you on my return.'

What remained of Cheyney's self-esteem disintegrated. She traced at once in her behaviour the shape of passion's own peculiar blindness. Christopher had left the prints of his faithlessness on all his recent actions. She had chosen to ignore them. Wanting only what almost any woman wants: to believe that somehow, in her own life, she has stumbled upon that near-impossible man for whom she and her love will be all-in-all sufficient. What else could the eruption of Christopher's compelling beauty into her daily life mean?

The Contessa's letter foreclosed upon that illusion. Impossible to make excuses. She sat on the edge of her bed for a very long time, Zazou lying across her knees. As if sensing her mistress's despair, she kept demanding to be stroked, coddled, cuddled. Every time Cheyney stopped, she was immediately pressed back into action by a lick, a nudge under her breast.

Hours later the door opened. A click, and the room filled with light. Dora and Lala stood framed in the doorway. Lala went at once to sit next to Cheyney. Dora was the first to speak.

'Mah, suggestion, ladies, is martinis. Lots of 'em, and no sad songs.'

'Might as well make it three glasses, Dora.' That was Cheyney. 'Doubles for our troubles, ladies.'

'Doubles,' both women chorused.

Dora left, humming 'Bye-Bye Black Bird.'

Cheyney folded the crumpled pages of the Contessa's letter as neatly as she could and placed them in an envelope. Then she wrote on a scrap of paper. 'The question is not whether I read this letter, but whether you left it here for me to read.' She slipped that in the envelope as well, licked the flap, sealed and posted it.

The pressures of business left her no time for introspection. Now there were lawyers involved. Every creditor seemed to have a lawyer fortified with threats. Accountants who analysed the books and advised her to cut her losses and file for bankruptcy. The mere work set Cheyney into a spiral of desperation. She refused. Every minute of her working day was devoted to forestalling that disaster. She pleaded with her advisers to issue assurances: if her creditors would only wait, she herself would carry all the debts of the three companies, and in time pay them off. No one was listening.

The last scheduled exhibition had just over a week to run. If she could only hold out. Day by day attendance at the gallery declined. There were some days when not one person entered to view the exhibition. It was a torture for her, as if she and the gallery were bleeding slowly to death. She needed only to keep everything at bay for those six days, to close, having paid all her artists, returned their property, and placed them with other dealers. And all without a scandal. Only six days to go, or so she thought. But even that was not allowed her.

She had been walking the dog in the park, and was just rounding the corner off Fifth Avenue into her street, when she saw Dora standing there waiting for her.

'Ah don't think you should go back in the gallery just now. Ah come to head yah off. Be better yah-all wait till aftah six, when da gallery's closed for the day. Just in case.'

Cheyney knew before she even asked, but had to say something. 'Just in case what, Dora?'

A sheriff and deputy had invaded the gallery. Cheyney had been forced into bankruptcy. She felt as she walked away from the gallery with Zazou on a leash in one hand, and a suitcase of clothes in the other – all that she had been allowed to remove – that she might never recover from her disastrous foray into the New York art world. She had been closed down and literally thrown into the street with a dog, a few dresses and two pairs of shoes. Notice of her personal failure was nailed to the door. It was a kind of death. Reincarnation seemed a flimsy faith to set beside that feeling. A life was over.

Chapter 12

In the two weeks that followed the abrupt closing of the gallery, Cheyney slipped in and out of deep depressions, fits of uncontrollable sobbing, usually when the friend she was staying with was out and she was alone. When she looked in the mirror her face was the same, except for the eyes. They belonged to a stranger. She recognised them as dead, like those of a fish freshly killed. Beautiful, clear, with nothing behind them. Just glaze, no life. She spoke only to her lawyer. Seemingly endless conversations. All the things she must *not* do: pay any of the creditors either with money or promises of money. Seek to obtain any of her remaining possessions. Make commitments of any kind to any of her past business associates. Talk to the receiver handling her case, or any persons who had been involved in the gallery, or her design company, without the presence of her representative. Thou shalt not.

Nothing. She was to do absolutely *nothing*, except to wait for a bankruptcy lawyer to be found who would take on her case. The receiver had already appointed his on behalf of the creditors, to counter any award of a discharge in bankruptcy. Which, as Cheyney's lawyer explained, was absolutely essential for her to win. It would prove that she had been innocent of any misconduct, and that she had lost the money and her businesses only after doing her best to succeed.

'A discharge in bankruptcy will wipe out your debts, and leave you free to start again. You've gotta win it,' was the lawyer's brief to Cheyney Fox. It was the *nothing*, the having to do nothing, being unable to have any say about what was happening to her. Waiting for events to carry her forward, where once it was Cheyney Fox who carried herself forward. She wasn't so sure. Her guilt at having lost the money was too great.

Della Robins could only be described as good people. She worked extremely hard, as junior executives managing large offices are prone to do. More than competent, she operated with both feet on the ground at all times. Della lived an uncomplicated but organised life. Even her paper clips were lined up in the same direction. It was a torture for her to see Cheyney in the state she was in. She actually feared for her friend's life.

Della lived in what was currently the most chic of the new glass residential towers erupting flashily over the city. This one was in Turtle Bay, overlooking the East River. She offered Cheyney – plus Zazou – her glass, her view, a ceiling over their heads. 'You must be my guest, for as long as it takes, Cheyney.' The act of a true friend. The twentieth-floor apartment, spacious and with a vast panorama of the city, boasted only one bedroom, one bathroom. There was a kitchen. But it was in the large hall dining area or livingroom that Cheyney spent most of her time.

Della offered Cheyney and Zazou safety, comfort, and a glimpse of an uncomplicated life. Day after day, one week following another, she was always there, with a smile, caring, sharing everything she had with Cheyney.

She never left the house except to walk Zazou. Once a pleasant, happy chore for her, rain or shine. No longer. Cheyney was fine in the elevator, going down the twenty floors. Even through the lobby and while greeting the doormen. But the moment she was on the city pavements, depression settled upon her. She was like an involuntary exile, in a limbo between what she had been and what she might yet be. After the first few days she never left the plaza and the gardens surrounding Della's apartment building. Her cramped walkabout with Zazou would leave her smothered in anxiety. Panicked, she would rush back into the building and up to the safety of her refuge.

Only thirty-five blocks and two weeks away from the world where she had been alive, in love, and a person of substance. A world hyped with promise and excitement, likely at any moment to challenge you with a vitalising choice, to probe your capacity for passion or intellectual involvement. Exiled from all that, she couldn't face the streets. Only Zazou, her beloved, devoted dog, her sole remaining responsibility, drew her into the street. And she could barely afford to feed her. The last humiliation: feed me, feed my destitute dog. Having to add dog-food to the charitable Della's shopping list. Self-sufficiency at least in that department became a desirable goal. If only she had enough money to buy a supply of dog food!

In the apartment things were little better. Her present nothingness clouded everything. Concentration was an early casualty. Make a bed, prepare a meal, wash the dishes: those were her limits. To answer the telephone was a major effort, to which Della compelled her by calling without fail every two hours. Often the conversation amounted to an extended hello. So numb was she that it took Cheyney a while to realise that Della saw herself as engaged in suicide-limitation.

That realisation shocked Cheyney. Because although she often wished that she were dead she would never dream of taking her own life. Why would she? Because she had lost all her money? Her lover? Her gallery? Because she had failed on what she deemed to be a massive scale? Certainly not.

She spent most of two weeks twenty floors above the city staring from a plate-glass window down towards the river, or up town to where she had once lived. Zazou lay asleep with her head in Cheyney's lap, or licked her hand, snuggling next to her, never leaving her side, doggily sensing her despair.

'You know you're welcome here for as long as you like.' Such generosity could create its own share of pain.

'I know.'

Cheyney was embarrassed by the concern in Della's face, so it was to please her that she finally accepted a dinner invitation from Tom and Paul.

She had refused to talk with them the several times they had called previously, but eventually it became unthinkable not to. The stress it caused her friend was more than Cheyney could take. She appreciated that they were all trying to help her. Still she was angry at being dragged into the stream of life, where she really didn't want to be.

She had always had, in the past, a soft spot for Tom and Paul. She kept telling herself that, if she had to see anyone, they would be the easiest. Wrong. The moment she set eyes on them, all the pain of the past became acute: they were too vivid a reminder of a distant dream she could no longer relate to.

They were charming, so pleased with themselves for getting her out for the evening. Cheyney felt the least she could do was double her efforts to come alive, at least while she was with them. They would need to be athletes of empathy to know fully what she was going through. She realised that her misery and the end of her life were a very personal affair, not easily off-loaded on even the most willing sympathiser.

She felt she had mislaid the art of being social and charming. She had lost herself, couldn't be the Cheyney they looked for. There seemed to be no self to articulate. The simple necessity of speaking to them was going to be an agony. She forced the anger she was feeling to some dark place in the back of her mind because their faces revealed how uncomfortable they were for her. They deserved better than that, and she knew it. She slipped an arm through each of theirs, and together they stood under the canopy and watched the rain pour down all around them. Cheyney winced at the shrill sound of the doorman's whistle trying to catch them a cab. The faint smiles they were able to summon allowed them all a sigh of relief. The evening might yet be all right.

It was a small restaurant: cosy, French, no more than twelve tables. Dim lighting, red and white checked tablecloths. The service was simple, and

97

the aromas and homey atmosphere of the place promised good food. One of those special little neighbourhood restaurants, with banquettes around the walls and an owner-chef.

They ordered Manhattans to banish the chill wind and the rain that had whipped around them while they hurried from the taxi. Over a deliciously hot celery soup, generously spattered with crunchy home-made croutons, Dover Sole *Véronique*, tiny parsleyed new potatoes, *mange tout*, an apple *tarte tartin*, served hot with lashings of *crème fraîche*, and two bottles of a perfect Chablis, they made polite conversation until the three of them were relaxed enough to stop skirting any mention of the art world, the closing of the gallery, or what Cheyney's plans for the future were.

'Is it terrible, the gossip about me? The closing of the gallery a scandal?'

'Yes, malicious. Perhaps you should feel flattered.'

'No, actually I don't.'

'Surprise. Anyway, it will blow over, be forgotten once you're on your feet again. If only you could have held out. That's what the kind ones say.'

'Does Christopher know what's happened? Where you are?' That was Paul.

'I don't know. Bad news goes the rounds. I think we can assume that he knows.'

'You're not just another notch on his cock, are you? He hasn't broken your heart, has he?'

'No. And you mustn't think that the mess I am in happened because I was escaping from some epic masochistic romance. It was bliss while it was bliss – if you know what I mean – and now it's over. Change of subject. How about you two? Bought anything recently to add to your collection?'

The men brightened visibly at the prospect of talking about art. 'Lots of things: we went shopping on Saturday.'

'I suppose Andy went with you?'

'Yes. And I'd better tell you: he wanted to come to dinner with us. We had to promise we would bring you over to his place for coffee afterwards, or we would never have gotten rid of him.'

'Oh, no!'

'Oh, yes!' said Tom.

'God, I don't think I'm up to this!'

'Which of us is?' said a smiling Paul.

'Please, Cheyney, just for a few minutes. If we don't turn up, we'll be considered enemies for life. The alternative is dinner with him. Then he'd pick your brains like a fishbone, till you tell him how to become a famous painter.'

'What's the difference – dinner or coffee? My brains still get filleted. Oh, those endless questions! What does one do?'

'Fob him off or tell him what he wants to hear, and be done with it.'

'That's how he gets everything. He pesters and cajoles. He never lets up. So you cave in. You give him what he wants. He's black-belt at wheedling. He gets a submission every time. That's how he's gotten where he is today.'

They all began to laugh. 'Where's that?'

'In his own little world making pots of money and crying poverty. He's got whole garrets full of skinny students doing the donkey art-work for his commercial illustration accounts. Feeding them the minimal diet of oats to keep them working, while he gallops around town trying to break into the big-league art game. He's convinced that the only thing in life that matters is being a celebrity in the wonderful world of art. A star in art – buy that! Oh, and there's the shopping. Never miss out on a bargain. Shopping and starring. A man of the times. A mensch for our season. No, nothing's changed for Andy.'

Cheyney was still laughing. It felt good. She asked, 'Has he bought a new wig?'

'No. No new wig. His theory, clean enough for last year, clean enough for this. Good old Rinso!'

'You're sure we have to do this?'

'A woman has to do what a woman has to do.'

'Well, come on then. Let's get it over with.'

The three stood huddled in the door of the restaurant. They looked across the street and up a few houses. The brownstone was dark. Just a hint of light to fool a lethargic burglar. 'Oh, good, he's gone out.'

'Never. He expects us. Just saving electricity. He'll be in the back room, his mother down in the kitchen.'

'There are things I'd rather be doing than this,' offered Cheyney. 'You watch, he'll carry on as if I am the same old Cheyney. Just been off on a two-week, arty-farty cocktail party. He'll drive me mad with questions that will upset me.'

'Forget it. One dash in, and one dash out, we promise.'

The rain had not let up one bit throughout dinner. Gutters gushed water, and still the rain sheeted down. Traffic seemed washed away. The three linked arms and dashed across the street, past several houses to Andy Warhol's front door.

An umbrella arched over them. Someone's thumb found the doorbell. It rang for an age. Paul pounded a dripping fist against the door jamb. A grimy lace curtain dangled on a sagging string across the glass set in the top half of the door. They peered through it.

Cheyney kept thinking, What am I doing here? This is madness. My shoes are ruined. She shivered. She had worn the wrong coat. Furious with herself for even being there, she announced, 'I'm leaving.'

'No,' they insisted. 'He's got to be here. He knows we'll bring you, and not let him down. Please, one more minute.'

Cheyney closed her eyes on her anger, and suddenly felt very disorientated, imagining she was somewhere on the upper east side of the city, Lexington Avenue, in the nineties. She became frightened, couldn't believe she was ever going to find her way back to Zazou and Della. She suddenly felt as if she had been kidnapped.

The lace curtain twitched. Nothing more, hardly a sign of light or life. Just a slight spasm in a dirty lace curtain. The three looked at each other. Tom shouted through the rain-spotted glass, 'For chrissake, Andy, open the fucking door. We're getting soaked out here.'

Three sallow, ink-stained fingers curved around the edge of the tatty lace. It drew back a few inches. Several wisps of dry hair, more dirty grey than blond; a cheap wig, more than a head of hair. Then a pair of dark eyes staring vacantly at them from behind the glass. A noisy bolt shot back, a key turned in the lock, a door chain dropped. The door was, at last, opened a crack.

'Oh, hi!' A look of utter surprise on the face.

'Oh, hi! Oh, thanks. Where've you been? We've been drowning out here for five minutes. You knew we were coming. Where were you?'

'The back room.'

'Well, are you going to let us in?'

'Oh, yeah, yeah. Of course. Hi, Cheyney. I thought you'd look worse. Yeah, come in.'

They dripped, just inside the door. Closing the umbrella, shaking off the rain, stamping cold wet feet. Paul flicked a wall-switch. A lantern in the hall-landing above them came to life and a dim yellowish light trickled down the stairs.

'Do we get to go upstairs or do we stand here, Andy?'

'Oh. Oh, yeah, sure.' But he made no move to lead the way. Instead he spoke to Cheyney. 'It must be terrible, all the awful things people are saying about you. Is it terrible? Was it awful when they threw you out of the gallery?'

I'm crazy standing here listening to this, she thought. She looked forlornly at her two companions, who returned her look, embarrassed. 'Well, what do you think, Andy?'

'I think it's too bad you didn't have more money. With more money, you'da made it. Everyone thought you had a lotta money. It's not the brains, it's the money and the success you need. You should'a had more money. You could've at least picked a lover with a lotta money.' This dissertation issued in a monotone from Andy's mask-like face.

Several stairs turned downward to a lower level. Andy bent over the banister and shouted, 'Mom, it's OK. They're my friends.' Cheyney saw a shadow fade from the stairwell below. More carpetless wooden stairs rose through the hall to the first floor above them. Sludgy, cold, and dingy, this was the Warhol residence.

Andy appeared to be just the same at home as he was in her gallery, or at Serendipity, or anywhere else. Just as much the alien, the odd-man-out, there as everywhere he went. Home may have been what he called it, but it was more like the annexe of a second-hand furniture and curio shop. It was chock-a-block with Andy's indiscriminate shopping, his Saturday bargains.

Everywhere she looked there were things, and things upon things. There were mahogany bureaux and dressing tables, and chests of drawers in walnut wood, and cherry and maple, some hand-painted; all shoved against the walls in between an Early American rocking-chair, a Chippendale settee, a garishly painted, life-size wooden Indian.

Everything was piled high with quill boxes and ivory boxes and cardboard boxes, glass bottles, books, wooden fruit, jugs, and Russell Wright plates by the dozen, stacked between yet more things. In a cup Cheyney saw a bracelet solid with moonstones, a necklace of gold leaves. Framed pictures in all sizes and shapes, watercolours, drawings and paintings peeped out from behind more junk or were stacked ten-deep facing the walls. A Victorian gold-leaf mirror, ten feet high, with more chipped gesso showing than gold leaf, half blocked a doorway.

Early American biscuit-tins by the dozen surrounded a wicker doll's-carriage, which held two Victorian dolls with cracked porcelain faces and torn limbs, a stuffed turtle and a cuckoo-clock, the yellow and red, cross-eyed cuckoo leering from the trap door on a spring gone limp. She counted five other clocks, and none worked, two Indian tomahawks and one feathered headdress, and they had not moved from the first-floor landing yet.

'Andy, you live in a warehouse!'

'Oh?' Puzzled, he looked around as if seeing it for the first time.

The radiators were hissing heat, and there was a grey film of dust everywhere. Cheyney had never realised just how pathological his passion for shopping was. He'd have shamed the proverbial squirrel, instinctively greedy, amassing his treasures for that cold winter day that could catch him unprepared. Cheyney suddenly took his greed personally. Her cold winter day had come, and, unlike Andy, she had no store of anything to fall back on. She had never been squirrel enough.

It was all too ugly. Twee, and camp. But, amid the ugliness, she was able to spot a really good painting, a fine drawing, slung in some corner. Andy's disconcerting gift was his ability to have the same enthusiasm for one of those choice articles as for a giant plastic Donald Duck, a tin drum, one Carmen Miranda shoe.

'Can we sit down?' asked Paul.

'Oh, sure, if you want to.'

He opened a door to the front room overlooking the street. The lighting was terrible, the place no less crowded than the upper landing and hall they had just quit. A salon of a hundred Saturdays' shopping. A merry-go-round horse with a shabby mane and a broken ear, its tail missing, loomed out of the shadows. And so did a large draughtsman's-table set near the window overlooking the street. A modern goose-necked lamp screwed to it highlighted an illustration in progress and its creator, a nervous emaciated young man, brush in hand.

'Oh, I forgot. Arthur's working in here.'

He allowed them no introductions, but hurried them from there to the back room, a larger version of the hall and the front room. Just another room of too much *stuff*. He emptied a grotesque Victorian wing-chair of a box of broken Japanese masks, so that Cheyney could sit down. Paul chose the arm of an Art Deco sofa. Tom removed a cardboard box of signed, glossy black-and-white movie star photos from a French butcher's table, dusted it off with a Chinese embroidered shawl, and perched on the corner of that.

'How can you live like this, Andy, with so much clutter? It would junk my mind. All these things. What do they mean? Why do you want them? The effort, the time it takes to collect all this. Don't you ever get tired of shopping?'

'Never. It's the most fun I have, shopping. You just never know what you're really getting, the value it might have after you've discovered it. So I buy everything. I'm not exactly a collector, I'm a many-kinds-of-things buyer. You have to have things. It's better to have things than not have things.'

'But you can be selective.'

'Why?'

Cheyney couldn't begin to answer that. She sighed, knowing it was a waste of time anyway.

'Part of the fun is just going into a store. You see something, you point to it, and it's yours. I like that, it's better than thinking about it. It's too tiring all that thinking: do I want it, should I buy it? I just like everything. Everything looks terrific. I don't buy things 'cause I need them or use them – well, eh, maybe sometimes – but mostly 'cause something catches my eye and I just want it. I like that. Fun-buying. It's all fun.'

'Instant recognition, instant gratification, and on to the next purchase, is that it?' asked Cheyney. She wondered how much of his stuff he looked at a second time.

'Sort of. I don' think about things like that.'

'What do you think about, Andy?'

'How to get rich. I go to church every Sunday and pray to become rich. I want to be the wealthiest, most famous painter in the world. A celebrity. That's all I think about, mostly.'

The atmosphere tensed, The pale, ghost-like Andy, immobile before the seated Cheyney, was aggressive, pushing, demanding without saying a word. The icy wave of his determination chilled her. 'Leo Castelli won't take me. He won't give me a show. And I can paint as well as Jasper Johns can. I'm as good as any of these new guys. I hate it when they say I'm too commercial, I'm not inspired. Inspired – what does that mean, anyway? Why won't he give me a show? Why can't I make it, Cheyney?'

'Andy, I don't really want to hear your troubles, or to talk art. The New York art world is not my favourite subject at the moment.'

'How can you not want to talk about the New York art world? You might just as well be dead.'

'Exactly.'

'But you're not dead.'

'Oh, but I fucking well am!' she shouted. 'Andy, for God's sake, don't you feel anything for what's happened to me? Don't you realise I have lost everything? Not just the gallery, but a lifetime of work and my whole credibility in the world of art? Lost. It's all gone.'

'No.' His tone was flat.

'No?' she repeated, tears brimming from her outburst.

'All that's happened is that you didn't have enough money to keep going. Hold on till some new wave of art hits big and strong enough to make real money, big bucks. That's all that's happened to you. You're the smartest, cleverest of the new dealers. With a hundred thousand dollars behind you, you would have made it.'

A hundred thousand. Cheyney rose from the chair, ready to leave, and promised herself that from then on she would not see Andy Warhol again. 'Andy, I will not talk about the art world. I didn't want to come here, didn't want to see you. Now I know why. I don't want to suffer just because you want to be an art star. And make no mistake, talking art is pain and suffering for me.'

Paul interrupted. 'Andy, why not get us some coffee? That's what we came for. Stop hustling Cheyney.'

'Coffee?' Again that dumb surprised look on his face.

'Yes, Andy, coffee.'

'You want coffee, Cheyney?'

She looked up from the floor. She had dropped her gaze so as not to look at the men in the room. Wanting to hide at least some of the anxiety smarting in her eyes.

'No, I don't want coffee. I don't even want to be here. Let's go.' The look on her face showed her pleading to be relieved of Andy's itching, trivial ambition.

He reached out to touch her. She recoiled. It meant nothing to him, he carried on. 'Wait a minute, Cheyney.'

He paused, and then he came out with it. 'Make me the most famous painter in the world.'

'You don't listen, Andy. I tell you I am a has-been in the art world. Who puts his money on a loser, if he's looking to be a winner?'

'I like having failures around me. I find it inspirational sometimes. It's fun.'

'Because they have nothing more to lose, and, in some perverse way might have something to offer?'

'That's too complex for me. I just like failures, that's all.'

'Oh, I see. It's more like "one man's shit is another man's flowers".'

'Yes, I guess you could put it that way, Cheyney. What you need to do now is to make me what I want to be. You know it all, and better than anybody. Just put it together. If you tell me what to do, I'll do it. Then I'll become the most famous painter in the world.'

'You're mad.'

'OK, I'm mad. Now just tell me what to paint. That's all you have to do. Tell me what to paint and how to get a show.'

'How much do you really want to be the most famous painter in the world? How far will you go?'

'I'll do anything, everything.'

There was silence and a shift of atmosphere in the room. Tom broke the stillness by switching on a lamp. Then he found another in a carton on the far side of the room, pulled it out and plugged it into the wall-socket. Paul found a lamp shade and placed it on the harp over the naked bulb. Something strange was happening. Andy, who at the best of times never looked quite alive, was the colour of ash, completely silent, all aggression gone. He was passive to the point of almost not breathing, whereas Cheyney, who had not moved from the wing chair, had come alive. The light caught her eye. She felt a surge of energy, a sense so positive and strong as to make her heart race. She emanated a confidence and excitement that transformed the room, without her saying a word or moving a finger. It was as if enlightening someone else might absorb the darkness that had all but extinguished the old Cheyney Fox.

'The coffee. Shall I ask your mother to make the coffee?' asked Tom.

'Never mind the coffee,' said Cheyney. 'It seems we have more interesting things to brew here. But I have two conditions. The first is that it will cost you.'

'How much?'

'Fifty dollars, before I say a word.'

Andy left the room, and returned almost immediately with a cheque and handed it to her. 'What else?'

'I want your word: if, after you have become the most famous painter in the world, you are not happy, it hasn't fulfilled all your expectations, you will not hold me responsible.'

'OK.'

'All right. Now tell me, Andy, what do you love more than anything else in the world?' Her catechism had begun.

'I don't know,' Andy said. 'What?'

'Money,' said Cheyney. 'Why don't you paint money?'

'That's a terrific idea. And nobody else has done it. Henry – you know, Henry Geldzahler, the curator over at the Metropolitan who's interested in the new artists – he keeps telling me I should develop new images. Ones no one else uses. But I couldn't think of any. Boy, money's a great one,' said Andy. 'He'll love that.'

'Now listen carefully, Andy. So you understand what this is all about. Your mistake until now has been that you have not understood that any great artist paints the things he knows best, whatever he loves or hates best, and understands, down to the core of his subject. With you it's money, and things. Most of all things, objects that are instantly recognisable, that you don't have to think about. It is not that you're too commercial a painter, but that you are not commercial enough in what you do. Your Bonwit Teller art is for the selected Fifth Avenue few. Money, kid, that's for everybody. That's art that everyone understands and wants to hang on the wall in one form or another. Paint money, and you will knock the stuffing out of the elitist art world.'

'What kind of money?'

'Dollars. American dollar bills. All denominations. Huge canvases of one-dollar notes, a fiver, a two-dollar bill, fifty, twenty, a hundred. Nice, fresh, crisp dollar bills of alluring proportions that will swallow up the viewer.'

'Faaaabulous!' exclaimed Andy. Cheyney wondered if she had made him see himself momentarily as Croesus or Midas. 'What colour?' No, he was being business-like.

'Money colour. Faded, bright. As seen in bright light, in shadow. Done in oils, pastels, charcoal and pencil, and on large canvases, enormous canvases. Or medium ones, small. The dollars can be drawn or painted as prim and proper portraits, or crumpled, or torn in half, or with their corners bent back. You could even paint dirty money. You could do an entire exhibition of the bills in their actual size. Lots of lovely money, all over the walls. People will adore it. Pay a fortune for a dollar.'

'Do you think Leo Castelli will take them?'

'Forget Leo Castelli, he has his new artists. You don't want to be where Jasper Johns is, or Rosenquist, Oldenburg. Roy Lichtenstein, Jim Dine . . . they've found a home for themselves. Don't look to muscle-in on their patch, find your own. Go up against them, create your own limelight in another space. Then you can think about sharing galleries with them.

'The dealers are nervous, taking chances, great leaps in the dark. And the more dealers who take a leap, the better for the ones who already have. It creates momentum in the marketplace. Momentum and a label for the newest movement in American art is what's needed now. One more inspired painter who can add to the Jasper Johns, Rosenquist and that lot's statement in paint, backed by a good gallery, should just about do it.

'You, Andy Warhol, will be what they're looking for, the new inspired image painter. And your work will push the art market over the edge for all the dealers. That's what we have all been searching for, our salvation, to get the market buoyant again. Somewhere to go after abstract expressionism.

'Just get that one-man show. That's all it'll take. A single one-man show. The timing is perfect for you. You have your idea. Why, you don't even have to think, just go to work.'

Cheyney was up out of the chair, bouncing ideas off various parts of the room now. Andy dragged out a large stretched canvas he had. 'What do you think? This size?'

'Yes, of course that size, and larger. Remember, the bigger the better. This is America and we're talking American art.'

'It would be easier in watercolour. Should I do them in watercolour? You know it'll be an awful lot of work doing them all by hand. Paint money by hand? I mean all that detail, painting money. It'll take hours, maybe even days. A long time. A whole show of painted money. Wow, but what a lotta work.'

'Well, what did you think it was going to be, Andy? Do you want to stamp your pictures out?' He seemed to brighten at the possibility.

'Well, that's not a bad idea.'

'You want to be a famous painter! You don't want to have to think. You're lazy. You don't want to work. Well, I hate to tell you this, but you're fucking well going to have to work at it, deliver the goods, *before* you become famous. That's the way the art game is played.'

'OK, so I paint a whole show of money, and I find myself a gallery to give me a one-man show. And what if it's a success? What if they ask me to have another show? What'll I paint then?'

'All right. I'll tell you what to paint next, and I won't even charge you for the idea this time around. After that, though, you're on your own, so far as I'm concerned. I think you should know that I am only doing this because I think it might just take as many as two shows to really get you up there where you want to be. But, remember, you must do everything exactly as I tell you. If you don't, it might not work.' Cheyney felt the power of talk.

'I promise I'll do exactly what you tell me.'

'It doesn't matter whether you've got your first show in New York or Timbuctoo, USA, just get a reputable gallery to give you a show, and make sure it's reviewed. You follow it up with a second show, as quickly as you can get one. The art world, the dealers and the collectors, will do the rest.'

'OK, but what'll I paint for this second show? It'll be terrible if I can't think of something.'

'I just told you, Andy, I'll tell you what to paint. It must be something just as familiar, as everyday, as money. Something so familiar that nobody even notices it any more. Something that Americans take for granted, just like money. Maybe a can of Campbell's soup. That's it. Most every American, sometime in his life, has to confront a tin of Campbell's soup. It's destiny. Our national pap. The nutritious American cream.'

'That's another great idea.'

'Yes, it is actually. It's a very great idea. Paint Campbell's soup cans.'

'How big?'

'Bring me your largest canvas.' He dragged one in. 'Nope. Not big enough.'

'Well, big like what?'

'Get a yardstick. We'll make the tin itself as tall as I am.' He found a tape measure, and they decided on her five foot seven inches, or close to it.

'What flavour?'

'Tomato, Chicken Noodle. It doesn't matter.'

'Make 'em all Chicken Noodle?'

'No. For your first one-man show you paint one tin about twice its natural size on a single canvas. Then repeat the process for every taste the company produces. Frame them, and hang them as neatly, as regimented, as the real thing is stacked in a supermarket. Just bare white walls of Andy Warhol Campbell's soup cans. The new art.'

'Wow!'

Cheyney began to laugh. There was not a sound from Tom and Paul. Andy asked, 'Why are you laughing?'

'I don't even know, but I have a strange feeling the joke is on me.'

'It's brilliant, Cheyney.'

'If you say so, Andy. But you mustn't let it end there. You must paint Warhol Campbell's soup cans in all sorts of ways. With their lids prised open, with torn labels, the cans dented, upright, lying on their sides, empty, upside down, *en masse* on one huge canvas. It will be fabulous. Everyone will want them. And, Andy, don't think about how much work it is. Think about the fame and fortune, the stardom, all your dreams come true. Oh, and make the Campbell's soup cans your first exhibition, money the second. Soup's more audacious – less meaningful than money. The impact will be terrific.'

The room seemed to buzz at the thought of manufacturing so much art. The three men and Cheyney appeared aware that they might have invented a rather special recipe. Stretched blank canvases were strewn everywhere, and huge sheets of watercolour paper slipped over themselves on tables, the floor, a chair. Nothing had been painted or sketched, and yet the Campbell's soup cans and instant art had transformed the dusty, junked-up room. It was no longer a storeroom of inanimate things. It was boiling over with excitement.

His questions went on and on into the night, and Cheyney somehow answered them all. Then suddenly it was over. She had given him what he wanted. She checked her handbag to make sure she had not misplaced the cheque. Cash was more solid than art or soup. It was her dog who needed a can of something right now. Ideas could pay for that. Art in America could look after itself for tonight.

Some curtain-call for you, though, Cheyney Fox, she mused. And what was it all about? An urgent need for dog food. A mournful bark. Ambition should be made of sterner stuff. Cheyney rose from her chair, feeling weaker than the banality of her inspiration warranted. She said, 'Over to you, Andy Warhol. I hope it's all going to be worth it. If not, don't blame me. I gave you my best shot.

CAIRO . NEW
YORK . ATHENS
AUTUMN 1963

Chapter 13

'Irving, you are something else.' Grant Madigan waved a cablegram at the short, dark man, who beamed a wily smile at him. Both pairs of eyes were simultaneously cruising the bar of the Gezira Sporting Club, sizing up the most attractive women.

Grant Madigan stood up, towering over his friend, and the two men shook hands, and walked together to a table where they could watch the women lusciously adorning the edge of the pool. 'The most beautiful women in the Middle East. And classy,' stated Irving. He sighed.

Grant Madigan read from the cablegram. 'Meet me favourite bar soonest. Irving.' 'How did you know I would be in Cairo this afternoon? I didn't know myself until I was half way here from Damascus on my host's jet.'

Irving Kirshner tapped his index finger against the side of his nose. 'Never forget, this is an Israeli nose you're looking at, old buddy.'

'And how did you know where I was staying?'

Irving tapped the side of his nose again. Grant Madigan shook his head in admiration of that percipient nose and called a waiter. He ordered a second malt whisky for himself and a vodka on the rocks for Kirshner.

'The last time I saw you . . .'

Irving chipped in, 'New York, four years ago, F.A.O. Schwartz, stuffed toy department. After a boozy lunch in the Oak Room at the Plaza, you bought a hippo and I snapped up a giraffe for Sidney Taylor's new-born son. You left me to deliver them. I watched you walk through those swing doors into a god-almighty rain storm and crash some good-looking chick to her knees. I thought: a bar in Singapore, a whorehouse in Paris, a three-day binge in Bombay, an orgy anywhere, would have been more our style. Insult to injury, I bet you even scored with that bird in the rain.'

'I had her in the taxi, but not the way you think. I had a plane to catch, and her vulnerability stopped me – you know how I shy away from vulnerable women. Too much trouble. But . . . more than once I've thought about her. She'd have been worth missing that plane for.'

The two men raised their glasses and drank. 'Well, this may not be Bombay or Singapore or Paris, but it is Cairo and I haven't changed my style yet, Irving.'

He raised his eyebrows. 'You mean a network prime-time mover like you hasn't been spoiled by fame and success? You telling me you're still the same hard-drinking, roving tomcat? The not-so-quiet reprobate who loves and leaves the ladies without a qualm? That no quiver has as yet pierced that steel shield you wear over your heart? The years haven't changed you? Come on!'

Grant Madigan gave his old friend a wry smile. As he was coolly checking out the women with an admiring eye, he evoked reciprocal glances at his own rugged American good looks, his adventurer's sensual, hungry eyes. Grant Madigan's discreet romantic liaisons were well-known to women in the diplomatic circles of Cairo. He had both notoriety *and* influence. He conjured for them the perfect image of a western romantic figure. An international celebrity, intellectual without being pompous, courageously sexy, but most of all the unattainable male lover-loner. It set women's hearts racing, their feet chasing. Irving looked with admiration at his old colleague and playmate in the love-stakes. He could not recall a single woman who had won his heart.

'Naw, I haven't changed either, Grant. Still the some sucker falling in love with any woman he fucks. Same old pattern: I home-in on my choice, enter the chase, bed 'em, romance 'em, and believe I'm going to marry every last one of them. Even years after I've left them. I really get off on those loves that chew me up. I'm still looking for *the* one who can last the course. I'm the same Irving Kirshner, that oh-so-nice, handsome, sexy, Jewish guy – a little on the short side, maybe; a bit crippled on the emotional side, too: from always tripping over his feelings and landing on his heart.'

That brought a smile to the face of each and Grant Madigan motioned to the waiter for refills. 'I love that warped image you have of yourself. You always play the *nebbish* like King Lear, Irving. Now, if only I had been born Jewish . . . my Hamlet, my Falstaff. I'd have dissolved you with my Macbeth.'

'Forget it, Grant. You can't be me, and you certainly can't be Jewish. Not a goy like you who *feels* just enough, and no more. I should be more like you – you never allow that sponge of a brain of yours to overcome your heart.'

'It's reassuring to know that a three- or four-year gap between drinks doesn't affect a long friendship. Jesus, it's good to see you, Irving. Where the hell have you been?

'Word has it that you've been working for the CIA, the French Intelligence Service, Israel's MOSSAD. The FBI has you listed on its books as a 'friendly associate'. And when I interviewed Golda Meir she was full of the part you were playing in bringing ex-Nazis to trial. A London friend of ours – name of M15 – reckons, if you hadn't been Jewish, you'd have won the spy-award of the decade. Now what the fuck does all that mean, Irving?'

'Not a lot.' He reached across the small table to the inside pocket of Grant's jacket to liberate a Havana cigar. Grant took another for himself, and handed over his cigar-cutter.

'What are you doing these days? What's new since you gave up journalism? When I heard you had, I was mighty angry with you. You were one of the best. Who are you working for?'

'Israel, of course. But not exactly.'

'If that isn't a typical Kirshner answer!' Madigan looked at his watch then at his friend. He tapped the crystal and said, 'I need the short version, Irving.'

'I know. You're being picked up in twenty minutes. OK, you're why I am here in Cairo. I need a favour. Don't worry, nothing that will compromise you, or your work. Paintings, works of art, are what it's all about.'

'I'm still not getting the drift of all this, Irving.'

'Bottom line: I'm after art-treasures stolen by the Nazis as they went through Europe during the war. Works of art that seem to have vanished for more than twenty years. But, of course, they haven't. They're stashed away in fancy private collections. Property of thieves, war criminals and their sidekicks and buddies. Most of them are the second-division Nazis who got away, and are now respected, wealthy and powerful members of the establishment.'

'That's some job, Irving. Who funds you? Where do you base yourself?' Grant Madigan was at once fascinated by Irving Kirshner's news. He knew Irving's quick wits and penetrating mind fitted him for the job. And he guessed Irving's discoveries could blow the lid off some very volatile secrets.

'I work privately, but am funded by various countries, institutions as well as individuals. I have offices in Paris, New York, Tel Aviv.'

'How successful are you?'

'Not bad. Better than anyone before me. Supposedly the best there is. And, besides prising beautiful things out of the hands of retired murderers, there is being involved with art. It's become a passion. I get off on art. It raises my spirits. There are other dividends too. It's lucrative. I met a lotta interesting guys mixed up in art, freaks and scum, rogues and villains. Even a few good guys. And things I've leaked have put a few more Nazi war criminals inside.'

Irving saw he'd caught Grant's interest. 'It started innocently enough. A good story. A feature article for *Time*: 'Lost And Found: One Nazi War Criminal'. Only it turned out to be not such an interesting story, stuff

113

we've all heard about before. Your run-of-the-mill fifth-rate Nazi was criminal. Just another sadistic camp commandant who escaped the net for twenty years. I dropped the story, but got hooked on the idea of this vast mob of the world's most despicable criminals reverting, in most cases, to cosy, well-heeled, bourgeois lives.'

Irving tapped the side of his nose again with his forefinger.

'It was all there, Grant. I was sniffing something out, but I had no idea what it was. It had something to do with the mediocrity of the lives these minor war criminals were living. Middle-class, boring, shit lives. Minor – what am I saying, *minor*? There are no minor Nazi war criminals as far as we Israelis are concerned! But there was a smallness about these guys the Nazi hunters were ferreting out, the men they were able to pick up and bring to trial. They were small fry, nothing compared to the big fish that were out there living it up. This nose of mine kept telling me: Irving, the biggest criminals leave a golden trail. Catch them by their greed.'

Grant and Irving were momentarily distracted by a brunette beauty who passed their table. Hadn't she been a former romantic springtime fancy of Grant's some years before? After a brief exchange of pleasantries, they continued.

'You know as well as I do that in intelligence work it's mind, not muscle, that's the key to success. These hunters were using both, but they were missing something. They were chasing around for facts, for evidence, and always missing something solid, concrete, to sink the bastards. To find a Mengele, a Martin Bormann, and the other fifty or more who quit Nazi Germany with enough cash, gold ingots and pictures to make fat cats of them for the rest of eternity, just follow the trail of their greed. That never changes. I had the key to it: the greed, the avarice.

'Then, one day, some months later, I was having a drink with Moshe Schratsky. You remember Moshe?'

'I sure do. He was a great help to me when I was in Jerusalem doing my interview with Golda Meir. What a bright guy.'

'I'll say. We were talking about Israel's intelligence network. It was Moshe who said, "Don't underestimate any intelligence service. The analysis, the piecing-together of disparate strands of information, may produce only tentative conclusions. But they have been known to dictate the survival of armies, the fate of nations. It's always been that way. Probably always will be." He tried to recruit me for MOSSAD, claiming that I have the intellect and ability to analyse for their kind of work. He tried to convince me that that, plus my instinct for sizing up a situation, could make me the perfect spy, or counterspy.'

'You a spy? Moshe must have been having an off day. Or he was desperate? Anyone who has ever met you for five minutes knows that you can't keep your mouth shut. And your womanizing alone would disqualify you.'

'That's what I told him. Only, in a way, that did not make me the schmuck you just described. I declined, explaining that the infidelities and materialism, all the vanity and ambition that drive people to betray their country, would be more fascinating to me than catching a criminal or playing I-spy. And in telling Moshe that, I realised I had stumbled upon something that really interested me – man's weaknesses and his failings. I could nail the bastards red-handed with their weaknesses, their vanities and their immorality.

'You should have heard Moshe. He was quite funny. He said—' and here Irving imitated Moshe's accent and waved his arms around ' – "What, trace their bank accounts? The Bormanns and Eichmanns and Mengeles of this world don't have bank accounts, Irving. Treasures, they live on their victims' treasures. All that fancy loot, art lost to the world. Thanks, Irving, thanks a lot."

'Their treasures! "Jesus, Irving," I said to myself, "that's it. Go for the lost works of art. That's the lock. Greed is the key." So I had the lock and the key. Trace them through the treasures they looted. I'd uncover the beasts as they off-loaded art-treasures plundered by the Third Reich, I'd go after their beautiful stash. A terrific adventure, a great story. And anything I could turn up for the Nazi-hunters, a bonus.

'It started as innocently as that. But, after six months, the Nazi art-treasures became an obsession. A magnificent obsession.'

They were interrupted again by a *sufragi*, sent by the doorman of the club to say that Prince Ben el Saud's car had arrived for Mr Madigan. Grant checked the time and told the servant to say he would be there shortly.

'Thank God for the local idea of punctuality,' remarked Grant. 'We have time for one more at least.' And he raised his hand to order another round of drinks.

Irving checked his wristwatch and said, 'We got twenty minutes before you gotta leave. The Prince expects to be picked up from the German Embassy exactly at seven, with you in the car waiting for him. You'll be joined by the man you're so anxious to meet, Helmut Furtwangler. That guy's private art collection is going to knock your eyeballs out, *if* you ever get to see it.'

'Uh-huh. So you suspect Furtwangler of being one of your Nazi looters for the Reich who then snuck off with the treasures. And the Prince? You have to have been watching him and me pretty closely to be so well informed about our movements.'

'Very good, Grant. Two out of two for good guesses. Helmut is a definite yes. And someday I'm going to get his stolen works of art back to those of his victims still alive to appreciate them. It may take years, but it *will* happen. Right now, we've only a few puny leads to go on. But they do hang together. And they add up to a pretty big network of private art galleries that go in for stolen works of art. A world-wide network, in fact.

'The Prince: sympathetic to former Nazis, no friend to Israel. But certainly no thief, no war criminal. He is unusual among the Saudi Princes. He's been collecting art since he was a young man. He got his schooling in England and France. They say he had a close relationship with the old Aga Kahn and his family. Anyway he picked up their French tastes, their passion for horse-racing. They gave him a lift into the arts. They made a collector of him.

'He knows a lot, Grant. He knows which stolen pieces are where. He's run his eye over quite a few of those mysterious private collections. I have plenty of evidence of that. But I don't know that he's ever bought anything for himself that doesn't carry a legitimate provenance. He's pretty canny about what he buys. Word has it that he intends to build a museum in Mecca for his collection. The plans are already on the architect's drawing-tables.'

'All hot copy, Irving, but I don't see where I fit in. And why choose right here and right now to put me in the picture, as you so divertingly call it?'

'Ah, the crunch. A little bird told me you are about to spend an evening in a house and get an eyeful of a collection that we reckon is mostly Nazi loot. The owner was a Nazi high-up though he claims to be a Belgian archaeologist. He's been shacked up in one of King Farouk's sold-off summer palaces since 1946. Forty-five rooms, stretched out beside the Nile and surrounded by a fourteen-thousand-acre farm. Two hours by fast car from Cairo. The place has several villages, a small town even. Plus a hush-hush army of uniformed hoods to run the estate like its own little country. It's a really shut-off place, out there in the desert. You see the Nile from in there, but you don't see in there from the Nile.

'This guy makes his own rules. He even squeezes a bit of respect from men like Helmut Furtwangler, and the Prince. Mossad has always suspected he's the Bormann they can't find. But can they get anywhere near the place or the man to prove it? He's just clocked up sixty years. Several of the top suspects on Israel's secret hit-lists are suddenly jetting in to Cairo for a twelve-hour stopover. I smell bandits. Something more like a class reunion along with the birthday shenanigans. And you, old buddy, are one of the guests. Specially invited, we suspect, by the birthday boy. Courtesy of the Prince, who dangled Helmut Furtwangler as bait. He knows you want a TV profile of the guy.'

'Irving, come on. This is way over the top. Why would a man like that

116

want me at his birthday party? I think your sniffer—' Grant tapped the side of his nose '– is out of order. You *are* playing I-spy.'

'I told you, Grant, that's not my game. Albert Semanan, the name the birthday boy has tacked on to himself, wants to meet you. He wants to go over your interview with Picasso. He has it on film. He's always playing it through. Picasso is one of his weaknesses. He has a fabulous collection of his works. You're going to be one of his best birthday presents. Hearing first-hand all about the man behind the artist.'

'Jesus, Irving, you've got some intelligence service going yourself. Who needs the professionals? Suppose all this is true – and it probably is, knowing that you wouldn't be here if it wasn't – I don't see how I can help you. I'll not inform for you. You should know that by now.'

'I'm not asking you to.'

'Well, what are you asking me, Irving? I'd like to help you find these missing works of art. I might even get a kick from putting them back where they belong. But I don't spy on people who take me into their confidence. It'd be unethical.

'Oh, but you can help – and without getting shit on that shiny lens of yours. Look, I got on to you, Grant, just by coincidence. When you were in Havana grilling Castro for TV, you visited the house of a German there. In Paraguay you stayed at the ranch of a man called Raymondo Oliveira.'

'Yeah, he's made himself a big number among collectors of Italian Renaissance Art. Big money, plus an extravagant life style, but buried in a jungle backwater,' interrupted Madigan. The coincidences were making him uncomfortable.

'Exactly. You and one other have shown up more than once at parties given by men I am interested in. A guy called Kurt Walbrook. Viennese, a collector of enormous importance. Do you remember meeting him or his mother, the Baroness Walbrook? Quite a formidable lady.'

'Can't say I do. And I still don't see how I can help you, Irving.'

'Grant, we go back a very long time. You know I wouldn't approach you unless it was important to me. And it isn't just me. It's hundreds of people who have been robbed of what they bust their asses to collect and preserve. And we're not just talking of big-shots, Grant. In fact, in most cases, just small people: well-to-do Jews, Polish and Czech aristocrats who collected these things as part of an already cultivated life.

'Walk the streets of Prague, Crakow, Budapest, and think of the empty walls once filled with Pissaros, Degas, Van Goghs, Rembrandts, Poussins, Russian icons, Greek and Roman antiquities. Do you think there were no Polish aristocrats who collected, had a love of beautiful things? No Jewish bankers who bought Renoir, Matisse, Manet, Cézanne? And what of Paris, Bruges, Antwerp, Rotterdam – looted and looted for their works of art? What does the world think? They hung calendars on the wall? When the Nazis came, a Monet supplied three people with bread for a month. A Van Dyck and a Reynolds went to a French butcher for one month's ration of meat for six. And those were the lucky ones, who dealt before their possessions were stolen. There are plenty of stories in my work for a man like you, Grant.

'But put all that aside for a minute. What I want is for you to tell me what's going on behind the scenes. I want to be able to send you photographs of works of art known to be stolen. Then, if you should ever see them, you might just let me know where. All I'm asking now is for you to keep your eyes open when you go to this birthday party. Just try to remember the pictures you see, the people you meet. It could one day make all the difference to us.'

The two men remained silent for some minutes before Grant rose from his chair. They shook hands, and then clasped each other in one of those very male gestures by which bonds of old friendship are called in and accepted. They walked together to the waiting car.

'When do you leave Cairo?' asked Madigan.

'Tomorrow or the day after. I have some other people I'd like to surprise.'

'What are you doing tonight?'

'Why? Have you got a number for me?'

'One of the best.'

'Good. Tonight's as good as any to fall in love.'

'598726. Her name is Caro Hamadi.' The two men exchanged a knowing smile. Grant Madigan slipped into the back seat of the white Mercedes 600, and was swept away towards his *rendezvous*.

Chapter 14

Ah, Egypt and the Nile. The land of Cleopatra and Queen Hatshepsut, the Pharaohs and the Mamelukes, Sobek, the crocodile-headed god. Cairo and the Immobilia Building, the Semiramis Roof. Falafel, kebabs, *moulukhiya*, the scent of garlic and jasmine. The heat and the sand, Alexandria, and the sea. The dust, the sun, and the city of the dead, the Wadi el Natrun, were never less than inspiring to Grant. Memphis, the Pyramids and the Sphinx who endures all – heroic, mysterious, no matter how many visits he made to them.

Gone was the old Egypt of Kings, of Pashas, the Wafd, the spoilt and decadent Farouk – and with them the final shreds of a bogus erotic romanticism fostered by Victorian adventurers and Orientalist paintings and watercolours, and several centuries of unspeakable maladministration of one of the most fascinating countries in the world.

Except, of course, in the imagination, and for the few Cairene aristocrats of great power and wealth who could afford to live out their fantasies in secret. In houses lost in a maze of dark and narrow streets of the old city, or in the Muski, the bazaar, or in tents deep in the desert, or behind the closed doors of beach-pavilions.

The new Egypt: a hamburger at the Hilton, an officer's cap instead of a frayed tarboosh, hard-pressed khaki drill everywhere in the streets. Reminders that the U.A.R. is not the Egypt of the Khedives or of Kitchener. Not even of England's Eighth Army. Its modern politics and wars held no less interest for Grant Madigan. For him the old and the new Egypt were as one. What it was, and what it had been, constantly engrossed him. A place where invariably he found a story.

The old and the new Egypt reciprocated alike the affection he showed them, both privately and in the various media he worked with. They were not unappreciative, although sometimes erratic. He had known the country for a good many years, which therefore included both the old and the new nations. The various regimes had alternated between expelling him from the country and making him an honoured guest. Egypt and Grant Madigan had an ongoing love-affair – but a volatile one.

He was their current blue-eyed western media man. He was, in fact, having a success all over the the Arab world – one result of his recent series on the oil industry and oil power of of the Middle East. Another was that he had been taken into the fold by Prince Ben el Saud. More than a year ago they had become good friends, which was why he was now speeding in air-conditioned luxury through the desert.

'Is it true that rage and revolution are tearing your country apart, Mr Madigan?' asked the Prince, his English edged with a distinctive Massachusetts accent.

'I doubt if it's anything quite so radical. But hope and change are on the move.'

'From *my* country, these appear to be deeply unsettling times for the United States. Your sit-ins and your civil rights, your anti-war, anti-bomb, anti-military movements. Your student marches. Not anarchy, Mr Madigan?'

'Not exactly,' said Grant Madigan, amused at the Prince's concern. 'This sixties generation you find unsettling is either a back-lash or a progression from the beatnik years of Kerouac and Alan Ginsberg, Gregory Corso – that lot.'

'A back-lash or progression? I don't know, Grant, I would have to think more about that. What I do see, however, is that already this sixties generation is drunk on liberation, without having had even a sip of the freedoms it's thirsting for. It has certainly not turned politics and society around enough for real change. I think it's inebriated on its own rhetoric, nothing more.'

He smiled at Grant Madigan, and continued, 'Oh, I do like the States and Americans, and your fads and short-lived fixations. Forgive me, but watching the goings-on in America now is like watching rebellious children in an opulent playground. What do you think is happening over there now, Helmut?'

Grant Madigan was alert for what Helmut Furtwangler might think was happening. He had targeted this man for an in-depth TV interview. The German was sheltering behind a pharmaceutical empire. With his vast wealth, he was said to be one of the most powerful men in Europe and South America. Heads of state in various countries felt obliged to acknowledge his influence.

'Is not the real foundation of all their movements fear?' asked Helmut Furtwangler. 'Fear of loss, of failure. Of falling from one of their numerous band-wagons: stardom, being famous for those few unforgettable minutes. Perhaps a higher ideal, and that freedom they are so anxious to wallow in. They are a loquacious lot, these young mavericks of yours. Maybe too much so. They're reaching other countries with their anti-establishment rebellions, their "age of Aquarius", their provocative music, their sexual liberation. It will be interesting to watch how your government will handle these dreamers. What mine, and other countries, may do about their influence. I know the States well, Mr Madigan. I can't help but wonder what will your average Mr Kansas and Wyoming, or Mr Texas, do about these cries for freedom – and nigger-power?'

The veiled fascism of these admonitions was no more than Grant Madigan had anticipated from the two men flanking him in the back of the Mercedes 600. The car was one of a convoy of stretch limousines tracing its way through the desert.

'Do I sense that you, sir, feel in some way threatened by what's happening in the States now?' asked Madigan.

'But of course he does.' That was the Prince answering. 'And well he might! They are setting up black-white polarities: America versus totalitarians, the law versus crime. Freedom against slavery, suburbia confronting the slum. Left versus right. And your young people are trying to force the world to take their side in the name of Coca-Cola, burned bras, promiscuous sex, a Campbell's soup can for art, and more fun. A higher ideal, equality for all. What has happened to the grey area, that place of live and let live, Madigan?'

'You know, Mr Madigan, the Prince has a point.' Helmut Furtwangler hesitated for a moment. He lit a cigarette, and then continued. 'In a democracy, where supposedly there is freedom for all, the intensity of the reaction against the students seeking change in your country tells me you're in turmoil. Unless your President takes a very sharp turn to the political right, he may not win a second term in office.'

They remained silent for a few minutes, pondering. It was not a happy thought for any of the three men. Although each of them had his criticisms and his reservations about President Kennedy, Grant Madigan knew they looked to him, as did most of the anti-communist countries, as their greatest hope. The first leader for a decade who looked as if he might bring lasting peace to the world. In spite of the Cuban fiasco at the Bay of Pigs, a kind of integrity beyond the mere glamour made him the world leader they had been waiting for. He was now keenly watched to see what he could deliver.

'Grant, you've spent a great deal of time with the President preparing for that extended talk you had with him on American TV. Do you really think your President Kennedy, his clan, and *his* Camelot, are in control of the situation? They are not, maybe, too liberal? Is it not possible they are playing the game of the right-wing liberal – to keep what your papers call the new left in check? A high-risk game. One can make powerful enemies on both the left and the right playing games like that.'

Before Grant Madigan could answer, the Prince held up his hand to silence him, and continued.

'I am, as you know, a staunch supporter of the United States, and in particular Jack and Bobby Kennedy. I like to think they are personal friends. But I am, in my country, a voice very much alone in this. My father is keeping his options open. But, I might tell you, he doubts that all this hope and glory, this fanciful drift to the left, will be tolerated by the right-wing factions that in the end dictate to your democracy.'

'Gentlemen, I think you have forgotten that President Kennedy is listening to the people, moving with the times, not bucking them. You surprise me. You were not far from him, Herr Furtwangler, when he said, "Ich bin ein Berliner". He's more the friend of Europe than you think. Why are you so afraid of his power as a liberal President of the United States? He's no more or less powerful than any of the Presidents we've had in the last thirty years. He just inspires more hope for a different future than most.'

'Precisely.'

There was a sense of menace in the way Helmut Furtwangler enunciated that single word. Its obscure insinuations stifled the conversation.

Their attention was diverted by the ball of orange-red sun sinking through a sky of bruised blue, mauve tinged with pink, behind the sand dunes. The limousines sped over a well-maintained track.

The dunes gave way to hillocks of crumbling stone and drifts of sand. The cavalcade of cars sped through a pass and into a canyon, out the other side to a hidden valley where the sand-swept terrain abruptly yielded to a dark earth rich in vegetation. A ribbon of green sprouting half a mile wide on one bank of the Nile, with golden desert on the other.

Between clouds of dust they could glimpse some distance ahead the palace of cream-coloured marble reflecting a bright coral-pink from the setting sun. A splendid, three-storey affair spread out along the river. Square towers of some elegance and grace rose from vast stone terraces and decorative marble balustrades, made more impressive by the curved staircases that swept down to the sumptuous gardens culminating in the banks of the Nile.

Still a good distance away, it appeared to sit in its exotic setting like a wedding-cake replica of the most elegant *fin de siècle* French *palais*. A confection of utter architectural delight. On white camels colourfully draped and tasselled, an escort rode out to bring the convoy of cars to the palace. World politics and America's sociological upheavals were drowned out as the riders fired rifles above their heads to proclaim the arrival of guests.

Grant had sensed that they were stepping back in time when they passed through the Nile villages. They had been greeted with subservient bows by the *fellahin*, peasants, in their turbans and kaftans, the women swathed in black, except for bare hands and feet. Silver jewellery, glass beads and bangles brightened their costumes. Dark, sultry eyes were outlined heavily in kohl. Swarms of scruffy, barefoot children laughingly chased beside the cars.

They had stopped at several check-points since they turned off the main road. Clusters of uniformed security guards, armed with rifles and automatic weapons, scrutinised the identity of those in the cars against their guest-lists. But now, as the cars pulled up to the grand staircase leading to the terrace, all that seemed primitive and superfluous, so refined, sumptuous and chillingly beautiful was the place. Even the sounds: Wagner's *Parsifal*, Grant registered, issuing from somewhere deep inside the palace.

Wagner on the Nile. A little heavy, that, thought Grant, and then, as he mounted the stairs, Why not? It's no more outlandish than anything else in this unlikely country.

The Prince and his party were greeted on the stairs by their host. The guests were drinking champagne as they wandered between the terrace and the grand salon, through tissue-thin, white silk curtains that covered the two-storey-high French windows capped with arched yellow canopies. It was a balmy Egyptian November evening. Grant felt for a moment mesmerised by the setting sun that had turned the palace bright coral, and seduced by the undulating silk curtains gently rippling in the evening breeze.

The man was handsome, looking more forty than sixty. Striking, but cold. An icy, somewhat inhuman handsomeness. Grant filed it as plastic-surgery handsome that had made time stand still for this face. The eyes were unimaginably cruel.

He emanated an air of powerful authority. Madigan's travelling companions were at once under his spell. The almost theatrical click of his heels, the drop of the head in the old Prussian bow, the tremble of excitement in Furtwangler's voice as he assured his host, in German, how honoured and grateful he was to share this evening with his old-time friend. Grant saw tears brimming in Helmut's eyes. He heard the man say, 'Helmut, Helmut, my oldest and closest friend, from those times when we worked together. What a life it has been – and still is. There are people here, our old colleagues, eager to see you after so many years.'

Grant recognised a Teutonic sentimentality he despised. He saw it too in other groups of men talking and laughing together on the terrace. If Irving were ever to ask how was the party, Grant would have to admit he'd been right: it was more like a class reunion. Goddam you, Irving, and your sensitive hooter, he said to himself. Furious because as usual his old friend had caught the whiff of something big before he had.

Albert Semanan shook Grant Madigan's hand. Their eyes met, and

123

Grant got the idea that he had just shaken the hand of some bad news for humanity.

His English was perfect, spiced with a trace of a French accent. 'I much admired your interview with Picasso. I have a film of it, and watch it often. I think you got the maestro to reveal himself more than anyone before you. I am obsessed with real genius, true greatness. I am fascinated by his genius, particularly. I met him several times in Paris. It would have been gratifying to have him here with us tonight. I own many Picassos, but never enough.'

A *sufragi*, dressed in a black kaftan and turban, his hands clad in white cotton gloves, offered tall crystal flutes of champagne. Albert Semanan chose one and handed it to Grant. 'After dinner, we will talk about your time with this great man.'

Their conversation was interrupted by other arrivals. Grant took the opportunity to wander among the other guests. With jade spoons dozens more of the black-clad *sufragis* served individual crystal bowls of the best Beluga caviar from heavy baroque silver trays. Slivers of crisp toast piled in pyramids on similar platters were passed among them.

Grant noted that no care had been taken to disguise the many armed guards wondering everywhere in their crisp white jackets. He could only assume it was a conscious attempt to reassure the guests that they were safe at least from anyone else's firepower.

This was a party of such elegance and style, it was difficult for Grant to equate it with murderers, plunderers, sadists. Yet, borrowing Irving's hypersensitive nose, he could imagine he caught the stench of brimstone beneath the heady scent of the jasmine, lilies and roses that adorned the room in lavish arrangements. Menace seemed more than usually discernible amid the rich fragrance of humanity on the desert breeze.

A dinner gong was struck, and the *sufragis* manned the French windows, drawing the curtains aside for the guests to enter the grand salon. That aroma of menace yielded for Grant, as he flowed through the hundred-foot-long reception room with the other guests.

The room was enviably filled with works of art. True art treasures of provocative quality and beauty. Picassos of every period, some of enormous size. Soutines, Roualts, Gauguins in eyebrow-raising numbers. Greek and Roman classical sculptures. Large, magnificently painted Greek vases and urns in glass cases. It was scarcely less impressive than walking through the museum galleries of Paris, New York or London, here all rolled into one grand showroom. But, of course, for Irving Kirshner it was not a gallery, merely the trophy-case of a Nazi looter.

A pair of grand pianos was distributing measures of Chopin to either side of the room. The guests wondered around in relative silence, awed by their surroundings. A flood of *sufragis* trailed in, carrying more silver trays with cups of hot lobster bisque. Albert Semanan collected a pair of cups from the tray and accepted two napkins from a *sufragi*. He handed one to Grant and said, 'I often do this. Serve the first course of the meal here in this room so people can enjoy the paintings. Most of my guests are only in Egypt for a few hours to honour me. This way I can at least honour them with more time to look.'

He was called away by a couple and that gave Grant time to observe. There were odd things about the guests. Their manner, their bearing, a certain pomposity and coldness, seemed common to all. They were replicas almost of one another. Most were German though there were several Americans, two ranking ministers from South American countries, several Arab Princes. The remainder were Europeans of dubious provenance.

And, among the black-tied men in evening dress, there were present half a dozen women. Gloriously young, beautiful, resplendently gowned and sporting priceless jewels. Kings' ransoms of rubies, emeralds and diamonds.

One woman stood out among the others. A woman of considerable age with honey-blonde hair worn in a rather old-fashioned manner. A wide braid twisted around her head in a crown and was held in place by diamond sunbursts. She had a marble-like, stoic beauty. She was dressed in black crêpe de chine, and bore a massive collection of gems, all diamonds, intended to swell her grandeur. She hardly spoke, but every person in the room paid respectful attention to her. She was introduced to Grant by Helmut Furtwangler. She was Viennese, the Baroness Walbrook. She acknowledged the introduction before dismissing Grant with hardly a glance.

She was a formidable if somewhat unnerving woman who carried in her persona a hint of moral decadence. He suddenly sensed glossed-over evil. Grant placed his cup of lobster bisque on the tray carried by a passing *sufragi* and headed for the terrace and a breath of fresh air. That was when he encountered her.

A ravishingly sophisticated beauty of blonde hair and fair skin, dressed in a strapless white silk jersey dress that barely covered the stunningly sexy breasts and fell to the ground in soft clinging folds. He watched her take the last few steps down the grand sweeping staircase. Her long, intricately designed diamond earrings, the only decoration she wore, sparkled as bright as the stars. They gave a glow to the no longer young but amazingly beautiful, experienced face.

On the terrace, he led her into the shadows. She resisted. Instead, led him to the balcony's stone balustrade where a shaft of light from the windows of the grand salon missed them only by centimetres. There they were able to see the lust in each other's faces, hear the sounds of people and music, feel the excitement of illicit sex. Time was not on their side. They felt the urgency, the danger of being discovered. It spurred them on. He reached out to ease her breasts from the silk. She resisted with a nod of her head, smiled, and from a chair dropped a cushion on to the marble, sinking down on to it on her knees.

She was magnificent. She took him wholly in her mouth and made love to him. He watched her face, and how she loved sucking his cock. She had to be one of the best. He was half in this world, half out. To see this calm, cool beauty devouring him. To see himself in the stream of soft light moving in and out of her amazing mouth. To feel the warm soft moist interior of this woman, and the tantalising rhythm of her sucking and squeezing on him. Oh yes, she was even more than magnificent. And then, in one swift act, he had her up on her feet, had spun her around, and having raised her dress up to her waist bent her over the balustrade. Naked except for white stockings held by long white lacy garters attached to a slim lace belt around her hips, the light and dark shadows playing on her, she was sublime, decadent lasciviousness, open and ready for him. He grabbed her by the hips, she raised her bottom and spread her legs as wide as she could to take him wholly into her cunt and used it as she had used her mouth while he fucked her.

'If someone comes?' she asked.

'They will see nothing more than two people looking at the stars.' The only words they ever said to each other.

When they returned to the salon cups were being collected and the guests were moving through the Great Hall towards the dining-room. They drifted apart and mingled with the crowd. Each of them would remember the interlude as the perfect romantic fuck, because they never exchanged names, never stole a glance at each other all through the evening, and would never meet again.

The entrance to the dining-room was impressive and dramatic with Pharaonic artefacts that might have been lifted from the Cairo Museum, and Italian Renaissance paintings seemingly snatched off the walls of the Uffizi. A more jovial mood seemed to have taken over the party. Laughter was louder, the people smiled at each other more, it was less tense. Grant felt the lightness with relief.

Semanan had the Baroness on his arm, and behind them a man was escorting a ravishing brunette. Grant recognised him from somewhere. Irving had said that Grant and another man had shown up in the intelligence reports. Grant remembered the name Kurt Walbrook but still had no memory of where he had seen him before.

The dining-room was resplendent in white damask, vermeil cutlery, crystal and gold goblets, gold plates, white lilies of every variety, and low candles by the the dozens, all alight. A *sufragi* stood behind every second chair. The walls were hung from the wainscot to the ceiling with priceless Impressionist paintings. Renoir flowers shimmered, Monet's water glistened, his water lilies begging to be plucked. Van Gogh suns burned, and Cézanne fruit invited tasting.

'As you can see, I am an obsessive collector,' Semanan told Grant. His smugness was repulsive. Wily old Irving, thought Grant, he's right. He'll catch this man by his greed.

He answered with, 'I have a friend who has recently become involved in the art world. He calls it his magnificent obsession.'

'Ah, that's very good. Most apt in my case, certainly.'

Grant Madigan could never recall exactly when or how the news arrived. Chairs had been pulled out from the table by the *sufragis* so that the guests could be seated. It was as the guests were settling down that he realised something had intruded upon the the stilted gaiety of the occasion.

A woman, an American opposite the Prince who was sitting next to Grant, lowered her head and covered her face with her hands. Kurt Walbrook at the foot of the table was rubbing his hand over his chin. He looked thoughtful, disturbed even. And was it tears Grant saw in the eyes of another guest? Both Semanan at the head of the table and the Baroness, who was seated on his right, appeared less disturbed. Helmut, on his left, was pale and very quiet.

All conversation trickled away. The room was perfectly still, the *sufragis* at attention behind every other high-backed chair. All eyes were on Albert Semanan. He looked suddenly furious, and rose angrily from his chair. It scraped the rose-marble floor. He flung his napkin down and in a rasping voice announced: 'It is my misfortune that this should have happened tonight, the one night in 1963 when you were all able to come from the corners of the world to honour me on my birthday, this 22nd of November that we have planned for so many years to celebrate. But it has, and I feel honour-bound to give formal recognition to the news. Let us observe a moment of silence, and then put it out of our minds and get on with our celebration.' Then he read out the message that had informed him that John Kennedy had been shot in Dallas.

Grant Madigan was the only one to walk away from the feast.

Chapter 15

When Mary Rosewarne hung up the telephone she returned to her Mixmaster. She switched it back on high, and hoped the cake mixture in the bowl had enough banana brandy in it. She had forgotten to measure. Two pots were bubbling over just enough to make a mess of the stove. The kitchen was warm and smelt delicious. But things were not coming out quite right. Not that it bothered Mary Rosewarne. She always kept going. An ambitious cook, she was not without her successes. Engrossed in her kitchen, she was hardly aware that her husband David had come home.

He went directly to the sink where she was scrubbing out a pan that she had somehow let burn on the stove earlier in the day. He put his hand on her shoulder and she half turned from her pot to him. He kissed her on the cheek, and she in turn kissed him on the lips. They loved each other in just that way.

She was wearing a navy-blue, taffeta, shirt-waist dress, with a diamond brooch and earrings of antique rose-cut stones. Her hair was dressed well and she was made up. She sped across the not-so-clean kitchen floor in a pair of high-heeled, open-toed, navy-blue calfskin shoes, around her waist a dirty apron. They were going to the country club for dinner with the Waverlys. She smelled of white lilacs and a touch of Ajax cleanser. She was not unlike a slim version of Marie Dressler with a Vassar degree.

It was all homey, upper-middle class until they spoke, and then you knew that it was upper, upper-middle class, or bottom-rung brahmin. It was perfect. She was perfect. David Rosewarne was content with his wife, his children, his work. His life was an ad-man's American dream.

'You're looking very pretty, Mrs Rosewarne,' he said, giving a purposeful pat to her bottom. She gave him a distracted smile and spoke to him as she stepped up her action on the burnt pot.

'Did you have a good day?'

'Yes. You?'

'Fine.'

'Where are the boys?'

'In their rooms doing homework.'

'Good. Mary, why are you standing over that sink? Where's Shirley? That's what she's hired to do here.'

'She's in her room. I thought I would clean the kitchen, give her a little rest. She's been washing and ironing all day.'

'Mary, you have a laundress for that. Now put that pot down and come into the study. We'll have a glass of wine before I go up to bathe and change.'

She duly relinquished the pot, washed her hands and removed her apron. She spread too much hand-cream on her hands and had to wipe it off with a paper towel. In the study her husband was removing the cork of a bottle of cold May wine. Two Baccarat crystal glasses, a strawberry in each, were waiting to be filled.

Mary sank into the grey, linen-covered cushions of the large, over-stuffed lounge chair and slipped into complacency. Gazing across the room she allowed herself a moment to revel in its handsomeness. *Her house*. It radiated cultivated New England taste and respectability. So did her husband. Like their life. She accepted the glass from him with a smile.

They up-dated each other about their family, their home, his golf game, her garden, his office. What she would do when he took the boys sailing in a few weeks' time. They had a second glass of wine, then a third. The Chopin nocturnes he had chosen came to an end, and they sat in the silence and comfort of their lives. A faint sound from somewhere in the house, unidentifiable to David.

'That's a strange noise. Can it be coming from the kitchen?'

Mary cocked her ear and listened. A whirring noise, and unmistakably from the kitchen. She took another sip of her drink and thought about it. Suddenly, she jumped from the chair, splashing wine on her navy-blue taffeta.

'Oh damn! The frozen banana pound cake, it must be ruined by now!' She ran from the study towards her kitchen to see if any of the mix was salvageable. David picked up the evening newspaper. She popped her head back through the study door.

'Oh, I forgot, Cheyney Fox called. Sounded mildly urgent, so I said you would call back as soon as you came in.' Then Mary was gone again.

A slight tightening somewhere between the gut and the heart. Wherever would-be adulterers feel such things.

Cheyney often thought about David Rosewarne's personal life. During the time that he acted on her behalf, she had seen at first hand similar scenes when she had consented under pressure to visit his family in Massachusetts. A window on to his relationship with his wife, his unquali-fied love for his sons, had a profound effect on her. The pride he took in being a leading citizen of his community, combined with what she knew of him as a successful, much sought-after lawyer, had only added to her

129

fondness and respect for the attractive, likeable man. He had let himself be persuaded by Cheyney's lawyer, an old Harvard classmate, to handle her bankruptcy problems.

David had taken her case on for several reasons. Money was certainly not one of them. His being a collector of contemporary art himself – a pastime both Mary and he had indulged themselves in passionately from back when he was a law student at Harvard – had something to do with it. The tale of her blackmail by Tony Caletti was another reason. Her courageous attempt to make her gallery work, yet another. They were factors, but his truest prompting had been her desperation. The pain he saw in her eyes. The lingering romantic in David Rosewarne had chosen to recognise Cheyney Fox as something special, rare and beautiful that was nly hanging on to life by a thread. He both feared for that life and wanted to help her, a potent emotional mix. But despite all this, he had not foreseen any personal involvement with her.

David had never imagined that her case would drag on for so long, or turn into such a bitter battle. He had fought hard to win. None of it had come easy. He could never understand the absolute determination of Marvin Weinstock, the lawyer representing the creditors, to hang a case of fraud on his client as well as to sink her under the weight of her debts. A common, vulgar man who wore white cotton socks under dark suits whose trousers were too short, he had displayed a vicious hatred of Cheyney right from the beginning. He believed she was a clever, manipulative criminal and pulled every string he could to prove it.

His constant interrogation of her had a crippling affect on her mental well-being. Many times during her ordeal, David Rosewarne thought that she would break down. He spent hours persuading her not to give up. Such intensity – and her beauty – had its effect on him.

Ever since the night that Cheyney had earned fifty dollars by telling Andy what to paint: money, how to earn more money, haunted her day and night. Now Andy Warhol had become a famous painter, much as she had predicted, the international celebrity he had wanted to be. And she was still down and out in Manhattan, living in penurious near-isolation at a good address.

She couldn't possibly take a responsible job: her mind was too tortured and fragmented for that. A stop-gap solution materialised. Waiting, zombie-like, in a boutique in the Village, while Della was trying on a dress, she got into conversation with the owner of the shop who asked about Cheyney's glass beads, and offered to buy them and anything else similar she might have. She sold them to him at once, happy to have some money in her pocket. The man explained to her that shops like his were always on the look-out for new things. That was how they survived, buying bits and pieces for cash, because it was a limited investment. The small quantities meant no risk. Four of something, six of another, a dozen of something else, was no big deal. On the way home Cheyney bought a pair of jeweller's pliers, and that evening tore apart what little ethnic jewellery she had, making nine pieces out of one. She sold it all to the boutique man the next morning.

She remembered, from her Andy Warhol days of camp lunches and banana splits, the shop cum restaurant, Serendipity, and the stream of forgettable figures with baskets over their arms who wandered in, pleading their wares. The owners always bought something, and paid those faceless suppliers immediately. She saw herself as one of them: invisibility appealed to her. She called in on Serendipity the next time she had something to sell. If they recognised her, they gave no sign of it, for which she was grateful. They bought, and she found a way to earn some money.

The Serendipity call was always the worst but the most lucrative for Cheyney. It was the only time she ever went above Thirty-fourth Street, except when she had to see her lawyer. She took the First Avenue bus up and then, with eyes lowered, she walked as quickly as she could across town to Serendipity. The journey alone put her in a frenzy. Walking the streets, seeing sights that had once been part of her life, filled her with despair, left her riddled with anxiety. She dreaded bumping into someone she knew from her art-dealing days. But maybe even worse than that was the idea that the boys at Serendipity would surprise her with Andy Warhol. They never did.

Once, she did have a strange encounter. It was a foul day, rain, wind, a bitter chill in the air, and she had several blocks to walk to get to Serendipity. She was reminded of another rainy day years before and of the handsome man who had rescued her from it with a taxi ride home. How good it felt when he warmed her with his body. How at 'home' with him she felt for a stolen moment in time. The street light changed and Cheyney hurried across. At the next corner there was another red light. And then he was right there, standing beside her, not in memory but in real life. She felt an instant pull, strong as a magnet. He looked and dismissed her with one glance. Cheyney wasn't surprised, she was barely a shadow of the woman she once had been. She almost spoke to him. But the light changed, and he dashed across the street into the arms of a beautiful young blonde standing under a black silk umbrella. She had scurried away, feeling more depressed than ever.

Cheyney developed a routine. Once a week she made her rounds of the boutiques and gift shops from Thirty-Fourth Street to Greenwich Village, selling her cash-and-delivery bits and pieces of ethnic jewellery from a straw basket over her arm. There was an 'on call' few hours a week stint of shop-sitting at a tacky antique shop that was more like a second-hand furniture store, on Lexington Avenue and Twenty-Ninth Street. On the first Monday of the month was her 9 a.m. meeting when the boys from Serendipity chose from the wares she designed for their shop with uptown camp in mind. Assembling collections of original Chinese folk art from the old traders in Chinatown, and selling them to the Brooklyn Museum gift-shop, was the best of the jobs she did. This was how she and Zazou had survived financially three appalling years of her life. Until a letter arrived from Lala and Roberto who were now living in Rome.

They had left behind at the time of their hasty departure two Etruscan pieces. Large, important. Would Cheyney sell them to the Metropolitan Museum for Roberto? They had insisted on paying her a thousand dollars, and a ticket to Rome whenever she wanted it, so she could come to them and be pampered.

It was an El Dorado for Cheyney. Her success, and Lala and Roberto's appreciation, meant little to her, except that she could give a thousand dollars to David Rosewarne against his costs, which kept piling up every day.

In those terrible years she filled her time mostly by walking when not defending herself in lawyers' and receivers' offices. She trudged where no one had ever heard of Cheyney Fox, where no one recognised her. The Fourteenth Street area, the Lower East Side, the Village, Chinatown and back to Turtle Bay. It was either that or wander through one empty room after another in her monastic island of peace, the apartment three floors above Della where she lived with Zazou and a few sticks of furniture.

Cheyney learned things in these three years. What real poverty means. How it can strangle the spirit. How demeaning being shabby can be. How wretched poor is, in a city where money can buy anything. That, when you're living in hell, it's hard to remember heaven.

She dressed very carefully. It was the first time since she had been forced from the gallery more than two years before that she wanted to look beautiful and chic. She resolved not to go for the final determination of her case looking shabby, down and out, and broken-spirited. It was not easy to be elegant and chic without money. But she worked hard at it on this morning.

In her Tregere suit with its frayed cuffs and shiny skirt – a left-over from her better days; cheap black shoes, at least styled to look like Ferragamos; coatless because she only had a yellow plastic raincoat Della had lent her; without a handbag, the good ones having been sold off years ago, she still managed to pull up from somewhere deep inside herself some pride and dignity. She shone and looked beautiful as she had not done since the bright days when the gallery was alive.

At David Rosewarne's insistence, she allowed him to call for her in a taxi on the way to the Court House. Nerves jangling, tense as a drum, Cheyney could barely speak. David had only to look at her to know what fear she was harbouring under the serene façade. He was wonderful. In the taxi, his assistant next to him, he said only three things to her. 'I understand how you must feel. We *will* win. You can begin your life again. Say nothing, do nothing, in the court room, and I will get you through this.' And he did.

It was all over before noon. Once out of the Court House he turned to her and said, 'You can let go now. Cheyney Fox.'

He offered her, in celebration of their victory, lunch at the Oak Room at the Plaza, the Colony Club, Romeo Salta's, the Harvard Club . . . Nothing he could do could convince her to go uptown with him. She accepted Number One Fifth Avenue, on the edge of Greenwich Village. A quiet, informal, yet sophisticated hotel with a large, quiet dining-room. Old New York in modern times, chic on the edge of Bohemian New York in sight of Washington Square.

As he placed his arm around her shoulder and pressed her to him in a hug of delight that her ordeal was over, she was unaware of anything different in their client–lawyer relationship. Likewise in the taxi going to Number One, when she saw the new warmth and the smile in his eyes for her. She could never quite figure out at what moment they fell in love. Over lunch?

Yes, that's where she thought it had happened. Or as David suggested, 'Number One is probably where we allowed it to surface, but I think I fell in love with you a very long time before that.'

David was probably right. After two Margaritas Cheyney began to relax. Enough for her to feel that everything from the moment she heard the announcement in court: 'The determination: Cheyney Fox, full discharge in bankruptcy, case dismissed,' was now the past, in the most finalising sense of the word. As if reborn, she found herself relating to David Rosewarne differently.

She saw him as a man, not simply as *the* lawyer. She felt a spark of joy rekindled, a flow of something of her old self stir within. For the first time in the years she had known David Rosewarne, they laughed together. He was enchanted by her smile. She was charmed by his dry sense of humour. They spoke candidly to each other about themselves. A candour beyond that of client and lawyer. She was surprised how attracted she was to his kind, respectable good looks; that she suddenly found him incredibly sexy. He was no less surprised by her smouldering sensuality which he had scarcely guessed at during the time they had known each other.

And then, as will happen, when the flame of a possibly illicit love flares, as it did now between Cheyney and David, conversation became superfluous. Desire, admiration, the beginnings of adoration, came into being for them. All those months of seeing each other, overshadowed always by distress, problems and the law, they had never seen or thought of wanting each other as they did now over lunch.

He said nothing, he made no move as their desire for each other grew stronger. She tried to distract herself from her feelings for him by talking about their meal. The *oeufs en cocotte*: she kept going on about how perfectly the eggs were cooked, just runny on the inside. His defence against his own developing feelings for Cheyney was to remind himself of his wife. It was her favourite egg dish, but she was unable to master it in her kitchen. Cheyney rhapsodised at such length about the poached salmon, it became ridiculous. More feebly, he mentioned that was what his wife had cooked for them the first time he had brought Cheyney home to dinner.

A long silence followed. In which she reminded herself of how much she had liked his wife, enjoyed meeting his children, admired the kind of marriage and life-style they shared. And now it shocked her to think of the many times she had thought of his marriage as a role-model for what she would like to have for herself.

He called for a Sauternes to go with the lemon mousse they ordered for dessert. They touched the rims of their glasses together. A look passed between them which gave Cheyney a nearly forgotten flutter of excitement. By the third glass she knew she had an admirer who would love her for the rest of her life, yet never do anything about it. There was a tremendous sexual desire in their glances, and it was equal for each of them.

She had no doubt that all she had to do was to say yes and he would make her his mistress forever. She sat there very silent for several minutes, drinking her wine, toying with the lemon mousse. She kept reminding herself that solid, stable, conservative men who love their wives, their children and the world they have constructed for themselves, don't lightly make moves that complicate their lives. A certain weight of passion is needed: nothing else serves. No matter how much they would like to think differently.

Cheyney and David's desire for each other became so intense, she had finally to speak. 'I want you so very much.'

'I want you more.'

His direct response left her weak-kneed.

She watched his eyes behind his glasses fill with tears. She believed him. That he wanted her more at that moment than anything else in the world. She reached across the table and took his hand in hers, turned it over and kissed the inside of his palm. Their eyes met. She watched him close his, so unbearable was his passion for her. He took a deep breath, sighed and gazed at her again. She raised the hand she still held and placed it over her mouth. Again there was the kiss to the inside of the palm.

Before he could say anything, her own voice trembling with passion for him had whispered across the table, 'So long as you understand I will leave you when I want more of you than I can have.'

She offered him a gracious exit with her eyes. He had declined, as she knew he would now.

Instead, they spoke of how they wanted to make love to each other, of how starved they felt for each other. The danger of their liaison, because their coming together would be explosive. All home-maker's caution, all restraint, would be replaced by passion. The sexual chemistry between them had incited a wild, unexpected raunchiness that delivered them into erotic ecstasy. Postponed. Until they could work out the moral side that pricked their consciences.

Cheyney whispered in his ear, 'November 22, 1963. My freedom from a horrible ordeal, and the day you brought me back to life.'

He answered, 'The day we were both brought back to life.'

Born-again lust for them both, each of whom had lost hope of such improbable renewal. It was like young love, erotic excitement, the joy of being out of control, of loving dangerously, of being less than perfect, of living a vital sensual adventure. Being alive again, with a new and fresh romance with which to embellish existence. There was no resisting it.

They covered their naked bodies and souls with eager lips, searching tongues, and caressing hands, and begged each other to let go and give in to their sexual yearnings. Only to be stopped by their fear of what their lust could do to them and their lives. The love they felt for each other.

Often after that first discovery of their passion for each other, he would say to her, 'You know, if you were to shout this across the rooftops of Cambridge or New York, or anywhere in the world for that matter, no one would believe you. They would say the woman is mad. It could never have been David Rosewarne, the conservative, staid, devoted family-man. The legal-eagle who never breaks formation. Impossible.

'Cheyney, I want you to know this has never happened before, and I am sure it will never happen with any other woman again. But you know that, don't you?'

'Yes,' she always answered. And always sounded as convinced as he did.

For too long now her life had been governed by having to prove that she was not and had never been a criminal. It was difficult to realise that period was over. It had been for months. She had won her discharge in bankruptcy. She had been proven innocent of fraud because, hard as Marvin Weinstock tried, he couldn't dredge up enough evidence to make a case against her. Then why didn't she feel that she'd won? Even when the bankruptcy court had reprimanded Marvin Weinstock for his methods and the vendetta he appeared to be acting out against Cheyney Fox in the name of the creditors. She had won her battle and her war, but at what price?

She was sitting on a bench near the old New York City Court House in lower Manhattan. She had a perfect view of the building: seemingly a late-Victorian version of an English Renaissance country house. Cheyney liked it. It made her feel calm, gave her hope. It was a symbol of justice, honour and the law. A reminder that rules were made to be obeyed and there might be a price to be paid if they weren't.

Balance, that was it. The scales of justice, and everything in balance. Cheyney was human: she could be happy with that. Wasn't that why she was there waiting for him? To put things back in balance. To explain it all carefully to him, so that there would be as little hurt as possible. Had she not had enough hurt to last her a lifetime? Her resolve was so strong that, much as she feared losing him, she was able to keep her emotions under control. But still, she didn't much like the prospect of telling him.

No, it wouldn't be easy to leave him. They had been through so much together. For the last few years he had been the most solid thing in her life. The kindest, most compassionate man she had ever known. The most honourable. That was why they simply could not go on. No, it most certainly was not going to be easy.

Cheyney watched the people going in and out of the Court House. They were well-dressed and well-groomed. There seemed, with their briefcases and the stacks of documents carried in their arms, to be purpose in every step they took. She recognised in them something of herself, a lifetime ago, and envied them. It surprised her because she was not a person usually prey to envy. She didn't much like the feeling.

She saw him just as he came through the Court House doors with a colleague. The two men shook hands and parted. David Rosewarne was looking for her. Cheyney rose from the bench on the small patch of green on the other side of the street from the Court House. She waved, trying to get his attention. He saw her almost at once and started down the stairs.

David waved to Cheyney from the other side of the street. He waited for the traffic to pass by. He always made her heart sing. If only he was free. What a wonderful lover he could have been, she thought. To be his wife, to build something solid with him. She put that from her mind immediately. It was because she had been thinking like that during the last few days that she was leaving him. No pain, with him or any other man, no matter how much she loved him. That resolve had become a priority in her life.

Now Cheyney picked up her basket and walked to the kerb to meet him.
'Hello.' he said.
'Hi. Good day in court?'

'Not bad. I made a reservation at El Parador for us. OK?

'Fine.'

He hailed a cab. In the back seat, he raised her hand to his lips and kissed it. They looked each other in the eyes and Cheyney had to look away. He placed his hand on her chin and slowly turned her face back to his.

'What's happened? Something's wrong.'

'Yes.' She could hardly get the word out.

'Tell me about it.'

'Over lunch. I'm really pleased we're going to El Parador. One of Carlos's Margaritas is just what I need.'

'That bad?' he asked.

'That bad,' she answered.

Cheyney really was relieved that David had chosen El Parador. The Mexican restaurant was only a short distance from her apartment. Now that she was sitting next to her lover she knew that it was a good thing to be that close to home. She was going to be very upset breaking up their relationship.

David did not press the point of her distress while in the taxi. He was too clever for that. Instead he changed the subject. He touched the sleeve of her dress worn thin from constant washing and pressing. 'Why don't you let me take you to Bergdorf's? Buy you a lovely summer wardrobe? You love beautiful things. I like you to have them. It would give me so much pleasure.'

'For the same reason I won't let you furnish my flat, or help me find new work. I don't want to be a kept woman. And you would hate yourself, your wife and me, because you had slipped into that role out of guilt, not pleasure.'

He looked embarrassed. 'Cheyney, there are times when you are just too wise.'

In El Parador, the Margaritas were all they ought to be. The first sip brought the rim of salt to her lips, it combined with the delicious cocktail and slid on to her tongue. She swallowed and her flagging courage revived.

'David, it's over for us. I'm leaving you.'

They were sitting in what had become their favourite booth, in their favourite restaurant. He remained calm. But Cheyney saw the immediate shock in his eyes. His face grew pale with anguish. He could not speak. He did nothing. She feared for him. What had she done? They remained like that for what felt to Cheyney like an eternity. She drank more of the cocktail and said, 'There must be something you can say.'

Her voice seemed to bring him back from where he had retreated. He drank deeply, and some colour returned to his face.

'Like what?' His voice was more bitter than she had expected.

'That you forgive me for wanting more of you than you can give.'

She felt her heart racing. For one weak moment she fantasised that he would offer her an alternative. That he would leave his family for her.

His only reply was to order more Margaritas. David Rosewarne, controlled on the outside, felt like a shattered pane of glass. He did not take his eyes off her.

'Do you love me, Cheyney?'

'More every day. That's the problem.'

'Will you have any more security without me than you do with me?'

That made Cheyney angry. He must know what he had to do if he wanted to keep her, and supply the security he obviously knew she sought from a relationship.

'That's an unfair question. Let me go, David. If I stay with you, I'll suffer, and I will have to learn to live with conflict. I want more than that. I want as much at least as Mary has. We both know – we've always known, from the beginning – that's impossible. At least, with you it is.'

'You love someone else.'

'No, of course not. But I'm going to look for someone like you who is available to love me and build a life with me as good as the one you and Mary have.'

'My life will never be the same without you.' He was trembling when he said these too-obvious words, and there was pain in his eyes. She had to lower her own not to cry, not to yield to him as she knew he wanted her to.

'You have six months to come back to me. After that I never want to see you again.'

She watched him walk away. He did not look back. She gave in to tears.

Chapter 16

Della opened the door. Zazou leapt up and Della caught her in her arms, and both were lost in dog kisses. Over her shoulder she said,

'Cheyney, you're just in time, They're re-running that marvellous interview between Grant Madigan and President Kennedy. The one Madigan did a month before the assassination. The TV Guide says he's going to do a live introduction. And after the interview there's going to be a discussion led by Madigan. His guests are going to be Pierre Salinger, Bobby Kennedy, and Ted Sorenson. We can have a good cry. We'll have dinner after that, OK?'

'Fine. Who's Grant Madigan?'

Della dropped Zazou on the sofa. Fiddling with the dials on the set, she chaffed her friend. 'Who's Grant Madigan? Just another Edward R. Morrow, that's all. And he's so dishy besides. Who's Grant Madigan? If you had a TV set, read the newspapers, magazines, came back into the world a little more, Cheyney, you'd sure know who he is. Wait until you see this interview. I did, when it was first run. And now poor Kennedy is dead.'

Grant Madigan's face filled the screen. Cheyney recognised him. The credits were still rolling when she said, 'I know him.'

'You know Grant Madigan?'

'Well, I don't exactly know him. He plucked me out of the rain and gave me a taxi ride to the gallery one day.'

'Honestly, Cheyney, I'd kill to know Grant Madigan.'

'Hang on, Della, I don't exactly know him. But I did have a rather intimate few minutes with him.'

'Intimate? You mean he . . . ?'

'Oh, no, no, Della, you've got it all wrong.'

'Shush, tell me about it later.'

That was the first time Cheyney had seen him on TV. The medium enhanced the good looks she remembered. The warmth she felt so briefly in his arms that day came to mind. Della had been right. The programme was fascinating. Madigan's intellectual grasp of complex foreign policy issues was masterful. Not one banal question, and no shirking the follow-ups. The President revealed himself to his host as Cheyney had never heard him do before. Perhaps Grant Madigan merited his reputation as the definitive press and TV man on the world power-players.

She was riveted by the energy, the excitement, coming off the screen. She felt inspired, full of hope. She watched and listened to the two men who knew how to raise the spirit, go for the big issues and win their points. At the same time she felt poignantly the Kennedy flame brutally extinguished. The brain, the mind, simply blasted away.

Madigan posed some tough questions. The man had a knack of zeroing in on his guest and probing weaknesses that even he had been unaware of. He did it so smoothly that it never offended, merely expanded the interview. Cheyney was suddenly reminded that Grant Madigan had done that to her when he had come to her rescue. Only he had been less smooth about it, more like a chastising knight who could see she was blind to her inability to protect herself. Had he not said something to her like, 'You're not even smart enough to get out of the rain. And that's basic.'?

There was a brilliance in the way he masked his ability to cut instantly to the core of things, in his relaxed use of a clear, quick mind that responded like the snap of a whip to a calm intelligence. He never lost your attention, not for one second. He was the best. And, watching him, Cheyney understood the extra something about the man that made him special. He radiated an enormous integrity. He framed his questions, forced his issues, with an apparent political impartiality that held his audiences and got them involved. He exercised his spell over them just as strongly as over his guests. They, too, were forced to face themselves and answer the issues in question.

The two women had problems with holding back tears during the Presidential interview. Dead, Kennedy's image seemed to hold even more the hopes and dreams of his America. But their spirits rallied with what they heard from Bobby Kennedy.

The TV switched off, Della insisted on hearing about Grant Madigan, as the women set the dinner table. At the end of her account, Cheyney added, 'Boy, was I sure of myself in those days! I thought I had the world by a string. All I had to do was work hard, look beautiful, keep stretching myself and my intellect, and life would take care of me because I was doing the best I could with what God gave me. I thought I was taking care of myself. If that isn't a laugh. On me, unfortunately.'

One look, for a moment, backwards into the past and fear wrapped itself around Cheyney and pulled her down into anxiety. She picked Zazou up and held her in her arms. The dog's mop of long hair, the warmth of her body, helped Cheyney. Zazou shook her head violently from side to side and wriggled, trying to attract more attention. Two bright black eyes appeared from under the mass of fringe covering them. As usual, Cheyney reacted. Zazou brought her back from herself, if not from the pit.

Over grilled lamb chops and baked potatoes, a fresh green salad, Della plucked up her courage. 'Cheyney, don't you think it's time to give up this reclusive life you lead? You can't stay below Thirty-fourth Street for the rest of your life. A telephone, a TV, making some real money – they're not beyond you. Isn't it time you wore beautiful clothes again, walked in a decent pair of shoes, and stopped tramping those empty rooms upstairs?'

Della was taken aback when she heard Cheyney say, 'Yes.'

'Oh, that's wonderful. What are you going to do?

'What I should have done in the last days of the gallery. Gather together enough money to run away. I have been too much the courageous fool. And the price I paid may have bankrupted me again. Only, this time, emotionally.

'You're leaving New York! To live where?'

'I don't know.'

'Don't you have a plan?'

'No.'

'Oh, Cheyney, you can't just run away. Think about it. Make a plan. Get some money together.'

'I do have an idea. As long as you're happy to keep Zazou, I want to sell off what stock I have left in my "basket-on-arm" business and leave as soon as possible after that.

'I've got to get away, Della. I'm not just running away from New York, I'm running away from David Rosewarne as well. He hasn't called, not even to offer me a "some day", and I'm constantly on the verge of calling him. That's too self-destructive in the long term for me.'

'Money, Cheyney?'

'My cheque came this morning from the Brooklyn Museum for the last collection I sold them. Selling the stock should give me about three or four hundred dollars. Roberto is still holding a first-class, round-trip ticket, New York, Rome, New York, in my name, with an open date. If I can use your telephone, I'll call him tonight after dinner, and ask him to send the ticket air-mail express. I will of course pay for the call.'

Della waved her hand to indicate that wasn't necessary. 'But Rome is so expensive, Cheyney. A couple of hundred dollars will get you nowhere. Not even if you stay with Lala and Roberto.'

'I'm not going to Rome. I'm not going to go to Italy. I am not yet ready to face Rome and the chic society Roberto and Lala run in. I intend to change the ticket for economy class and book it to Athens. That's where I'm off to.

'Athens?'

'I was happy in Greece. The life-style suited me. It's cheap, I know the city, the islands. It's the last outpost before the east, so I will still feel I am in the western world. A good jumping-off place for other countries. I'll take a room for a month and do a reconnaissance. See what really fine folk art I can collect for the museum. What I can find to import from there and neighbouring countries for the boutiques and shops I sell to. And to see if it can become a lucrative way for me to drift around the world until I can find the right place.'

'But that takes money – being an importer. Where will you get the capital to start a business like that?'

'I don't intend to start a business that I have to invest my own capital in – or anyone else's, for that matter. Not ever again. The museum and my other customers seem to think I have an eye for the rare and beautiful, the sort of thing they find hard to buy. They will pay for what I buy for them on bills of lading or documents presented against letters of credit at specific banks designated by me. It's not altogether a crazy idea. The enthusiasm is there. The rest is up to me. According to the director of the gift department, good reliable buyers abroad are hard to find.'

'And if it works, what then?'

'Well, then will be the time to see about that, won't it, Della? For the moment, living the lazy care-free life of the expatriate for a month while I look around can't be bad for me. The worst thing that can happen is I will return with nothing in hand, and have to scrounge around the jobbers' lots, assemble at night and peddle in the day, as I have been doing. Sit for the boys at the antique shop when they need me. I can always have a job there.'

'Did you choose Greece because of Christopher?' asked Della hesitantly.

'No.'

'Are you sure you're not still in love with him?'

'Absolutely.'

'Well, that's a relief.'

'Are you sure you don't mind taking Zazou for a month? Everything hinges on that.'

'No problem.'

It was after midnight in Rome. Exactly the time for Cheyney to catch Roberto and Lala at home. They were night people, but was Kurt Walbrook? Roberto and Lala daren't take the chance to find out. Their friendship could hardly survive a miscalculation in such a matter. So the couple decided to wait until morning to call and tell him the good news. Cheyney Fox was finished with her romance. She was free now from both

her legal and emotional commitments and ready to accept the ticket they
had been keeping for her. That was the good news. They were less eager
to share the bad. Cheyney was not accepting their invitation to come to
Rome and be pampered by them.

They had been entertaining: after talking to their friend, they went back
to their guests and forgot about Cheyney and Kurt Walbrook. The
rosy-fingered Roman dawn for some reason brought the subject to mind
again. Lying in his arms Lala asked, 'Roberto, darling?'

'Yes, darling.'

'Do you think Kurt really loves Cheyney?'

Roberto plucked a cigarette from the box on the table next to the bed,
struck a match and lit it. The tip glowed in the dark. He took a deep pull
on the Gitane. The glow momentarily brightened his aristocratic features.
Lala lovingly traced them with a finger and kissed the tip of his nose, then
snuggled even closer to him. Finally he answered.

'Yes, I do.'

'You don't think that Cheyney is just a rich man's whim, Kurt's play-
thing, do you?'

He took another long draw on the cigarette, taking his time before
answering. 'No. No, I don't think so.'

Lala rolled on her side and kissed him on the cheek. 'Why, Roberto.
Why do you believe him?'

'Because of the way he has chosen to pursue her. The elaborate plans he
has made to help her help herself without her knowing it. The way he has
disciplined himself to stay away from her until, as he puts it, "She is
whole again. Until she is ready for me." I don't care for his terminology,
but I see what he means.'

'Don't you think it's strange that he doesn't care how long it takes? It's
been years already,' said Lala, feeling concern for her friend. She pulled
herself up to a half-sitting position against the pillows.

'That doesn't bother Kurt. Time is irrelevant for him when he wants
something. He's tracking Cheyney the same way he tracks a great work of
art. I have seen him do it a dozen times. He bides his time, lets all other
contenders make their mistakes and fall out. Then, when he senses the
time is right, there is no opposition. He makes his bid and walks off with
the prize.'

'Tracking a work of art, my foot! It's more like he's stalking his prey. It
gives me the shivers. He's so cold and controlled about it.'

'That's how he always gets what he wants. Don't get worked up about
it, darling.'

'I can't understand the man. He watches Cheyney from way off, clings
to any news of her we can give him. He wants her, yet he showed no

143

jealousy when we told him about her affair with David Rosewarne. Remember, his only remark was, "It's the best thing for her now." A real red-hot Romeo there! I expect he'll just nod when we tell him her affair is over.'

'I expect he will.' Roberto blew out a smoke ring.

'Well, I will grant him one thing. If she's on the back burner, he does at least keep checking the temperature. And he's found a neat way to boost her income, having us ask Cheyney to act on our behalf and pay her for her trouble.'

'Not bad for us either. Damned good of him to put it about that he uses us as agents, without telling anyone that we are, after all, just his puppets with him pulling all the strings. It does our art dealing here in Rome no harm to be associated with a number-one collector.'

'I know that, Roberto, and that's all wonderful. Wonderful for Cheyney and for us. And, God knows, he is more than generous with money. But . . . why? What's his motive?'

'You know why. For just the reason he told you. He wants Cheyney Fox. He wants one day to pluck her from the world and place her in his life and keep her there for always. But he is not going to approach her until he is certain she is going to go with him.'

'I find that scary, Roberto, real scary.' Lala slipped down from the pillows and huddled tight up against him. 'In fact, I find Kurt Walbrook more than a little scary when I think about him.'

'Don't think about him.'

Lala ignored that and continued, 'When I am in his company, like most everyone else, I go for the smooth Viennese charm, the old sensual magnetism, and the fantastic life-style. All that patrician presence, the shining white hair, the piercing blue eyes, and the total respect and obedience he commands from everyone. He suffers fools gladly, and that scares me, even though I know he is very fond of me – in spite of my being, as he has so charmingly said, deeply, deeply silly. He is scary, Roberto, and what he is doing with Cheyney is too. Why, he could go tomorrow and pluck her out of New York. He could make her life so easy, with chunks of real money, instead of his two thousand dollars here, a thousand there. I think the largest amount we have ever paid her at one time was three thousand dollars.'

'He would never get Cheyney that way. He is smart enough to know that he can't buy her. That she has to earn her way back up again, or he would have a basket-case in his bed. If he wanted her just for a one-night stand, Kurt Walbrook would have bedded her the only time he ever met her, that night at the Tinguely exhibition at the Museum of Modern Art in New York.'

'He's such a schemer, Roberto. It's like he's stalking Cheyney in the dark.'

'Yes, but Lala, darling, he demands nothing of her. All he has for his efforts is the hope that her psychological scars will heal enough for him to make his move one day.'

'And shoot her down for himself.'

'Well, I wouldn't put it exactly that way.'

'And if she doesn't?'

'Then she doesn't. She will have not been good enough for him, and he will have helped a woman he was intrigued by. You have got to admire him, Lala, it's very romantic.'

'No more romantic than us.' Lala took the cigarette from between his fingers and crushed it out in a marble ashtray.

'No. Different league from us, my darling.'

'Would you have done that for me?'

'I have done more, my dearest heart.'

They made love. He was half asleep when Lala put one last question. 'Roberto?'

'Ummm.'

'What if Cheyney does turn herself again into the woman he fell in love with, and then says no to him in favour of someone else?'

No answer. Lala shook him by the shoulder to see if he was awake. 'Couldn't happen,' he mumbled, en route to a deep sleep.

Roberto and Lala did not find Kurt Walbrook in Austria. Or at the telephone number in Paris. They found him in Montevideo, where the three spoke at length. He was clearly delighted to hear that Cheyney was on the move. He made arrangements for Roberto to meet him in Venice. Three days later Lala was waiting for Roberto's return. His plane had already landed and he was on his way in from the airport.

Lala was still miffed at not having been invited to Venice with him. She had kept going on about it all the way to the airport the morning of his departure.

'What will I do while you're away?'

'Lala, darling, I'm only away for a day. Not even a day. For lunch, altogether maybe ten hours. Surely you can find something to do. Do what you always do.'

'What's that?'

'Go shopping.'

She perked up at that. 'You won't be cross if I'm a *little* extravagant?'

'Shopping, but *not* extravagant. And I will bring you a surprise from Venice.'

She did go shopping, and she was extravagant. By the time Lala arrived on the Via Condotti, two chic shopping bags already in her hands, she had forgotten about Cheyney Fox. And Roberto in Venice. Even about not having been invited to the Palazzo Borgano, the Walbrook Venetian residence.

That was where she bumped into Giovanna Buchelli, and found out that Kurt Walbrook kept a mistress in Vienna, a German, a great beauty. But that it didn't mean a thing. He had another in Paris, and that didn't mean a thing either. 'They are like convenience-food to Kurt. I should know. I was once part of the menu. He devoured me and I loved it, and I saw – as all his women do – myself as his Baroness. My dear Lala, as long as the present Baroness, his mother, is alive, he will not marry. You can depend on that. She is monstrously important in his life.'

'You mean he has a mother-complex?' Lala had scanned her *Reader's Digest*.

'Oh no, not at all. I could've handled something as routine as that. No, this is more complicated. If anything, she has a son complex.'

They had a girls' lunch together, and Giovanna drank too much. She broke down and confessed – in strictest girls' – lunch confidence that Kurt Walbrook was the most exciting lover she had ever had. That he could get some surprising erotic tricks out of her. She called him a sexual Svengali, and rhapsodised over his prowess. The wine drew from her the intimate details of the sex-life she had shared with him. She had been heartbroken when it was over between them. Lala raised an eyebrow at the news. All Rome knew Giovanna's sexual reputation, and how hard her heart was even by Roman standards.

'It happened so quickly. We went to a private exhibition at the Museum of Modern Art in New York, guests of Aly Kahn. And then, just like that.' Giovanna snapped her fingers. The sound was quick and sharp, puncturing the hum of other gossip around them. 'He saw a woman on the edge of the crowd, and he walked away from me. When we went to reclaim him from her, I saw it in his eyes. He was finished with me. Just like that.' She snapped her fingers once more. A gossiping diner accorded her a glance.

Lala nearly choked on her wine as her lunch companion said, 'If I ever see that woman again, I will grind my heel in her face.' The woman had, of course, been Cheyney.

Lala made a quick exit after that. What delicious gossip she had for Roberto when he came home! Feeling guilty about her extravagances, she made an effort with an antipasto, selecting for it all the things she knew he liked. The antipasto and the drinks were waiting on the terrace. And Lala sat in the library awaiting Roberto and wondering what was going to happen to Cheyney. Secretly she still believed that Cheyney had met the great love of her life in Christopher. No one would ever replace him.

Roberto arrived and presented her with a beautifully wrapped gift. All silver paper, gold and silver and bronze ribbons. A minutely carved snail of chased silver, the size of a plum. A compact for face powder. Delighted she read the accompanying note.

'Be assured I will never harm your friend. Kurt'.

Typically all her doubts about Kurt Walbrook vanished while the snail held her attention.

'Roberto darling, isn't it gorgeous?' Visibly delighted, she bubbled with enthusiasm until she asked him about his day-trip to Venice, and remembered that she had not been invited.

'I suppose this is an apology because he didn't ask me to go to lunch at the Palazzo with you.' She held the silver snail up, opened it, and looked at herself in the small mirror on the inside of the lid. She plucked out the white, swan's-down puff and dusted the tip of her nose. 'Why didn't he, Roberto?'

'The first thing I'm to tell you is that Kurt would like us to visit the Palazzo Borgano sometime very soon. A time when we can stay for a few days. He said no more than that, but I understood from what I saw that his mother was in residence and entertaining, and not he.'

'Oh, I suppose I forgive him, then. And actually I do know that he finds me amusing and likes my company. So I really can't take it too personally. And, well, I gotta lovely snail!

'We're having drinks on the balcony. So come along and tell me all. You first and then, golly, have I got some hot gossip for you! And it's about Kurt Walbrook. Is the palazzo divine?'

'Unimaginably grand, yet warm and inviting. It has to be one of the finest palazzos in Venice. On the Grand Canal, once the palace of a ducal family whose members tended to get themselves elected Doge of Venice. Restored impeccably. And the things in his collection – quite unbelievable. Where, how, he was ever able to assemble such a collection of art and artefacts is beyond the imagination. Several lifetimes' work. The furniture, the mirrors, and, and, and . . . A priceless library. It just kept going on.

'I was given a personal tour by his librarian, who explained that I couldn't see Kurt until after he had dined with his mother and her guests. A long-standing luncheon-date he could not cancel. I was given lunch on the library balcony.'

'The linen, the silver, the goblets, the food – what about all that?' asked a voracious Lala.

'Baroque French silver, eighteenth-century Venetian goblets, Burano lace on the table. I don't remember the china. Oh, yes – Sèvres.'

'The food, Roberto. What was the food like?'

'You will be furious, you'll pout the rest of the evening if I tell you.'

'I won't, I won't! Promise.'

'Ravioli stuffed with lobster and scallops.'

'I am *furious*. What was the sauce?'

'A lobster sauce. That was followed by thin strips of veal cooked in Marsala and covered in two-inch-thick shavings of fresh white truffle, mange-tout, and a potato thing that melted in the mouth. Small puffs, deep-fried. The wines were excellent.'

'I can't bear it. I'll pout. Yes, I can. Tell me, what was the dessert?'

'Warm Zabaglione.'

Lala stamped her foot, and he laughed at her. She playfully snatched away the antipasto and announced, 'Roberto, you don't deserve this. You will have to make it up to me tonight by taking me out to dinner at the Osteria Del Orso.'

'Delighted, honoured.'

She poured him another Scotch on shaved ice, and then asked, 'What about Cheyney? What did he have to say about her and what she's doing? Wait, wait, I don't want to miss anything. OK, so you saw the palazzo and then you had that sumptuous lunch overlooking the Grand Canal, and then what?'

'Then he appeared. About four o'clock. Lunch over, he excused himself just long enough from his mother's guests to meet me in the library. We spent an hour together.'

'Roberto, *caro mio*, that doesn't tell me anything. You're dragging this out. Teasing me. What's happened? And I want all the details.'

'Well, as we already knew from speaking to him on the telephone, he was delighted about Cheyney leaving the lover and New York. I think he sees it as a move towards him, even if she is unaware of it.'

'Did he say anything, show any flicker of emotion, about David being out of the picture?'

'Nothing.'

'Nothing? What a cold bastard.'

'No, Lala, he's not a cold bastard. He's a man. Stop expecting him to behave like a woman in love. And he's an Austrian, who can deal unemotionally with the reality of his situation.'

'Well, maybe he isn't an icy bastard. But how can one tell? He's such an enigma. Maybe what scares me is what Giovanna Buchelli calls his Svengali charm. You must admit, Roberto, he's a man not easy to figure out. And from what I heard today . . . well, never mind. Go on, what happened next?'

'The upshot of our meeting is that he wants to help Cheyney to be happy in Europe. He sees it as a stepping-stone for her, and for him and his purpose. Kurt believes she needs some real successes, and that he has the means to put some work in her way that will give her a chance to achieve them. He was very straightforward with me, Which took me by surprise. He said, "I want her in Europe. So we are going to see that she has enough interesting work here to contemplate making a permanent move. My plan is simple – if you will work for me, Roberto, as you have done before.

' "I intend to ask you to front for me on some things I want to buy. You will do nothing more than pass the deal over to Cheyney. And, for your trouble, you will split between you the buyer's fee I am prepared to pay. The original purchaser, that's me, will of course remain anonymous. You will be able to explain that to Cheyney by saying your client deals with you on a condition of strict confidentiality. I will assemble some fine works of art, and both of you will benefit financially. *En plus*, Cheyney gets a psychological boost. A beginning, Roberto, for what I hope will ultimately be a lifetime of happiness for me and this woman who intrigues me so." '

'Roberto, that's wonderful news. You did, of course, say yes?' asked Lala, a look of concern on her face. She knew how soft-hearted he was. He could easily have played the grand gentleman that he was and offered to do it for nothing.

'Yes.'

A sigh of relief. Gentlemen needed money too.

'I told him that I thought it an excellent way to help Cheyney, and I believed we could get her to act for us, just so long as it had nothing to do with anything in the contemporary art world again.'

'What did he say to that?'

'Nothing. He just gave me a smile that told me he was thinking, "Don't bet on it". What he did say was, "We will begin by luring her back into the art world through buying antiquities. In that field she has no failures to be reminded of. I want her to be the vital, sensuous creature I saw and have been enchanted by ever since. That's the way I want her, for me, of course. But, if not for me, then certainly for herself.'

Roberto stopped, moved by the hint of a tear in Lala's eye, and waited for her to say something.

'The man *is* a romantic. I would never have believed it. The cold fish. I'm speechless.'

'Good. Then let me tell you the immediate plans. I am going to speak to Cheyney this evening. I have already sent a cable from Venice asking her to call us tonight, midnight, our time. I will tell her that I have two projects pending in Athens, and I want her to take them over and complete the deals for me. Payment, a thousand dollars and my eternal gratitude. She is to check into the Grande Bretagne, and we'll meet her there any day she chooses. She is not to worry about the money because the client picks up all expenses.'

'*We're* going to Athens?'

'Yes, *we're* going to Athens.'

Chapter 17

Athens continually enchanted Cheyney by resisting the metropolitan chic that veiled the charm of so many capital cities. It would always remain for her simply the biggest village in Greece, no matter how man strove to urbanise it. Too bad if the 'cradle of democracy' did not appreciate that its village mentality, wedded to its magnificent ancient past, was its greatest asset. It was what made a cross-section of the world want to flock there and bask for a time under its sun, or to stand in the shadow of its Acropolis.

Cheyney had first arrived in the city in 1958. More than half of it was still sun-baked Neo-classical buildings, and ancient architecture, sculpture, art and artefacts. It raised the spirit and dimmed the vision against all the poured concrete – that lethal amoeba, spreading across the city in the guise of *polykatoias*, apartment buildings. In their basements, hundreds of handsome young would-be architects sketched their urban blueprints. But no inspired modern architecture arose. Just functional, boring, concrete blocks with terraces. Now, ten years later, a Neo-classical building was getting harder to find. And a newly spawned dictatorship promised even fewer of them. Concrete was on the march faster than ever, part of the promise of an orderly, modernised Greece.

Athenian intellectual life before the military coup of '67 that ousted the King and probably destroyed the monarchy in Greece forever, had been modest but graceful. It swelled to something unique because of the French, English and American artists and intellectuals who chose to pass through the city en route to somewhere, or indeed to linger in Athens or on the islands, sensing some remnant of their ancient allure that can still energise the creative spirit.

In those days Athens' intellectual life flourished in a hearty village atmosphere. Simple and easy. The vitalising part of it was less what it finally produced, than the lifestyle it offered its artists. A communication between men and women able to ditch their egos in their studios and absorb the sun at a *cafeneon* in Kolonaki, in the bar at Orphanidis or the Grande Bretagne. At Zonar's for a side-walk lunch, a *taverna* in Plaka. Exchange the day's gossip for hours, pronounce upon world events, pontificate upon their favourite subject, politics. All the time watching the world stroll by, and letting it know who was in town. An effortlessly rich and inspiring place to be. In that Athens could rival Paris any time.

Cheyney had arrived with Zazou and six suitcases on the last flight into democratic Greece, which was still under its monarchy. She awoke next morning to the rumble of tanks affronting the slender streets of the city. First the shock of what the coup meant. Then Cheyney realised that she lacked the hard cash to quit Greece as a fine gesture, so she learned to live in her adopted country as her Greek friends did. Cautiously, and in the hope that in time there would be a counter-coup, and democracy would be restored. A fascinating and repellent time to be in democracy's home town.

In some respects, the Greek lifestyle Cheyney had moved to Athens to enjoy changed little under the dictatorship. Her Greek friends were deeply saddened and depressed by the political stifling of their country, and filled with fear for the arbitrary power the Colonels wielded over their lives. Men could disappear for telling a joke against the regime. Paranoia had become the Greek disease. Absurd phobias surfaced. Intellectual life shrank correspondingly from within and without. Many of the more famous foreign writers, painters and scholars stayed away. And yet, even under those extraordinary pressures, much of the day-to-day living in the city carried on as usual.

It was still difficult to be lonely, poor, a failure, a stranger, in Athens, even if you tried. The hum, and rattle, crash and bang of the city as it kept on the move day and night – except during the sacrosanct siesta – and the Greeks, with their extravagant hand and arm gestures that seemed to go with the exaggerated volume of their voices, their music, their generosity, would never allow it. You could be penniless in Greece, but you couldn't be poor. Their fear of silence or isolation kept them a people who enjoyed living in the streets. Only, these days, discretion entered the Greek armoury, a new and necessary skill. It was not an easy thing for them to learn, but they did, and fast. Eventually, it was what changed the Athenians and the city.

The first time Cheyney flew into Athens she knew nothing about the city, nor a soul in it. Nor anything about the Greeks – except what Kazantzakis, Henry Miller and the history books had made them into. Hers were the same romantic expectations of the city for which millions of other travellers made the journey.

She had therefore been prepared for the much-vaunted brilliance of the light of Greece. Or she thought she had, until the plane circled the airport. Below her was Athens, all white, and the blue Aegean Sea, luminous with it. She was dazzled for a few minutes, then seduced. Greece was going to outshine all that she had imagined.

And it still did. Yet many things had happened to both Cheyney and

152

Athens. Certainly not all of them good, some much worse than just bad. But there were things that stayed essentially the same. There was little difference between her arrival ten years before and when she had returned to make the city her home in '67.

Or for that matter now. A year after the Colonels' coup, you still had to go through the same trial by fire to get into Athens from the airport. Passport control, find your luggage, customs, the taxi ride – all horn and riding the brake. The blaring *bouzouki* from the tinny radio, the constant taxi-driver chat-up, the near-misses among the after-siesta traffic.

That, like so many other things that were part of the fabric of Athenian life, had become in part Cheyney's life. She never took any of it for granted, feeling always the foreigner, a mere guest in the country, no matter how hospitable the Greeks were to her. She still felt the same vibrancy about living in Athens as she had the first time she saw the Acropolis. Yet she knew that the vibrancy came from Ancient Greece and Athenians who had been dead two thousand years. The rest was something else. A carnival, a fiesta of living, or a great clinic for the spirit, where the patients come to be healed. If they make it, they leave.

Having had an on-again-off-again Athenian life for nearly a decade before she had moved permanently into the city, Cheyney slipped easily into it: work, street cafés, bars, tavernas, the cinema, and crowds. The lonely days of solitude were still there, but there were fewer of them.

In Greece to find someone dining alone was like finding a pearl in an oyster. The Greeks liked to eat, drink, laugh, talk, go to the movies, the theatre, a concert, anything, in groups. The *pahraia*, their own little clique of friends, that almost every Greek finds life unbearable without, was as important as family. The Greek sense of humour, sense of honour, open-heartedness, had always appealed to Cheyney. What she learned now was that, when a Greek grabs your hand, he grabs it forever. That, after her New York experience of transitory friendships, was a kind of restorative for Cheyney. Such kindness stood out amid the gloom engendered by the Colonels. And Cheyney enjoyed not one but two *pahraias*. One Greek and one of expatriates. She had become a social animal again.

Cheyney Fox got her life together. She thought about the past only after the recurrent nightmare she occasionally suffered. She even accepted that she might one day return to New York, but told herself through gritted teeth that she would make sure she was a millionaire before buying the ticket. Once again she began vaguely to savour contemporary paintings. Savour, yes, but think about them, talk about contemporary art, never. When it came to that, she simply switched off. She wasn't there.

Pop Art and Andy Warhol were the phenomena of the sixties art-age. She never spoke about her part in that world: to friends in Greece or Egypt,

153

those in Europe, she was just a lady with a random eye for art, who bought antiquities and folk art. The pose suited her just fine. Cheyney Fox's preferred profile was low.

On that first trip, when Roberto and Lala had flown in from Rome to meet Cheyney in Athens, once all their business discussions were over, the two women had had a girly gossip in Cheyney's room. Lala had pointed out in her inimitable way that, 'Europe is not America, Cheyney. We Europeans don't insist that you fall in love every time you land a good fuck. And try and keep in mind we come from the old school of sexual morality. The alma mater has just erected a new wing: it calls itself the permissive society. Sexual freedom is all the rage. It's a joy-ride, a merry-go-round, a carousel. I know you, you love too much. Take a rest. My suggestion is that you hop on, grab the golden ring and have a good ride.'

Cheyney had been amused by Lala's 'we Europeans', and the way she never shed her fantasy. She had also listened well to Lala's advice, and took it. She learned that her friend was right: nobody bothered any more to use love as an absolution for sex, Sex was, like the *pahraia*, fun.

In the past few years she had had her share of 'fun'. Sundry mini and harmless sexual affairs that had been conducted with a good deal of affection, if not with love. She had even had sex with Christopher in the Greek island house. He had been thrilled. For her it was an exorcism. They both knew it, and never tried again. It had been a muted ending to so passionate a love. But neither of them had wasted tears on it; they went their separate ways.

For Cheyney, there had even been an affair that still lingered, with a famous Parisian surgeon. A man dedicated to the science of healing, always duelling with death, who had the temperament and the soul of an artist. A man in constant conflict with his emotions, because torn between the *bourgeois* man of science that he was and the free-spirited creative human being he would like to be. When he and Cheyney began their affair, they opened worlds for each other they both yearned for, but were unable to live with. Each had what the other wanted, but not enough courage to do anything about it. They grew apart, and Cheyney was left with yet another love affair that fell short of its promise of a romantic, erotic passion with something solid on which to build a life of love and togetherness. Christopher, David, Claude, they had all given her much, but nothing of that extraordinary warmth and oneness she had experienced for those fleeting few minutes in the arms of Grant Madigan in the back seat of a New York taxi.

If Grant Madigan had not yet entered her soul he had most certainly entered her psyche. A brief thought, the occasional yearning to experience her more thrilling sexual encounters with him. The ridiculous fantasy

154

even, that he would one day ride into her life, as he had done once before, and fill the hole in her heart, the void in her soul, that disappointment in love had inflicted upon her.

Afternoon heat. Coffee-time at Zonar's. Cheyney was having a cappuccino with several members of her expatriate *pahraia*. She had tried changing the subject under discussion several times. No dice. She gave a languid ear to what so gripped them.

'The case has been going on for two and a half weeks. Not just in the courtroom. The papers are full of it. The artistic and moral issues are all bound up together. Everyone's using them to fight his own corner. Seems this guy Barry Sole has taken half of them for one great big Pop Art ride. If it's true, an awful lotta heads are going to roll right into the basket. The art world is screaming for justice, *the facts, the facts*.'

For days, the two men, a Chicago painter and a Toronto poet, had been talking about little else over lunch with the other foreigners. The painter, the bitchier of the two, clubbed two somnolent bluebottles in quick succession with a rolled up *Time* magazine. He swept them from the table to the ground. Then, tilting his chair back, he leaned against the glass window, and let the hot October sun do its enervating worst.

He tossed *Time* across to Cheyney. She caught it by the cover. 'What do you think about all this?'

'I try not to, Ben.' She returned the magazine via the man next to her. Someone else at the table took up the subject.

'As I see it, Barry is being sued by the people of the United States for fraud on the art world. Is that right?'

'Just about.'

'Now why would the US Government go and do a thing like that?' Yet another person at the table got involved.

There was even a sun-seeking lawyer-friend of Ben's from New York to explain the public dimension of the case. Now the whole table was listening. Cheyney was about to switch off, but he was so pompous she couldn't resist hearing his interpretation. The sun was hot. She was a long way from the events that were for the moment shaking the art worlds of Paris and London as well as New York.

'Seems a complaint was sent to the District Attorney's office by a famous art collector. That complaint stated that the said collector, as well as any number of other collectors, big and small, had been collecting the works of Barry Sole for the past ten years. He had been assured by Sole, along with other reputable people and institutions, that Mr Sole's paintings were of a serious nature.

'Now, the indictment against him claims that this is not true. That the millions of dollars invested in the work of the Pop painter Barry Sole, as

155

well as other Pop Art painters, have been made virtually worthless by the recent actions of Mr Sole.'

Ben sniggered. Cheyney began to be irritated by the lawyer. She thought the whole thing a bore. Someone else did too. A blonde hippie, dressed in fringed doe-skin and dripping with Navajo jewellery, all hammered silver and chunky turquoise, from Madison, Wisconsin, began fumbling with her boyfriend's shirt-buttons. 'Doreen, I wanna hear this,' he whined. More fool you, thought Cheyney. She had decided to leave as soon as she finished her coffee.

'I can shut up if I'm boring you,' said the lawyer huffily.

The table opted for him to get on with it, and he continued. 'The evidence submitted was that Barry Sole found a salvage company in Miami, Florida, with a warehouse full of candy bars, covered with chocolate and filled with caramel. A shipment damaged in a freight-car accident. The bars, all in their original silver and green wrappers, were crushed, broken in half, or melted into odd shapes, or with their wrappers blackened from smoke damage. Sole snapped up the candy – all one hundred thousand bars.

'He divided them into three categories. Then he had all the bars sprayed with a half-inch-thick, clear resin. That made the chocolate bars airtight.'

Cheyney's ears perked up. She just knew what was coming next. She did, after all, know Barry Sole and his quirky, Dada mind. She wanted to burst out laughing right then and there. She put her hand to her mouth and bit hard on to the side of her index finger to hold back her laughter.

'Now he is selling them all over the world. Hundreds of dinky little art galleries are passing them off as fine works of art. A bar with a stamped signature of Barry Sole is priced at ten dollars. There's a batch with a stencilled signature of Barry Sole: that costs twenty dollars and fifty cents a bar. The third price is fifty dollars. For that you get a bar signed with a Magic Marker "Barry Sole", and dated.'

At this point Cheyney did burst out laughing. The more she laughed the funnier it seemed to get. So far, the others at the table had not seen the funny side of the candy bars. But Cheyney's laughter caught on. Even Ben, who was annoyed by it, succumbed to a twinge of a smile, then continued,

'OK, now may I go on? The collector behind this investigation claims that this is an art scam. Sole handiwork of one Barry Sole. Motive: pure profit. That it has nothing whatever to do with art. Surprise. That it's no more than an exploitation of his name. And the said works of art, the candy bars . . .'

Cheyney had heard enough, and brought herself under control, intending to leave the table as soon as the 'prosecutor' paused for breath and she could decently make her exit. No call to look rude.

She didn't have to wait for a pause. She was saved by a waiter, Basili. He handed her a bunch of violets and a note written on a folded white paper napkin. A quick tilt of his head and a raised eyebrow showed her the man who had sent them. She could only just see him across the crowded tables. A shock of white hair, part of a profile. She unfolded the napkin and read his note,

'The last time I saw you, you were laughing as you are now. From your soul. Perhaps you remember?'

Cheyney looked up from the note. The group at the table was looking at her. The note, for the moment, was more intriguing than Barry Sole and his art scam.

'Something more interesting than listening to me, Cheyney?' asked the lawyer, unable to keep the note of bitchiness out of his voice. He had just lost his audience.

'It is to me,' she answered, her face still radiant with laughter.

Alex, an English travel-writer, who was sitting next to her, placed an arm around her shoulders and teased, 'Another admirer, Cheyney? This one can't be Greek. Your Greek fans never spoil flowers with a note.'

'True,' she answered, holding the violets under his nose to share their scent.

'If he were Greek, by now there would be meaningful looks aimed at your heart, every one an arrow, courtesy of Aphrodite.' That was Nancy getting her tease in.

'Drinks would have been sent over for us all. And you would have asked him to join us – hoping that way he wouldn't follow you home,' said Karen.

'We all know the routine. We've all been there, Cheyney,' added Nancy.

When she rose from her chair, she had still not been able to remember the last time she had laughed with such abandon. She laid money on the table to cover her share of the bill and it was not until she found herself winding her way around and between the small marble tables of chattering Athenians that she realised she did not want to walk away from this stranger without at least thanking him for the flowers. A first clear view of the man, and she recognised him at once.

He rose from his chair at her approach, smiling. She felt happy, as if she were being drawn towards him by fine, silken threads, invisible to the eye. She liked his power, sensed mystery, a promise of magic.

The years had been good to him. He was no less handsome, perhaps more sexy. Her surprise gave him an advantage. He spoke.

'Hello. You remembered.'

'No, actually I didn't. Not until I saw you.'

'Ah.'

Kurt Walbrook said nothing more. He walked round the small table and withdrew a chair, offering it to her. The glance into each other's eyes. It took only a second, that glance that passed between them. A moment of exquisite togetherness. An intensity that goaded the senses, made their everyday worlds stand still. An instant that was suddenly gone. Both would from then on treasure it. No need to register in words that fleeting moment of oneness between them. Enough that they understood what had happened. Two personalities with the strength to grasp such moments in life, they controlled themselves. The momentary gift did not pass unsavoured.

From behind her, his hand under her elbow, as if guiding her into the chair, he stepped close up against her. He moved his hand cautiously, held her now with his hands on her upper arms and eased her that few inches back up against him. Kurt felt her give in to his embrace. He brushed his lips against her long, shining, black hair just at the nape of her neck. It wasn't enough. He pressed his hands deeper into her flesh and pulled her a fraction closer. Then let her go, and stepped gingerly away. Cheyney sat down.

It had all happened quickly, a sensuous coming together under the eyes of laughing, gossiping, politicising Athenians at the tables at Zonar's. Cheyney hadn't even the time to be surprised or overwhelmed by it.

She watched Kurt take command.

'What may I offer you?' he asked her.

'I have a weakness for pastries, cream cakes. My small Grecian vice.'

He ordered a selection, and two Greek coffees for them. Then he turned back to Cheyney and gave her all his attention, 'Well, that's one wicked thing we have in common. Vienna. The capital city of that pardonable vice, pastries and whipped cream. Our chocolate cake, Sacher Torte, is delicious to the point of decadence. One day I will ruin you with cream cakes in Vienna.'

His voice, that soft, sensuous undertone to his faint Austrian accent. It charmed, it warmed and embraced her. Delight, there was no other word for it. An air of luxurious delight elevated their gourmandising chat.

'You remember me?'

'As vividly as you remembered my laughter. You asked me to marry you. And then promptly walked off with another woman, and never looked back. I am not likely to forget a proposal like that.'

He smiled and his eyes teased. 'Reach back,' he asked. 'Do you remember anything else?' She hesitated, concentrating on that night so long ago, when she had in fact been smitten with the gallant, mature man who flattered her with his attentions.

'Oh, yes, I do. You said, "One more time, we'll meet one more time, and then I will marry you."'

'Very good. I have often wondered what you thought about that.'

'Presumptuous, how presumptuous, that was my first thought. My next was that you had the best line I had ever heard a man throw a woman. It was terrific.'

'Presumptuous? A line? Certainly not.'

'What, then?'

'Exactly what I said.'

He was looking at her matter-of-factly. 'You do mean to marry me?' she said, stunned by the realisation, surprised at how much his intentions fascinated her.

'Yes,' he answered, looking very happy.

'Do you always get what you want?'

'Yes.'

'I like my freedom, living without any serious commitments.' That was more an automatic reflex than a statement.

'And I like mine. But one day . . .'

What could have been a tense moment, intruding upon their delightful flirtation, was avoided by the arrival of Nesselrode and Florence and Frangipane, cream-cake slices, puffs of choux pastry bursting with whipped cream and dripping with dark sweet chocolate, slices of *millefeuilles*, tartlets of custard, tiny, bite-size eclairs oozing mocha chantilly, and puffballs of meringue draped in maraschino *crème fraîche*.

'Oh my lord, what a parade!' Cheyney exclaimed playfully, covering her eyes with her hands for a second.' It looks as if I don't have to go to Vienna to have you ruin me.'

Kurt was delighted. She seemed to be toying with the erotic connotations of his earlier words.

The waiter hovered with the two cups of Greek coffee and two glasses of cold water on a tray. Where to put them? He turned to the two men sitting at the table next to Cheyney and Kurt and asked, '*Sus para calo*. Do you mind?' And, before the men could answer, he plunked the small tray down on their table and flounced off.

No amount of apologies or insistence that they could manage without disturbing the two men could retrieve their coffee cups. The two elderly Greeks didn't mind at all. In fact, they would be insulted if they were removed. Cheyney couldn't stop smiling: if this sexy old smoothie opposite her thought he would get another chance to practise his charm on her, he was wrong. She knew what was about to happen.

Cheyney and Kurt reached for the cups only twice before the Greeks began rearranging things. The tables were pushed together. They suggested which order the cakes should be eaten in. They looked so good they ordered some for themselves. They interrupted Cheyney and Kurt's conversation to give their opinion on whatever was being said. Now they were a party of four, everyone plunging a fork in everyone else's pastry. A well-known painter walked by, and joined the two men, then an out-of-favour politician, and their party grew larger.

At last they made their escape. He said he would walk her home. 'Is it always like that?'

'Almost always.' She slipped her arm through his and said. 'You should have seen your face. You were wonderful, the way you just surrendered and enjoyed it all. That's Athens sidewalk café society for you.'

'Why do I get the feeling you're laughing at me?' he asked good-naturedly.

She whispered in his ear as they walked, 'Because I am.'

Chapter 18

Their walk, arm in arm, was leisurely, while everyone else was rushing home for the siesta. Up Voucarestiou Street, then Kanaris, through Kolonaki Square, up towards Lycavatos. They watched the streets emptying and relative quiet descend. They stopped, balanced on a kerb, to let the dwindling traffic pass before they attempted a crossing.

'Why do you want to marry me?' she asked.

'Because you're beautiful, very beautiful. You are exquisitely sensual, erotic even. I like your soul, your passion for life, art. I admire your courage. Let me say, the courage of a lioness. I like your independent spirit, your own special kind of love and loyalty, and you're intelligent. How's that?'

'Is that all?' she teased, eyes sparkling. They braved the street. Once across, he grabbed her hard by the elbow and pulled her sharply up against him.

'No, one more reason. I like your body. And especially in a dress like the one you wore the first night I met you. It was the perfect covering for it. Your body spoke to me that night. It told me everything I might want to know about you. I actually crave your body.'

His look was intense, his voice tight. Then he relaxed, let go of her arm and the teasing twinkle she had seen earlier in his eyes was suddenly there again. He laughed at her, 'With me you will have to expect to get as good as you give.' He slipped his arm through hers and they walked on. Now she was confused. Had it all been mere teasing? She made no attempt to find out. He was a seasoned player of the game of seduction.

'And why will *I* marry you?' Her Freudian slip? She had meant to say, 'Why would I marry you?' He turned his head to look at her. She kept her eyes straight ahead, not daring to take in the expression of delight she knew must be there. He noted her mistake and the advantage it might one day give him. He answered her.

'You suit me. And you will marry me when you realise that. So, for that reason, and because we can have a wonderful life together.'

'And love?'

'We already love each other. And every day we know each other, we will love that little bit more.'

'You *are* a presumptuous man. You take my breath away.'

'So I see.'

'I know nothing at all about you.'

'Yes, you do, you just haven't put the pieces together.' That perplexed her.

'Not even your name.'

'Don't you like a mystery?'

'Yes, I do like a mystery. I'd better, I have one here,' she quipped.

'Adventure?'

'Of course. Without an adventure, what would life be?'

'Then think of me as an adventure, and forget about names, at least for now.'

They stopped at the bottom of a street a hundred worn, white marble steps high. It was flanked on one side by Neo-classical houses, each one more finely detailed than the last, and on the other by a garden of luscious green pine and juniper, springing from hard, dry earth. Towards the top of the stone-banked tiers of trees, a scattering of empty wooden taverna chairs and the odd wooden table, white cloths flapping in the breeze. Very quiet, just a few birds twittering, and the muffled hum of city noise borne in from the distance.

'That's where I live. Top of the steps and around the corner. A penthouse apartment on top of a *polykatoia*. There's no need for you to make the climb. I'll say goodbye and thank you – for all that evil whipped cream.'

She held her hand out, intending to shake his. He took it and held it. Suddenly the idea of his leaving her hurt. She didn't want him to go. Yet again, those invisible silken threads seemed to draw her to him. She wanted him terribly. It rather shocked her how carnal she felt about this stranger, who suddenly didn't seem at all like a stranger, but more, as he suggested, an adventure. A grand adventure.

He kissed her hand, and something within her dissolved. She felt giddy, almost missing what he was saying. She made an effort to concentrate on his words.

'Dine with me this evening.'

He knew that she would. He saw her say yes with her eyes. He placed a finger to her lips, as if asking her to keep her silence, and then traced their outline. He pressed the soft sensual lips, a caress. 'Good. I know just the place.'

'Where shall I meet you, and at what time?' asked Cheyney.

He took her by the arm. She liked being touched by him. They started the climb up the steep flight of steps. She wanted to say, 'There's no need, it's such a tiring haul to the top.' But what was the point? She knew he had no intention of leaving her.

162

In the hall of her apartment building she wanted again to suggest to him that they meet later. The words were not forthcoming. Crammed so close together in the tiny lift as it slowly creaked up to the penthouse, she felt his magnetism so strongly she had to fight her instinct to succumb. His own special, sensual male scent was intoxicating. Attractive, dominating, a strong sexual charisma. It felt good to be close to him. More than good. But, beyond those things, there was the pleasure she derived from knowing he wanted her. At the door to her apartment he took the key from her and unlocked it. She gave up.

Inside he showed no reaction to the sparsely furnished rooms. The vast terrace with a spectacular view of the city and the Acropolis way off in the distance, a ribbon of blue, the sea.

He was much older than she was, twenty years older, maybe. But he moved like a young man. The handsome, older-man good looks and the courtly manners, so smooth, oh so smooth and charming. The accent, the voice. Such blue, blue eyes that held you in his spell. The straight nose and strong chin, the sensuous lips, the way he looked at Cheyney and the other women at Zonar's and in the streets. He didn't woo them with his eyes, he penetrated them. It was only now as she watched him that she thought he was most probably more than just a womaniser. A sensualist, for certain, a libertine possibly. She felt quite nervous at the thought of where he could take her sexually. Nervous, but filled with desire to go there with him. This was ridiculous. And the whole afternoon has been bizarre, she told herself, trying to steady her thoughts.

'Why don't we take Zazou with us?' he asked.

'Yes, she'd love that. We both would.'

'Good, then it won't matter how late we are getting back. We'll leave as soon as you are ready, we need some time to get there.'

'I must have at least a short siesta. At least an hour.'

'Fine, an hour then, we'll go after that.'

Before she realised what was happening, he was leading her to her bedroom. It was too late for protest, and much too exciting. The hot October day, an interesting sexy man who professes love and offers marriage, an adventure – what was there to protest about?

She felt embarrassed about the bedroom's stark white walls; on the floor, in the middle of the room, an oversized mattress covered with black goatskins. A bowl of yellow dahlias set on a four-inch-high, black lacquer box. And nothing else. She waited for a reaction. He displayed none. He said nothing.

He opened the French doors to the balcony, and pulled the shutters closed and then the glass doors behind them. Light banished, the room turned sensuously dim. He removed the dark grey and beige Harris-tweed jacket he was wearing and walked past her to the wardrobe. He found an empty wire hanger for the jacket. The hanger buckled but held. He removed the red wool tie and then the Turnbull and Asser, Delft-blue cotton shirt and handed them to her. No chair in the room to drape them over. With the last available hanger in the cupboard now gone, he had little choice. Cheyney made no apology for the sparseness of her life, but found room for his clothes in her closet.

His body surprised her. No longer young, not particularly muscular or in any way dynamic, it was nevertheless without fault. Naked he was earthily male, frighteningly sexual. It was a strong body, the wide shoulders tapering to a narrow waist, the hair on his chest still dark. This body held the promise of a masterful eroticism.

He was so sure of himself standing naked in front of her. It was unnerving for Cheyney that he felt no need to float seduction upon a flow of banal words. He obviously sensed there was no ice to break. He slipped the red silk scarf from around her neck and placed it in her hand. Then he undid the three buttons on the mocha-coloured fitted suede jacket she was wearing, turned and walked to the bathroom.

She heard the shower. He would be back soon. Her imagination shifted into high gear. Her body tingled with anticipation. Hurriedly she undressed. Yet, a drowsiness suddenly took command of her. She held a dressing-gown in her hand ready to slip into. He reappeared and, taking it from her hands, stood back and looked at her in the half-light. He tilted her chin up, wanting better to see her face, before kissing her on the lips with an infinite tenderness. Nothing more.

Unnerved by the seduction, she slipped away from him and into the shower. The damp heat and hot water cleansed and soothed, and did its work. All she wanted was to sleep.

She slid between the cool, white linen sheets. He turned on his side to face her.

'An hour, we can only sleep for an hour. Be happy, I am going to give you everything you have ever wanted. You are going to have a better life than ever you dreamed of,' he whispered. The voice was sexy and smooth, the accent mesmerising.

He stroked her hair. Her eyelids, heavy with sleep, kept closing. She was fighting to stay awake. He liked the straight slender nose and traced it with his finger. 'Sleep, sleep deeply, my love,' he whispered in his honeyed, sensuous voice.

She was so drowsy. It was like swimming through gossamer, trying not to founder. But she wanted him, wanted him to take her. She was his.

He put his lips to hers and kissed her. He tantalised her with his kisses, sensitised her body with them. They were hungry for her breasts, all her hidden erogenous places. His lips, his mouth, his tongue, velvet explorers fired with passion. Weighed down by drowsiness, and her own private lust, she was unable to resist his exquisite seduction of her. With every gentle caress, every lick of his tongue across her flesh, she dissolved a little bit more. He drew from her a stream of light, sweet, orgasms. She whimpered with the pain of such ravishing pleasure.

She wanted to reach out and touch him, to feel the weight of his own sex in her hands, to feel the taste of him in her mouth. Impossible. In her half-dreaming state she was beyond an active role in their lust for each other. Instead she absorbed his luxuriously slow, loving thrusts. Revelled in that most exquisite feeling of being filled to bursting with a relentless penis. She could only give him pleasure by coming again and again and again. She was mesmerised by his desire to pleasure her, and glided away into a dreamless sleep.

When she opened her eyes to see him lying next to her, he was dressed. Shirt opened to the waist, trousers, bare feet. She ran her fingers through his hair.

'Was I dreaming?' she asked.

'I don't know. Were you dreaming?'

She flushed with embarrassment, remembering the blissful sensations she achieved in her orgasms. How he had satiated her. But had it been a waking bliss, or had she been dreaming? She hardly knew, yet felt that he did.

'You're not going to tell me, are you?' she asked.

'No, not now. Not ever.'

She knew he was playing with her, but she also felt that he meant what he said. She might never know whether they had experienced such a fiercely erotic coming together or not. Cheyney made up her mind to resist asking again.

Gathering some of her hair in his hands, he kissed it, and then touched her cheek with his lips. A moment of tenderness and then it was gone, and he was up on his feet, straddling her still prone body. He held his hands out to her. She took them, confused that that was all he wanted. Surely he must have known she was his sexually for the asking? He couldn't have missed her signals, he was much too clever and quick, he knew women too well for that. He had her puzzled. Women generally know when a man fancies them sexually, and she knew down to the marrow of her bones that this man wanted a sexual scene with her that had been smouldering for years, ever since that first time he approached her in New York. Or had he had it? There had to be, at the very least, a little of the sexual devil in him to leave her tortured by that question.

He pulled her up, she tried to pull him down. He set her on her feet. She still wanted sex with him and was disappointed that it wasn't going to happen. Or had it? Again the torture of not knowing. How had he mesmerised her into that half dream-state, so he could play with her like this? The way he fucked her with his gaze, and caressed her nakedness with his hands as he helped her into her dressing-gown, proved one thing to her: whatever had happened in the last hour, whatever reason they were not having sex now, he still wanted her, and more than ever. Of course she was right.

For him to subside into sleep after he had made love to her had been impossible. He had still wanted her long after he had fucked her to sleep. Kurt had done it deliberately, seduced her in every possible sexual way to lull her into dreamland rather than to excite her into wild, passionate sex. That would come later, when she wanted more with him than that. When she wanted marriage.

He was boundlessly happy to know how much her own lust suited his, no matter how sure he had been that it would. What keen joy he had had with her. But it was nothing to what they would have together once they were married, and then for the rest of their lives. Having at last had sex with her, Kurt confirmed what he had always suspected: part of the joy of marrying Cheyney Fox would be teaching her the ways of the erotic libertine, and the great sexual game they would practise together. The seduction of Cheyney Fox had only just begun.

Of course she knew very well that they had had intercourse, that they had both come and revelled in their comings. He understood her need to have it confirmed to her. That was no insult to his lovemaking, but a compliment. He had learned long ago from an accomplished mistress of his father, a Eurasian beauty, what a rare pleasure it was for a woman to have sex with a man in that way. She had taught him well. He was more than accomplished at it. There was a trail of women strewn across the world who could attest to that. Women who still yearned for him, as he knew Cheyney would from that day on. In her case, it was only their beginning. There would always be more for them. Here was the one woman he would never abandon.

He hadn't planned any of it. Not meeting her at Zonar's, not sending the note, not having sex or making love to her, none of it.

He had been in Athens only for the day. There to assess the authenticity of a rare Byzantine icon secretly on the market for a discreet buyer, who would deposit the money in Switzerland. Under the present regime, increasingly works of art in Greece were finding themselves released from private collections. In normal circumstances, that would not have happened. But to secrete money abroad had become one of the major concerns for many Greeks now.

Of course he knew that Cheyney lived there. But he had had no intention of looking her up. First he had heard her laughter, then he had seen her. After that, there had been no choice. He sent the note.

Now, waiting for her to finish dressing, he sat in a canvas chair on the terrace. An orchard of potted olive trees rustled in a still-warm autumn breeze blowing in from Africa.

He was thinking about the icon. He would not buy it. Perfect as it was, it lacked that special something he expected from everything he collected.

Cheyney appeared in a terracotta-coloured, buffalo-suede suit. The fitted jacket was perfectly cut, with its row of six decorative gold buttons on each sleeve and on each of the small breast pockets. Under it a pencil-thin skirt. She had drawn her long black hair into a voluptuous twist at the nape of her neck. On her ears, huge gold earrings from Senegal. She was barefoot and held a pair of shoes in each hand.

More, much more, of the old Cheyney he had seen that night he had fallen in love was now coming through, as she stood dressed in her best before him.

'High heel or low heel? It all depends where we're going. I wouldn't want to break a leg. And, keep in mind, I do have a tendency to fall down. I'm not a woman who always looks where she's going.'

'High heels for your legs and for me. But the flat ones for the Agora. I think I would like to walk through the Agora with you.'

He watched her slip into them. She pleased him so much. There was no question about it, she had an impressive personality. She did not have to say much because every action she took, no matter how large or small, was clean, clear and sure. She was like someone who lived in a small world of her own. Only her world seemed to be the whole world.

During sex, she had listened with her body and taken all that he had to give, and given back again and again at just the sensuous moment. He divined that was the way she must be all the time. She was a glorious woman.

'A lovely idea, but the Agora will be closed at this hour.'

'Not for us.' He rose from his chair. 'I think you look lovely. You are one of the prettiest women in the world. Let's go.' In the few hours that she had known this man, he had several times elevated her with compliments, flattery even, and then not taken advantage of it. It did something to her, something good. It made Cheyney want to raise herself just that little bit higher than where she was.

The driver rushed around to open the rear door the moment they appeared. Cheyney recognised the Mercedes as belonging to the German Embassy.

167

'I hope you don't mind. I used your telephone while you were asleep.' That was his only explanation. Settled into the soft white leather of the back seat, she realised that they had not asked each other one personal question. It was strange, they didn't even know each other's name – or so she thought. Something Lala had said came to mind: 'You don't have to love them to fuck them.' Right on, Lala, 'Maybe you don't have to know them to like them, and want to fuck them.' How glorious it could seem, this permissive society that loosed the shackles and set you free. Even if it lasted no longer than an interlude with an exciting stranger. She almost had to pinch herself to make sure this was real. She had come so far from West Hartford, Connecticut, survived New York, and still had the spirit for an adventure.

She was amazed that the guard let them into the Agora. They had the famed archeological site to themselves. The afternoon light animated the ruins.

'I find the Agora so romantic. The ruins speak to me, and I hear them, and I learn from them. Once, when I was very young, I sneaked in here with a woman on a blistering hot night. Under a perfect full moon we made wild, passionate love among these broken marbles. In those days there was hardly a guard about. My lady and I had no need to stifle our cries of ecstasy. They echoed among the spirits that dwell here amid the marbles. Oh, the golden vanities of youth. I thought to spill my seed amongst these old stones and magnificent maimed statues. It would, after my death, allow me to join those august ghosts who through the centuries have made this place their home.' He laughed at himself and slipped his arm through Cheyney's.

'I am so glad we never met then. Well, we probably couldn't have. Perhaps you hadn't even been born then. But had we met, it was then you might have been able to call me presumptuous, and with reason. When I look back, which I don't very often, I must have been insufferably arrogant. Come this way.' He took her arm so as to move her faster.

They were walking towards the west entrance to the Agora. Of the three, it was the best. It afforded them a sublime view of the romantic ruins, with Mount Hymettos in the background. A little further on, set on a rocky plateau, was the well-preserved Temple of Hephaistos. A perfect jewel of architecture. They sat down to rest there, and for a few precious minutes became a part of the Agora. After a while they reverted to the present and, remaining where they were, simply enjoyed the view. He turned to her and asked, 'Would you have bought one of the "candy bars" you were laughing about this afternoon?'

'Only if it had been edible,' she joked, and they both laughed.

'But you like the things?'

'Oh, yes, but the concept more. It still makes me want to laugh. Do you know about the scandal of the chocolate bars?'

'Yes, some of it. Only what I read in the papers and have overheard people saying about it.'

'What do they say about it?'

'Everything and nothing. It's perfect cocktail-hour chat. Actually that – as you have discovered yourself – it's more comic than significant.'

'They aren't seriously hoping to win this case against Barry Sole?'

'Is a serious case possible against anything so intrinsically unserious as that creature?'

She began to laugh again. He couldn't help a smile. She said, 'I find it *so* funny. It's difficult to believe they have been able to make a case out of this story, and have got it before a jury. The mind boggles as to what the lawyers will do with it.'

'Oh, they'll go down many different paths to keep the case from being thrown out of court. It's in too many people's interests now for that to happen. They will try to prove that this choc-bar scam is nothing more than an art swindle, a fraud. It also happens to devalue Sole's paintings. They'll argue that what he is up to is as fraudulent as a stocks and shares swindle for those who have invested in him. And for himself, as a well-known and respected Pop painter.

'The prosecution will try to prove that Barry Sole, wilfully and with intent, created a fraud. Obviously, Mr Rosewarne is going to try to prove otherwise.'

Kurt watched her face for a reaction to her former lover's name. He was not disappointed. She stiffened, the smile in her eyes dimmed. He was sorry for her, that the pain connected with this man had still not all gone. He would tough it out, bring it out in the open, in the hope that it would help her get rid of it.

'Is something wrong? You look upset?'

'No, not upset. Surprised that David Rosewarne would take on a case like that. I knew him, he helped me once.' The light came back into her eyes and she sighed. 'That all seems like a lifetime ago. I am sure I was another person then. His name evoked the past for me for a moment. It made me feel strange, almost as if the me who knew him was now dead.'

She gave a visible shiver. Wanting to distract him from herself, David Rosewarne and her past, she asked the first thing that came into her mind. 'What do you think will be the upshot of "the candy bar scam". Might it just melt away?'

'Only if someone stops the lawyers getting their teeth into it.' They both liked her pun.

He took her hand in his, lowered his head and kissed it. Then her cheek.

She was moved by something in the way he kissed her. She knew he understood exactly what she had said, that he understood her pain. Amazingly, she felt as if he had kissed that particular pain away forever. Who was this man? A Svengali, a magician?

'Yes, I think that's just about what will happen. It will melt away, and leave a smudge. Guilty or not, Sole has raked up the Pop Art muck, and that whole world is slithering about in it. Only a few, if any, will emerge with the smell of roses still on them. This man Sole will blossom and no doubt enhance his creative *esprit*. The American Abstract Expressionist painters will feel as if they have been freed at last from a terrible dictatorship, Pop Art. Perhaps they'll abandon the resistance movement they have worked behind these past few years, to take their places again in the open, and ignore the dictator.'

Cheyney was stunned. She had asked him, and he had given her a sensitive and intelligent interpretation of what he thought might happen. Fair enough. But one that displayed a certain knowledge of art. Normally she did almost anything to avoid becoming involved in a contemporary art conversation such as they were having. Now, somehow or other, she was right in the middle of one, yet not panicking about it. The wariness, doubts and second thoughts that normally taunted her at every word uttered about the art world, though not gone, seemed, as she sat in this Temple with this stranger, foolish, unnecessary. Another thing to be relegated to the past and buried. She listened to him say,

'Pop Art and Andy Warhol, and the sixties in politics and music and society, morals and myths, have, for good or for bad, had a tremendous impact on the world. The time has touched us all in some way, no matter whether we reject it or open our arms to it. Now it's nothing more than a question of how much it has affected us all, and where do we go from here. It's not life, you know, only a small moment in a life. Enough of "candy bars", never enough of the Agora. Alas, one last look. We have somewhere else to go.'

Cheyney had listened, no longer torn by bitterness about the art world. She felt sober, cool and calm; in fact, downright unemotional about it. Unemotional, yet with a twinge of interest in it. She was free. After so many hard and unhappy years she was free. The last of her guilt over her past role in the New York art world died that afternoon, with a stranger, in the Agora.

170

Chapter 19

The car climbed towards Sunion. He told her, 'I have known Greece for most of my life. I'm always amazed at the lasting effect it has on people. The changes it makes in their lives. You go away, and yet it always stays with you. Whenever I come to Athens, I touch base again with the Acropolis, the Agora and Sunion. How nice for me, this bonus of having you here with me.'

'Is that often?'

'No. You see, I touch base in many places. Machu Picchu, Angkor Wat, Luxor, the Valley of the Kings, Ephesus. Even Eleni-Kamini. I wish there had been more hours in this day, I would like to have taken you there for dinner. It's a small cove on a Cycladic island I know, with nothing more than a taverna on the beach. You get there by caique from the old port. We would have sat near the water's edge on weather-worn wooden chairs placed on a beach of stones that the sea has washed smooth. There is a breathtaking view: all sea and sky, and some deserted islands off in the distance that seem less to rise from the sea than to have been plucked from the underworld by some god, and carefully laid on the surface of the water to float in place for eternity. At dusk and at dawn, a mysterious, milk-thin mist appears and veils them, then moves sensuously around and between them and vanishes. The evening visitation of some unhappy god. Or so the locals have claimed for as long as the island has been inhabited. We could have had ouzo and *octopodi* cooked over a charcoal grill, and watched the sun set over the sea.

'One day I'll take you there. Yes. We'll go in late spring when it's hot, and the air is still fresh and full of the scent of night and flowers. Out there the sky is simply a blanket of stars broken by millions of pieces of dark blue night. Would you like that?'

'Of course,' she answered, hoping that it might one day happen.

They laughed a great deal when he asked, 'Tell me about *your* Greece?' She supplied him with her interpretation of a certain type of foreigner who falls in love with Greece and the Greek Islands.

'To sit on a Greek island, let's say Hydra or Mikonos, in the blistering heat, under an awning in the old port. You drink Demestica or a cold Fix, cheap Greek beer. You watch the caiques bobbing up and down in the water, hearing its lap and slap against the boats and the quay. I love it. The curtain has gone up, the scene is set, and here's a play that runs twenty-four hours a day. Surely, if you have been to those islands, you will know such scenes.

'The boats when they disgorge their passengers and freight – dogs and chickens and goats and tourists. The whole island down at the port, waiting to see who bought what in Athens, who has arrived, who's leaving. The beginnings of new sagas and the endings of old. The pinched and exhausted look of the returning locals. The Greeks never travel well, they just pretend they do. The cautious, hungry but happy eyes of the foreigners. They have already fallen in love with the picture-postcard port and the island of their dreams. They step on the quay and, snap, something happens to them.

'No one knows how, but suddenly under the burning sun, the magic light, in Greece, and especially on the islands, new life surprises them.

'The fairies sprout wings, the closet queens quit the closet, the spinsters turn into instant nymphomaniacs. Happy suburban husbands let their sexual fantasies fly in every direction, male, female or whatever. The butch girls and gay boys unzip their dreams and tuck their instant loves under their arms. They flower proudly in the sunlight. And the islanders just help them along, feeding them with their own needs.

'Then, one day, as suddenly as it began for them, it's over. The holiday has run its course. They fold up the subconscious like some old soft hat and pack it away for another year. They leave with memories of their dream-island stashed away in the core of their being. Some return as soon as they can. Some just can't leave.'

'That's very funny,' he said, truly amused.

'Yes, it is,' she answered, 'but it always worries me that, in this particular theatre, the viewer is just as much one of the actors. There are moments when I ask myself, "What are you doing here?" '

'Do you get an answer?'

'Well, I haven't yet.'

It was dusk when they arrived at the Temple in Sunion. Perched on the top of a precipice rising two hundred feet out of the sea, the very tip of Attica, it had always been a beacon of home for ships returning to the Saronic Gulf.

Again they were fortunate in their timing, they were the only people there. A magic few minutes, walking among the Temple of Poseidon's slender, luminously white marble columns. 'More Ionic than Doric. Perhaps the same architect who designed our little Temple in the Agora. At least, that's what the archeologists have suggested.' He took her hand and led her across the worn marble floor. Together they went as far as they could to the edge and looked across the water. 'The sea, this marvellous Greek sea,' he said.

It was vanishing right before their eyes, swallowed in the impending darkness of night. 'I suppose I ought to quote you something of Seferis, or better still Cavafy. But this place seems for the moment to have silenced even their voices in me.' She would have liked to have offered him poetry as a gesture of thanks.

'That would have been perfect.' She thought she saw a far-off look come into his eyes. And he walked her to the car.

Riding away from the Temple back towards Athens, Zazou kept leaping from the rear-window ledge to his lap and up to the ledge again, then down into Cheyney's lap, a game accompanied by barks and doggy cries. He was pleased, Cheyney relieved to have the distraction. It filled a sudden distance she had felt growing between this man and herself as they had walked in the dark from the Temple to the car.

At last Zazou settled down. In silence they sped through the darkness, travelling the winding Cape Sunion road for some miles before he reached out to take her hand in his.

Kurt was more than smitten with Cheyney Fox. To have known her, learned to admire her, as he had had to from a distance for all these years, had been a challenge he quite enjoyed. A taste of her now had proved to him the search to uncover her real qualities, her weaknesses and strengths, would be well worth his efforts. If the game had to be the courtship process to get her, then so be it. All the more fun for him. One day he would explain to her that he had only to look at her once to know that in many things they were the same: like him, she too was seeking someone of substance, someone of quality. That he knew a time would come when the nest-building instinct would get the better of her. A time when the life-creating instinct would get the better of both of them. And for them, it would have to be with the right person, or not at all.

He switched the car's interior lamps on. They cast a soft, warm light. 'We only have a few hours left before I have to catch a plane, and I don't intend to waste them struggling to see you in the dark.'

Cheyney was not surprised by his announcement of an imminent departure. Something like that was bound to happen. She was, however, disappointed. He had been an exciting adventure, a more than interesting man, one who had quietly brightened her life, and all in a few hours. Too few. She would have liked him to have stayed at least the night.

There was something else. She did believe he intended to marry her. Otherwise there would not have been the visit to the Agora, the pilgrimage to Sunion. They would have remained in her bed, and they would have had sex together all afternoon and evening. She knew almost nothing about this man, except that she found him to be cultured, and highly-sexed, a seducer of women.

'Two strangers meet . . .' she began.

He interrupted her. 'Ah, but that is not strictly true, if you are talking about us. You must begin, "Two people meet again." '

'All right. Two people meet again, if you prefer. They like each other, they want each other.'

Again he interrupted her, a smile of approval on his face. 'Ah, that's good, that you want me. Now we have a real beginning.'

He turned off the light and slid over the seat to be those few inches closer to her. Taking her face in his hands, he drew her head forward and kissed her. A long, slow, passionate kiss that kindled an uneasy flame within her. Then he placed his arm around her shoulder and drew her close against him. In that one kiss he managed to upset her poise. She struggled to regain her equilibrium, and continued, an edge of huskiness in her voice, 'They come together.'

Yet again he interrupted her by taking her in his arms and whispering in her ear, 'You see there was no need to ask me if you had been dreaming. We were wonderful, we were sublime, whether in your dream or in the real world.' Before she could ask anything, he kissed her with even more passion, his hand caressing her naked breast, her nipples reacting to his measured touch. She felt dizzy, and was relieved when he gently released her, took a long, lascivious look at her still-naked breasts and closed her jacket, buttoning it up. She had scarcely been conscious that he had opened it.

She sighed, and leaning back against him, was silent while she composed herself. Finally, when she had recovered enough to speak, she murmured, 'Maybe I should have worded that a little differently.'

He laughed. Then added to his laughter, 'Yes maybe you should have.' It happened so quickly. He did it with such finesse. He released his massive erection from the confines of his trousers, raised her skirt to her hips, and whispered huskily, "Guide yourself onto me, Cheyney.' Then he pulled her hard down on to him, impaling her on his outrageous lust.

She gasped as the head of his full throbbing penis rent open her lips while he caressed her naked bottom. She did as she was bid and guided him up into her but still could not wholly take all of him inside her. A moment of exquisite pain for her as he pulled her yet further on to him until she could feel him pressing tight and desperate to the very opening of her womb. She could barely catch her breath for the excitement she felt, sitting upon his lap that way.

174

She whispered, 'We are mad, what will the driver think?'

'Nothing. Just my lady being cuddled lovingly in my arms.' And he whispered in her ear, 'You feel wonderful to me.'

'And you to me,' she whispered back, as she raised herself a few inches off him and then slowly slid down, able now to take every bit of him into herself aided by the silky smoothness of her orgasm. She repeated the exercise yet again, then relinquished him in a slow luxurious withdrawal that was as sensuous and raunchy as his own behaviour.

Now it was he who seemed at a loss for words, he who had to compose himself, by asking in the darkness of the speeding car, 'You were saying, before I so rudely interrupted?' The tremor of passion he felt for her was impossible to disguise.

She switched on the light. 'I was trying to say – and no more inter-ruptions, please – I find it strange that in the times we have been together (a few minutes in New York, a few hours here), neither of us has posed a personal question to the other. No, are you married? what do you do? where do you live? All those banal questions that are supposed to be important when two people meet. I know nothing about you, and I don't care.'

'I know everything about you, and I do care.'

She pulled away from him, just enough to take a good long look into his eyes. She was trying to see if he was teasing her or not. It was difficult to trace a smile on his lips.

'What *do* you know about me?'

He was on the verge of telling her all he knew, but changed his mind. Not yet, not quite yet. This wasn't the moment.

When she had turned to face him, she had brushed his cheek with hers. He touched it now, and said, 'I know you make up your face beautifully, so skilfully, and I like your scent, lilies and jasmine, and your chic suit. I know that you are a glamorous woman, full of life, yet living in some kind of a retreat, or you would not be in Greece. You would be in Paris, New York or London. You discriminate finely when it comes to men. You are not a woman to snap up the first thing that comes along, or you would have been married long ago and many times. And there are no signs in your personality or the way you live of your having done that. Oh yes, you live simply, but have not always had to do so. Shall I go on?'

He was teasing her. Well, she could play his game. 'Oh yes, why stop there.'

'I know that you have an interesting mind. The kind of mind that likes Tinguely, the concept of "chocolate-bar" art, Pop Art. You can see and understand them for what they are, and laugh at them.'

To himself he added, 'And you persuaded a strange man into the

175

strangeness of painting Campbell's soup cans. And that caught the imagination of some very artistic people.'

'A clever mind? An intelligent mind?'

Again to himself, 'Is it a scheming mind? An art-genius mind?' That he didn't know yet.

'I know that art must have its special place in your life,' he told her with sympathy in his voice.

Cheyney was genuinely surprised. 'You are perfectly right. You do know a great deal about me, and, I now suspect, more than you're telling me. You speak about art, not for the first time today, as if it were important to you. Is it?'

'It's my life. My magnificent obsession. Art is everything – well, almost everything. Perhaps I think of it as being an expression of the god Eros. A great force, which is sex and love and desire. Art is the human soul at its most cunning. For people like you and me, art is the fundamental method of explanation. That is putting it rather pompously. What I should have said was, for you and me and all the rest of mankind, art is a means of truth, even with all its conniving and tricky ways. That's why you should not be so hard on yourself for loving it. I'm not. I'm proud that it's my great passion, my soul.'

Cheyney felt her own attitudes to art and its ambiguities take shape within this man's phrases. At a loss for words, she slipped her arms around his neck, placed her lips upon his, leaned her body into him and kissed him. A kiss where she took command and they dissolved into each other. On this occasion, it was she who released him, and it was she who was calm enough to tease him.

'You had better be careful, stranger. You have just given me enough reason to think about you in the context of marriage.' She sat back, leaning against him, enjoying him and what she had learned about him. A moment so different from their moment of pure lust but equally as exciting. Neither of them spoke for some time.

They were on the outskirts of Vouligmeni, flashing by more traffic lights now, with more houses scattered among the hills. Soon the intrusive *polykatoia* of the wealthy would be appearing. It was a sign to her that this odyssey was nearly over. She felt strengthened and happy, full of vitality.

It was she who broke the silence. 'Haven't you anything to say about that?'

'What shall I say? Men propose and women do the choosing. That's the way it is, and that's all right with me. I proposed. I can wait for you to choose to marry me. It's just a matter of time, my darling. Nothing but a matter of time.' There was a lilt in his voice.

'Are you playing with me?' she asked, at this point so happy she couldn't have cared if he was. So she was not taken aback when he answered, 'Yes. The game is called courtship. Isn't it wonderful and exciting? All the arts that have ever existed have been created around this game. It's a game of love without pressures, and there is nothing wrong in that. A game that offers great sport. And the only game I know where both players can win.'

'You really have it all figured out. But just suppose I turn out to be a Holy Roller, and you happen after all to be a Lubavitch Hassidic Jew?' The possibility provoked their laughter.

'That is too impossible even to contemplate.'

'OK, what about if you are a Buddhist and I am a zealous Muslim?'

'Why look for religious differences? They cannot exist for us,' he answered, still very amused.

'Why not?'

'Because I believe that true religion is simply the absolute expression in our lives of the good. Nothing more, nothing less. A person either embodies that expression in his life, or he doesn't. Religious affiliation is only the trappings, the decorations.'

'Are you a religious man then?'

'Only on rare occasions. I am more a pagan man.'

'And you are happy with that?'

'Oh, yes, and so will you be. Happy and appreciative.'

'You think you've got me on this, don't you?'

'Yes, I do,' he answered, quietly enjoying himself.

'Relativist,' she countered. 'You confine religion to morals, behaviour, ethics.'

He faltered for a moment. Then, 'I think the expressing of what I call "the good" leaves room for the transcendental . . .'

For the remainder of their ride into Vouligmeni and to a private yacht-club where they were to have dinner, they became embroiled in a semi-philosophical tussle about true religion. Her determination to have her say in the matter amused him at first. Later he was taken aback when she lectured him with, 'Man starts yearning, pretty soon after birth, for oblivion. That's what he seeks in the arms of Eros. The spirit must have something absolute, or it goes crazy. Good needs evil, and evil needs good to bounce off from. That they only exist by contrast. Maybe the spirit goes crazy anyway.'

They had finished their conversation within sight of the club-house. Now he waited patiently for her while she primped, enjoying every minute of it, and watched her concentrating as she adjusted the twist of black hair at the nape of her neck.

He admonished himself, 'Kurt Walbrook, if you think you have her pinned down to a type, think again. She has sprung neatly away from it

177

more than once today, and left you wondering. No, no type-casting for this lady. And forget pigeon-holes to tuck her away into. Yes, labels would sit uneasily on her.

It was an exclusive yacht-club near the Astir Palace Hotel. The yachts moored at the club or in the bay, where the water was deep enough for these grande-dames of the sea, gleamed with the aura of wealth, power and unrelenting beauty. Somehow even more so for the darkness. Their lights shone on white hulks of marine architecture, like foam on the black of night.

They walked on a dimly lit cobblestone path flanked by shrubs. Only the sound of their footsteps broke the immediate stillness of the dark. Close to the entrance of the club-house an arched trellis covered with vines, deep in their winter sleep, rose over them. Among odd leaves that were still green and not willing to die, one white flower. They stopped. She raised herself on the tips of her toes and stretched to pick the flower. It was perhaps a trumpet-shaped lily. She couldn't quite reach it, and so he stood very close to her, almost touching her, and held the branch down so she could pick it. They glanced into each other's eyes. It felt to each of them like their last intimate moment together.

Neither seemed sad about it. On the contrary, theirs was a feeling of pure pleasure for an interlude well spent. She plucked the flower. It still had a faint scent.

'Allow me?' he asked, and took it from her hands. He walked behind her, then carefully placed the brave blossom in the twist of hair at her neck, securing it with one of her hair-pins.

'There, it looks lovely.' And arm in arm they walked into the club for dinner. They were greeted by the maître d', a Frenchman who obviously knew Cheyney's escort. The two men shook hands, but didn't exchange names. It was a slight disappointment for Cheyney, if she had thought so easily to gather a revelation about this half-mysterious man. Her disappointment quickly faded. Nothing could spoil this perfect intermezzo.

The elements of romance and sex and danger. And, yes, there was something decidedly dangerous about this liaison, that had not only diverted and excited her. It had also charmed her. It would have been little more than the satisfying of her curiosity to know who this attractive man was. To know could hardly have embellished an already perfect day.

Entering the restaurant was, after the day they had spent together, like finding themselves transposed to Monte Carlo, Nice or Cannes. The reek of chic. Of southern France, the Riviera. The room was perched on a promontory. It overlooked just sea and magnificent yachts, ocean-going cruisers. The interior was all plate-glass walls and white marble, navy-blue and white glove-leather chairs and banquettes. The curved bar, of white marble streaked with a rich, blue-black vein, reclined like a piece of sculpture. Standing behind it was the bartender, serving a man and a woman, languid sculptures of wealth and ease themselves.

'Not very Greek,' she said. 'It's as if you have said, "Hey presto", flicked a magic wand, and here we are in Monte Carlo or Cap Ferrat.'

'Pleased, then, to be swept away – for an hour or two – from all that moussaka and olive oil?'

She smiled. 'Everyone loves a little "frightfully chic".'

'I have a confession. Greek food is not one of my passions in life.'

'Somehow or other that doesn't surprise me.'

So, a sumptuous dinner: *fruits de mer*, an assortment of the delectable crustaceans to be found in the Mediterranean; a bowl of *bouillabaisse* that might have been sent from France; and a *loup de mer*, the succulent sea bass, served with a light langoustine and scallop sauce. A bottle of sublime Montrachet. They talked about the things they liked to do in Paris, Rome, London. He whetted her appetite for Cairo, too.

Their conversation was easy, comfortable. Several times he took her hand in his and kissed it. They had become romantic friends.

Other people drifted into the restaurant, were made a fuss of, and took their tables. They were the Greek tycoons and their friends, another class of people. No one recognised Kurt or Cheyney, no one disturbed them.

A Cussy – a round base of genoise, its centre filled with a salpicon of fruit bound with a thick apricot sauce and covered with poached apricots, coated with meringue and browned in the oven – was served with a jug of hot apricot sauce laced with Kirsch, and a bowl of whipped cream. A delectable pudding of some sophistication. They ate it unashamedly, then took their espresso standing at the bar where they went to choose an Armagnac. And then, quite suddenly, it was over.

He said nothing. Just guided her with a hand under her elbow through the restaurant to the entrance. She noticed that he didn't pay the check. Outside, a chill October wind had come up. Not one but two cars were waiting with their engines running. Puffs of white exhaust swirled into the night. The chauffeurs were standing at attention by the open rear doors. At first she didn't understand. She was about to get into the Mercedes, expecting him to follow. He stopped her and they stood gazing into each other's eyes.

'Forgive me. Our time has run out. I'm sending you home in this car. I'm taking the other. A plane to catch at midnight, and not much time to make it. Thank you for the most unexpected, wonderful day. I'll call you.'

She was taken aback, but knew better than to show it. 'I don't know what to say. Except thank you for everything,' was what she managed. She plucked the white flower from her hair and placed it in his hands, then quickly slipped into the back seat and glided across it to the far corner where she could see him, the better to wave goodbye.

179

He ducked into the other car, slipped across the seat to be next to her for a second. He found her hand and kissed it, not without some emotion, she thought. He said, 'Remember, fortune favours the brave. *Au revoir, chérie,*' and was gone. The last she saw of him was through the rear window of the Mercedes. He was walking briskly towards the black Rolls-Royce. They waved.

Riding back into Athens, she could only wonder if she would ever hear from him again. It had taken them more than three years to meet this second time. She sat bolt upright at the realisation that he had not even asked her name.

Ah, she told herself, he had you at times even believing him. A little flattery got him where he wanted to be. She had to laugh at herself, but only half-heartedly. She had responded to him as the most attractive man she had met for a very long time.

She conjured up her image of him, wanting to remember as much as she could: the distinctive white hair, the mesmerising blue eyes, the long silky eyelashes – how seductively he used them. The way he kissed her hand. What an attractive brute he was, naked, for a man his age. The way he clenched his amber cigarette-holder between his teeth, how delicately he held it between his fingers. How he had dunked sugar cubes in his coffee and transferred them to his mouth. The way he closed his eyes while still speaking, when expressing deep emotion. The voice, that seductive, honeyed voice, and the softness of some of his words. He pronounced *charming* as *sharming*. Would he, one day, she wondered, call her 'Sheyney'?

She found a small white calling-card on her pillow. He had bold but elegant handwriting. It read:

And so it begins
Kurt.

She sighed, gloriously happy that they were going to see each other again. 'His name is Kurt.' She walked around the room repeating his name aloud. She had never known a Kurt. She turned the card over. Beautifully engraved, she read, 'Kurt Walbrook'. The name registered at once. Stunned she collapsed on the bed. One of the world's more famous art collectors. For as long as she could remember, there had been travelling exhibitions of the Walbrook Collection.

How tactful he had been not to give his name. He knew she would have been intimidated by it, or if not that then certainly in awe. She reached back in her memory, trying to remember where she had read he was international high society's connoisseur of art – and women. A collector of both on the grand scale. A rush of warmth coloured her cheeks. The sex had been no dream.

Chapter 20

She lay down to go to sleep, but there was no sleep in her. She remained in the dark, waiting for it to come. There was still a hint of his scent on the sheets, a reminder that the hour of sex they had together had been real. How foolish she must have seemed to him. Whatever did he think about the way she lived? Forget all that garbage, Cheyney, she had told herself, it was a great time, and that's what it's all about. The telephone rang. No time for it to occur to her that it could be him. She picked it up on the second ring.

'Sheyney.'

'Kurt.'

'Ah, my handwriting remains legible, good. Just to say good night, Sheyney, and thank you. And you were superb, in every way.' She knew what he meant. He made it sound so erotic she squirmed in the dark. 'I will call you, or write, or something. And we will meet again, soonest.' A click, and the voice was gone.

Cheyney's life slipped back into its Athenian routine. Perhaps a little livelier than before, because she was riding on a high, living off her romantic interlude with Kurt Walbrook.

Della called from New York, and Cheyney told her what a great time she had with a man who claimed that he was going to marry her. Della, ever the realist, said, 'Sounds a great line. He's probably a bum. Don't get your hopes up. Just wait and see what he does.' What Kurt Walbrook did was nothing. Not a word in any form.

Two weeks after her 'thing with Kurt' – that was all it had come to mean to her now – she received two parcels. She had gone through a minor Greek hell at the post office. All the obligatory pushing and shoving, shouting and begging, turning from a sympathetic human being into a raving bitch. This entitled her to sign a stack of forms and lick a feast of stamps. Her reward: to be allowed to accept a parcel, torn open, man-handled by the censors, and now shoved into her hands, tied with a snapped rubber band. Inside, a bundle of clippings on the Barry Sole story that Della had promised. A prize Cheyney would willingly have done without. She had become just interested enough to label it 'The Chocolate-

181

Bar Caper', but mainly because, even in Athens, everybody was talking and mostly laughing about it. At least in the circles Cheyney frequented.

She was trying to revive herself after her exhausting experience at the post office with a cup of tea, when the second parcel was brought to her door. It seemed that the German Embassy was Kurt Walbrook's post office, the chauffeur his postman. Of course, she knew who had sent him as soon as she opened the door and recognised the man.

The parcel was a large dress-box, wrapped in brown paper. It was addressed to her. The dress was long, the colour of sand. Made of the finest hand-spun raw silk, an Arab robe discreetly bordered with a single row of seed pearls. It had been laid in the box with great care. A long necklace of Burmese amber, several more strands of seed pearls, and yet another of antique Egyptian gold beads, were intertwined and placed at the neckline. A pair of Phoenician gold and ruby earrings, worthy of any museum of antique jewellery, completed his gift to her. She picked up the calling card. It read,

Flowers would not
have sufficed
Kurt

The night that Cheyney and Kurt had parted, the private jet had touched down in Athens airport only long enough for Kurt Walbrook to board. It had on deck four polo-playing friends, twelve polo-ponies, his German mistress and two French ladies. Saying good night to Cheyney seemed important enough to have kept the jet engines revving, and his friends waiting, that little bit longer.

The plane had been en route to Cairo from Deauville, where the polo team had its permanent home. The other members were already in Cairo making ready for the charity tournament they were to play there.

Once on board, Cheyney Fox became for Kurt a thing of the past. Not that he forgot her. He was simply one of those men who did not allow love or passion to inhibit his getting on with the next thing. Relegated to the back of his mind she might be, but in his heart he would carry Cheyney Fox up front for always.

Although he wanted Cheyney as a life partner, he had no desire to possess her. He had never felt possessive of any of the women he had loved. He wanted to love and be loved by Cheyney, for them to share a life together. But not to the exclusion of freedom for either of them. That for Kurt Walbrook was part of his definition of real love. The woman he would marry would understand that.

Once settled on board, his mind did hark back to the delights of the day.

Not the least of which had been his discovery of a lasciviousness in Cheyney he could build on. He was also pleased to have stirred in her the revival of interest in the art world.

Remembering that, he wondered if this – a time when the art market was low on trading, while everyone waited to see what was going to happen as a result of the candy-bar saga – might not be the best time to buy the works of several Abstract Expressionist artists he had for a long time admired. He had always wanted to have their work in his collection. He would also consider buying a Pop Art painting or two. There was no question that without a representative or two from among them there would be a hole in any serious collection of American contemporary art.

Cheyney Fox, love of my life, to think that you were once a part of all that, he mused. That gave him an idea. And suddenly he felt a pulse of excitement. Here was a way for Cheyney to test the waters and see if she was ready to step once again back into the stream of life. He would call Roberto in the morning.

It was then that Maria, his German mistress, had laid a long slender hand on his, and asked, 'Is it what you have done in Athens today, or our week ahead in Cairo, that has you so excited?'

'A little bit of both,' he answered diplomatically. Not insensitive to her elegant good looks, he kissed her hand. She whispered something in his ear. He began to laugh, and asked her to wait. There was their bedroom in Cairo. She kissed his cheek, fondled his hand. But she could not distract him from thinking about art.

The Walbrook Collection had within it a small but fine collection of American art. But he was a discerning buyer – it was not often that he found an American painting he wanted to own. He had often thought of expanding his collection beyond the purchase of the odd painting. But, with his many other interests, he had not devoted to it the time necessary to do so.

The Walbrook Collection employed five curators. Maybe this was the time to think about keeping a sharp eye for a sixth. There would have to be one in a year or two if he did go ahead with his plan. He would think it over well this coming week in Cairo. For the remainder of the flight he put art and Cheyney away. There were ponies to be discussed with his team-mates.

Several times he was distracted by the laughter of the women who were sitting together. Maria never missed a chance to meet his glance and dart him a meaningful look. Maria von Geller was the perfect mistress. Aristocratic, well-educated, pampered, spoiled, a lady in public, a depraved bi-sexual in bed. Every glance she gave him was a sexual promise. The French women had been brought along by Maria. And everyone on board knew they were there to flirt with the team by day and entertain Kurt and his friends at night.

She knew about his woman in Paris, his many infidelities. She was capable of real bitchery, and horrible scenes in the privacy of her bedroom in Vienna, but never in his presence. She believed he would never marry and he would never leave her, she had told him that many times. As he looked at her that night on the plane, he knew that he would have to keep her even after he married Cheyney. Not just as a sexual distraction, but because there was a hint of madness in her depravity. Though he felt no responsibility for it, he would not abandon her to it. And there was, too, something else. He revelled in depravity, it suited his libido.

He remembered, 'The spirit must have something absolute, or it goes crazy. Good needs evil, and evil needs good to bounce off from. Maybe the spirit goes crazy anyway.' Cheyney's words only a few hours before.

He had known Maria for many years. Her background, her attraction towards the depraved when not held in check, was something akin to evil. He knew the cause: her basic amorality caused her to be concerned only for herself. Her attitude was, 'I want this, I don't want that. What I don't want, if it doesn't get out of my way, I destroy.' She would never lose her Nazi heart. He himself was not unaware of the charm and magnetism to be found in the company of evil. Had he not been surrounded by it, lived and breathed it all his life?

Before the plane landed, what had begun as a whim was now formulated into a plan. There were any number of better people to consult than Roberto and Lala about Kurt's intention to buy several Acton Pace paintings. That, he had decided, was the artist he much admired, and had neglected for far too long. But had he done that, there would have been no way now to get Cheyney to act on his behalf.

In the few deals she had completed for him, she had proved an excellent dealer. More than that, her selections for his approval had been faultless. In each case he had purchased every item. And that had nothing to do with altruism or love. She was just very good. What a plume in Cheyney's hat, to return to the New York art world with a blank cheque-book. That is, if she would accept the job. He placed the call to Roberto.

He spoke at length with both of them. All was well. Maybe too many questions from Lala. But in the end she agreed to handle things as she was told. Roberto and Lala had been dispatched to New York forthwith to see Rowena Sicle, Acton Pace's dealer, and several others who handled the artists whose work interested Kurt. He was sending in the infantry: Cheyney was to be his armoured division. They arranged for a meeting as soon as he was available. A surprise that emerged from the conversation was that Acton Pace adored Cheyney Fox. He had been trying to get in touch with her for years. That was how Lala happened to have his studio's unlisted telephone number.

Kurt made two more phone calls. One to Otto Furtwangler, to tell him to make available to Kurt a bank-draft made out to Cheyney Fox at the Wall Street branch of the Chase Manhattan bank. For four million dollars. The money was to be released to her upon presentation of bills of lading. Kurt owned twenty per cent of Otto Furtwangler's conglomerate, a legacy left to him by his father.

He didn't relish the second call. It was to Albert Semanan. He knew that Semanan would insist he go to stay with him for a few days. Especially since Kurt's mother was there for her annual visit. He would rather have used that time in Cairo, but Albert Semanan could not go to Cairo to visit Kurt. He remained always in his palatial prison with his magnificent art treasures. Fear of kidnap or assassination governed his life. Semanan ought to have been the world's most wanted Nazi criminal. He knew that, but did the world? His true identity had so far remained his own secret. But always with the numbing proviso: for how long? Well, Maria would be happy and so would Kurt's mother. The Baroness adored her son, and even approved of Maria von Geller.

Kurt Walbrook made his last call, and then emptied his mind of all of them while he played through a week of glorious polo.

Chapter 21

Most of the collectors and dealers whom Roberto and Lala knew in New York, who had in the early sixties pooh-poohed Pop Art, had by now embraced it with a vengeance. It made garish their walls and their lives. They were drugging and drinking and swinging a sixties pop-life. It was difficult for the newly arrived Roberto to get a clear picture of the art scene. And not for him alone.

Think yourself into a helicopter, flying low over Fifth Avenue, Upper Fifth Avenue. If you looked to the left, you would see the plush green of Central Park with a few cars nosing towards its various exits. To the right, a series of buildings, all very elegant, in stone and brick, with the façades broken by windows draped in beautiful velvets, silks and satins. Here and there a sliding Shoshi screen instead of the usual draperies. If the helicopter hovered, you could see through these windows into one luscious apartment after another, Louis Quinze furniture in one, Marcel Breuer chairs in another, a Queen Anne dining-room in another, Directoire and Knoll Associates all flash by. The smartest of the smart and the richest of the rich.

Maybe you could see the walls, and so review some of the best paintings in the world. A fantastic vision of the rich, the elegant and the beautiful. The calm, solid façades of these buildings with the jewels of the world inside.

Must not the owners be wonderful, like their collections? How could they not be? To know them, to be with them, to exist alongside them – yes, the people must be jewels too. Well, own jewels, anyway.

Occasionally the helicopter might descend a few floors, only to show more of the same. Then up a few storeys, to see the Fifth-Avenue terraces and roof-gardens.

At one point it might pass a solid glass turret clinging to the front of one of the buildings. From the helicopter it would look like a huge, domed, three-sided birdcage. Inside, might be perched two humans.

Larry and Tina Finn, superstar collectors of Pop Art, sat at a round glass table. It stood on a white plaster sculpture of a locomotive by the Pop artist Nick Dakota. This sculptured base was entitled Choo-Choo Train.

It was seven-thirty in the morning. This was the only hour of the day when Larry and Tina could sit quietly, having their breakfast, suspended in space over Fifth Avenue. The blue sky above, the green park in front of them and their ice-white bedroom, with all its Pop sculpture and paintings, behind. Underneath them, over the black tarmac, rolled all the chrome-plated bolts that secured the wheels that earned the money that made them the stars they were.

This was their hour of togetherness. An hour when they sat and talked through their plans for the day. Who they would see, what they would do, how they would spend their money, where they would dine, who with – life in all its grim essentials. The remaining hours of the day were spent in maintaining their positions as superstar collectors of Pop.

Tina was looking really lovely this morning. But her hair needed doing, and so she had it wrapped in a turban of heavy, hunter-green silk with ruby-red lettering spelling out LOVE all over it. St Laurent. She had on no make-up but Estée Lauder Wild Rice lipstick and Germaine Monteil paprika rouge gel. Her thin, pointed face and lovely blue-green eyes with their heavy, dark lashes made her look fresh and clean. Her perfume was slightly sweet, made up for her exclusively by one of the more famous couture-houses of Paris.

She had the fashionably lean body of a young boy. No boy ever worked harder keeping it that way. This morning the top of that body was encased in a T-shirt of ruby-red, silk-knit jersey with an inflated portrait of herself on the front in yellow and green. The work of Barry Sole. She wore wide green Missoni trousers of knitted jersey, and a pair of handsome green patent leather shoes by Pierre Cardin. Her earrings were gold and rubies by Dali. Around her neck she wore a choker designed by Calder, and on her arm were bangle bracelets made of gold and enamel – they were Life Savers, Milky Way Bars and Almond Joys by Oldenberg. More great Pop Art. Her only ring was a wedding band of gold.

She was pretty and decorative, even if it was all a bit on the hard side. Forty, looking twenty-eight. She was elegant, she was 'now'; she was art and Pop. Her image out-popped Pop.

Her husband, Larry, who sat opposite her, had on a mocha-brown suit in the style modelled by Mao but made by Cardin. It had a smart, wide white zip up the front and one on each wrist. Larry had any number of these outfits. They gave him his own special Pop look: they were his own grey-flannel suit, with Peking-populist chic.

He had mouse-brown hair, streaked with grey, dark brown eyes and a round face. Average height and weight. Shame about the flabby double chin and the bulbous nose though this was not too unacceptable with his style of suit: it raised hopes of some Maoist sayings from his lips. He wore chocolate-brown, suede ankle-boots by Cardin, and no jewellery.

He had the nasty habit of paying cash for almost everything, and so he kept two wads of bills. The wad of hundred-dollar bills was held together by a money-clip of gold, inset with huge diamonds and rubies, in the shape of a dollar-sign – designed by one of the Pop painters, executed by Cartier. That was always placed in the left-side slash-pocket of his trousers. In the right pocket were the wadded bills of tens and twenties. They were held together by a clip designed by a lady Pop artist. It was a miniature of his wife in tiny mosaics made of precious jewels and executed by Boucheron. He never bothered with small change. He too out-popped Pop.

Some extra tension was in the air this morning. The newspapers were waiting in the car downstairs. Larry would read them as he always did on the way to the office, so they were not available to relieve the atmosphere. Tina had gone over the morning mail in the library before breakfast. No mail either, then, to distract them as they faced one another. There were only the yellow daffodils on the table, their breakfast and these two Pop people in their glass cage. Nothing to do but talk about it.

Tina was being awkward. She simply sat there silently, drank her coffee and waited. Larry was being made the one to break the silence. He looked across at her and told himself, She has deliberately worn that Sole shirt to make a point. Ignore it. Make-believe it doesn't exist, that I don't even see it.

Finally he broke the silence.

'Tina dear, don't be upset about what people are saying. I promise I will see we are on the right side. Please listen to me. We cannot be divided about this, we must stick together, there's too much at stake. All you have to do is stop supporting that little faggot.

'Look, Tina, if we take that stand, we have a chance to sue the dealers we purchased from, and the museum directors who led us into spending a fortune on Pop Art. We have a chance to recoup our money. Now, for Christ's sake, get yourself into that dressing-room and start thinking the right way for a change. And take off that fucking Sole shirt. He is out.'

'Has it ever occurred to you, Larry, that Barry Sole might increase in value even if a new American Art movement replaces Pop Art? Or what our social position is, vis-à-vis Barry Sole and Pop Art?

'You must see that our entire social status depends on how we stand in the Pop world. Sole right now is at the very top of the pile, not just of Pop society either. It wasn't you alone, Larry, who bought all those paintings of his. It was *my* father's money that bought those pictures. You who decided that Jonas Sandies was a brilliant dealer. It was you who decided with Jonas what to buy and what to sell, what institutions were the right ones to accept *our* generous donations of Barry Sole paintings. And when to do it so as to get those huge tax-deductions. It was you who thought investment, investment. Corner the market, and then art. You didn't even like half the paintings you had to buy to sustain the market and our image.

'It was all money, money, and wheel and deal for you. Out of all that, we built up a social standing in this city. I may not like all the paintings we have in our collection, but I like the society and life that it has brought us. Barry is my little faggot-companion, Larry. It saves me having a handsome gigolo.

'You may think we invested twelve million dollars for paintings instead of stocks and bonds. What I see is we invested twelve million dollars of my father's money to get out of Astoria, Long Island, and the chrome bolt and screw business and into American art-world society, jet set, call it what you will. I am not going to throw that down the drain. I like my life now, I like being in the society columns, the art magazines, *Vogue*. I happen to enjoy being known all over the world as a patron of the contemporary arts. Everywhere we go, we're recognised: Tina and Larry Finn, the famous collectors of Pop Art. And I love it. It was and is worth every dime of my father's money.

'We will be made to look fools if you turn against Barry Sole and our collection, and start dumping it on the art market. I mean to keep Barry's friendship. I will not take off this T-shirt.

'I intend to remain Barry's constant good friend – whatever is said about him or his work in this ridiculous court-room drama that's going on. We can deal with this problem together and win all the way, no matter what happens to Barry or the collection – if you will only think of me and my position in all this.'

Tina Finn looked at her husband. She noted the large vein twitching just under the skin of his right temple. She felt sorry for him. They had come a long way together, and she was proud of that.

'Larry, don't be upset. Darling, you be the businessman – hard, ruthless even, if you have to be – and I'll be the patron of the arts. That means not dropping Barry. For the moment at least.

'Have you looked at our calendar? Have you seen how many invitations we have? Barry will be at every one of these places. I will play it right down the middle, support you in whatever you do with our collection, and at the same time be as sweet as I can be to him.

'What I think you should do, Larry, is take the position that you are protecting *our* investment, but you feel the same as you always have about Barry Sole and his work. He is a friend. The art world's socialites will drop Barry Sole if Pop Art collapses. We don't have to put ourselves out on a limb and do it. Now doesn't that make sense?'

'OK. There's something in what you say. But keep this in mind: if we don't sell off our Barry Soles at the right moment and put the money into some new art movement, I'm gonna look foolish anyway. You, too, if you are constantly showing yourself all over town with Barry, defending him in public. Can't you cool it, just a bit? Now, I ask you, would it hurt you to change your shirt? Just little things like that can make a difference.'

Just then a helicopter flew low, right past their glass cage. The windows shivered.

'Well, that's the limit! There's a law against that. Is there no privacy left? Oh, by the way, I think we should begin buying a few antiques. Maybe even a few Renaissance paintings, that sort of thing. You know, slowly. Let the world know we are interested in all the arts. I think it might be a safe thing to infiltrate some antiquities into our collection. Then when the crunch comes, if it does come, we will seem to have been more general patrons of the arts. Renaissance men. You know?

'It will give us a chance to move up into a different circle of society in the art world, one we've been shut out from 'til now.'

'Matter of fact, I was talking to Wildenstein just yesterday. He has asked me to go by the gallery tomorrow – with you, of course – for a drink and a private viewing of a Poussin. How does that fit in with your day?'

'I have Halston for a fitting at four, but I suppose I could meet you after that. I was trying to figure out what made you buy that book on Poussin. I was starting to think you'd gotten interested in art.'

He ignored her bitchy remark. 'OK, five at Wildenstein's. Leave the Poussin book here.'

'But we can't stay too long. Remember drinks at five-thirty at Chryssa's studio.'

The Finns sat silent now, reflected in their glass cage, as each drank a final cup of hot black coffee.

The court at the Barry Sole trial being in recess, only added to the frenzy of their lives. The case was still dangling before the art world, and would until it resumed in a few weeks' time for the summations and a verdict. That appeared to justify even more parties, gossip and fun than usual.

Lala and Roberto got nowhere with their reconnaissance, the motive for their being in New York. They got swept up instead by Tina and Larry Finn, who dragged them from one good time to another. The Finns entertained them lavishly. A week of luncheons, dinners, parties, art gossip and shopping, before they made a concerted effort to talk to Rowena Sicle.

Under strict orders from Roberto, Lala had been discreet about which artists interested them. And that was not easy for her. It was much more her style to blurt out who their client was, what he wanted, and how much money they had to play with.

Rowena Sicle was a bitch, and had no time for Roberto and Lala as dealers. But she did see them. She never took a chance on losing anything. She knew that Lala and Cheyney were friends. The first thing she did was to use her bitchiness against Cheyney. That was bad form, but what was worse was she had no Acton Pace paintings to sell anyone. He would only release a painting when he needed money, and nothing would change his mind. Since every painting sold was in the six-figure range, one rarely came on the market.

The shock loosened Lala's tongue. Only a swift tap on her shin from Roberto saved her from throwing discretion to the winds. In the street, she could not hold back the tears. How could this happen to them? The break of a lifetime, and they were unable to take it. Roberto calmed her the best he could. He told her she could go shopping with Tina after lunch, while he checked if there were any works by Pace for sale anywhere. On one condition: no gossiping about their business with anyone.

It was definitely not going according to plan. And Lala simply could not stand it. Nor could she keep her mouth shut. She called Acton Pace and spilled the beans, saying that Cheyney and she were in a position to be able to buy several of his paintings, but she wasn't sure Cheyney wanted to deal in contemporary art again. Acton's insistence on speaking to her friend obliged Lala to call her. Roberto was furious. Cheyney as yet knew nothing of their project – or Kurt Walbrook's instructions.

So instead of flying home to Rome to wait for their meeting with Kurt, Roberto and Lala were obliged to fly to Athens to explain to Cheyney how much they needed her to work with them. There was no way they could acquire a Pace painting unless he released them. But getting one would give the three of them more money than they had probably ever earned in their lifetime. She was their only hope, since Acton had made it quite clear he would talk to Cheyney, she was to call him, but he had, for the moment, no intention of selling any paintings.

Now both Cheyney and Roberto were angry with Lala. Cheyney chided her, 'Don't you see that you have placed me in an untenable position? I don't speak to an old friend for years, and now you want me to call him and insist he does something he does not want to do. I will not ask him to sell us his paintings. I find the idea of doing so, under these circumstances, abhorrent. How could you, Lala?'

'But what if he wants to?' Lala insisted, tears in her eyes.

'Well, that's quite a different thing, isn't it? Why didn't you call and tell me about our prospects of forming such a collection before you went to New York?'

'It all happened so fast, and I had to do some last-minute shopping, and then we had to catch the plane. And then we had planned to call you on our arrival there, but got swept into the art scene. And, well, you know what New York is like, and believe me it's more crazy and exciting than ever. Anyway, what's the difference?'

'I'll tell you "what's the difference". I would have stopped you from seeing Rowena and calling Acton. I would not have known he was stockpiling his paintings. I might have called him and been in with a chance to ask him if he were interested in selling me some of his works. Now I can't even do that.'

While listening to Lala describe what her mystery client wanted to purchase, Cheyney became excited at the prospect of assembling such a collection. But that quickly faded. It had been nearly eight years since she had had anything to do with the New York art world. Desire for a return, and especially with a project like this one, flickered, but only just. You needed a flame burning bright to pull this deal off. Acton, his wife and his dealer were not easy, and it meant coping with a world she had bombed in. Was she ready for that? From what she had been hearing about it, the art world was a place she no longer knew. Now that had been confirmed by news of the goings-on there. And then Lala torpedoed the very idea of being involved in the project with the news of her visit with Rowena and her call to Acton. Now what?

The one thing that Cheyney was convinced she had to do was talk to Acton, who from Lala's account was anxious to talk to her. They spoke for three hours and through a dozen telephone disconnections. Their friendship had always been close, something very special.

Acton had picked Cheyney up in Greenwich Village at the Cedars Bar: watering hole to New York's famous artists. She was seventeen, beautiful, wide-eyed with wonder for the new world that had opened up for her as an art student in New York City. He befriended her on sight. She had youth, a loving spirit. She was quick, intelligent, and she wore her sexuality like a second skin. He was not only enchanted by her, but besotted. And for Cheyney, what better way to start a life in the art world than to have a companion who was already a well-known painter? She was won over by his genius, his sensitive sweet soul, his brilliant but complex mind, and his constant attentions. His desire to teach her everything about life and what art was all about. She was a willing student and he taught her everything he could about the adult world. He was instrumental in turning her from a girl into a woman, specifically an erotic woman.

Thirty years older than Cheyney, he was flattered by her receptiveness, her youth, her virginity. That she should want to give them all to him, and without reservation. He rewarded her with being the perfect first sexual encounter, the perfect first man in her life. He taught her how delicious, how succulent, sex could be. He gave her her first orgasm, and sexual oblivion. Until Acton Pace sex for Cheyney had all been over-sexed boys: a great deal of heavy breathing. Hard, crass, inexperienced penises and bruised breasts. His reward was a burst of creative energy in his middle age that shot him to the peak of his career and from which he never looked back.

Theirs had been a romantic interlude that metamorphosed into a special friendship. His last fling with youth, her first serious adult affair. Neither of them could ever forget what they had meant to each other. They did after all come alive together.

It was therefore difficult for Cheyney to explain to Acton how, even now, healed as she might be from her gallery ordeal, talking to him was not easy. She had only just got rid of her guilt for having failed so many people. Coming back into the big world was hard. There was something in his voice, in the things he had told her about his life these last years since they had met, that frightened her. He had become a recluse, or nearly. That she could sympathise with.

The following day she flew not to New York but to Boston, changed planes and flew on to Provincetown. Reha and Acton Pace were waiting for her on the dock where the sea-plane landed. Roberto was on his way to Cairo for a meeting with Kurt Walbrook, and Lala was reluctantly waiting in Athens. Neither Roberto nor Cheyney was very happy. Lala was, she knew they were all going to be in the money. In spite of herself Cheyney would get the paintings. Art was just as much in her blood as it was in Acton Pace's – and Kurt Walbrook's.

Cheyney found everything to worry about during the flight to Boston. Would she miss a call from Kurt Walbrook? Would he even call? Could she cope with seeing Provincetown and the Paces? Listen to all the art talk she once loved so much? Did Acton believe her when she said she was coming for him, not his paintings? That was important to Cheyney. She found herself digging deeper and deeper to find things to worry about.

The letters of credit in her pocket that Lala and Roberto forced her to take 'just in case'. She hated that 'just in case'. It meant they expected her to make some sort of a deal. And so did the telephone number and instructions they pinned to it of Judd Whyatt, the lawyer their client wanted her to call, if a lawyer might be necessary. She was armed with more support than she could stand, for someone who was not going for the paintings. It looked so calculating. She was resolved not to mention to Acton the buying of any of his works. And she didn't. It was he who insisted he wanted her to help him dispose of some of his paintings.

It was extremely odd. Stepping off the plane on to the dock, Cheyney was in a near-panic. She felt the way they say a drowning person feels. Her past art-life flashed by her, so many images, there and gone in seconds.

And then, even before she set eyes on the Paces, it was over. She suddenly felt wonderful. As if time had stood still. As if nothing bad had ever happened to her in her life. She was there, and the time was now, and there was Acton. She rushed into his arms. They hugged each other long and hard, and then she gave Reha a hug and kissed her on the cheek.

Acton looked wonderful to her. The house on the dunes was like a homecoming for Cheyney, which was very strange since Reha made no effort to hide her resentment at the visit. Reha of the barbed tongue, who had always resented the special relationship between Acton and Cheyney. She watched them, their every move, listened to their every word, when Acton allowed her to be in their company. She retreated after the first twenty-four hours. Then the pair of them walked the dunes and the beach, and talked and talked, and spent endless hours in his studio, where he pulled out from the racks one beautiful canvas after another. They were high on art and beauty and friendship.

She was therefore very concerned when Reha got her on one side and told her that Acton had to be watched nearly all the time. That he suffered from severe depression. He had had no exhibitions for the last few years and refused to sell any paintings. He had definite ideas on the way he wanted his work handled, yet it seemed that he had no intention of sharing these with anyone. Reha was rarely let into the studio. He became more and more possessive about his work. The only compliment she gave to Cheyney, in between the most bitchy and spiteful things she could possibly say about her bankruptcy and subsequent behaviour, was that Reha had not in the last five years seen Acton look so happy and well.

It had been a simple request. Well, that at least was how Acton saw it. Really it was far from simple. He wanted Cheyney to buy twenty-nine paintings for three million dollars, on condition that the collection should remain together, always. Three million dollars was a fraction of their value. Twenty million would have been a more correct evaluation. No, he didn't want twenty million. Only three. He was insistent on that. If she could get her client to spend some of the other seventeen on a one-room museum to house them, and only them, well, that would be a different matter.

Cheyney's condition for the purchase was that she call in a lawyer to witness the sale, and that Reha be present. Once they agreed, she initiated a round of phone calls. Cheyney to Lala in Athens, Lala to Roberto in Cairo, Roberto to Kurt Walbrook, Kurt Walbrook to Judd Whyatt, and finally Judd Whyatt to Cheyney. The client agreed, but had a request and a question. Would Acton Pace sell him another five for the client's personal collection, since he intended to abide by the artist's request? And was there a particular country in which Acton Pace would like the collection kept?

194

Acton said yes to the first, and no to the second. A price was fixed between Cheyney and Acton for the extra five.

And then Acton and Cheyney spent all the night and most of the morning selecting the paintings. Reha was banned from the studio, which was nothing out of the ordinary. Cheyney spent the most exhilarating night of her life in those hours with Acton. They sat on the floor and ate bacon and eggs, and huge wads of Jewish rye bread, smeared thick with butter, and drank Mouton Rothschild amid a blaze of colour and form, abstract impressions of a man's life painted on canvas.

At one point he broke down and cried. From, he claimed, relief that she had come and this was happening. He had intended to burn his studio paintings before he died. When she looked alarmed, he told her that it was not such a crazy idea. He hated the wheeling and dealing in them, and they were, after all, his to do with as he pleased. Now he and she, together, would have saved them all. 'Three million smackers well, five now – in one lump will shut Reha up for the rest of my life, anyway. And I'll not burn the rest. She can play the grande-dame artist's wife while I'm alive. And count her canvases after I'm dead.'

The first idea Reha had that something out of the ordinary was happening was when a helicopter landed on a sand dune near the house. That was when she met Judd Whyatt. She was finally let into the studio with Judd, who met Cheyney for the first time. Acton took command of the situation. Chairs were found for everyone, and large crystal wine glasses filled with more Mouton Rothschild, his favourite wine. Then he sat down next to Reha and, with great love and affection, explained how deeply unhappy he had been for years with the state of the art world, and that it was he who had persuaded Cheyney to help him. She had done so. Then he stated what was about to happen.

Of course, he had been terribly clever. There was no way Reha was going to say a word against what he was doing. She never even thought of it. She was too overwhelmed at him having become a millionaire literally overnight. When the moving van arrived from Boston with a team of ten packers, she happily made coffee and sandwiches for everyone. Part of the agreement was that the sale of the paintings should not be made public until the purchaser desired it. It was done, it was over. And Cheyney was back in Athens forty-eight hours later.

Those days with Acton had been such a personal experience for Cheyney that only after Lala had crushed her to her bosom in a near paroxysm of happiness, repeating, over and over, 'Cheyney you've done it! We're in the money, the real money. Oh, Cheyney,' did she realise she really *was* in the money. Two hundred and fifty thousand dollars in the money.

Cheyney had been on the poverty line for so many years, and then living hand to mouth, albeit well, for the last few years, that the idea of having no more security than that had become a part of her life. With the realisation of the money came a feeling of overwhelming relief, and then one of utter exaltation, What wealth confers is the freedom to do what you want, when you want. Cheyney now had that. She placed her arm around Lala.

'And all thanks to your big mouth, old girl.'

'Yes,' she answered, beaming, 'I take full credit for my part in this.'

Lala took a room for her and Roberto at the Grande Bretagne and waited for him to return from Cairo. Cheyney slept for a day and a half. When she woke she called Acton to say thank you, needing reassurance that he was happy with the deal. She felt some pride when he said, 'Cheyney, you gave me the only thing I ever wanted for my work: understanding, a passion for it, and now a house all of its own to live in. Even enough money to retreat into my studio and lock the world out. What's not to be happy? For the second time in my life you have come into it when I needed you.'

While she was dressing to go and celebrate with Lala and Roberto, she was reminded of something Acton had said. 'How many times have I climbed *my* Everest to reach the pinnacle of my dreams? How many more ascents do you think there are left in me? I sometimes think I'm too battered, deafened, and wearied by the elements to enjoy my victories. Not so you, my beautiful Cheyney, mistress of my erotic fantasies, my dear friend and soul-mate. You've only made a brave attempt once. There are a great many more climbs left in you. You'll make the top of your Everest And, when you reach the pinnacle of your dreams, you enjoy every last one of your victories. I do, with every canvas that works for me.'

Cheyney looked at herself in the mirror. She saw what everyone else might now see. A beautiful, successful, independent woman. She placed a hand on her cheek to feel her own skin and she marvelled at how elated she felt.

Walking down the marble-stepped street on her way to meet Lala and Roberto, it occurred to her that, much as her friends wanted to hear every last detail about her part in their art deal, there was only one person who would truly appreciate her experiences with Acton Pace. Kurt Walbrook. It was then that it came to her. And, once the idea came into her head, she knew it had to be true. Lala and Roberto's mystery client for Acton Pace's paintings was Kurt Walbrook. Why wasn't she more surprised?

Chapter 22

Acton Pace lay back in the old bentwood rocker, his left foot on the floor with his right leg crossed over it. Only his fingertips touched, raised as if in some abstract form of prayer.

He was as if mesmerised by the painting on his easel. He sensed his body as something light, ethereal, being drawn towards it. Acton Pace felt himself dissolve into his latest painting. He and the painting merged, became one. They shared the same life, the same acute awareness of everything around them.

Sharpness and detail; everything vivid and alive. He could hear the tiniest note of the smallest bird as if it were sitting on the rim of his ear drum. Outside the wall of window-glass, scrubby pines sunk deep in the sand dunes trembled in the wind. The ink-blue waves of the Atlantic crashed coldly on the deserted shore under a bright sun.

Forty feet across the room, behind him, the walls where his paintings were stacked in neat rows. Bin upon bin to the forty-foot ceiling above. In the middle of that wall a door – and what lay behind it: the fine beige crystalline sand that slips into the sides of your shoes as you both sink and walk across the dunes the quarter of a mile to the barbed-wire fence with its gate and rusted padlock. There a sign on the fence signalled 'Private Property, Keep Out Unless Invited.' Neat, chromium-red paint.

He could hear voices from the terrace above him. A dull but steady hum and rumble. His wife, his dealer and his oldest friend, Simon North. They had arrived with a man, a lawyer called Judd Whyatt. He knew what they were talking about and he wasn't interested. He figured his wife and Mr Whyatt were the hums, his dealer, Rowena Sicle, and Simon North the rumbles. He knew what Judd Whyatt wanted, and that Simon, Rowena and his wife Reha could handle it. They had no need of him.

Simon was just as famous an Abstract Expressionist painter as he was. The testimony on their kind of painting that Judd Whyatt sought from him would be erudite. It would serve. Simon was good with words but great with paint.

Pace listened. Words, words, rumbles. They had come to hear what Acton Pace had to say. Why? For years he had been telling them he had nothing to say. Still they asked for words. Were his paintings not enough? Would they ever be enough?

His wife Reha and his guests would press no further for him to join them. They would be sensitive to his mood and smart enough to leave him be. 'Only if you want to help us out,' they said. 'We'll be upstairs. We won't disturb you again,' they said. Considerate of them. So why didn't they all go away? Why all the rumble, the hum, why?

Now he saw himself pass into the painting, slip through the thin film of oil paint. The moment his body first touched the surface of the canvas he saw himself change form, flatten into a flesh-coloured wash of pigment, covering every inch of the canvas. He felt and saw in the same instant the painting's colours and forms absorbing him.

Acton Pace felt himself a five-by-seven piece of linen canvas, stretched taut, painted and signed by the body sitting in the rocker. He looked out from the easel he sat upon and started his daily dialogue with that other Acton Pace sitting in the rocking chair.

'Made your farewells to anyone?'

'No.'

'Not even your wife?'

'No.'

'Any regrets about that?'

'No.'

'Listen.'

Again, very loud and clear, the twittering of many small birds. To a background of waves and rustling pines. Over all this, dimly, the hum and rumble from the terrace above.

'There's some artists would try a goodbye to the sights and sounds of the life around them.'

'Not me.'

'I say only, go with care, Simon, and you too Rowena, but go without me. Support Abstract Expressionism causes with all your verbiage, if you like, Reha, my dear wife, I love you. But you are my enemy, because you insist on defending my life and my work when it needs no defence.

'Barnet Newman and Rothko and Pollock and De Kooning, and, yes, even me, Acton Pace – our paintings are not threatened by Pop Art. Just challenged to a contest created by the likes of you.'

End of dialogue. Acton Page felt himself separate from the pigment and found again the self rocking in his chair. He listened to the sounds of life around him. His eye took in his painting. He rocked to and fro, again and again, his gaze travelling to the painting, up to the ceiling, back down to the painting.

Some time later he rose from the rocker and went to the cupboard. With the rope that was there he made a noose. He placed a box exactly where the rocker had been. He did what men have to do in order successfully to hang themselves.

Judd Whyatt and David Rosewarne, two men living in quite different worlds except for their profession. Two men who thought so differently on most things in life. Their only knowledge of one another was that they were adversaries in a courtroom, exercising their abilities. One defending Barry Sole, the other prosecuting him. One would win and one would lose. They would then return to their own worlds, more than likely unchanged by the experience, and never meet again unless in another courtroom. Or so they thought.

Yet the strands of a net of circumstance were meshing to hold them closer than they could have expected.

Take today, for instance. Judd Whyatt was flying in a small plane with a man called Simon North, a famous American painter, to Provincetown, Massachusetts, to meet another famous American painter, Acton Pace.

Approximately twenty miles outside Provincetown the pilot swooped down low over the bays and beaches. They passed over a picture-postcard bay, one that was almost a closed circle. It was surrounded by a scrubby, windswept golf-course on the cliffs above it.

Almost dead centre in the circular bay was an elegant black sloop with burnt-orange coloured sails. Two boys were handling the boat and a man was reclining on cushions, reading.

The man was David Rosewarne; the papers in his hand, the Barry Sole brief. The particular page he was reading, a list of artists likely to give evidence against his client. Acton Pace, Provincetown, was what he read as the plane flew over the boat.

David Rosewarne looked up. He watched the plane climb and circle the golf course. Judd Whyatt asked the pilot to make another low pass over the black sloop, then wondered why he had made the request. When the plane swooped down for the second time, David stood up to have a better look. He kept his eyes on the plane until the sky was empty.

'That was a nifty four-seater Cessna, Dad. I sure would like one like that.'

David Rosewarne eyed his son Joshua and said, 'Sure you would, Josh. It must be going to Provincetown.'

Hours later, Judd Whyatt was helping to cut Acton Pace down from his studio rafter. It was just about the time that David Rosewarne looked up at the sail and yelled over to his son Calvin, 'For God's sake, Cal, how many times have I told you to be neat? What do you think "ship-shape" means, son? Look at that rope swinging in the breeze. Good heavens, boy, that's how accidents happen! And what's a noose doing on the end of the rope?'

They found him hanging from a rafter of his studio. His back was turned to his last painting. Judd Whyatt was deeply shocked by the suicide of Acton Pace. He could not but think he was in some way a part of that tragedy. All the time he had been sitting on the terrace right above the man, dealing with words and issues, Pace was acting out what he felt about those very words and issues. Had he not said 'Do something definite and absolute about the manipulations of art and the artist, or shut up'? Well, what Acton had done was undeniably an absolute response to manipulation.

Judd Whyatt had never seen a hanged man before. The thing that stuck in his mind the most was the weight of the man when he had cut him down, and the fear that he might drop him.

Judd Whyatt had wanted to lay him down gently, carefully, because although the act was such a violent one, there was an enormous calm over the studio and its corpse.

The moment he touched the cold, stiff body, Judd Whyatt had known that Acton Pace had left only the shell of his self there in the form of his body. The essence of the man was alive everywhere in the room. It looked out at him from the painting on the easel.

The powerful presence of Acton, so vibrant and alive, and the feel of Acton's cold corpse in his arms, was a lesson in life and death that Judd Whyatt would be forever grateful for. Tears brimming in his eyes, his heart bursting with compassion for the dead man, he had the most overwhelming desire to kiss Acton Pace goodbye.

They had met only once for a few hours, that two weeks before, when he had acted as legal adviser to Cheyney Fox on the completion of the sale she was negotiating with Acton Pace. And then he had been alone with the artist, at Acton's request, for no more than fifteen minutes, because he insisted that Cheyney Fox should have three paintings as a gift from him. He had already made the offer, which she had refused. Acton could not accept her claim that she had to decline his generous gift because Lala and Roberto's client, and indeed her associates themselves, might think there was a conflict of interest.

Acton Pace had been in total command of his faculties then, and known exactly what he did and didn't want. He had been even more than that: he had been shrewd enough to make it legal and binding. Together Judd and he had worked it out. The paintings which he had already selected for Cheyney were to be sent to storage in Boston, and would be delivered to her upon his death, along with a document signed by him. The document stated that she had the right, if she so wished, to purchase from his own private collection twelve paintings over a period of twelve years, at the cost

200

of one hundred thousand dollars a painting. She could then exercise the right to keep or sell them on the open market. Acton had indeed never forgotten that, with Cheyney Fox, part of himself had sprung to life, like a second coming.

Judd remembered vividly when Acton's wife had been called back into the studio and read the document. She ranted and raved, and kept repeating, 'What will Rowena say? And this man is not even our lawyer. And all that to a woman! You're giving all that to a woman who betrayed the Abstract Expressionists? Have you forgotten who thought of Campbell's soup cans? I won't have it.'

Pace had answered: 'You will have it, and you will abide by it. And you will say nothing to anyone about it, and you will give your word on that or you will have nothing but that cheque in your hand. I will burn every last one of my paintings unless you do.' She gave her word. She had to. There were more than a hundred completed paintings in the studio's storage racks alone.

Judd rarely came across such tragic and emotional circumstances as he found himself in. He was a high-powered, international corporate lawyer, not a family or criminal practitioner. In order to accommodate two of his firm's wealthiest clients, he had found himself dragged into the art world with the Barry Sole litigation, one of the great art sales of the decade, and now this tragic death.

The artist's wife, his best friend and his dealer, were devastated by the hanging. The tears, rage, despair of losing Acton so shattered them that it fell to Judd to take over the things that had to be done immediately. Down to him to find the doctor, to call the police, to insist Reha call her own lawyer at once. It had also been Judd who, filled with compassion for the corpse he had held in his arms, covered it with a sheet of linen canvas and silently blessed the man and wished him *bon voyage*.

Everyone was upset. The art world registered shock but no surprise. Rowena Sicle, his dealer, bought his last painting for herself from Pace's widow not too long after the funeral. The dealer purchased it with many tears and much emotion. Had she not been, after all, his devoted dealer for twenty-six years?

When art had duly canonised its latest suicide, the Vatican Museum blessed Rowena Sicle for offering to sell it to them. Dry-eyed now, she accepted a dozen times the widow's price for this last relic of Acton Pace.

How he would have hated that.

Chapter 23

Cheyney did not hear about Acton Pace's death until six weeks after he had committed suicide. And then it was under the strangest circumstances.

That night in Athens, when she and Roberto and Lala met to celebrate their obtaining the paintings their client wanted, Cheyney stated that she would never work for the couple again, unless she knew who their patron was. That put both Roberto and Lala into a flutter of protest. And ensured that Lala would tell all, or as much as she could without getting into trouble with Roberto and Kurt.

'I am under oath not to disclose his name,' a flustered Roberto had said. 'But I will ask him to change his mind.'

The two women's eyes met. They had known each other for too long not to understand what that look meant: 'I'll give you the hints. You stitch them together.' Lala wasted no time.

'Cheyney, I've been meaning to ask you, any divine new man come into your life lately?'

'Yes, as a matter of fact, a man called Kurt Walbrook.' Roberto choked on his drink. A drop splattered over his tie. Lala handed him a napkin. Her shins happened to be out of range of his foot. He was tolerant beyond belief, but not stupid. He knew how women communicated. He wanted to leave the table but daren't.

'You don't happen to know him, do you?' continued a mischievous Cheyney.

'Yes, actually. We've met him, on and off, socially for years. We have on occasion helped him find things he wanted.'

'Lala!' Roberto's foot had abandoned its probing beneath the table.

'Yes, darling. All right, I promise we'll stop the girly-gossip right now, so we can hear all the details of the deal.'

Later, on the way to the restaurant, when Lala whispered in Cheyney's ear, 'I'll tell you all the gossip about him when we're alone,' Cheyney had whispered back again, 'No, I don't want to know. Leave it alone, Lala.' She gave her friend a look that silenced her.

The following day Cheyney surveyed her apartment and her wardrobe. A cup of tea, and the realisation that she no longer had to live with nine orange-crates and a borrowed mattress on the floor, made her also take stock of her way of life. She could afford more than a few dresses and a box-spring to put the mattress on. There could be a few more luxuries in her life, and possibly a widening of horizons. A holiday, a real holiday. Kurt Walbrook had whetted her appetite for Egypt, and long before him, Lawrence Durrell and Cavafy and Napoleon, who had once conquered it, and Shakespeare whose words kept Cleopatra and her Antony alive, and every Pharaonic art and artefact she had ever seen.

A phone call to the museum in New York to say she would be shipping from Egypt, if they were interested. They were. She had no intention of changing her lifestyle just because she had earned some real big bucks. She was off on the afternoon plane with Lala and Roberto for Rome. There could be no better place in the world – well, possibly New York or Paris or London – for her shopping spree. For Cheyney Rome would serve.

She had planned to stay in Rome for ten days. That became impossible. It was a case of too much, too soon, too rich, too fast. Or some such pleasurable dilemma.

She bought Missoni and Valentino and Gucci handbags and luggage, and the most glorious hand-made shoes she could find. Six pairs of them. Jewellery from Bulgari, even a piece of silver from Buccellati. A Fendi sleeveless jacket of leather and sable, mostly dark, honey-coloured leather.

After the simplicity and antithesis of chic in Athens, plunged now into Roberto and Lala's ultra-chic Rome with its parties, balls, beauty and style, money and success, and the evenings of tittle-tattle and serious gossip, Cheyney was not so much bored as over-indulged.

There was something else. Rome was a city where flirtations were an occupation. Here Cheyney had a problem. She had been looking too long at men as people and not men. She found playing the game exhausting. A handsome new Italian escort every night, and a string of them waiting for dates. She was simply not in training for it.

Cheyney had forgotten how hard Roberto and Lala could laugh and play. She looked and felt beautiful, ravishing, even, and was amusing and charming and fun. The old Cheyney was back in town, and everyone wanted to know her.

She had no idea how or why it happened, but a huge wave of sadness overpowered her as she realised how frivolous she was being. Frivolous and extravagant. It was, as usual, Lala who snapped her out of it in a second by saying, 'Cheyney Fox, frivolous? So what? Extravagant? Don't lay that number on me. You can afford it. For God's sake, good times are here to roll.' She handed Cheyney a long, slim joint, and looked over her shoulder to make sure Roberto was not in the room.

*   *   *

Cheyney knew that she had made a mistake picking up the telephone, before she even put the receiver to her ear. She really didn't want him to have to give up his game. He recognised her voice at once.

'Sheyney?'

Her name flowed off his tongue, as if in letters of liquid honey. She liked the sound, just hearing his voice. She imagined the piercing blue eyes, the sensuous lips. Or had he closed them, as he did when he spoke with emotion? She stretched her imagination that little bit further and saw his long, thick eyelashes. Just his presence on the other end of the telephone made her feel sexy, think of his mouth, his kisses.

'Yes, Kurt.'

'Then you know?'

'That you are the client whom Roberto and Lala are working for? Yes. I guessed that, after my return from the States.'

'I thought you might have. I am extremely pleased with what you have done for me, Sheyney. It's only the beginning. Together we will build a museum for the collection. You have managed one of the great art sales of the decade. How proud you must be. I want to hear all about it when we meet. Darling?'

'Yes, Kurt.'

'Does it matter to you that we keep this art-transaction a secret, at least until I have worked out what I want to do with the collection?'

'No.'

'Good. Oh, by the way, I received your note of thanks for the bits and pieces I sent from Cairo. How clever of you to send it through the German Embassy. Do you have a pencil? Write this phone number down. You are to use it if you want to find me. We will see each other as soon as I am back from Rio. I fly there in a few hours. I love you, Sheyney.'

He gave the telephone number, and his voice was gone. Yet again she realised they had not asked a single personal question of each other. They hadn't even thought to. She was aware of how free she felt, how much better that was than being in that 'in-love' state, where those dozens of possessive questions come into being. The where are you? Who are you out with? Where did you go? Are you happy? When, where, will I see you? Free and just sort of in love, not a bad feeling.

She dressed in her new togs, packed her Gucci bags, and thought herself shamelessly elegant. With a list of the *right* people to know in Cairo and Alexandria stuffed in her new handbag, she kissed a pouting Lala and the ever-understanding Roberto goodbye, and took the next flight from Rome to Cairo.

Grant Madigan and his crew had been in Cairo waiting around for the call for three days. It had come and this was the day. Now it was a matter of the time and location for the interview. They would be contacted. That was why they happened to have been at the Gezira Sporting Club, playing bridge and drinking nothing but lemonades for the last five hours. A *sufragi* interrupted their game to announce that two army officers were at the entrance to the the club-house ready to escort Grant Madigan and his crew to their meeting.

At last. The cards were at once abandoned on the table, chairs were scraped back, jackets retrieved, the air of bored marking time gave way to adrenalin, enthusiasm, action. The *sufragi* was sent to the pool to fetch post-haste the other two crew members, who were not swimming but chatting-up two Cairo beauties.

They were on their way to a well-kept secret. President Nasser was ready for his interview with Grant Madigan. Grant and his crew were leaving the club-house when he saw Cheyney Fox for the first time. Or so he thought. She was with three of Cairo's most attractive hostesses: all women in their early middle-age, beautiful, wealthy, socially chic. He had had a short liaison with two of them. But his eyes were only for Cheyney. It was an instant carnal desire for her. She was the dark-haired, fair-skinned, sensuous, vibrant kind of woman he most liked to bed. But in the case of this woman there was something in the face . . . A kind of completeness of beauty that comes from hard living, not the beauty that is merely conjured from the face-cream pot. Here was a woman who had been through some-thing more than Elizabeth Arden's red door.

Cheyney's own feelings were not far off his. She did something she had never really believed happened to people. One look into his eyes and she fell in love, and with it came an overwhelming awareness of a person as someone other, separate from herself.

They took a step towards each other. But they were blocked from even a smile, an introduction. One of the army officers strode up to shake hands with Grant. One of the women in Cheyney's party called to him, 'We expect you to dinner. See you then.' And Cheyney was swept away.

He never showed up. After the first course, his chair was removed from the dinner table, the place-setting cleared away. The *sufragi*, when chang-ing the plates for the next course, rearranged the two settings flanking the absent guest's place. Grant Madigan's space vanished.

So much for seeing a man as a man, thought Cheyney, more disap-pointed than she really wanted to think she was. From the time she had seen Grant Madigan earlier in the day, she could not get him out of her mind. She remembered those few short minutes when they had been in a taxi together years ago. She had felt towards him then none of the attrac-tion that she did now. But how could she have? Christopher was such a great part of her life then, there had been no room to be interested in any other man. Albeit, over the years, Grant Madigan had often come into her thoughts. She had even wanted him, his warmth, his sex.

She tried to shake him from her mind, filling it with her feelings for Kurt. She and Kurt Walbrook . . . so perfect together. She had become whole in his arms. The most exciting man who had ever entered her life and possessed her with sex, his grasp for living and fun, and who shared with her his grand passion, art. That same obsession she once had and lost and found again under his tender care. Kurt who loved her but allowed her to remain her own independent self. A man who wanted her, and pursued her relentlessly, offering her marriage and love and security and an exciting lifestyle that she could share with him while stretching her own special creative self. Every day she grew to love and respect him more and flower in their relationship. It was all there, but what she felt for Grant Madigan was something else. A natural, inexplicable chemistry that can happen between two people.

How was it possible to fall for a man with nothing more than a look to go on. Childish, teenage, romantic love? She thought she was long past that by now. Cheyney dropped her fantasy of having sex with him. She put right out of her mind a look he had given her that suggested a thrilling carnal love affair, if nothing else. She distanced her passion for Grant Madigan by involving herself with the other guests.

His session with the President went on for hours. Then there had been a post-mortem of the filming with the crew. That was how he happened still to be drinking malt whisky in a corner of the darkened lobby of his hotel at three o'clock in the morning. His way of unwinding.

The first he saw of her was when the night attendant unlocked the front door of the hotel, and she tried to say good-night to her escort there. He hadn't been sure it had been her until she came further into the hotel's entrance. The man was not taking the all-too-obvious hint. He followed a few paces behind her. Grant watched her deftly side-step the velvety advances of an Italian diplomat. Once, twice, she stopped and unwound his arm, removed his hand. He had staying-power this young lover, right up to the concierge's desk. Persistent buggers, those Italian lovers, thought Madigan, greatly amused to see her practically frog-march him back out of the hotel. Back at the desk, she received her key from the night porter and, as she handed the man several bank notes, he heard her say, 'This is for you *not* to give him the key to my room. Do you understand?' As if he did not quite understand such up-Mediterranean ways. The man agreed, smiling in a way that was not encouraging.

She slapped several more notes in his hand, and he said, 'I understand.' Language was not the problem.

He heard her mumble to herself, 'Thank God for that.'

Grant thought, Am I looking at a woman who knows how to take care of herself? He liked that. He gave her a round of half-ironic applause from deep in the shadows of the room. She swung around. She could barely see him in the dim light, as he walked towards her still clapping his hands. The night porter bent forward and whispered, 'That's Mr Madigan from America. He makes movies and is in the television. He and his crew always stay with us.'

'You did that nicely. But I would have been very disappointed if such a romantic ham had outplayed you.'

'Me too. When in Rome, do as the Athenians do.'

He offered his hand for her to shake. 'Hi, I'm Grant Madigan.'

'Yes, I know. We almost met this afternoon at the Gezira. We almost dined at the same table this evening. I'm Cheyney Fox.'

'Good name, Cheyney Fox. It suits you. Well now, Cheyney, what should we do?'

'Do about what?'

'About us.'

'Is there an us?' she answered. His approach lacked elaboration.

'Isn't there?'

Direct, but more than that. An intensity in his gaze that told her she was not alone in that overwhelming awareness she had felt earlier at the Gezira Sporting Club. That intense desire for intimacy united them. Each of them sensed it. The heart had its reasons even if reason itself wasn't having any. Come in, Pascal, she told herself. To feel so deeply, almost violently, and so quickly for another was at once thrilling and frightening, not to mention awkward. Yes, awkward, if the feeling was not to be reduced to something less than what it was, to something vulgar. Because what she felt for Grant Madigan was a deep passion that knew no rules, put up no bars. There was nothing merely vulgar about that.

'I would like to play coy, flirt with you, say something dazzlingly female and coquettish like, "We'll have to see, won't we?" But it would sound pathetic, cheap, and there is something cheap about how I'm feeling, standing here talking to you. And if I did do that, I think you just might turn your back and walk away from me.'

A look of pleasant surprise lit his face as he said, 'I'll take that as a yes, then. Come on, let's get out of here.'

'To go where, at this hour?'

'A night club where we can drink and hear Arab love-songs sung by a woman with a voice to melt your heart, and something special in sensuality. And then to a very private place where I can make delicious, depraved love to you. You and I, Cheyney Fox, are going to have a wonderful time.'

'Such promises. Clearly I am with a deceiver,' she said, falling in step with him unresistingly.

'I am. I feel an amazing intuition about you. No, it's more of an insight, the inner you that is rarely if ever revealed to others. It excites me, makes me feel good. I know you almost better than you do yourself. Don't be frightened,' he whispered in her ear, 'I'll never harm you.'

She watched him haggle with a taxi-driver. A promising start, if this man was her destiny. The whys and wherefores of a relationship with him were irrelevant. She only knew that she wanted to be a part of his flesh, and to give herself up to him.

The haggling over, they climbed into the back seat of the old black Buick. It sped them through the near-deserted streets of Cairo towards Giza and the Sphinx and the three great pyramids of Egypt.

Just before dawn was no bad moment to feel the sensuousness of Cairo as a city. A night sky full of stars, and a nearly full moon slipping in and out of a few low clouds. A cool breeze drifted through the hushed city, raising more of the powder-like dust off the sands of the desert. They rode down the *Sharia el Nil* and watched the dark silhouettes anchored in the Nile: the Egyptian *feluccas* that have plied the length of the river for as long as man has navigated the Nile. A caravan of camels being driven to market had to be negotiated. The sound of tinkling bells on maltreated, apathetic donkeys pulling flat carts of produce in from the country. The odd taxi or car was all the traffic at that hour. A city asleep that from sun to sunset was usually teeming with people and whose life's force was one of the sacred rivers of antiquity, the Nile.

Cheyney felt the heartbeat of Cairo. She knew she would love it all her life. Just as she would the heartbeat of the man next to her. She made up her mind not to hold back with Grant Madigan.

'I want to know everything about you,' she said. 'How tall you are, how much you weigh, what your politics are, have you ever slept with a black woman, a man, a Chinese, been in love, been hurt by love? Whether you like *escargots*, steak, ice cream. Where you live, has there been a wife, children, is there a dog, a cat in your life? Do you play poker with the boys, are you wealthy, mean with money? Everything, even some serious things . . .' He kissed her quiet. And she happily gave in to his kiss.

'I'll tell you anything you want to know. But not all of it here or now. Now I want to tell you how much I want to make love to you. No, that's not wholly true, I want that and more. I want to plumb the depths of life with you, to have sex with you that is more thrilling than either of us has ever experienced. I want to do things with you, have experiences with you, that I have never had with any other woman. I want us to die together in our orgasms to everything else in the world, again and again. And to rise

208

together, to be fresh and renewed. And I want to know everything about you. I want us to talk and talk and hold back nothing of what we feel.

'And I don't want to be dishonest either. I want you to know the dark and the light side of my nature and for you to understand my worst faults and to love me in spite of them. And I need you to be big and brave and strong and independent because I'm a cad when it comes to women and commitment. I don't make bonds for myself ever. I don't want a home, I like living in hotels. Room service and restaurants might have been invented for me. I live by them. I hate anything that reeks of domesticity, babies, wives and children, home or hearth. Traps – I see them as man-traps, except for other men. I enjoy being part of those things in the lives of my friends, but only there. And when I am old and still a crusty bachelor, there will be no regrets because I will have chosen to do other things as rewarding as those I gave up. My love affairs are short term, Cheyney, because I make them that way. They are numerous because of a strong libido, and an admiration for women in general. I especially like beautiful women like you. But I could easily walk off with an ugly duckling of a lady, if there was a sexual rapport between us. When I am with a woman, I become everything to her because she becomes everything to me. And when it's over, the taste always lingers. But I still get on with my life. Until a time when we can come together again.

'I sense a kind of destiny for us. But I want you to know right off what that destiny does not entail. When we have to part, I don't want you to feel a moment of misery, never mind the overwhelming misery I have seen other women suffer for some men. I have the uneasy feeling that ours could be a lunatic love, for both of us. We were bound to meet. Cheyney, I don't usually pick women up as I have done with you this evening, in two minutes flat. Or spill all this out to them.'

'No? How long does it usually take? An hour?'

He liked that. That she doubted him and was not afraid to tell him. That she, like him, cut past the chase and got right down the path to where they were headed. Her emotional stability excited him because here was a woman he was less likely to hurt.

'Look, Grant, we're safe, maybe not from wanting each other, but certainly from wanting to destroy each other's lives. I have a friend who taught me something I never knew before. "You don't have to fall in love to have a happy fuck with somebody." She and this liberated age of the hippie sixties have set me free. I have even learned that you can not only fuck 'em, you *can* love 'em and still let your partners go free. My days of a lunatic love are over. So don't give me that speech.'

'You're angry.'

'No. Not angry, a little embarrassed by your pomposity. If I didn't want to be here, then I wouldn't be. In fact, I am not so sure I *do* want to be here. Not sure in my head anyway. But my body, my heart, the lust inside me, say something different.'

'You are one terrific lady. Absolutely terrific. I think I am already talking myself into love with you. You're up-front. You deal a straight hand. I like that. Cheyney, I don't mean to be pompous, even if that's the way I come across. But it is something I am adamant about, not hurting women. When I get something going with a woman, I don't want to play the cad. I know who I am, what I am, and my image can stand up to the truth, just as I am certain yours can. Otherwise we wouldn't be having this conversation. But there are a great many people, more people than not, who can't handle the truth about themselves or those they want. I have the right to the life I want for myself, and some women don't want to believe that.

'There are men, many men, who do not want marriage and children and the responsibility all that entails. But they still want a woman to make passionate love with. They want her to want them, it inspires them to give themselves up to her. I'm one of those men. The greatest ambition of women is to inspire love. It was Molière who put that across best, and he still gets my vote. I also believe it is the greatest contribution to man that a woman makes. Where would we be without women who inspire love? I've covered enough wars as a journalist, seen enough gore, listened to enough dictators and world leaders, interviewed enough wealthy power-players, to tell you that, without love, the world would be a burned-out, hollow place. Even more than it already is.'

'And I inspire that in you!'

He pulled her across the seat, tight up against him. 'You know you do, or I wouldn't have you here.'

'That was not a question, just a statement to let you know I know where we are with each other, Grant Madigan. And I like it very much.' He squeezed her hand.

'This is the best I can do,' he said. 'For the moment, anyway.' They rode in silence for a short time, and then he added, 'I think you are a beautiful and exciting woman, and I want you, and I know we will never ruin what we will have together.'

The night club was in a large tent in the desert some distance beyond the great pyramids. On the way there they passed the Sphinx, bereft of tourists, with only the moonlight and the stars for company. She looked like something that transcends time and place. She was magnificently mysterious, and her silence spoke to Cheyney's imagination and probed her heart. The Sphinx, this ancient creature of stone who had for thousands of years probed the hearts and minds of other humans, so stoic and alone, who had

210

withstood so much and might for thousands more, fixed its questioning presence in Cheyney's soul.

Grant was not an insensitive man. He watched her being seduced by the Sphinx, then drew her roughly to him and on to his lap, and filled himself with her scent of jasmine and roses, while she watched the colossal statue turn from seeming some intangible thing that was more than stone back into the Sphinx of Giza. It grew smaller and fainter, and finally disappeared from sight through the rear window of the old Buick.

The largest of the three pyramids rose up in front of them. The moon cast a white light down the sharp edge where two sides met. Cheyney actually gasped, so powerfully dramatic and magnetic was the sight. It kept drawing her back in time, reminding her how transient her stay on earth was. Yet it reminded her, too, to live, and live to the most fragile edge, like the one accentuated by that shaft of moonlight running down the pyramid.

Grant laughed at her. It was a laugh of approval. It was cold in the desert, and black black night, with little but the sound of the Buick. He rolled down the windows, wanting to listen to the nothingness and keep her warm with his body. The taxi sped crazily across the sand at high speed. Ten minutes later they were there.

A huge tent with crazily parked Rolls-Royces and Bentleys and extra-long Mercedes by the dozen, a few taxis. Out here they were nothing but dark forms in the desert. It was so still nothing moved, not even half a dozen camels squatting in the sand, their riders rolled up asleep in mats next to them. So quiet even here, except for a faint hum coming from the tent. It chilled and excited the senses. Cheyney clung to Grant's arm. They found the entrance. Someone heard their arrival. Two men flung the huge tent-flaps back, and bowed them in.

The contrast was astounding. The tent was filled with men and only a very few women sitting at tables that circled the interior. Candle-lit desert lanterns hung from the tent's ceiling and were set on the tables. Aisles radiated to the centre of the tent where the carpeted desert floor was empty. The Arab sheiks and Saudi princes, Egyptians and Kuwaitis, Iraquis and Iranians, the wealthiest of the Arabs who came to Cairo to play, were there to hear the singer they were passionate about. The air was aswirl with smoke from hookahs. It smelled of hashish, and Indonesian grass, expensive cigars from Havana, or just plain tobacco. It mixed with the scent of a rose garden and roast lamb. A room of talking, laughing, sex-hungry men waiting to have their emotions stirred by the sensuous voice of Shammamam.

The owner rushed towards Grant, recognising him at once, and found them a table after shifting and moving several other tables and people.

Fifteen minutes, she was to sing in fifteen minutes, whispered the *sufragis* from table to table, and that generated more excitement. A bottle of Krug, an excellent vintage and chilled perfectly. A heaped platter of lamb cutlets grilled over charcoal and herbs, another of crisp fried potatoes and onions, were placed on the white damask cloth. The only fare served at the club. Except for platters of fresh fruit, peeled and sugared, and bowls of dark, rich honey to dip them in, which came later. A hookah was made ready for them and brought to the table. A lump of hashish, Lebanese Gold, smouldered in the embers.

'I'm not the only civil barbarian in this room who thinks you're a beauty and would like to ravish you. I dare say there's not a man in this room who doesn't envy me.'

'Ah, then you really do find me beautiful,' she teased, knowing very well that he did.

'Oh, yes, and more. But you know that.'

'Yes, I guess I do,' she said. 'But I certainly didn't the first time we met. And I don't mean at the Gezira Club.'

'But we have never met before.'

'Oh, but we have. You knocked me down in a rainstorm. In New York, in front of F.A.O. Schwartz's toy shop.'

He recalled nothing about the incident. She described it to him, and they laughed together about the rude things he had said to her when he took her home in a taxi. About the way he behaved towards her, his kissing her and fondling her breasts, how angry she was with him because he assumed he understood her. She was gracious enough in prodding his memory to add, 'As it turned out, you did understand me better than I did myself, but that is another story. And that was years ago, and this is now.'

They were distracted from themselves by, 'She comes now, she comes.' Word spread around the tent. The *sufragis* stopped serving and rushed to stand mutely against the black cloth walls. A hush like an indolent wave rolled slowly across the room. Complete silence for several seconds, and then a spot-light beamed a path for her down one of the aisles. She entered the tent and walked seductively through the light. Men reached out to touch her, pick up the hem of her skirt to kiss it as she passed by them. With one voice, a roar of admiration for her filled the tent. Men stood up, some clapped, others waved their arms, others called out in blood-curdling yells or banged their fists upon tables. She stood in the centre of the tent and turned a full circle, bowing to them, her arm-gestures bidding them to calm down.

Her skin was a coffee colour. She had green eyes outlined heavily in black, a face of sensual beauty with its high cheek bones and pointed chin, its long slender nose. A feline, fox-like face with an expression of sweetness that could melt the coldest of hearts. Her lips, large and fleshy, were crimson. Her hair, long and bushy, a mass of crinkly waves, stood out like a seductive snare. Over it, pinned on the top of her head, a traditional black head-scarf that fell over her shoulders and flowed down to the ground as it billowed out around her, emanating a dark seductive aura. Her dress, again black, fitted tightly across an ample bosom and a narrow waist that accentuated wide, fleshy hips and a voluptuous bottom, such as Arab men favour. The black braid of the bodice of her long dress was buttoned tight up to a long and slender neck. On her ears, large golden earrings set with diamonds and rubies.

Her performance was backed by an orchestra of Arab instrumentalists, who sat in clusters at the four corners of the tent. While Shammamam was still taking bows and trying to settle her admirers, four *sufragis* rushed down an aisle carrying a simple, narrow, wooden day-bed and placed it off to one side near the centre of the tent. Two others placed cushions upon it, then disappeared. Finally the men quietened down and she began to sing.

Cheyney had never heard such a sensuous voice. The guttural sounds the woman drew from the back of her throat, the way she caught a note on a breath and manipulated it, her timing. Arabic holds such exotic sounds when spoken well, like its calligraphy, all sensuous twirls and flurries on the tongue, the roof of the mouth, deep in the throat. She tore out the heart of every man with her singing, the movement of her hands, a turn of her head, a tilt of her chin, the way she used her eyes, moved her hips, made as if to caress her audience with her head-scarf. She lured them further and further into a trance-like state with every voluptuous note.

Each song many times as long as a western song seduced her audience and refused to let them go. By her fourth musical extravaganza even she seemed to have worked herself into some sort of trance. Several more songs and the erotic pitch broke all bounds. Shammamam tore open her bodice and presented her magnificently large breasts to her audience as if she was offering them to every man in the room. They flowed over her hands, and their nipples with their large nimbus rouged pink, with tattooed blue arabesques around, were more an erotic gift than a vulgar gesture. Cheyney heard men softly weeping, others panting with excitement, others who looked lost in the words of her songs.

She finished. The centre light followed her as she collapsed on to the day-bed. The crowd went wild with applause. The *sufragis* rushed down the aisles to carry her on her bed from the tent. Men were throwing banknotes on her and on to the carpet at the centre of the tent. Jewelled bracelets and necklaces, pearls and diamonds, were draped on her breasts by men trying to kiss and caress them, her lips, a cheek, a hand, a finger, a foot. She tortured them further; drew her knees up, raised her voluminous black skirts to above her thighs and opened her legs wide, giving them a brief glimpse of her most intimate self while she writhed in her own sexual lust on her bed of jewelled tributes until she was gone, rushed away by her bearers. But not before Cheyney saw an Arab, in princely robes, roughly snatch from a mistress's neck a necklace of cascading diamonds. He flung them between Shammamam's legs into the shadows of her skirt, making an attempt to stuff them into her yearning cunt while he bit hard into her fleshy thigh. Pandemonium! When shoved off her, he was seen to have Shammamam's blood on his lips, in his mouth.

On the way back to Cairo, to a large and grand house behind closed iron gates that were opened by the night watchman standing guard, they said not one word to each other. They couldn't; so enveloped were they in the dark aftermath of lust, words would not suffice. On entering the car, Grant placed an arm around Cheyney's shoulders and pulled her tight against him, grasping her hand. Once he raised it to his mouth to kiss her fingers. He sucked them moist and bit hard into one of them until he saw the tears brimming in her eyes. But they did not speak.

The house *sufragis* ran before them up the grand marble staircase, lighting the way. In the bedroom, he thanked them and sent them away, saying he did not want to be disturbed. Then he turned to Cheyney. They drew together in a powerful urgent lust that dissolved all emotions save one and knew no restraints. Cheyney heard the tear of silk, felt his hands upon her flesh. They excited, but she burned with desire for more, and to that end, she tore at his clothes, and bit into his lips, and covered his face and then his body with wild passionate kisses.

Cheyney and Grant, driven by the thrilling exhibition of unashamed erotic abandon Shammamam had seduced them with, and with a boundless desire to share with each other nothing less, ravaged each other and constantly sought more and more from the flesh. It was passion to the point of violence. Erotic madness that went beyond the realms of reason. Each magnificently erotic act inducing another and another and another. And erotic gave way to lust and lust to decadence. But to two willing partners steeped in sexual oblivion, what Cheyney and Grant once might have classed as depraved, decadent, sexual acts lost their labels. They became, instead, shared sublime erotic freedom governed by trust and love. Their sexual coming together was as natural for them as if they had been waiting all their lives to meet and surrender themselves completely to each other, and their fantasies and dreams of all that is sex.

They remained together for three glorious days. Cheyney never left Grant's side, night or day. They could not get enough of each other. And then they had to part. He was flying with the crew to Khartoum to interview the Mahdi. He promised to meet her in Luxor in three days' time. He never arrived. Instead she received a cable: he was flying straight to New York, she was to call him there on her return to Athens, regrets and love.

A week later Cheyney was sitting on the running-board of a battered old Chevvy, fending off the midday sun with a large black silk umbrella. The car had broken down just beyond the Valley of the Kings, where she had gone to a village to see if she could buy some water-pots for the museum. She had sent the driver back to the village on foot for help. Three hippies with rucksacks came down the dirt road on foot. They gave her a drink, offered her a joint, and promised to send back the first car they could stop to pick her up. She convinced them that she couldn't abandon her wares or the car without the driver. One boy, who claimed to be called Pandor, tossed her an old *Newsweek* magazine to while away the hours. And that was where she read about the death of Acton Pace. And then wondered what she was doing, stubbornly pursuing pots in the desert. She felt lonely and alone and broke down and cried for the loss of a great painter and a fine friend.

Of course Cheyney had no idea, as yet, how guilefully generous a friend Acton Pace had been to her. Only Reha, Judd Whyatt and Kurt Walbrook knew that.

Chapter 24

Home from her travels for the first time in nearly two months, Cheyney was barely through the door of her Athens apartment when the phone rang. Grant Madigan wanted her in New York as fast as she could get there. Just the sound of his voice would have been enough, but there had been more. Love in his words, warmth, passion.

She crossed the ocean, and faced New York without a second thought, just to be with him for two days. That was all the time their busy lives allowed them together. But they had been two days of never to be forgotten lust and love and had ended with no tears and the promise of a future – that was never defined.

Now here she was, four days after his departure, sitting with Della in a New York courtroom waiting to hear the summations of the Barry Sole trial.

Waiting for the judge and defendant to appear and be seated, the courtroom to be called to order and Judd Whyatt to present his summation, Cheyney sized up the courtroom. The serious formality of it all: the solid dark mahogany of the room, the bare windows, the empty chairs, the wooden railings and dais where the judge sat. Impressive, dramatic even, the lines of empty chairs where twelve people boxed into justice, six upon six, would soon be seated. Her mind wandered. She could not help but think of the two days she had spent with Grant in his rooms at the Waldorf Astoria.

Love, that's what those two days were about. Two people who feel for each other intense sexual love, who are in that in-love state that blinds them to all else but each other. Days that were made even more intense by the very fragility of such powerful feelings. Days and nights when they used the gambit of intimate relations. Maybe too intimate. Too revealing to live with. They had allowed themselves the ultimate luxury *vis-à-vis* relationships. They held back nothing, gave themselves up completely to each other. Showed themselves from the lightest most loving side of their nature to the darkest most secret and depraved side of their being, and came out loving each other even more for what they had been able to give and accept. They loved flaws and all, Cheyney was certain of that. But could they sustain such a love as they felt for each other?

In those two days they lived in the present every minute of every hour. It was as if the past and the future did not exist for them. They asked not a question about each other's lives or loves or dreams. They lived in the now of their passion. The scent of Grant Madigan, the taste of him, the feel of him inside her, possessing her, the joy of submitting to his every sexual demand without question or thought, repeatedly, were even now more exciting and rewarding than she had ever imagined a woman might feel about loving a man. But he had submitted no less to her, and more than any other man had done before. They held the power of love over each other, and that was a sobering thought for Cheyney. It pushed the memory of those two sublime days out of her mind, for the moment at least.

The scene in the courtroom conferred a certain perspective upon the overpowering intensity of feelings instilled in them by the lust they had shared. Their intimacy challenged the ordinary barriers that separate a man and woman. It left them psychologically bare and raw. Little but the seeds of life itself to build on. And now he was gone. Gone for two years.

She could not forget his words. 'I don't know when we'll be together again, but we will. I'm going away, off into the field, for two years, possibly three. It's research on all the wars since 1945. I have a contract for a book and a lengthy TV series. Be happy for me, Cheyney, it's a magnificent project. Algeria, Palestine, Cyprus, India and Indo-China. Suez – I already have a great deal of material researched on that – Vietnam . . . wonderful contacts there.' Then his mood had changed. He took her in his arms and said more feelingly, 'There has been nothing in my life as intense as giving myself up to you. It blinds me momentarily to anything else. But it's not enough, not for either of us. We'll meet. I'll send for you, or come to you.'

She was happy for him. She could have wished for more of Grant Madigan for herself, but that hardly crossed her mind. They belonged to each other, no matter where they were, even if they were never to see each other again. She was sure of that, enough for her to get on with her life. That had entailed moving in with Della for a few days. And making a call to Judd Whyatt, in response to the urgent message she had received to call his office. It was he who had arranged for Cheyney and Della to be seated in the courtroom.

Della had been concerned as to how it would be for Cheyney, facing so many people in the art world for the first time since she vanished from that scene after the disastrous collapse of the gallery. Eight years was a long time. But was it long enough for Cheyney to accept failure, call it the past, and forgive herself?

She had watched how carefully Cheyney had dressed so as to look absolutely stunning. Her fur and leather jacket over a long tweed skirt that covered the tops of her suede and leather boots, all her hair tucked under a sable cossack hat, she looked every inch the successful art-dealer. But to them? Cheyney had seen at least a dozen people she had known. Most had cut her, a few greeted her coldly. Reha Pace had been more curt than rude. Not at all the way she had been with a five-million-dollar cheque in her hand the last time Cheyney had seen her. But then, thought Cheyney, Acton had been alive.

The swing-doors flew open. In came Marion Tree, David Rosewarne's assistant. Behind her a very subdued, neatly dressed, smoothly clean but shuffling Barry Sole. Then the scrubbed, kindly lawyer from New England, David Rosewarne. They all took their seats at the table to the right of the plaintiff.

A side door in the courtroom opened, an officer of the court stood aside. The jury filed in and took their seats. Ten minutes elapsed before the judge entered and order was called in the courtroom. The bailiff called out, 'All rise. All persons having business before the Supreme Court of the State of New York come forward and be heard. The case of Finn, Head and Elizabeth Lacey Foundation for Contemporary Fine Arts versus Barry Sole.'

David Rosewarne rose from his chair. 'Your honour, ladies and gentlemen of the jury, my client is not guilty of fraud. Yes, he had an intent. It was to make himself into a successful painter. He did so. By his art, and by public acclaim.

'For ten years the public supported Barry Sole. They were free to reject his work, but they chose to support him. He has stated any number of times that "One element of my art is to use everything that comes before me, no matter what it is, or who brings it to me". These are, in fact, Mr Sole's own words. Why then did the art world accept him? Why do they turn their backs on him now? Why do they all cry fraud, after using him up?

'He is in this courtroom today because he is their scapegoat. He was their escape-goat, their way out of a bleak period in the American art market when the art world needed a fresh new brush. Barry Sole and the images he painted served them well. Until now. And what I see here is that once more they are using him as their escape-goat. This time, to supply an exit from a burnt-out movement called Pop Art. Both times, Barry Sole has been used as a catalyst in the art world. Used because he has the gift of making things happen.'

Cheyney was riveted by David's summation. It put the knife into the art mafia.

'Barry Sole never misrepresented his art. He did not claim it was great art, he never suggested that it was anything other than what it appeared to be. I would like to point out here that the definition of fraud is the wilful untrue representation of an existing fact with the intention that the other party rely on it to his detriment. But it must be proved. That fact has not been proved in this courtroom.'

People began to whisper among themselves. Della leaned towards Cheyney. 'David's fantastic. I can't believe the way he has turned this thing around to make Barry look the innocent victim.' Cheyney saw some well-known art faces begin to sweat. Larry and Tina Finn, conspicuously sixties-trendy, were haggling among themselves. Larry was also trying to slip a note to Judd Whyatt. The judge banged his gavel. The courtroom was silenced except for David Rosewarne. He continued.

'I think it was best summed up by the Abstract Expressionist painter, Simon North, in this very courtroom, when that most eloquent man made the point that painters paint what they have to say, and the public has a choice to understand or not. To buy it or not.

'I will now let my case rest before you, only leaving you with the one perception that I feel is relevant here – that, if a crime has been perpetrated, it is upon my client, in this case being even allowed to come into the courtroom. Thank you, the defence rests.' David Rosewarne sat down.

Half the court broke out in applause. The other half looked very solemn. Did they think they had lost their case? And if so, which one, the financial, moral or artistic? The judge looked impressed and Barry Sole looked confused. Judd Whyatt stood up and addressed the court with his summation.

'Your honour, ladies and gentlemen of the jury. I will be brief and to the point. The case that I plead before you is not a very complicated one. In fact, it leaves my request for a conviction of guilt hinging on one fact and one word. Intent. Every thing that Mr Sole has spoken in this courtroom can be judged in the light of that one word, intent. In short, intent is at the heart of this case.

'Mr Sole is *guilty* by the fact that he intended to use anything and anyone in a number of fraudulent ways to make of himself a successful painter. He has admitted before this court – and I quote – "All I wanted to do was to be a successful painter, just like any number of other hungry painters before me." But what he has failed to admit is that he has sold works of art that he knew in his own mind to be worthless. And sold them for high prices. That is the fraud.

'If justice is to be done today in this courtroom, you have only to find Barry Sole guilty as charged. There can be no other verdict. I rest my case, and thank you for your attention.'

Whyatt sat down in his chair. Silence fell heavily over the courtroom.

Barry Sole and David Rosewarne were notably disturbed by the summation. Sole was more the colour of uncooked pastry than his usual pale self. He was getting to look more like Andy Warhol every day. Larry Finn was flushed almost purple. A kind of anger seemed to be lurking in the lower half of his face. The jowls, lips and chin had a set to them. The jury was impassive.

The courtroom was abuzz. Journalists were still frantically scribbling notes. Several people took advantage of the commotion in the courtroom to leave, Cheyney among them. She told Della she had had enough, and would meet her at home.

When Judd Whyatt left the court, he found no Cheyney Fox. He was annoyed, and snappily asked Della to make sure Cheyney was at his office the following evening at six.

The following day the court re-convened and Judge Whitfield charged the jury, and retired to his chambers.

The verdict made the TV news-casts and all the evening newspapers. Two-inch, heavy-type headlines:

FRAUD CASE : NOTHING FISHY ABOUT SOLE

BARRY SOLE 'HERO FOR ART'

But the headline that covered the entire front page of a New York tabloid was the one with letters four inches high. The one with which Barry Sole could flatter himself for life:

BARRY SOLE POP ARTIST ANOTHER AMERICAN DREAM

There was no man happier in the world that evening than Barry Sole. He loved every word, every letter of every word. His wingless imagination got lift-off. He saw the black ink slip into a dark purple and then a blood red. Then the red dissolved into letters of ink as yellow and hot as the core of a burning sun. The words changed, shifted, and the letters altered shape. They were four inches wide and one inch high. They began to spin around and around on themselves, tiger-stripes chasing their tail. They all melted into a puddle. Slowly they blossomed into an oversized yellow plastic chrysanthemum. The centre petals opened out with a blood-curdling, ear-splitting roar and then changed into the Metro Goldwyn lion.

Chapter 25

Cheyney crossed town from Second to Fifth Avenue walking on Thirty-Fourth Street. It was cold. A biting wind sliced through canyon-like walls. Less than two weeks before Christmas the city was all dressed up for the arrival of Santa Claus, and anyone else in the world who was in the business of buying or selling or giving. Cheyney's intention was ambitious. Her plan was to window-shop up Fifth Avenue to Fifty-Seventh Street, meet Della at the Russian Tea Room for lunch, and then do the Fifty-Seventh Street galleries. Last stop, Rockefeller Center and Judd Whyatt's office.

Della was stunned when Cheyney revealed over breakfast her plan for the day. Surprised and thrilled. After the cool reception Cheyney had had from some of the art people who had known her in her gallery days, Della feared she would turn her back on New York and flee.

It was a perfect day – if you didn't mind the cool wind coming off the East River – for what Della called 'the Christmas walk'. The beginning of the week, crowds not too bad, every window at a peak of decorative imagination, each out-shining the other in Christmas fantasies. A good day, too, to view exhibitions.

Cheyney walked along the Thirty-Fourth Street side of B. Altman's department store. The windows were sensational: all Austrian castles and fairy-tale figures in the snow, glitter and subdued colours; icy blues and frosty pinks and pearly mauves. In the winter-wonderland stood magnificent articulated three-foot-high dolls: Cinderella and her Prince, pumpkin coaches and ugly sisters, gleaming Hansels and Gretels. The Old Woman in her shoe, Beauty and her amorous Beast . . . Music-box tinklings from hidden speakers. Cheyney felt like a child, wanted to clap her hands with joy, unable to check the smile spreading across her face. The crowds in front of the window were, even at that time of the morning, three-deep.

She rounded the corner. Her first step on to Fifth Avenue for eight years. A street teeming with people dressed in furs and winter woollens, weighed down by multiple shopping bags and packages, struggling against that bone-gnawing wind. The doors of Altman's swung constantly in the slipstream of shoppers. Bursts of welcoming warmth escaping every time

221

the door opened tempted even Cheyney to enter. Santa Clauses, in over
the top woolly white beards, were bellowing jolly 'Ho, ho, ho's' on every
corner, and stamping their feet to keep warm, ringing their bells for the
Christmas poor and needy. 'Rudolf the Red-Nosed Reindeer' out blared
Bing's 'White Christmas' and Como's 'Winter Wonderland'. Salvation
Army bands, blind violinists and young buskers took their chances on the
wave of yuletide noise.

For as far as she could see, it was a never ending stream of the same thing
on both sides of the street. A Christmas wonderland, a Christmas circus. If
there is such a thing as a serious shopper, it was here setting its face against
the tide of canned music, commercial merriment, and just plain com-
merce. A losing battle. Everywhere she looked, strained faces broke into a
smile. Someone found time to open a handbag or reach into his pocket to
toss something into Santa's black iron pots swinging on a tripod. New
York and its Fifth Avenue Christmas: infectious as an epidemic. Dollars
taken and given with a smile. Santa with no claws.

Cheyney laughed, just threw her head back and laughed, thinking, Oh,
Fifth Avenue, how I've missed you. It's good to be back. She allowed
herself a twinge of self-pity that she would not have Grant on her arm to
share this walk with. That they would not spend this Christmas together.
And how long would it be before she was to feel his heat caressing her
womb, the delicious taste of him in her mouth? Dizzy with desire she
laughed once again, this time at herself for having carnal thoughts in the
middle of Fifth Avenue. She dropped them. It had been sublime being
with him, and there had been love and she had no intention of spoiling
that, even if the price of having it was always to let him go. Miraculously,
she was happy with or without him on her arm.

She started her slow window-walk up the Avenue, criss-crossing the
street for the more spectacular of the windows. Lord and Taylor's, a dream
of silver gauze and ribbon, silver everything: she stood there for five minutes. Saks Fifth Avenue, not to be outdone, was all shimmering gold
displays of chic. Could there be anywhere in the world a Christmas tree
more spectacular than Rockefeller Center's? Aglitter with luminous
Christmas balls swinging in the wind. St Patrick's Cathedral, adapted
French Gothic in unyielding granite with flying buttresses and sky-high
twin towers, a richly carved counterfoil to the Rockefeller Center across
the street: an oasis of conservativism shrouded in green spruce and red
ribbon. She almost went in. Best and Company . . . she stood against the
wall where she had stood in a rainstorm years ago, just before she was all
but knocked down by Grant Madigan. The memory drew from her an
inward smile. She resumed her walk.

Mark Cross grudgingly dressed in red. Tiffany's windows were jewels themselves, the diamonds displayed like hunks of stars. Bonwit Teller's and she felt she had come home. She wondered if they still had a B. Wragge department in Ladies Sports. Bendel's all-white window displays that glittered, Bergdorf's all black, with showers of silver snow-flakes. She thought about long white kid-gloves with pearl buttons, and evening dresses and lovely hats and handbags and perfume. It was an adult's Disneyland, a window on all that was wonderful. It triggered memories of the good times without quite erasing those terrible years when she couldn't bring herself to walk up the Avenue. Dimmed them, yes. But still not enough to induce Cheyney to penetrate any of those gaudy temples for a Christmas shopping-spree.

Lunch at the Russian Tea Room had not changed. Maybe it was more like a dining-club than before. Everyone knowing everyone else, or want-ing to. Diners table-hopped, drumming up 'good relations' with a not-too-discreet 'do a little business?' attitude. In between, conspicuous consumption.

Della and Cheyney parted on the corner of Fifty-Seventh Street and Fifth Avenue, Della going downtown, Cheyney going cross-town. Her first stop was the Sidney Janis Gallery. On entering the exhibition rooms, a strange thing happened to her. It was something like *déjà vu*. Her bad times in the art world faded, as if they had never existed at all. She had that same enthusiasm, felt the familiar excitement, enjoyed that same feeling of exhilaration she had experienced at every exhibition of worthwhile paint-ings. She visited four other exhibitions in the building. As she descended in the elevator, the other gallery experiences of the past crept up on her. None more vivid than that of the first exhibition of De Kooning's 'Women'.

Cheyney spent three hours in some of the city's finest art galleries. During that time, not one dealer had came forward to speak to her. Not even a dealer's assistant. The occasional nod from one or two, but that was all. They had forgotten her and her failure, the gossip, the rumours and the lies. Either that or they were practising that well-known New York indifference. She simply didn't exist for them. Was she offended? Not in the least. She just saw how foolish she had been for far too long. She could have returned sooner. It had been crushing guilt and a shattered ego that kept her away, not the art world. That realisation was a hard pill to swallow.

Cheyney arrived at Judd Whyatt's office on time. She was impressed by the sophisticated, bookish elegance of the penthouse suite of rooms at the top of Rockefeller Center. He did not keep her waiting, she was shown into his office immediately on her arrival.

At their first meeting at Acton Pace's house on the dunes, Whyatt had appeared attractive, and extremely competent. His had been a calming influence. His mind simply snapped shut against anything irrelevant to the deal. Impressive. Any other lawyer might have dragged his feet, turned it into a long-drawn-out, complex, emotional haggle. But although his many attributes registered with Cheyney, she had been completely absorbed in Acton, his paintings, and the buying of a Pace collection. She had been surprised to receive Judd's letter asking her to please call him on a further matter to do with Acton Pace and his paintings.

It hurt to talk to anyone of Acton so soon after his death: the paint still so colourfully alive, the artist simply extinguished. So she had postponed the call until she was in New York, and even until Grant had left for the wars. She had felt no urgency. Whyatt's letter had been more than a month old by the time she had received it.

Until she entered his offices, she had not given much thought to Judd Whyatt. Here he was, though, sitting with his back to a glass wall and french doors that led out on to a balcony planted with Japanese pines, hemlocks and cypresses in large wooden tubs of wood and bronze, among old weather-worn bamboo chairs and tables. This was where he sat on calm days to read his briefs. It was like seeing the man for the first time.

She stood before him, looking through the window, past the balcony of trees bending to the wind, and down onto the cityscape of steel-and-glass skyscrapers. 'What a wonderful place to work,' she said as she shook his hand.

'Isn't it? Please, take a seat.'

On top of the long Chinese-Chippendale table he used as a desk was an imposing Arab box of inlaid ivory and silver. It had drawers of various sizes, in which Judd kept all his personal papers, pens, pencils. The remainder of the huge highly polished, mahogany surface was neatly arranged with stacks of his current work papers.

He saw that she was riveted by the Arab box. 'Lovely, isn't it? A gift from a client, an Arab prince whom I was able to oblige.'

'Yes, I can see you like beautiful things. Mind if I ask why you took on the unbeautiful Barry Sole case for the prosecution? You must have known he would be acquitted.'

'No, I didn't know that. I only assumed he would be. And fought against it the best way I could. I doubt that any other lawyer could have mounted a better case against Barry Sole.'

'Oh, I wasn't thinking anything like that. Just that you had an impossible case to win. If you had, it would have been such a blow to every creative artist.'

Suddenly Cheyney looked ill-at-ease. 'Oh, dear, it's very tactless of me to go on about it like this. Losing, after all you have put into the case, cannot be easy to swallow. I know that from my own experience. I feel such a fool.'

'No need,' he said, sliding gracefully off the end of the desk. Walking between a pair of oval-backed French cane-armchairs with black patent-leather cushions on the seats, part of a crescent of four around his desk, he proceeded to a round, pedestal table. He picked up a folder and brought it back to his desk. He gave Cheyney a conciliatory smile.

'Oh, come now. No need to feel uncomfortable. I have lost cases before, you know. Not many, granted. If it will make you feel easier, I will tell you that I didn't want to take this one on. I did so only because of an obligation to two of my clients. As you may know, we are a firm of international lawyers. Corporate law specialists. We are also the lawyers for several individuals, major stockholders and owners of some of those corporations and companies we represent.

'Two of our clients, men who spend not millions but tens of millions of dollars funding museums of contemporary art in this country, determined that the case should be settled in a court of law. They wanted our firm involved. A folly they could not be talked out of.'

'Your clients can't be too unhappy, even if they have lost. The trial was lengthy. It may have created a great deal of dissension among the various people involved in art. For better or worse, it'll have shown the seamier side of art in big business. But it has probably quadrupled the value of your clients' collections.'

Judd Whyatt was impressed. She was no slouch, understanding that prices were about to go through the roof for all contemporary art. Kurt Walbrook definitely had taste, spotting her potential and grasping it with both hands.

'Well, if it hasn't, it will.'

Now that he had agreed, Cheyney felt better. She smiled at Judd and said, 'So you've lost your battle and your war, but still come out the victor?'

He was even more impressed. 'Yes,' he answered, 'I suppose you could say that. You make it sound as if we should celebrate. How about a glass of champagne?'

'What will we be celebrating?'

'Your good fortune.'

He flicked a switch on his intercom to ask his secretary to bring in a chilled bottle of Roederer Cristal and two champagne glasses. He flicked the system off, and added, '"Fortune" being the operative word.'

'Mr Whyatt, what is this all about? I've no idea what you're hinting at.'

'Acton Pace chose three paintings for you and had them placed in a repository in Boston. They were to be given to you upon his death. A legacy, so to speak, because you would not accept them while you were acting on behalf of someone else.'

A knock on the door. He rose to open it. Passing Cheyney, he placed a comforting hand on her shoulder and said, 'The wine has come at just the right moment. You look like you could use a drink. Compose yourself. It's a legacy, not a writ.'

Life is an education. It teaches you there is no such thing as a free lunch. Twenty-five years into it, you no longer expect unsolicited good fortune. And when your friends die, the good they brought you is almost blown away with the funeral ashes. So the first few legacies come as a shock. Cheyney had received gifts before, but not like this, from beyond the grave, and on such a scale. The mysterious part of himself left by Acton Pace in those paintings was also a kind of blank cheque for her. His notorious suicide made each painting a well-publicised relic. A commodity. He had created her market for her by the manner of his going. This was a strange, extreme extension of friendship.

It all seemed like some extravagant dream: that she should have, at this time in her life, a small nest-egg of hard cash and three Acton Pace paintings. *En plus* love and sexual fulfilment with Grant Madigan and what she sensed was to be a *grande amour*. She placed her hands over her eyes and closed them.

Compose yourself, she thought. Instead, she heard a faint pop. The champagne cork. Removing her hands, she opened her eyes to see Judd Whyatt pouring the wine. He walked across the room to her, and she saw him in the context of his room: moneyed, like the Matisse, the Gauguin, the Roualt, hanging on the dark, rich wood-panelling. How could he possibly understand what a trauma it was for her to have so much and so fast, after so little for so long?

He drew a chair closer to her and sat down. Touching the rim of his crystal champagne flute to hers, he said, 'They say one swallow doesn't make a summer but with champagne the first swallow is always the best. To your good fortune, Cheyney Fox. May this be only the beginning.'

The vintage Roederer Cristal was only that little over-chilled, but Cheyney was grateful for it. The cold seemed to snap her to greater attention. It felt so good in her mouth, and she drank to quench a thirst she had not realised she had. The wine instilled an immediate sense of well-being. She relaxed.

'That's better, you went quite white. If that's what good news does to you, I hope I am never a bearer of bad.'

Cheyney touched her forehead and then her cheek with the back of her hand. 'I'm all right now. It just took me by surprise. I never dreamed I would ever have an Acton Pace. Now I have three.'

'Quite a little trinity, in fact,' he said as he rose from his chair to refill their glasses, returning to sit behind the desk. Opening the folder, he looked across his desk at Cheyney and said, 'Brace yourself, Cheyney Fox. The three paintings: one, title "Mystic Moon", painted in 1958, size, four feet by five feet.' Judd Whyatt then slapped a large coloured photograph of the painting smartly on the polished surface of his desk in front of Cheyney. Number two was 'Homeward Bound', six feet by nine feet. Another coloured photograph was placed neatly in line with the first. The third painting, done in 1965, 'Moon, Mist and Sand', seven by nine. Whyatt placed a third photograph into her hands.

Cheyney drank from her glass and remained silent for some moments. That gave Judd a chance to study this unusual woman. He sensed that there was a bond between them, forged by Acton Pace, that would always remain strong. Finally, she spoke.

'I know those paintings well. We spent the night before you arrived at Acton's studio together, going through his work. Looking, admiring, being transported by it. Assessing each painting. We set those three aside, agreeing that for us they were in the top thirty of his best work. There is not a museum in the world that, if it had the funds, would not buy them. And he has left them to me . . .

'Mr Whyatt, you simply cannot imagine what this means to me. They are an enormous responsibility. I could live with those three paintings and nothing else for the rest of my life. They are a world of beauty and love and hate, and birth and death and rebirth, on three canvases. I find it hard to believe that Reha will let me have them.'

'Oh, I can assure you she will. Acton has seen to that. They are legally yours. There actually isn't anything she can do about it.'

'The insurance alone is going to put me back in the bankruptcy court.'

'That's being just a little negative about a very generous gift, don't you think?'

'Well, of course it is,' answered Cheyney, more annoyed with herself than with the lawyer for pointing it out. 'I make no apologies for being slightly overwhelmed by Acton's magnanimous gesture. He would have understood, where you can't possibly. Unless you know that my life has felt like climbing Everest barefoot these last ten years. Now, suddenly, I'm well equipped to go for the summit.'

'Then what you're saying is that you're overjoyed, of course, but don't know it yet?'

'Yes, something like that,' she answered, already feeling more at ease.

'Good, because, Miss Fox, Acton Pace must have wanted to make certain you have every chance of conquering your mountain. He left you the paintings and more. The paintings he left you are yours to do with as you like. No strings attached, so to speak, and Reha can do nothing about it. And frankly, I don't think she will even try. Acton Pace left you something else. I have here a document, legal and binding, because signed by him and witnessed by Reha Pace and myself. You have the right each year to buy one painting of his from his estate. Any painting of your choice, at the price of one hundred thousand dollars a painting, for the next twelve years.'

'But that's mad. Why would he have done that? He might just as well have left me millions of dollars. Reha will never stand for that.'

'Well, she will for a few years, but, I have no doubt, in time she'll try to find a way round that agreement. She hasn't much chance of doing it. He was of sound mind when he made it, though it's a recipe for strife. I didn't know the man. I met him, what, for a few hours? Spent fifteen minutes with him alone. He was a great artist, a remarkably kind and loving yet very introverted man. Not a happy soul, at least not for many years, I'm guessing. A man who, I think, felt that he had been manipulated and abused enough by people who wanted control of his paintings. If he hadn't wanted you to have these gifts, he would not have gone to the lengths he did to make sure they would be yours.

'May I suggest to you that you set a precedent about the purchasing of these twelve paintings? Put it into a legal document that we can send over to the Pace attorneys. A document that states you have accepted your legacy, and that you intend to exercise your right to purchase a painting a year for the next twelve years. That, to make it easier for all concerned, you will choose that painting on a specific date, the same date every year. Establish it as an annual event, so the Pace estate can swallow the pill once, and then deal with it as a matter of form.'

'That's all very well, Mr Whyatt. But you are assuming I will always have a hundred thousand dollars on hand to buy a painting.'

'Well, of course you will! You buy your first one, and if you have to, or want to, you sell it. Invest the proceeds from the sale in safe bonds, and you have enough money, and more, to buy all the others. Unless of course you have, or can raise, the money for the first purchase. If that's the case, then you can keep your first acquisition, and sell it when and if you need money to buy the second, and carry on like that.'

'Of course, I'm still thinking in pennies. But, Mr Whyatt, to earn enough to spend a hundred thousand dollars a year, every year – that's something I doubt I can handle. It's a great deal of money. But I think I understand why Acton has done this, in just this way.' Cheyney stood up. She began pacing back and forth in front of Judd Whyatt. 'He wanted me to become an art-dealer again. But only if that's what I wanted to do. So he has funded me with his paintings. Of course I can earn enough to buy a painting a year. Just dealing in his work alone, I could do that. And that doesn't necessarily mean selling his paintings. As you can see, Acton could be very shrewd when he chose to be. He knew I could use my collection of Pace paintings as bait to deal in other works of art if I chose to. How generous and clever he has been! He must have loved me very much, believed in me beyond my failures. And of course he knew that I would have earned a large chunk of money from the commission I would receive for putting together the deal for his collection. That I already had the money to buy the first painting.'

'By releasing the paintings to you at the rate of one a year, Acton Pace has set you up for life. And protected you from being wiped out by any business catastrophe. The guy was one artist who knew what he was doing.'

Cheyney sat down once again in her chair opposite Whyatt. He filled their glasses yet again. They drank in silence. After some minutes, he broke the silence.

'I have no idea about your finances, but I do know this – you are a very wealthy woman. Now, if the firm can be of any further service to you, let me know. Or I can pass these documents over to your own attorney.'

'Mr Whyatt, I have been handed a great legacy, and I don't intend to blow it. It meant too much to Acton when he gave it to me, and it means everything to me to have it. Not just the wealth, but the paintings themselves and the manner in which the gift was given. I'm going to have to think hard what I want to do about it. Luckily, I have all the time in the world to think things through.

'This much I can decide. I would like to ask you to act as my representative in all legal dealings concerning my Acton Pace legacy. I have about two hundred thousand dollars. A hundred we will spend immediately on the purchase of my first Acton Pace painting. As you know, I live in Athens. That means under a military regime. So I will not take my paintings to Greece. Too dangerous. For the moment, we'll move them from Boston to a strongroom I'll have to rent at Manhattan Storage. I will invest the hundred thousand dollars I have left in something absolutely safe, and live off the interest and what I can earn for the next year. That will give me enough money to buy the second painting, and to decide what I want to do with my life and my art collection. And that's all I can think about for the moment. So . . . will you handle my affairs in this matter, since you are already involved?'

'Normally yours is not the sort of work this firm handles. But, yes, I will, because I do have what has come to be an unusual personal involvement in all this. I originally came to the Acton Pace matter, as you already know, only to accommodate your client.'

'Kurt Walbrook. Yes, I know who the mystery client is.'

'Oh, good. That involvement extended to my helping Pace to arrange these matters for you. I suppose that it deepened as a result of going to visit him once more after my initial visit when you were there. You see, it was me who cut him down from his studio rafters. I would like to see that everything he wanted me to do for him comes to fruition. If I can help I am at your service.'

One look at Cheyney and he realised she had not known the gory details. He had assumed that she knew because, somehow, despite all the influence he had used to keep the true facts from the press, someone had leaked the story in all its gory details, and it had made nearly every newspaper. It had to have been one of the two women, either the dead man's wife or his dealer. They had both been very angry with Acton Pace for taking his life and even more for what he had done with his paintings in those two weeks before his death. No, it was certainly – he assured Cheyney, after explaining to her what had happened that day – a woman's revenge.

Chapter 26

'I don't know why we're making this ride to the airport. It's six days before Christmas. Why can't you stay for the holidays? I hate to see you go.'

'Athens is my home now, Della, and I want to be there for Christmas.'

'But surely that's all changed now, Cheyney? You can afford to move back to New York.'

'Not yet I can't. And I don't know that I ever will return. Try to understand – I really feel like I'm going home. Bad as it is with those putrid colonels; bad as it can be at times being a foreigner living in Greece; for the time being, it's my home, and will be until I feel the time has come for me to move on. And there are other reasons why I must return. I have work commitments and friends who are going through hard times: I can't drop them just because my luck has changed. Also, I'm committed to send several shipments to the museum. I've got orders to fill for my boutique-clients. I have to think out the art-scene in New York and what I want to do about that. Once I have fulfilled my obligations, and figured out how and where I want to live, then I'll make a move.'

'Oh, Cheyney, this is the place for you.'

'Maybe so, but not now.

'And what about your Acton Pace paintings? Aren't they something to come home to? And your relationship with Grant Madigan? New York is where he will be when his work is completed. Don't you want to be with him?'

'Using Grant is a cheap shot, Della.'

'I know, but I'm getting desperate for reasons to keep you in the States. You know how red, white and blue I can be. I hate to see you going all European on me.'

Cheyney put her arm around her faithful old friend. Trying to defuse Della's sentimentality, she said, 'I don't, for the moment, have a home of my own where I can bring my Acton paintings. And I've made up my mind not to leave them in the Manhattan Storage. Acton didn't paint them for that, not for private avarice, not just to blush unseen. He painted them to be looked at, admired. Maybe to raise consciousness. Hell, to give pleasure! He painted them to be experienced. His paintings were created

231

to live with people. So after the holidays, I will be putting my working life in order. And that includes picking the museums I am willing to loan them to for a one-year showing. After that, another museum, unless I am settled enough to have a place for them to be with me.

'Now, please, no more about my leaving. Change your mind and come to Athens for Christmas.'

Only when the plane circled the city did Cheyney feel relaxed. Her body even went nicely limp on her. She wasn't humping the world around on her shoulders any more. She had not felt so happy and at ease since Grant Madigan had kissed her goodbye before he stepped into the airforce cargo-plane, with his crew and all their equipment, bound for Vietnam.

She had borne the pressure well, and only realised at touchdown on the Athens runway how great a strain it had been. The Barry Sole trial, seeing all the people from the art-world again after such a long absence, New York itself all dressed up for Christmas. Doing the galleries. And then the legacy, and its aftermath. Establishing her right to buy the Paces, and then making her first buy. All that seemed to vanish into the sun playing on the water, the white houses spread out, 'the biggest village in Greece'. The thought made Cheyney smile. She even hugged herself, so happy was she to be back.

The wheels bumped on the tarmac, and the plane shot forward at what Cheyney always felt was too great a speed. She followed her own routine for landing at Athens airport: closed her eyes and hoped that they wouldn't over-shoot. For once she was not annoyed at the airport drama. She smiled at everyone and seemed determined to say hello to any airport attendant who looked the least bit familiar. She even laughed at the Athens taxi-driver sounding his horn: short, sharp blasts every five seconds. He kept calling her 'Kukla mou', my doll, punctuating his complaints about the traffic, the weather and radio-static, which he tried controlling with a fist. The weather was actually good, sunny and warm enough to sit outside at a street café. There was hardly any traffic, which was extraordinary. When Cheyney pointed that out to him, he banged the radio in protest and reverted to moaning about the lack of tourism and the cost of living, now laying on the sultry, 'what you need is a Greek lover' look. Even that didn't bother her. She told him she had one: the Minister of Transport. The possibility made him quiet and respectful the remainder of her ride into Athens.

The temptation to linger near the Acropolis was resisted. But not that of stopping at Zonar's. She had a Greek coffee and greeted several friends. At the Byzantium in Kolonaki Square, another coffee, more friends, and a promise given to return later in the day to tell them about New York.

On the short ride from there to her apartment, she mulled over life's little labyrinths. How your circumstances can fluctuate, and yet your life not change, unless you choose to change it yourself.

232

Only days now before Christmas. Not a word from Grant. She was, frankly, not so much disappointed as surprised.

It was the early hours of the morning before she returned from a night out with the Greek *pareia*. In bed, too tired to sleep Cheyney thought about the two men in her life. Her heart ached for Grant Madigan, a resurgence of that carnal passion that seemed to bind them together despite their fear of the power they might wield over each other's lives because of it. Her very soul ached for him. That did not diminish her desire to be caressed and made love to by Kurt Walbrook. She fell asleep, yearning for his lips and his tongue to be upon her, to feel that slow steady coupling that had given her such endless sexual satisfaction.

His telephone call took her by surprise. No less the sensation of delight she felt on hearing his voice.

'I would like to be with you for Christmas and New Year, but that's impossible. I have other commitments. I would be happy to have you with me, but I don't think you would have a good time. And so, what can we do?'

'Wish each other a merry Christmas?'

'Oh, I don't think that's enough. Wouldn't you like to see me, be with me? At the very least for us to be in each other's arms to kiss each other for Christmas, Sheyney?'

That voice, that mesmerising sensual voice, the way it whispered and spoke out clearly at the same time. It provoked shivers of excitement. Cheyney was unaware of what she was doing. She opened her blouse and touched a naked breast, caressed a nipple. She unashamedly closed her eyes and felt her breathing quicken as warmth coursed through her body. Against her will, she was charmed by his voice, seduced by the words. She had to control her voice when she answered, 'As a matter of fact, I find I would, very much.'

'Good. Today, tomorrow . . . are you free?'

'I can be. Where are you?'

'In Paris. Would you like to come to Paris?'

'Oh, Kurt, I don't think I could bear to get on a plane right now. So much has happened since last we met. I've only just come from New York, and when we meet I have something to tell you about that. And there's Zazou, I simply can't leave her again. But, no, I don't think I can come to Paris.'

'Then I must come to Athens.'

'Oh, would you?'

'Ah, I like the enthusiasm in your voice. Of course I will. And I will arrive like Santa Claus, laden with presents. But I shall only be able to stay for a short time. I will have to leave you in time to be in Austria for Christmas Eve.'

'Then when shall it be – today or tomorrow?' she asked, elated at the prospect of seeing him.

'Today *and* tomorrow. I will be there as soon as I possibly can. Do nothing, buy nothing. I will bring our entire Christmas with me.'

'Am I at least allowed to offer you a gift?'

'I thought you had, when you said we could be together for an early Christmas. I love you, Sheyney Fox, and I will see you in a few hours.'

For some time after she had spoken to Kurt, Cheyney sat quietly thinking about him and the effect he had upon her. Whenever they talked on the telephone, she felt as if she were in a half-dazed state. And most certainly on that day they had spent together. It was as if he honed all the rough edges off her life. He affected her like a powerful morphine: the pain instantly dulled, herself wafted away to some earthly paradise. Cheyney felt she could become addicted to Kurt Walbrook. She wondered what it was going to be like to be with him, now that each knew who the other was.

The day he had picked her up at Zonar's had been very exciting. Their sex had been mysterious and thrilling – because they had been no-name strangers to each other? All that was changed now. But his voice hadn't changed nor had that magnetic charm. She looked at her watch. She had no more time to waste anticipating something she would know about in a few hours' time. There were things to be done before his arrival.

Cheyney knew only a fraction of Kurt's involvement with her since the time he had first seen her and fallen in love with her. But it was enough for her to appreciate that he cared deeply for her, and had helped her greatly from the background of her life. Although she had no facts, she sensed that she owed him a great debt. He had helped her to become whole again. If he could go on a shopping-spree for her in Paris, she could do the same in Athens.

She had not spent years in Greece without locating the best private collections of arts and artefacts in the country and identifying their owners. Antiquities that could be legally exported, and those that could not be. Her mind began to roam, eliminating most of the things she knew were for sale. She narrowed it down to three, and then one. A piece she had always coveted for herself: a life-sized Etruscan head of a youth, a boy so beautiful that it made one want to weep, in a yellowing, white marble. Fifth-century work. Once determined to buy it for Kurt, Cheyney made several phone calls. Two hours later, she sat in her flat surveying the sculptured head, resting in the open, blue-velvet-lined travel-box the collector had made for it. The export-licence lay on the table next to the box.

The perfect gift for Kurt Walbrook. And she half-luxuriated in the spectacle of having spent so much. Ten thousand dollars on a gift for a man! There was no way she could explain even to herself the mad extravagance of the outlay. Not just the impulse to buy something superb for a man of Kurt's discrimination, but a real *desire* to do so. She closed the lid and wrapped the pig-skin box in a not very pretty Christmas paper, all that she could find. She clinched it with a much prettier bow of wide red and white candy-striped satin. No easy task, since the box was heavy and cumbersome to enfold. She had spent the money she had allotted for up-grading the furnishings in her Athens flat. Well, that would now have to wait. The mattress on the floor for another year? She would have to just live with that. And so would Kurt for the next two days, or check them both into a hotel. Well, a man has to take a girl as he finds her. Cheyney discovered in herself a case of the jitters. Slight, but unmistakable. Her slight trepidation had hardly faded when she heard his voice over the intercom.

She felt the rush of excitement women feel for their lovers. She waited for what seemed a lifetime for his appearance from the little elevator that rose through the floors to deposit him in front of her door. Whatever her anxieties, they vanished the moment she saw him step out. A Christmas wreath over one arm. He laid it on the hall table outside her door. Then, tilting her chin towards him, he kissed her on the lips.

'Merry Christmas, my love. You declined to come to Paris, and so I have brought Paris to you. *Voilà*!' She heard the commotion of people trundling up the stairs long before they arrived, the distinctive timbre of French speech.

A chef, a butler, a maid, a designer, and two workmen with boxes stacked up to their noses, of all shapes and all sizes, wrapped in the most glorious Christmas papers and ribbons, and Christmas trees of pine, and what seemed like forests of fresh green spruce and holly and mistletoe. Cartons and boxes trooped past the couple as they stood in the entrance to Cheyney's apartment. Huffing and puffing from the climb, people managed big open smiles and greetings: '*Joyeux Noel*.' 'Oh, *mon dieu*, such a climb.' '*Chère Madame*, Merry Christmas. *C'est très romantique*, such a Christmas.'

Zazou added her barks, scampering between everyone's feet, until she spotted Kurt and leapt into his arms with yipes of joy. She licked and kissed his face, unaware of or ignoring, for the moment – impossible to tell which – the four-legged intruder Cheyney was holding. Kurt had to usher Cheyney back into the apartment. She hadn't moved, so surprised was she by it all.

'Kurt, I don't believe all this.'

'Well, my dear, you had better believe it. I've brought them all so we won't have to do a thing.'

Then he introduced them one at a time. Henri, to do the Christmas decorations; Jean Louis the chef. He whispered, after that introduction, 'I told you I hate the Greek cuisine. It doesn't suit my palate at all.' Mimi the maid: 'So you don't have to press a thing.' An English butler was introduced, and lastly various fetchers and carriers.

'First things first.' Kurt held Zazou high over his head in front of him. 'Romeo is his name, Zazou. He's two years old, of impeccable breeding, and loves the ladies. I expect you to play Juliet to his Romeo, and with no nonsense about it. It's about time you had a lover of your own.' Zazou let out a curdling howl, Romeo a commanding bark that silenced her. Good shock-tactics. She remained silent and docile when Kurt placed them both on the sofa, just long enough for Romeo and Zazou to sniff and lick each other's fur and affect canine love. Their future relationship resolved, they hopped off the sofa and chased each other round the apartment like unhouse-trained schoolkids.

'OK, I believe this, a Paris Christmas in Athens. But Zazou allowing another dog in the house? You should apply to be Secretary-General of the UN.'

'That's been suggested before. I'm taking over your home for forty-eight hours. Well, a few hours less than that. Tell me you're pleased, or I'll feel like an intruder.'

'Of course I'm pleased. A little overwhelmed, but really pleased that you should want to do all this for me.'

'Us,' he corrected.

'Us. Kurt, you're always surprising me.'

'This is the way it's going to be for us. Fun and excitement and surprises. Maybe not all the time, but certainly much of it. Now we have just one delicate matter. Your bed.'

'You mean my mattress,' feeling very foolish that she had not made it a priority to go out and get for it at least a box-spring.

'No, Cheyney, I mean the bed I have brought you from Paris, a Christmas gift, along with Paul Chabrey, the man with the skill to assemble and drape it for us. Tell me you're not angry, but frankly it was that or a hotel. And I knew you wanted to be in your home for Christmas. It's an attractive bed, and rare. A campaign bed large enough for two. Wrought iron, with a domed canopy and all its draperies. A travelling-bed that was used in the Napoleonic campaigns. You are not angry with me?'

'Angry? I'm thrilled!' was what she said. She did, however, marvel at the Napoleonic assurance with which he assumed she wanted to share her bed with him.

'Oh, good. If you don't like it, I will take it back with me tomorrow evening. I would not want to impose anything on you that you don't want. It's not my way. Not with furniture, at least. Now, enough. We must leave everyone to their jobs. So you and I, we will walk down to Zonar's and begin where we began before, over coffee and cakes. When we come home in a few hours – *voilà*, it will be Christmas.'

Romeo had captured Zazou's instincts, and the walk to Zonar's seemed a miracle to Cheyney. Zazou for once spared Greek ankles, and Cheyney didn't have to keep apologising for her spoilt dog. Greeks in general felt a proper contempt for pampered animals and their owners. She could not stop thinking 'He even mesmerises Zazou. A dog! How many times had she tried a dog with Zazou, and it had been a disaster! On the walk, Cheyney told Kurt about the Barry Sole trial. She made him laugh a great deal, and then she told him about her Acton Pace legacy. She knew his pleasure at her good fortune was genuine.

Of course he already knew about it. He knew everything about Cheyney, even Grant Madigan.

At Zonar's he was introduced to some of her friends. With little exertion he impressed them. Invitations to them both for the evening followed swiftly. Kurt was the first person she had met who could emphatically decline an invitation and yet step back from the *pareia* without an argument, excuses, or having them turn things around so they joined Cheyney and him. Instead they gracefully accepted his rejection. She had never managed to accomplish that, and rarely seen anyone else do it. It was a trivial enough thing, but it made her realise what a powerful presence Kurt Walbrook had. The natural authority he wielded over others. Though it was exciting, it was, too, a kind of charisma she found just a little bit sinister.

On their return home they stepped into a Christmas wonderland of pine trees draped in white fairy-lights, and shimmering silver balls hand-painted in sumptuous designs and colours. Red ribbon and Christmas carols. Dozens of presents wrapped in exotic papers and luscious bows were stacked under the trees. The aromas of a magnificent cuisine mingled with displays of fresh spring flowers, lilacs and tulips. It was already dark, and you could see through the windows on to the terrace that circled the apartment. Boughs of spruce and holly and mistletoe studded with more fairy-lights and draped in red ribbons and bows were wrapped around its banister. The city lights sparkled below and beyond like jewels.

Placed in the centre of the bedroom, the Napoleonic campaign bed: a skeleton frame of iron gracefully shaped to culminate in a cage-like dome, draped in transparent handkerchief linen, its curtains tied back at the slender turned posts with white suede thongs. It was made up with white linen sheets and pillow cases trimmed in cream-coloured lace. A blanket of chinchilla lay across the foot of the bed.'

They ate a regal dinner. Fresh *foie gras en croûte*, oysters, followed by fresh asparagus. Then the main course: roast goose, stuffed with chestnut, apples and sausage-meat. There was Christmas-pudding ice cream covered with meringue and baked in the oven, topped with brandy-flavoured whipped cream. With the Stilton and biscuits a vintage port was served. Everyone left with orders not to return until Kurt called them. Cheyney and he sat on the floor near the trees and opened Christmas presents. Cheyney was touched to see that he really did mean to share his Christmas with her. He had transported his gifts all the way to Athens to put under her tree, and open with her.

For Cheyney there were cases of wine: vintage Château Margaux, Montrachet, Pichon Lalande, a case of Dom Pérignon. Chocolates, and hampers of delicacies from Fauchon. St Laurent dresses and evening gowns, hats, gloves, handbags, A cashmere cape from Dior, a lynx coat from Revillon, diamond earrings from Van Cleef and Arpels. Even beautiful shoes and boots. Everything pretty and chic, feminine yet classically beautiful. All the things any woman would delight in receiving for Christmas.

She dived in and out of clothes and shoes, modelling for Kurt. She marvelled that everything fitted, not just about but perfectly. How could he have known the sizes? Lala, perhaps? Of course, he must have called Lala for her sizes.

Then it was time for his gift, the last present to be opened. They had to wade through hills of tissue-paper and opened boxes spilling out their contents, before they could reach the box which Cheyney had pushed far under the tree. He helped her to pull it out where he could open it. He looked terribly happy. When she gave it to him, she kissed him on the lips. He seemed reluctant to let her go. Then she said, 'Merry Christmas, Kurt. I don't know it all. I don't even want to know it all. The things that you have done for me that have helped me to get where we are now. But I know that it is much more than you will ever let me know, and I hope that this gift will be a way of saying thank you for that, and for all this, a Christmas I shall never forget.'

His response was unexpected. He took her in his arms and kissed her deeply, with an uncontrolled passion that set her aflame. Then he released her and opened his gift. He held the piece in his hands and admired it in silence. It was so remarkably fine an example of its kind that it threatened to make everything around them look like dross. He said, 'If I say any more than that it is superb, and that I am touched very deeply by your generosity, and that I thank you very much, then I will say too much. I would rather show you how I feel.'

With that he took her by the hand and led her to the bedroom. This time he chose not to lull her into a half-daze with his lovemaking, but to excite her lust with his erotic demands. He allowed his long-restrained appetite for her to take command of them both. They were imaginative sexual cravings, responses to erotic fantasies she had heard about but had hardly experienced before now. He hushed her fears of being subjugated totally to his sexual will with the mesmerising erotic lust reflected in his eyes, and his soft, honeyed voice that promised her sexual delights she would never have experienced, and his love forever.

She thought her heart would burst, it pounded so hard from that sweet combination of fear, anticipation, the thrill of the unknown, of being untried at the mercy of the god Eros who took them both over. He knew every inch of her skin, had kissed and licked and made love to it. He was a forceful lover whose thrusts had drawn from her copious orgasms they both revelled in. She swallowed his come on demand and had never known such sexual ambrosia until then. He watched her enjoyment of him, and sex, and he knew that he had always been right about Cheyney Fox. She could be taught to appreciate the wilder side of sex. His kind of sex, the forbidden sex he craved, *she* would crave. He wasted no time. He rolled her over in his arms and laid her on her front and lay on top of her, kissing the back of her neck, her shoulders, down the centre of her spine, while he tied her wrists to the bed posts. Then he caressed her bottom with his hands and kisses and raised her on to her knees. The scent of jasmine and roses enveloped her before she felt the oils caress her skin, his searching fingers seduce, the slow deflowering where no other man had ever been. He silenced her protests with kisses and erotic poems and long, slow deep thrusts until she was open and coming as he took her alternately first in one place and then another, again and again, until she was lost in licentious oblivion.

He promised her that was only their beginning and drew her into a web of new and exciting sex that triggered her own erotic fantasies. He had command of her as not even Grant Madigan had had her. And yet, when he left the following day, there was a fragment of Grant Madigan in her heart that Kurt Walbrook would never be able to remove. He called her from Austria on Christmas Day, and New Year's Day, and they settled down to loving each other.

Among her other calls on Christmas Day had been one from Saigon. Grant told her that things were much worse than he had been led to believe from the reports he had heard previously about the Vietnam War. That although he was there to do research on the war from the time the French had command of the country, he was being increasingly drawn into the present conflict. How good it felt to be a journalist in the field again! Yet this war was something he could not just research and run away from. That he felt, with his connections to the power-players in the conflict, he would have to do a few programmes on the immediate problems while at the same time working on his book and his series. And, all the while, she kept thinking, Grant, don't let me slip away into a life with Kurt

Walbrook. I don't want you to lose me. He said nothing to indicate that he loved her in anything like the way she loved him.

Cheyney would not suffer for this love of Grant Madigan. She had made up her mind about that when she saw him off to Vietnam. It was as much what passed between them during those two days together as his leaving for his wars that had decided her. He had been so angry about the deep carnal attachment he had with her. He would not let her force him into some sort of a love-commitment as a result of it. He obliged her to confront this: whatever he felt for Cheyney, it would always have to be a thing of the moment and nothing more. His call only reinforced her resolve. She would do nothing but what her own life – not any man's life, but Cheyney Fox's life – dictated. On Christmas night, at a party she raised a glass and silently toasted the two men she loved.

Chapter 27

It was a vintage year for Cheyney, 1969. She assembled a large collection of handicrafts from the Middle East and shipped them to the museum-shop in the States. She travelled to Syria, Lebanon, Egypt, Sudan, Ethiopia. She worked by day and played by night with friends made through Kurt. She felt the heart-beat of the countries she travelled to, learned about their political and economic problems in a world made ever more hectic by instant communication, where money and arms were the real heads of state. Where indigenous extreme-right factions feared westernising liberals and exercised their paranoia on anything politically left. Even more so if they were leaning towards Moscow. She listened, and learned, and began to understand what power-playing was all about. She made few judgments. Cheyney's view of the world was expanding, and her reward went far beyond job-satisfaction or monetary recompense. Making new and interesting friends, she was growing as a human being. Occasionally she thought of Grant Madigan and what she was missing by not being with him, that special kind of oneness with another human being. A corner of her heart was not happy.

She placed her four Acton Pace paintings in a travelling exhibition that went to the Fogg Museum in Boston, to the Carnegie Institute in Pittsburg, to the Chicago Art Institute. The show culminated at the Jewish Museum on Fifth Avenue in New York, where, six days a week, it was drawing lines of people that stretched around the block. She shocked the New York art-world without ever appearing in it. Especially Rowena Sicle, who had never seen the paintings, not been told that they existed, let alone that Cheyney Fox owned them. It was claimed that they were some of Acton Pace's finest works. Reha Pace, more angry than ever with Cheyney, now felt betrayed by both her dead husband and his friend. The Metropolitan, the Museum of Modern Art and Whitney Museum, all suffered institutional indignation that they had not been offered the collection for exhibition, that it had gone to a somewhat obscure smaller venue. Acton would have approved, she knew. Cheyney Fox suddenly found herself courted by the three big museums in the city, and dozens of others around the world.

She chose and bought her second painting from the Pace estate.

Both she and Kurt agreed that, if she were to deal for him on any works of art, it would only be fair to do so by dealing just as they had before through Roberto and Lala. That arrangement still worked for all concerned. She bought three items for him from private collections, one from Damascus, one from Montevideo, and another from Lisbon.

Kurt and she took several holidays together. A week in Rome and Venice with Roberto and Lala. They stayed in his palazzo. That was where she began really to see how he lived and worked, to sense his wealth and the power the Walbrook Collections and his curators wielded in the art world. They stayed with his friends in extravagant houses, rich in art treasures, in Rio, Caracas and Buenos Aires. Her favourite holiday with him was when they went alone to the Galapagos Islands and Patagonia. Together they selected an architect to design the building for Kurt's collection of Acton Pace paintings.

In 1969, Grant Madigan called Cheyney just once, from India. He spoke about his trip to China to interview Chou-En-lai. Now he was to see Mrs Gandhi. In July, the call came from Algeria. He was setting up base operations there for a few months. After that, he was returning to Vietnam. He was making a last attempt to have talks with Ho Chi Minh. He scooped every other journalist with that interview. Ho Chi Minh died in September. Madigan's piece became a kind of autobiographical obituary.

The next year Cheyney changed house in Athens as a concession to Kurt and the new decade. She would make no decision to leave Athens to live in Paris, London or Rome. By now she knew many more of Kurt's friends, some of whom she liked very much while others stirred her distaste.

Another job for Kurt. She purchased two of the finest Van Goghs she had ever seen. Long after she left Paraguay with them in tow and delivered them to Roberto in Rome, those paintings and the man she bought them from kept haunting her. The corn-yellow haystacks against the cobalt-blue sky at night studded with stars, an image so vivid she often had physically to shake her head to try to free her mind from it. It was a troubled painting, wrenched from a tortured mind. There was such outrageous beauty in it. The violence almost leapt from the pigment. And there was something about the owner that had repulsed her. A thin little weasel of a man, with the most hateful eyes she had ever seen. Arrogant, with a stiff, formal manner, he was almost impossible to deal with she was so appalled by him. That he was evil she only figured out on the plane, with the carefully wrapped paintings occupying the seats next to and across from her. How could such a terrible inconsequential little man, living in an upper-middle-class suburb of a fascist country like Paraguay, have come by such magnificent paintings? It had been Cheyney's first inkling of something not so right about some of the collectors she met through Kurt. When she tried to speak to him about it, Kurt had smoothly evaded her questions. The subject was dropped.

She received a cable from Grant. 'Thanks change of address and telephone. In touch.' That had been in the middle of the year. It was pathetic that her heart should still jump a beat when she heard anything from him.

She made only one trip for handicrafts, and Kurt joined her for a week of it. He marvelled at her in the field, working to try and save the crafts as old practitioners died out and a new generation neglected their skills in favour of migration to the cities and menial work for faster money. He had to admire how clever she was, furnishing villages with an oven, a well, a schoolteacher, in exchange for their crafts. It did more for them than money. All over the world ancient crafts were dying out. Cheyney Fox was doing her admirable best to save them. But even she was beginning to see that it was a losing battle. She had gone as far as she could. Now it was simply a matter of keeping what she had organised going. She had grown beyond it. Time to move on. She began training a Greek friend to take over from her.

That gave her more time in Athens to realise that her world had widened and life there was no longer as much fun as it had been. She had long since been healed even of the psychological wounds that her hard fall in New York had dealt her. If not completely, certainly enough to leave Athens and start again somewhere else. But there was no rush. She would know when it was time to go.

She had more time for Kurt. They made several trips to South America. In Peru they skied in the Andes and in Lima they saw the finest private collection of Inca gold artwork ever assembled. Their host presented her with a priceless necklace once worn by an Inca prince. They sailed down the Chilean coast of South America, stopping to visit Kurt's friends who entertained them on a lavish scale. He bought her a vineyard that stretched from the mountains to the shores of the Pacific Ocean and had on it a small romantic villa set in a semi-tropical garden high up on a bluff with nothing but the Pacific Ocean and sky for neighbours. It was there and on the ski slopes of the Andes that she felt herself falling more under Kurt's exotic-erotic spell. In Argentina he played polo and cut yet another dashing figure for her to contemplate as something permanent in her life.

They went on a mystery holiday which turned out to be a week in a white marble palace, floating in the middle of an Indian lake. A week of sex and sleeping and drinking and eating and swimming in the mother of pearl pool in an open courtyard in their bedroom. Of being pampered and spoiled by servants who answered their every request, who massaged their bodies with scented oil of jasmine, gardenia, rose, and knew ways to excite their erotic desires Cheyney never imagined possible. Masters of Karma Sutra made of her an admirable pupil. Kurt watched her rise to every erotic occasion. Taught by a sexual guru how to let herself flow in a steady stream from one orgasm to another she was fast becoming the sexual instrument he wanted her to be. Soon she would, as he had long planned, fall at last into his arms forever.

He draped her in saris of transparent silk embroidered in pure gold and set with tiny diamonds; others in silver and semi-precious stones. But mostly he kept her naked, draped in fresh flowers: white orchids and roses and jasmine, ropes of tiny yellow lilies whose scent was in itself an aphrodisiac. Or draped her in necklaces of priceless pearls, diamonds, emeralds. Their imaginative sexual games often culminated in a priceless gift, as when he inserted one by one real pearls the size of cherries into her vagina and then fucked her slowly with deep thrusts. The sensations of the pearls and his cock simultaneously rubbing and clinging, rolling against her sensitive vaginal walls, up against her cervix, tantalising her womb, tortured her with pleasure beyond anything she had ever known. She squirmed on the bed and begged to be released. He continued, knowing he could give her yet greater pleasure. Her protestations slowly changed to whimpers and then cries of ecstasy. Tears streaked her cheeks. He watched her flush pink, revelling in her own passion as she began to come, again and again. He felt her steady flow of orgasm. It drove him on until he thought she might actually swoon with exhaustion. He came and then sucked the pearls from her cunt one by one and placed them in her hands.

The more time they spent together, the more Kurt Walbrook was able to bind Cheyney closer to him. They both knew she was under his spell. They made their most memorable trip together to Tibet where she saw the spiritual side to this fascinating and complex man's nature. They spent an hour with the Dalai Lama that affected her profoundly. She returned to Athens to contemplate on what to do with her life.

By this time Andy Warhol had given up being a celebrity painter in order to become an even greater celebrity. After his successful exhibitions of Campbell's soup cans and money in the early sixties, there had been frantic cablegrams chasing her. 'What should I paint next?' 'Have you any ideas for me?' 'Call Andy.' She had never answered any of them. Andy Warhol and Cheyney Fox were worlds apart now. It was therefore rather embarrassing when in London, walking down Bond Street one summer's day, their paths crossed. Surrounded by the freaky entourage he was now famous for, Andy confronted her in silence. All he thought to utter was: 'Oh, I thought you were dead,' before he was swept away. The same ghost of a human being, but even less interesting now that he has become nothing more than a media machine, had been her only reaction. What bliss anonymity could be.

In September, Kurt took her for the first time to Austria. To Schloss Garmisch-Konigsberg, his favourite house, the place he really called home. She met his mother. Cheyney found her incredibly cold, and somewhat unnerving. She sensed an unhealthy adoration of Kurt by his mother. Disturbing, even though he was a most extraordinary man. Cheyney spent an uncomfortable half-hour alone with the Baroness, during which time she told Cheyney, 'My son is besotted by you. I can see that you would make him a good wife, even though I don't approve of you, for reasons outside your control. Do you know that you love him? You had best accept that. The sooner the better. There are many women who would like to be the next Baroness. Are you one of them?'

'I am not sure, madam,' Cheyney had answered coldly.

'I know my son. He has made up his mind to make you happy. So he will. Don't behave like a stupid American, thinking you can change him. He is a complex man, a far deeper person than he presents himself as being. He holds many secrets, and never reveals himself. He is devoted to me because I have given him everything and asked for nothing. And I allow him his private world. I suggest you do the same, or you will suffer. He has been grooming you to be a Walbrook for years. I recommend a long engagement. It might be preferable, until you are very sure you can obey his every wish. That is, if you intend to be the next Walbrook matriarch.'

'My God, what a bitch you are!' snapped Cheyney. She was immediately furious with herself. She had lost her poise before the Baroness.

'Yes, that's quite true, and how American of you to come right out and tell me so. You see, that is my point. If you marry my son, you will have to cultivate some manners and many changes of attitude. Common behaviour is unacceptable to him.'

Unsurprisingly, Cheyney and the Baroness avoided each other after this skirmish. They met twice – once in South America, the second time at Kurt's mother's birthday ball in Vienna. But they never spoke to each other again, beyond an exchange of greetings. Kurt said nothing about it to Cheyney or his mother. It was a characteristic of his never to involve himself in other people's disputes. On both occasions he showed respect and attention to his mother, love and adoration for Cheyney.

She could not bring herself to ask him about the coterie of men who danced attendance on his mother. Men of all ages. Some, the younger men, were almost caricature Teutonic army officers. Others mimicked a Viennese charm, intended to play down the evidence of ruthless, unbending minds, inclined to rigidity during conversations on world

245

politics. Nearly all of them were fascists. Kurt's only answer to her questions: 'It would be good to remember that they are my mother's friends. They were devoted to my father, and, as such, I am devoted to them.' Cheyney did take note that his real friends were nothing like these people. They were wealthy sportsmen, men of letters, scholars, a handful of international playboys, a brace of industrialists. And several quite remarkable women who were all in love with him. One day Cheyney might think she was the woman closest to him. The next, she wasn't sure she knew him at all. But it didn't seem to matter. They were happy together, and Grant Madigan was not there to challenge that happiness.

Once, in a fit of pique after a particularly unsavoury conversation at a dinner-party, she attacked Kurt. 'What is it with your mother and the Walbrook family friends? Do they ban the poor, the middle classes, anyone who's not Aryan? Everyone I meet is powerful or power-mad, wealthy and avaricious, white and well-bred. They are all so polite to me, generous with their attention. But lifeless and formal. They never really speak to me. More at me, or past me. I think they resent my being an American. No, don't say a word. They don't count in my life, anyway.'

Kurt's mother's birthday – a grand dinner and a ball in their townhouse in Vienna. In the previous months, Cheyney had come to accept more and more the idea of marrying Kurt. He never pressed her with the question of when they would marry. He didn't have to, he had made it clear that he didn't want her until she was ready for a lifetime commitment to him. It therefore came as a surprise to him when, in bed one night after an extravagant display of sexual intimacy, she said she would like – if he would – for them to consider themselves engaged to be married. Leaving open the time and place of the ceremony, of course.

One of the things that prompted Cheyney to take that next step in their relationship was that, having been beside him in many places and at a number of large public functions, she had recognised that Kurt Walbrook, for all his celebrity, knew how to retain his privacy. Having to live with him constantly in the public eye would have been for her death by a thousand camera-cuts.

He did after all keep several different lives going at the same time. Several different images as well: playboy-jet setter, society-bachelor, dilettante, patron of the arts, owner of the Walbrook Collection, philanthropist on a rather large scale. Some of which made the gossip columns around the world, but not too often. Cheyney envied his ability to keep his profile low in the midst of such celebrity. Or was his old money less interesting in the sixties than Pop money? Or maybe his judiciously chosen friends managed to keep his activities up-front in the glossies, while fading out his personality? Cheyney herself had been aware of him and his collections, yet had not known the face behind the columnists' legends.

They agreed to announce the news at his mother's birthday ball.

Kurt did try to prepare Cheyney for the celebrations. He explained to her that all his relations, and his father's friends, were devoted to the Baroness. They would be flying in from all over the world for the event. 'It will be a formal affair, with a good many of my mother's generation looking back on a world long lost to them. So you mustn't mind too much their sentimentality. It will be an occasion for reminiscences. They may bore you, but they need not bother you. They are their reminiscences, not ours. We have yet to create our own.'

The birthday ball was the first time she visited the family house in Vienna. It was a turn-of-the-century mansion, set behind iron gates in a three-acre garden. By then Cheyney had learned never to be surprised by anything to do with the Walbrooks. The more she saw and learned, the more fascinating they became as a dynasty of the Austrian elite. However, on the very night of the ball, Cheyney was less dazzled by Kurt Walbrook's world than she would have liked. For the first time she recognised what the sinister undertone was that she found in the admirers of the Baroness Walbrook. It was, after all, not that difficult when confronted by men in evening dress, the Iron Cross worn on a ribbon around the throat, Third Reich campaign ribbons across the breasts of their jackets. The women wore elegant gowns and jewels of a splendour to match those of the best royal households. For the most part, they seemed to have been spared the Nazi regime's highest decorations. The Baroness herself delighted her party-guests and shocked Cheyney by wearing a sash of red, white and black across the bodice of her silver-lamé gown. Fetchingly pinned to it was an Iron Cross framed in diamonds. She wore other magnificent diamonds in her hair. Around her throat, a necklace of blinding beauty and brilliance. She sported bracelets and rings of huge diamonds in sophisticated Art Deco settings. She presented herself to her guests for the first toast in champagne by sweeping down the curved staircase into the hall where they were all assembled.

A woman standing next to Cheyney, dressed splendidly in black and emeralds, leaned over and whispered, 'You know, our leader believed her to be the most intelligent and clever woman in Germany. They say he was in love with her. I was there when he presented her with the Cross she wears tonight. He adored her and her family.' The woman had tears in her eyes. Riveted as she was by the spectacle, Cheyney felt duly sick and left the hall.

Someone entered the library. Cheyney heard the click of a lock. She recognised Kurt's step as he walked towards her. She turned from the window where she had been standing to watch a light snow fall. Faint

247

sounds of an orchestra in the ballroom above them playing. Spry Viennese waltzes. He looked very handsome as he came towards her. He wore no wartime decorations. She had known that, but now she found herself checking his appearance for them anyway. It was the sort of occasion when one might have materialised. She simply could not bring herself to mention how revolted she was by his mother's friends. The deadly glamour of it all precluded anything so trite.

'Now I understand why you have all the security men in the gardens and all over the house. It's nothing so up-to-the-minute as a drugs raid you worry about. Nor burglars hauling off your guests' jewels. It's for secrecy. To make sure they can celebrate their slice of history without getting caught doing it. How can they wear those decorations, Kurt? It's grotesque! And you? My God, don't tell me you were a Nazi. I can never believe that.'

To let her bitterness diminish, he took his time fitting a cigarette into his amber holder. Then he lit it, and savoured a few puffs. He took Cheyney by the hand, led her to a chair and asked her to be seated.

'Is it any more grotesque than the Americans, the Allies, the Russians even, wearing their decorations? No, Cheyney, don't interrupt me. Hear me out.' There was no soft slurring of her name as he spoke to her this time. 'The men and women of Germany and Austria fought and lost a war. There were those such as my mother who believed passionately, however misguidedly, in the new Germany and Hitler, those like my father who did not. Men like myself, who left Germany and chose to remain neutral, but never – and I do mean never – deserted my family because of their beliefs. Could you possibly have believed that every Nazi sympathiser, even after the débâcle of 1945, would forget his glory days? The men in that room are some of what is left of Hitler's most competent high-ranking officers. They may be respectable citizens in their own country, living constructive, affluent lives. But in their fat old hearts, though they know they will never march again, they remain as devoted as ever to what they fought for. They're human. It's not twenty-five years since Germany was defeated. That may be enough time to come to terms with their defeat but it's not long enough for the men who designed and fought in that war to forget it. It was the time of their lives. Each life only gets one such time. History supplied Hitler to give them theirs.

'Most of the people in that ballroom do not admit, even to themselves the atrocities their war unleashed on humanity. For them it is over. All they have left is what they retreat to in their memory. They have run with their spoils of war. When they dare, as they do this evening, or in their splendid houses behind bolted doors, they display the medals of a dream lost forever. You can see it as the fag-end of a nightmare, dwindled to fancy-dress. It means little. It is their business, and has nothing to do with us. I have been deeply involved with some of these people all of my life, and will always remain so. I refuse to be judgemental on this issue. I cannot stop you from being so. We have discussed this now for the first and last time. The subject is not open for discussion, not now, not ever. If that is clear, and you are still unhappy about being here, you can go up to our room. I will join you there as soon as I can.'

There was nothing in his tone to lead her to believe that he was angry or disappointed with her. He was stating the facts and letting her know quite emphatically the stance he had taken and intended to maintain. For him, the parade was no more menacing than a fancy-dress ball.

He reached out his hands to Cheyney, who took them. Touching him, she felt his warmth and his love. It coursed through her body. Their eyes met. She sensed what he saw. She was dressed in a black silk damask gown that was simplicity itself. Slender shoestring straps on the shoulders and cut to the waist in the back, a tight bodice that accentuated the shape of the breasts, the narrowness of the waist and gently flared over the hips into its bias-cut skirt and train that voluptuously trailed on the floor behind her. At her neck a slender ribbon of diamonds, a single white camellia pinned to one side of it. Her long black hair done in an elaborate twist at the nape of her neck.

He closed his eyes. She caught the emotion in his voice as he said, 'Sheyney,' and drew her towards him. 'I love you. Nothing, no matter what our differences may be, now or in the future, can ever change that.' He opened his eyes and she was, as before, mesmerised by the strange sensual power that drew her to him. 'We will be happy together for always, you wait and see. Please.' Then, reaching into his jacket pocket, he produced a square-cut diamond, larger than Cheyney had ever seen, a gem of such splendid fire and beauty as to make her catch her breath. 'Accept this ring, it's my engagement present to you. Wear it for me, for us. But I think it best we don't announce our engagement here at the ball. This is supposed to be the beginning of the happiest time of our lives, and you don't look happy about being here. So only you and I will share this special time. We'll be selfish and keep it for ourselves. Is that fair?'

'Fair enough,' she echoed equivocally.

As so often, he had handled her in a manner that smoothed the roughnesses between them. Cheyney accepted the ring. Not having to share that special moment with the others in the house brought relief. She relished the beauty of her ring, and told him she loved him. He showed her his feelings. He slipped the straps carefully off her shoulders and lowered the bodice of her dress to caress her naked breasts with hands and kisses. On the sofa he lifted her skirts and continued his kisses. They returned to the ball, he with the taste of her pleasure still on his tongue, and she that little bit more in love with Kurt Walbrook.

Then why did she still ache for the loss of that something special she only felt in the arms of Grant Madigan?

In the months that followed, Cheyney and Kurt saw less of each other than they had expected. She returned to Athens and remained there. The trip to New York to buy her third painting from the Acton Pace estate was cancelled. She arranged the transaction by telephone. A trip to London to see the paintings of Acton she was lending to the Tate Gallery, and to meet several people in the contemporary art world there, was about the only journey she made abroad. On her return she began thinking seriously of what she was going to do with the rest of her life.

Where was Grant? Would he ever be there for her, just her? She would happily settle for that. But she knew the answer almost before she formed the question. She had to come to terms with the fact that as much as he was her magnificent love obsession, a life together to build on there would never be. It takes two for that and he was still running away from love.

By this time Cheyney knew that her life was bound up with Kurt's. There were bonds there that might never be broken. A kind of love and sexual interdependence that tied her to Kurt Walbrook. The dark side of his sexual life was fast becoming their shared dark side, one which, in spite of herself, she enjoyed enormously. She was not unaware of just how much she had slipped under his Svengali spell. But there was, too, a desire in both for them not to be merely enslaved by each another. They had become a formidable couple, with more than most going for them.

It was actually his love for her, his obsessional desire to make a fulfilling life and home for them, that ate into the very fabric of Cheyney's independence. But never in a negative way. That again was thanks to the eversensitive Kurt, who always tempered his desires until she was ready to share in them. Cheyney conceded that there might never be any other man for her to make a life with. Not so long as Kurt was alive. She had to dismiss the nagging memory of Grant Madigan. His restless spirit was in his work.

The alternative? To stay as she was with Kurt, move to a city where she could open a small gallery. That certainly held no interest for her. The very thought brought back too many bad memories. Keep working with Lala and Roberto on the odd job? As a wealthy woman in her own right, thanks to her investment in Acton Pace paintings, she had options. What seemed to beckon most alluringly was that of sharing a life with Kurt Walbrook. There was something else: what it was becoming fashionable to call her biological clock. It was running down, and Kurt was not a young man. There were only a few years in which to have a child before she turned forty.

They had their usual very private and early Christmas together in

250

Athens, and celebrated their first New Year's Eve together. 1971 was rung in on the promise of a wedding before spring. Two things delayed their plans.

On the Ides of March, Kurt's mother was found dead in the house in Vienna. A heart attack, said the obituaries. Years later, Cheyney would discover that, her hair dressed beautifully, her make-up applied to perfection, she had dressed herself in the silver-lamé gown she had worn to her birthday ball, and wearing her sash of honour and no other jewellery except her wedding band of gold, she had lain down on her bed and injected an overdose of morphine. Her favourite drug, introduced into her life by another of her admirers, Herman Goering. The papers in Austria omitted such detail, recording rather her wealth, her generosity to children in need, and her having been among Europe's greatest female patrons of the arts. A statutory period of mourning, and time to settle her will: then a date was set for their wedding.

One bright April morning, seated outside in the sun, reading the *International Herald Tribune* and drinking a coffee at Zonar's, Cheyney looked up from her paper to see Grant Madigan, a beautiful Chinese nymphet clinging to his arm, together with another man. The three had stopped to greet someone and then the party of four wound between the tables in search of a place to sit. Grant spotted her.

She gaped, stunned that he should just pop up like that on the pavement.

For him to have been in Athens and not to have called her – had she deserved that? Not even a call to tell her he might be there. Well, of such is the kingdom of the foot-loose. Yet, from the moment their eyes met, he settled his companions at a table, apparently intent only upon going directly to her. His mere presence at the café was bad enough, but now he was walking towards her. It brought her slowly to her feet.

Neither seemed able to speak. At last it was Cheyney who broke the silence. 'A long separation.'

'Yes, rather prolonged. I think you are more beautiful even than I remembered.'

'Oh, then you do remember?'

He began afresh. 'How are you, Cheyney?'

'Weren't you even going to call, Grant?'

'I've been thinking about it.'

'How much thinking does it take? How long have you been in Athens?'

'I arrived two days ago.'

'Two days to find a phone! Or to find something to say, for chrissake.'

'There hasn't been time, not time to reflect at all. This has been my first free morning. Why am I making excuses?' He looked angry with himself, or with her for making an issue of it.

251

'I don't know. I shouldn't put you on the spot. Look, if you'd wanted to call, you would have called.'

She gathered up her things, dropping first the newspaper, picking that up only to drop her handbag. Her distress was obvious and she seemed unable to keep it from spiralling towards farce. Grant grabbed her by the arm. 'Cheyney, come and join us. Have a coffee, a drink, anything you like, with us. I'll get away from them as soon as I can.'

'Forget it, Grant.'

He increased the pressure on her arm. 'Why are you doing this?'

'Figure it out.' Her distress now turned to anger. She wrenched her arm from his grip and walked away from him, tears brimming in her eyes.

He caught up with her two blocks on, just about to step into a taxi. He grabbed her by the arm. 'I have to see you. I have to be with you.'

She felt weak-kneed with desire for him. Her heart pounded, her mouth suddenly dry, and tears of frustration formed in her eyes and made her more angry with herself than with him because she wanted Grant so much. She pulled away from him and jumped into the taxi. He was right behind her. He closed the door. 'Go away. Please go away, Grant. Go back to your friends, your little Chinese fortune-cookie. Jesus, she's a baby!'

'Oh, I see, that's what this is all about.'

'Well, of course that's what this is all about,' she shouted at him, and quickly gave the driver her address.

'I can tell you that little cookie would never behave as badly as you are now. Uncomplicated, easy, no demands and no commitments from that little lady.'

'Girl. Get it right. I'm a lady, she's a girl. And who ever asked you for any commitments? Certainly not me, and you can be sure I never will. Now, please, get out of my taxi!'

'You're even more beautiful when you're angry. Stormy skies – they bring out the sun. Your anger has given me instant recall. It's the first time I remember you as a woman in the rain, in another taxi, years ago. You were angry with me then. Not quite like this, though.'

'You haven't really seen much of me, have you? Get out of my taxi.' She ordered the driver to pull up to the kerb. 'We started in a taxi, now let's just finish it in a taxi.' She leaned over him and flung open the door. 'Out.' She was trembling with rage.

He slammed the door shut and ordered the driver to go on.

'Are you married? Is there a man in your life?'

'It's none of your business.'

'Don't be angry. I didn't say it was my business. I asked you a civil question.'

'OK, you want this taxi, you can have this taxi.' For the second time she ordered the driver to the kerb. Tears of anger stinging her cheeks, she scrambled out.

'And what the fuck are you doing with those two stupid, noisy animals?' he shouted at her back.

'At least they come when I call them, and have no hang-ups about commitment!' she shouted over her shoulder as she ran down the street and away from him.

She fumbled with the key, and almost fell over. Inside her flat, Cheyney closed the door behind her and leaned against it. She dropped her things where she stood. She was shaking, quite unable to control the tremors of feeling. Unable to take another step forward into her own home. She remained where she was, and finally calmed herself. Her sobs subsided. She had no idea how long she had been standing there. She jumped when she heard the knock at the door. Her heart leapt. It had to be Grant. She wiped the tears from her cheeks. Yet another knock. 'Are you going to let me in?'

'Just go away, Grant.'

'Let me in, Cheyney. Or so help me, this door comes down, and that is not just a threat.'

At last she found the energy to move. She turned around to face the door, and then she opened it to him. Silently she stepped back and let him pass into the apartment. He closed the door behind her, and pulled her roughly into his arms. Grabbing a handful of her hair, he pulled her head back and pinned her to the wall with his body. He placed his other hand around her neck.

'What is it with you? You're forever erupting into my life, always sending me out of control. I have only to see you and you trigger something in me that's both basic and base.'

Cheyney could feel his anger as if it were her very own. He crushed her with a passionate kiss, sucked her lips into his mouth and bit them. She slipped her arms around his neck and grabbed his hair with both hands, pulling as hard as she could. He did not let go. Instead, he lifted her off the floor by her waist. She tried to wrap her legs around him. Hindered by her skirt, he ripped it from the waistband to the hem. It fell to the floor. Now she clung to him with her legs around his waist, and he supported her with his arms.

He did not stop kissing her lips. Their tongues made hungry love. His kisses found her eyes. He pulled the earrings off her ears, and threw them away, and sucked on the lobes, the flesh at the side of her neck. He was in a wild passion for her. He tore her silk panties first down one hip, then down the other, and roughly yanked the remnant from between her legs. His hands caressing her naked bottom seemed to drive them both into a greater

253

carnal frenzy. His searching fingers probed between fleshy cheeks, reached under her and found what he was after. He kissed her with his fingers as deeply as he could, once he had breached her vaginal lips. His mouth and tongue found hers, eager now to please him.

While he carried her thus from the hall, she clung by her legs, wrapped tight around him. She tore off his tie, ripping open his shirt. She rubbed her face back and forth across his naked chest and licked him with her tongue. Her quick hands darted beneath the opened shirt. To feel his body in her hands, the touch of his skin, his flesh in her mouth as she passionately sucked on his nipples. She mouthed huge lusty bites of him, leaving deep red teeth-marks. She must unbuckle his belt, get it free of its loops and fling it into the room.

Their anger had blazed into lust for each other. Her fingers scrabbled at his buttons and zip. She grabbed the pants and his shorts together on his hips and pulled as hard as she could leaving him naked to his thighs. She loosened her grip on him, and he swept her away from him to impale her with one forceful thrust of his penis. She let out a cry but muffled it with her hand. She tightened her grip on him with her legs, driving him that precious bit deeper into her.

He couldn't wait. Slowly he sank to his knees. Then he took her on the cool marble floor, half in the hall and half in the drawing-room. Afterwards, he carried her to the bedroom. Time for gentler explorations of their passion for each other. It had hardly subsided when they dozed enfolded in each other's arms. Their mutual urge to realise all their sexual fantasies for each other drove them on.

Years of sex with Kurt had made Cheyney into a more adventurous, even more responsive sexual partner than Grant had known her to be. Now there was nothing he need hold back from her. Not even the most nakedly outrageous sex. He spent in her his last, most intimate self.

It had been less difficult for her to do that. She felt no shame that he should see her lust for his seed, know her desire to be filled with it. Why shouldn't he know how she loved the taste of him in her mouth, the feel of absorbing the fruit of his orgasms into her womb? What did she care that he knew how vulnerable she was in his hands? How she wished she could keep alive every drop of his sperm, have it cling to her, so she could nurture it, as she wanted to nurture him.

It was dark outside when he woke her, with yet another passionate kiss. She was surprised when he switched on the bedside lamp to see that he was dressed. Well, as dressed as he could be with a buttonless shirt held together by a well-knotted tie and a tweed jacket over it. She touched the sleeve of his jacket with a tenderness they had shown sparingly to each other that day. She sensed that he wasn't pleased by her touch. She pulled herself up against the pillows. Cheyney had the feeling she was not going to like what was coming. She tried to fight it off. She fixed a gaze on his handsome rugged face, as if she were trying to burn a vision of it into her memory forever. A bad sign, she thought to herself. He had a bruise on the side of his chin and on his lower lip. They had made love like rutting animals.

'This is all there is for us. It's more than most people have in a lifetime. Learn to live with it, and remember it's no easier for me to live with that knowledge than it is for you. But that's the way it is. I may be back one day. If I'm not, what we have had together for these few hours should serve as a good lesson to remind you why I'm not. You wouldn't want to lose what we share any more than I would. Being together the way you would like would kill that. Don't wait for me. Get on with your life, I'll be doing the same. I'm not difficult to find.

'If ever you need something, anything, I'll be there to help you.'

And he walked out on her.

He scarcely listened for her whispered 'Goodbye.'

Chapter 28

Why wasn't she upset or even angry? She felt neither deserted nor alone. She felt no malice towards Grant Madigan for so coolly walking out on her. For not wanting to include her any more in his life. She would never be with him again. For the first time that seemed a reality. They might never have the thrill of being two bodies and one soul as they had been in the hours they had just spent with each other, as it had always been for them, right from their first coming together. Never again. Rather than indulge herself in sadness, Cheyney chose to savour every memory of this overpowering love they felt for each other, that seemed only able to express itself in mutual lust.

She turned out the light, and slipped down from the pillows to lie in the dark. Grant Madigan had given her, for the moment, everything he was capable of. And he had been right: it was more than most people had in a lifetime. She was reluctant to get up and wash away the scent of him, his touch, their orgasms. Instead she caressed herself with loving hands, for a last time seizing pleasure in what remained of their lust. He could be hers for a few more hours. Thus she slid into sleep.

When she woke, she felt fresh and free of Grant Madigan at last. Because there had been no choice, her goodbye to him had been genuine. But that was not to say she didn't understand her great loss, or realise that she would have to live with it for the rest of her life. But now she was ready to make her commitment to Kurt Walbrook for ever.

She turned on the light. The room was a shambles where she and Grant had left a trail of strewn clothes, sheets, blankets, and pillows everywhere in the wake of their love-making. The bathroom was no better: towels, terry-cloth robes, powder and open jars of cream, perfume. In the drawing-room she was reminded of their violent passion by an overturned table, a chipped vase, an abandoned cushion, an open champagne bottle, a broken glass. There was a scattering of the flowers he had placed in her hair, before he had made love to her. Romeo and Zazou were silent, nowhere in sight. She found them asleep in their baskets in the kitchen where Grant must have put them. Canine indifference to human carnality.

Closing the door quietly so as not to rouse them, Cheyney went back to the drawing-room. She found one of her earrings he had flung away, then spotted the other on the far side of the floor. In the bath, the jasmine-scented soapy water brought out the bruises on her body. A cherished reminder of the violence of Grant Madigan's passion for her.

The following morning, she was dressed and out on the streets of Athens by half-past six. She walked all over the city, the old parts and the new. She made several pilgrimages: the Agora, the Acropolis, the Odeon of Herodes Atticus, the Roman Agora and the Tower of the Winds, where she drank coffee on the street at a café. She walked through Monastiraki and Syntagma Square up to the Benaki, and then down-town again to the Archeological Museum. Down old narrow streets, the backwaters of Athens, to cafés she had known and tavernas where she was welcomed. She spoke to the tradespeople she knew, friends she bumped into. In the late afternoon, exhausted and unwilling to walk another step, she found a taxi. She went ten miles out of Athens to the Byzantine monastery church of Daphne. She wanted another look at the mosaic of Christ Pantocrator in the dome.

She arrived back home at nine o'clock that evening. She realised she had been saying goodbye to the city. Cheyney Fox was through with Athens and Greece, ready to move on. The voice of some fundamental change within herself told her so.

All day it had been creeping up on her, a kind of excitement and enthusiasm that kept growing stronger with every step she had taken. Now, waiting to hear Kurt's voice come on the line, she felt happier than she could ever have expected to feel.

'Sheyney?'

She closed her eyes, feeling a thrill at the sound of his voice. She wished she was there, right next to him, so she could put her arms around him. She would kiss him, and let him know how happy she was that he was a part of her life.

'Kurt.'

'This is the first time you have ever called me. Does it mean what I think it means?'

Cheyney began to laugh, 'If you think it means what I think you think it means, which is that I have called to ask you to marry me, then you'd be right.'

His laughter was filled with sunshine. 'When, this eager bridegroom would like to know? Today, tomorrow, the next day?'

'The sooner the better. But you mustn't say anything to anyone, or do anything about it, until we have a talk. Promise me that.' He promised. She arrived in Venice two weeks later.

It was unseasonably warm that afternoon. She felt that Venice had never looked lovelier. Kurt met her plane, a private jet that detoured to Athens to pick her up. He managed to send the other two passengers off with the luggage in a motor-launch while he captured Cheyney for himself in the Palazzo Borgano's gondola and took her in to Venice.

Once they were settled under the canvas canopy against the daffodil-yellow Fortuny cushions, he kissed her face, then her hands.

'It's good that you are really here with me at last.'

'No "at last". Well, not yet. Not 'til we have had our talk. Can we go for a coffee in the square? I really have to talk to you before we go home.'

'Of course.'

The Piazza San Marco was more visibly enticing than ever. The tourist season had not quite begun. It was, for that much-peopled Piazza, virtually empty. They sat at their favourite café, drinking Americanos in the afternoon sun. The resident musicians sawed their way through Vivaldi.

Finally he asked, 'What is it you're so anxious to tell me, Sheyney?' A flower-lady passed by. From the basket over her arm she offered a nosegay of spring flowers, their stems wrapped in silk ribbon, trailing in long slender streamers. Neither of them could help smiling: it was so like a miniature wedding-bouquet. Kurt presented it to Cheyney and paid the woman.

'I almost don't know how to begin. Because, you and I, we never talk about our personal pasts. We hardly even talk about yesterdays. We seem always to live in the immediate present, without questions, without queries about each other's lives. We seem to be two people happy to leave each other our separate secrets. I don't even particularly want to know about the other women in your life, your mistresses. And that seems to be all right. It seems to work for us, and I hope it always will. But . . . I want to marry you, and something has happened, and I think I have to tell it to you, because unless I do I will always be afraid that you'll think I have married you for some other reason than loving you and deciding at last I am free enough of my past to go forward and make a life with you as your wife.'

Kurt took her hands in his. He lowered his head and kissed first one palm, and then the other. She felt a tremor of pleasure. Warmth flowing from his hands to hers. When he raised his head, his eyes were still closed. His seductively long, thick lashes shivered, and he opened his eyes. His provocative look drew her to him. His fatal charm, that combination of raw male sexuality, power, adoration, caused her to stumble over her words.

'His name is Grant Madigan. I have only been with him four times over a period of ten years. It's a strange love-story. It hardly existed until the day before yesterday. And now, it's over for ever.' Cheyney was brief, dispassionately honest about her affair with Grant.

Experience had withered the rampant masculinity in Kurt Walbrook into a calmer understanding of women. He could absorb all she told him of Grant

Madigan. He sensed that when she said she was finished with Grant, she probably was. And the man seemed finished with her, no matter what. Kurt recognised that, but for the intense sexual encounter the couple had shared two days before, they might never have resolved their relationship. Then he would not have been about to marry the only woman he wanted for his wife.

It was possible that he loved her that little bit more. Less for her honesty than for the maturity she brought to understanding the relationship between her and Grant Madigan. He knew instinctively that Cheyney Fox's love for him had become even stronger because of Grant Madigan and what had happened in Athens. Their marriage was going to be all he had always hoped it would be.

She seemed calm, not at all ill-at-ease for having told him her only dark secret. And he liked that. He kept her waiting no longer. He asked, 'Would you like to stay in Venice and marry me here? You won't even have to go back to collect your things if you don't want to. We can send for everything, ship it all to Garmisch-Konigsberg. We could make that our real home. I seem to recall you said it was a place where you could live forever.'

Unable to hold back, she burst out with, 'Oh, I'm so happy! I love you so much, you know.' She threw her arms around him, almost toppling him and his chair over, while she kissed him. Titters from the tables all around them brought a blush to her face. Yet again, Cheyney sought to regain control of herself.

'I think this calls for champagne, don't you?'

'Oh yes, those wicked champagne cocktails they do here.'

'Quite right. The house wickedness it shall be.'

Cheyney watched him give the order and was thrilled that he looked so happy. It occurred to her dimly that she might have lost him over Grant Madigan. The very thought came as a shock. She would have coped, she knew that. But the loss to the quality of her life . . . only now did she realise that it would have been incalculable.

'Cheyney, I have something to say to you about you and Grant Madigan.'

'Yes?'

'Have you thought what you might do if he has made you pregnant?'

His question surprised her. 'Why do you ask?'

'Such things happen.'

'Well, yes. There are precedents, now that I think about it. But you must believe me, Kurt, the idea never occurred to me.'

'Calm yourself, Cheyney, I believe you. It's surprising how often people tend not to. I am only asking you to think about it now. It makes no difference to me, but it might to you. We should talk this out, now.'

259

'But, Kurt, I wouldn't have suggested that we marry if I had thought I might be pregnant.'

'Cheyney, stop protesting. I told you – and I do mean it – it makes no difference to me. Only to you. If it were so, what would you want to do about it?'

'Have the baby, of course. But I wouldn't want Grant ever to know.'

'Are you so sure about that?'

'Oh, absolutely. He would hate being trapped by a child. He has made that clear to me in no uncertain terms. But, of course, we cannot marry until I know, can we?'

'Why not? We can marry and be happy together, whether you are pregnant with his baby, or mine, or not pregnant at all.'

'I don't see how, Kurt.'

'Quite simple. You let me be the baby's father, no matter if the natural father is Grant Madigan. Cheyney, I am no longer a young man. It has been a long time since any of my female companions has claimed I've made them pregnant. And look at us, there has been no pregnancy for us as yet. I wouldn't want to deprive you of having this so-far imaginary child, if you want it. Nor would I deprive Grant Madigan of his child, if ever a time came that you wanted him to know he had one. But one thing you must understand: once we marry, I'll never give you up for him. I would embrace his child as if it were my very own. Because it's yours, I would like it to be ours. As far as I am concerned, that's all I have to say about our marriage and a child – if a child should happen along. So you see, these are things you have to be very sure of. If we agree on them, to the altar we go. And I, for one, say, the sooner the better.'

'You mean that with all your heart, don't you, Kurt?'

'Yes, I do.'

Their drinks arrived. They touched the rims of the glasses and silently drank a toast to each other. Kurt put his glass down and began to laugh.

'Why are you laughing?'

'Because, if you have conceived out of such an intense love-encounter as you have had, you and I had better do some quick catching up. That way I can at least be almost a part of this baby. Lots of sex is called for, Cheyney.'

'I think you are teasing me, Kurt.'

He placed some money by their bill and said, 'Let's go home and see.'

They married four days later, a short distance from Venice, on the island of Torcello, deserted except for the restaurant famous for being another arm of Harry's Bar in Venice. Ernest Hemingway was said to have written *Across The River And Into The Trees* while living in the rooms above. In the ancient ruins of a church, and in the presence of thirty of their closest friends, Cheyney and Kurt took their vows. Della and Roberto and Lala were there, together with two of Cheyney's best friends from Greece. Kurt's best man was a playboy prince, the other men handsome and amusing polo players and Austrian boyhood friends of Kurt, with their glamorous wives groomed to perfection. A string quartet and marvellous food and wines combined with the romantic setting to give their wedding distinction.

Valentino was rushed in from Rome. He brought dressmakers to conjure a wedding gown for Cheyney from a two-hundred-year-old length of Belgian lace, a gift from Kurt. It was a Walbrook family heirloom. Like the large, transparent-brimmed horsehair hat she wore, it was the colour of champagne in the sunlight. She carried a cascade of four dozen white moth orchids. It was the day of Cheyney's life.

She hadn't realised how much she had already merged into the pattern of Kurt Walbrook's existence. If she had any doubts that her husband was a remarkable man, a law unto himself, then they were dispelled during their first weeks after marriage. For someone as intimately involved as she had been with him for so long, she knew relatively little about Kurt. Every day she discovered a little bit more of the remarkable life he so carefully cultivated for himself, and now for her.

They had made a joint decision: Cheyney would retain her name, though she was by law the Baroness Walbrook. And everywhere they went he would introduce her as his wife, Cheyney Fox. It was no small thing, her retaining her own name. It served to remind them both that, as two strong and independent individuals, they would remain within marriage their own autonomous selves. Kurt Walbrook and Cheyney Fox detested the idea of merging into 'the Walbrooks'. To be swallowed up by the institution of marriage was not what they were about.

Kurt was not at all naive about the power of his position in the world, or his wealth. He had seen time and again how daunting it could be. There had been many a man and woman working either for him personally, or for the foundations he subsidised, or for his collections of fine arts and artefacts, ruined by the Walbrooks' power, position and wealth. He had no intention of letting that happen to Cheyney. But then he had no intention of over-protecting her either. And so he doled out the responsibilities of her new position in life, as his wife and a part of his whole little empire, in palatable doses, and watched her take them in her stride and assimilate them into the life of Cheyney Fox.

Every week he presented her with yet another piece of jewellery from the family's collections of gems, rather than overpowering her with it all at once. Had he done that, she might have rejected it as too important a collection for her to wear. That would not have pleased him. She was, after all, still the same person who, only a short time ago, had been walking the streets of New York, hawking her pathetic wares from a basket over her arm.

One of the many reasons he had married Cheyney was to pass on all he had into her hands. He sensed she could withstand the pressures of such vast responsibilities, having a strength of character honed by some pretty hard times. Another was her creative spirit. She never disappointed him.

Six weeks after they married, Cheyney Fox found herself walking down the curved staircase of the Walbrook family home in Vienna, on the arm of her husband. But this time it was to greet the five hundred guests assembled for Kurt and Cheyney's formal wedding-reception. There was the same heavy security surrounding the house and gardens. A similar number of guards at the door, checking invitations and ID cards. Discreetly gun-laden men prowled the house. But there were no watery eyes for Hitler and the glorious days of the Third Reich, no campaign-ribbons worn on proud chests or Iron Crosses dangling menacingly from ribbons around stiff and wrinkled Nazi throats. They had been warned: the new wife of Kurt Walbrook, Cheyney Fox, was not one of them. She was no Nazi neophyte, and, in her home, discretion was the better part of Valhalla. It was twilight for the old Nazi gods. She had put them in the shade, where they belonged. She was greeted with nothing more menacing from her guests than applause, good wishes for her future happiness, and exquisite Viennese charm wherever she turned. They mingled with other guests from London, Paris, New York. To all appearances, they were no more than they seemed: cosmopolitan European old-guard high society.

Cheyney responded not with silver-lamé and a king's ransom in diamonds but a red taffeta ball-gown with dramatic puffed sleeves in a silk cabbage-rose print, worn off the shoulders. With it she wore around her slender neck a ruby the size of a pigeon's egg set in a wide band of diamonds. She descended the stairs with pride of self, dignity and beauty, an outsider, a rebel in their midst. If they could not take her to their hearts, they could at least admire her. Most of all for luring Kurt Walbrook where no other woman had – to the altar. One jealous woman was heard bitchily to say, 'Our modern-day Empress Elizabeth, American-style, I think.'

Cheyney stood in the reception line to receive her guests. She recognised men who had flown in from Paraguay, Rio, Caracas, Montevideo, Lima. Otto Furtwangler was there, together with her favourite Saudi prince and so many more she had met briefly. Their attitude towards her now that she was married to Kurt was different. She was uncertain how, but she could guess why. There was, too, an even greater respect shown by these men to Kurt. Cheyney put the near-fawning attention they paid to her husband down to the death of their heroine, the late Baroness. She learned a lesson from that evening: that Kurt would no sooner turn his back on these men and women than his mother had. Not for her or anyone else.

It was impressive, that ball. Yet not at all uncomfortable for Cheyney. She had found a way this time to mingle with them. She determined likewise to find in future a way to deal with them on her own terms. But until then, she had only to enjoy the ball.

Already, by the night of the wedding-reception ball, they both knew that Cheyney was pregnant. They were both delighted. They sat down and carefully worked out the dates. There was no doubt about the father. It had to have been Grant Madigan.

The dramatic changes that kept flowing in a steady stream through Cheyney's life for the first nine months of her marriage were made easier for her by the huge staff of retainers who had helped keep Kurt Walbrook and his mother, and their lives and interests, ticking over.

The greatest lesson that Cheyney would learn from her husband was how to delegate while remaining independent and in control. He was a grand master at it. The luxury of having the right people to delegate to was in itself enough to change the habits of anyone's lifetime. Arrange that luxury for yourself, and the mind opens and expands. Life gets its chance to change you. That was what was happening to Cheyney every day.

She was slower to appreciate the idea of motherhood than Kurt thought she should be. But he was patient and said nothing. If anything, he grew every day more besotted by his pregnant wife. Her pregnancy made his always-strong libido a voracious one. His sexual stamina, more remarkable than most men's she had been with, seemed to feed on their every sexual encounter. That did wonders for Cheyney, and her ego, at a time when it might have been fragile. It enhanced their already excellent erotic relationship. It was his constant sexual hunger for her, and his eager involvement in every detail of the coming birth of her child, that finally brought home to her the momentousness of what was happening within her own body: that she was going to have a baby for them. Thanks to Kurt, she learned in those early months of her pregnancy to love that unborn child and its natural father for what he, however reluctantly, had given her.

Kurt Walbrook had what he had always wanted from Cheyney Fox. He had wooed her strangely, with his secret benevolence, and had won her heart forever. It was evident to both of them that she could never look at another man as long as she was with him. He could see that in her eyes, hear it in her voice, and his utter domination over her sexually, and her enjoyment of it, was his reward. Yet her strange self-possession daily led him on to play his game of courtship with her. He adored her for that.

One of Kurt's many projects, dear to both their hearts, was the building of the museum for Acton Pace. The site once chosen, and the architect's preliminary plans approved by both Cheyney and Kurt, the Walbrook Fine Arts Foundation issued a press release. The Kurt Walbrook Gallery For Acton Pace Paintings was to be built in Boston, Massachusetts. It would be a gift to Harvard University, with Cheyney Fox as its lifetime director. Kurt entrusted the entire project to her. Of all his gifts, this one touched her most deeply. She was no longer dabbling in the art world but back as a mid-field player. The American art world buzzed with the news of the magnanimous gift from the Walbrook Collection.

Cheyney Fox at last had a real home for her own Acton Pace paintings to come to. She reassembled them from the various museums that had them on loan, and redecorated one of the large morning rooms in the Schloss Garmisch-Konigsberg as a room of her own to work and play in. It was there that she hung them.

And it was from there, in the months before her child was born, that Cheyney was once more launched in the grandest and most secure fashion back into the contemporary art world. She was welcomed with open arms. Not so much as a hint of memories of bankruptcy, failure, fraud. The words had apparently vanished from the vocabularies of every art person of significance in New York. But not from Cheyney's. No matter how far back in her mind she pushed the memories those words evoked, the past was still there.

She had never been happier than when she was pregnant and living with Kurt in Schloss Garmisch-Konigsberg. Their life was more exciting than ever. Within weeks of the announcement of her directorship of the gallery, she had enough letters and phone calls – from instant friends, in or on the fringes of the international art world – to flatter a film-star. The greater number were of course from Andy Warhol. She found it a bitter irony to receive so many offers of friendship and work in the art world now that she didn't need any. Kurt was amused, and as usual was able to teach her to be amused too. She gave in to him, saying, 'I can afford most of the things that make people happy. I suppose I can also afford not to be bitter.'

He had laughed and answered, 'Well, if you can't, I would surely like to know who can.' She fell on him with kisses, and they made love on her new white marble desk.

Nurseries were being made ready in each of their three houses. Kurt was as puffed with pride as if he were really the father. While she bought teddy bears and prams and played with the Walbrook period baby-clothes, he brought back baby-wardrobes from Porthault in Paris, shops in Zurich, London and New York. He had already made arrangements to put the boy's name down for Eton. He was booking an education, masculine and English, a decade in advance. Yes, he had decided it was going to be a boy. He laid down a wine cellar, he admitted for him or her, conceding that a

264

girl could drink. Bought him an elaborate antique train-set, and her a collection of antique articulated dolls with porcelain faces, and period costumes, from France. He took over the decoration of one of the nurseries himself. He presented it complete, down to the nappy-pins, to Cheyney as a surprise.

They each had their work, their love for the other and their social life and travelling. Yet, with such an outgoing life, they still managed to keep it a very private one. It was not easy to get to the Walbrooks.

Cheyney bought and paid for her fourth Acton Pace painting. It was as good as lighting a fuse under the explosive widow Pace. Combustion was postponed when Cheyney, heavily pregnant, and flanked by Kurt on one side and Judd Whyatt on the other, selected the eight other paintings she wanted to buy. She placed eight hundred thousand dollars in escrow, to be released at the rate of one hundred thousand dollars a year to the widow Pace. Neither Cheyney nor Judd would make any other concessions to Reha. They were determined to follow as closely as possible Acton's instructions, issued in his legacy to Cheyney.

They had Christmas and New Year holidays at Schloss Garmisch-Konigsberg, with a houseful of guests who included Lala and Roberto and Della. A house-party fit to make the huge hunting-lodge echo with laughter long after they all left. It was now only a matter of weeks before the baby was due. Kurt infiltrated the idea that it should be born in the States. Cheyney wanted the baby born at home in the Schloss.

'I think your son should have an American passport as well as an Austrian one.'

That surprised Cheyney. 'I thought you would be so pleased to have our baby born here.' She was talking to a man who had seen frontiers and nationalities dissolve before tides of history that rubbished frail European documents overnight.

He simply said, 'I would like nothing better. But I don't think we should deprive the baby of being born in his own country. Both his natural parents are, after all, American. Our world can be a very unstable place. Even with all that we have – all that we will always have – that will one day be his, I think it would be better if he were born in the United States rather than here as an Austrian. Please don't ask me to go into it any further. I have very deep personal feelings about it. I hope the hint will be enough for you? However, if you can honestly say we are being fair to that child, and to Grant Madigan, by having him born here, that's good enough for me.'

Taggart was born in the Lennox Hill Hospital in Manhattan. Kurt Walbrook was at Cheyney's side for most of her ordeal. And it was an ordeal. Whereas her pregnancy had been an amazingly comfortable and easy one, the birth was not. She was in labour for forty-two hours, but was finally delivered of a perfectly beautiful, healthy boy. Only once did she think of Grant Madigan, and that was when they placed her new-born son, still womb-warm and wet, at her breast. She experienced the most intense moment of sensual yet pure happiness of her life, in spite of all the pain and devastating exhaustion. How uneasy the experience would have made Grant: it could have bound them to each other for the rest of their lives.

Cheyney had never told Kurt about her abortion. It was one of the things about her past that she instinctively chose to keep from him. For the first few days after Taggart's birth, she was tortured by memories of that searing experience. She kept slipping into half-sleeps where she relived that night, again and again. Kurt listened to her restless sleep, and watched her closely, affected by the look of sadness in her eyes at a time he knew she was happier than she had ever been. One morning he arrived in her room with yet another armful of flowers. He kissed her and whispered, out of nothing more than intuition, 'Sheyney, banish the past from your thoughts, my darling. We three have a lot of living and happiness to get through.' A few days later she had regained her strength enough to do just that, and the dreams stopped.

The rich years of early parenthood rolled by, and their life was full. Only imperceptibly did they adapt their established lifestyle. They just added Taggart to it. He was never denied the right to know who his natural father was, or what relationship had existed between Cheyney and Grant Madigan. At the age of eight, he was told the whole story by Cheyney and Kurt, and with such sensitivity it seemed only to add to his life. Once he knew who his real father was, he began following his 'other famous father's' career. That was the way he referred to Grant, innocently flattering Kurt in the process, and talking openly about him to his mother and step-father. Mercifully for Cheyney, that was not very often. She didn't much like it but held her counsel, sensing that it was the right thing.

Thanks to the wise and intelligent Kurt Walbrook, and his close relationship with his step-son, the boy grew up happy with the father who was present, and waited with ease and minimal anxiety for the time when he felt he was ready to meet the father who had never been there. Taggart was a handsome, quick, intelligent child, who grew up with few of the insecurities of a child born out of wedlock – because, in any sense of the phrase that mattered, he wasn't.

Chapter 29

In the year that followed Taggart's birth they pursued their remarkably cultured and cultivated existence, but with doubled happiness. Three months after Taggart was born, Cheyney became pregnant again. Their sexual intercourse became an even greater focal point in their marriage. Cheyney found herself rising to Kurt's every sexual demand, no matter how adventurous and unusual. He still had that mesmerising effect on her, drawing her into loving him and expanding herself through his obsessive love for her. Her appetites for a more exotic erotic life were now as sharp as his, her urge to satisfy them no less compelling.

Her second baby boy was born in the Schloss Garmisch-Konigsberg, after another long and difficult birth. Cheyney was thrilled to be able to give Kurt a natural heir, a gift of thanks for all the love he had bestowed on her and Taggart. From soon after Andrew Charles was born, however, Cheyney sensed a subtle difference in Kurt's attitude towards their baby from that he had towards Taggart. There had always been in her mind a nagging little worry that Kurt, with a son of his own, might lose interest in their first born. But quite the opposite seemed to be happening. Though she said nothing to him about it, quite quickly it became obvious to everyone that he favoured Taggart. Step-father and son seemed to share an exceptionally close loving relationship.

His attitude towards baby Andrew, although it hurt her sensibilities, seemed to make no difference to the relationship between Kurt and Cheyney. As soon as they were able to resume their sexual life, she was assured that all was well by his tremendous ardour towards her. She convinced herself he would come around to loving Andrew as much as he loved Taggart. They made two trips, shortly after she gave birth, one to Egypt for a visit to Albert Semanan, which she was not especially happy to make. She always found him a cold, sinister personality, but she had no intention of letting Kurt down. With them, at Kurt's insistence, they took a nanny and the children.

Since the time Taggart was born, they had taken him with them on their travels. A precocious twenty-month old child, he was as always a joy to have with them. During their week with Albert, Cheyney was able at least to relax and enjoy the luxury of living among an unpleasant man's most pleasing works of art.

When Cheyney was not riding with Kurt in the desert, or visiting temples close by, her greatest joy had to be seeing Taggart playing with Kurt. Which happened most of the boy's waking hours. Kurt even took the boy with him when he was in private conference with Albert and his friends. Seeing the genuine bond between her son and Kurt, she could forgive her husband anything. For mother-love instructed Cheyney that love and security, a happy family life for Taggart and Andrew, came before all else.

Two important things were brought to light for Cheyney by that visit. The second night they were there, Kurt slipped something new into their sexual life. Another woman. Never short of charm, he cast an irresistible seductive net and ensnared Cheyney into the sexual threesome in a way that made it impossible for her to resist. They often liked to have intercourse with both of them lying on their side, Cheyney with her back against his chest, her bottom tucked tight against him. He could then slip a leg over one of hers and enter her between her legs. Penetration was deep and the angle seemed to touch her most sensitive spots. On that particular night he delivered her into sublime sexual ecstasy that had been especially thrilling. Cheyney was not a selfish lover. He knew that she would do anything to give back to him the pleasure she was experiencing. Breathless, she came in a long and exquisite orgasm and whispered huskily in the dark, 'Now, it's my turn. I want to make you come in a passionate frenzy, the way I have been coming.'

She tried to ease herself around in his arms but he held her tight and thrust deep inside her, pinning her to him with his penis. She relaxed in his arms. He kissed the back of her neck, her shoulder, caressed her breasts with his hands and sucked and bit hard on a nipple. He felt her tighten with the pain he was causing her, and so he released the nipple and licked and kissed it before he said, 'Good. That's what I want too.' And he moved in and out of her with a newfound zest. Then he switched on the light and, never stopping the sexual rhythm, kissed her on the ear and said, 'Isn't she lovely? I have bought her for us for the night.'

And he kissed Cheyney hard on the lips and moved faster and faster in and out of her, and the beautiful tall slender Chinese girl who appeared soundlessly and as if by magic lay down and took Cheyney in her arms, and began to kiss and caress her and Kurt with hands and lips and cunt. It was there at Semanan's house that more bizarre sexual adventures became a part of their life.

In the sun, by the pool, the following day, Cheyney had to come to terms with the fact that her husband had slowly, cleverly, yes, Svengali-like, corrupted her. What was so dreadful was the realisation of how much she enjoyed it. After their third night of sensual debauchery, Kurt dismissed the man and the woman who had intensified their sexual games. He confessed to Cheyney that he loved her more because she fulfilled every fantasy that he projected on to her, and more. And that he loved her son Taggart as he never dreamed he could love a child. He hardly mentioned Andrew. Kurt then presented her with a necklace of emeralds that he had purchased from Albert, telling her, 'They were once offered by King Carol of Rumania to his mistress. They're yours, for giving me Taggart and Andrew. But the Botticelli is mine. I have waited thirty years to get it away from Albert. It's mine, and when I die I will leave it to Taggart.'

She wanted to say, 'Is this what being friendly with all these decaying fascists is all about? Waiting to pick up their treasures for yourself?' But how could she be so churlish to a man who had just presented her with such a gift of words and jewels? And there was another reason she couldn't say anything. Her assumption touched areas where Kurt would tolerate no probing.

It galled Cheyney that a man like Albert Semanan should possess even the smallest work by such as Botticelli. That a man like the one in Paraguay from whom she had bought the Van Goghs, who positively radiated evil, should own two of the finest paintings in the world. Again that question niggled. How did they come by these magnificent treasures in the first place? Why no competition for Kurt from other collectors for the works of art he pursued? It was not a thing she could ask him about. Previous experience silenced her. She recalled the sharpness of the speech he had made to her at his mother's birthday ball.

Mystery surrounded her husband. Cheyney nursed a desire to unfold it. But any enquiry would have to be subtle, because Kurt never answered questions. Not hers nor anyone's.

She relegated the worry to the back of her mind. There were other things to occupy her. A still fascinating, somewhat complex husband, two children, the soon to be opened gallery in Boston for the Acton Pace collection, two exhibitions she was organising: one at the Museum of Modern Art in Amsterdam, and another in Dallas, Texas.

To all the world, Cheyney seemed to lead a charmed life. She could do no wrong, and luck was with her. That was true, but Cheyney and Kurt had their share of pain too. They buried their child, Andrew, before he was four months old. The only natural child they would ever have.

An articulated lorry swerving out of control crushed Andrew Charles Walbrook to death in his pram. It propelled the nanny into a coma and on to life support machines, condemning her to a non-life until someone had the courage to pull the plug and leave her to die a natural death.

They were crossing the road ten blocks from the family house in Vienna when the lorry struck. The enactment of a parent's nightmare. Kurt and Cheyney were at home waiting for Andrew and the nanny to return. When the hours began to slip by, Cheyney panicked. The hospitals came up with no records suggesting the nanny and a baby had turned up there as accident victims. In the police and hospital logs for that afternoon only a woman was recorded as having been run over by a lorry. The police were called. Everyone's first thought was a kidnapping.

At midnight, one of the Walbrook servants saw the accident reported on TV news. He recognised one of Andrew's teddy bears that had been thrown from the wreck. No body had been recorded on entry into any of the hospitals because, until the TV cameras found the teddy bear, no one knew that baby and pram were lying somewhere within the twisted wreckage of the lorry.

Living a nightmare, Kurt Walbrook contacted the police chief. The man did what he could to redouble the efforts to lift the wreckage and try to save the baby. There was no baby left to save. Not even enough of Andrew to allow Cheyney the luxury of a last look at her dead child, to be able to kiss that beautiful baby goodbye.

The sudden bludgeoning out of their lives of a baby: no parent will ever forget it. Cheyney and Kurt had no stronger defences against that than any one else. Although their relationship was as solid as ever, the death of Kurt's only natural child caused a hiatus in their marriage. The loss of the child sent Cheyney into a state of deep grief. For months she was inconsolable. It was appalling coming to terms with such a devastating loss. But she finally came to accept it, and the fact that, for whatever reason, Kurt did not feel the loss quite as she did. Nothing could possibly make her forget Andrew, not even time. With brave faces and a void in their hearts, Cheyney and Kurt resumed their life, and she grieved silently for Kurt and Taggart's sake. But grieve she did for her baby every day of her life. Kurt managed his grief in his own way, becoming more devoted than ever to Taggart. Not quite to the point of obsession, but certainly after the baby's death he drifted away from Cheyney towards Taggart – more so every year.

With Taggart's growing, the greatest pleasure Cheyney had in life was to see him flower into a stable and secure child, bright and quick in mind and body. A mischievous, happy boy, curious about everything and everyone. A boy who had a natural aptitude for art, and a love and respect for his surrogate father. Taggart treated Kurt Walbrook as his first and real father. Every day Cheyney could see the best of her sophisticated, Viennese-aristocrat husband, with his faintly mysterious past and his current fame as art-collector and patron, imprinting itself on the boy. He was the husband she would have chosen had her sole aim in marrying been to find a father for her child.

Through the turbulent seventies, Cheyney's marriage to Kurt became increasingly a partnership in art-collecting and dealing. For her it was an education in the ways of the artistic world, a final rending of the veil of idealism from her childhood dream of art. As she journeyed with her husband, and when possible with their son, from one artisic milieu to another, they became even more involved as partners in the business of art. Cheyney came to know people whose involvement with art dated with sinister exactitude from the final years of Hitler's war. In the castles and houses they visited in Europe and South America, in Egypt and Syria, there were breathtaking art treasures in abundance, all suddenly acquired at that time by the families from whom Walbrook wished to prise them, by his charm and his money, without asking whence they came.

The realisation was like a worm gnawing within the otherwise supportive structure of their marriage. Kurt seemed unaware of it, so far as Cheyney could tell. She gradually had to recognise the probable sources of her husband's own collection and wealth. And once that fixed itself in her mind, she had to brace herself and confront Kurt with her concern. Questions, asked by her with increasing precision and alarm, were brushed aside. Finally the topic was specifically banned. And she realised that already, from opportunities created by him for her, she had unknowingly compromised herself by the tempting deals she engaged in. She knew success as a dealer of modern art again, but she knew the gnawing remorse of lost integrity.

She began to feel they were becoming increasingly estranged as lovers, even as art partners. But their closeness as sexual partners and as a family remained strong, its cornerstone always her husband's love for her and Taggart. She nudged away the feeling of loss, pretending it existed only in her imagination.

Cheyney's marriage to Kurt had been founded partly on his mesmeric attraction as a suave older man offering her immediate successful re-entry into the world of art where she had previously encountered defeat and humiliation; partly on the security he offered her and her child, because he had planned it that way. Because he was certain that was the life they both wanted. The mix had in the end been irresistible to her. She had for years enjoyed the sexual life he weaned her into, not only for her own pleasure but largely because of his. By this time in their relationship, she endured the sexual demands he made on her. The sex was not the problem, he was too clever not to make sure she enjoyed – not just enjoyed but craved it. It was more that the years with Kurt, as wonderful as they had been, were soulless. Not for one second had their souls come together and made love. She still, with all he was able to give her, missed that oneness with another human being that she had had with Grant Madigan, and knew she would never have again. Kurt's sexuality was now irreversibly entwined with his own psychological needs, which she must serve. It was for his pleasure first, her pleasure, and because her child's well-being came before all else that she loved Kurt and forgave him his lost soul. Slowly she grew to realise that this match was making a subtler but still more corrupting demand upon her than she was comfortable with. The strain on her was enormous.

'Irving Kirshner!'
'Jesus, Grant Madigan!'
Irving Kirshner rose from his chair. A thump on the back for Grant. Hands warmly grasped.
'What brings you here, you old hound dog?' asked Grant. His smile showed how really pleased he was to see his old friend.
'I'm here for the poached turbot. What are you doing here?'
'I'm here for the turbot too.'
'Like hell you are! My information has it you're in Paris to have lunch at the Elysée Palace. So what happened? If you spill the beans, I'll pay for the turbot. Deal?'
Grant accepted the invitation and was introduced to Irving's guests. The Israeli Cabinet Minister Grant had met before. The fellow American was CIA. Grant sat down, tapped the side of his nose, and began teasing Irving. 'Still in the same business I see, Irving.'
'Still in the same business, Grant.'
Sam White arrived at the Hotel Crillon Bar. Knowing all the men at the table, he stopped briefly to shake hands, say hello, and then sat down at his regular table. It had come to be more like a desk, and the Crillon a second office for him. The Crillon was one of Grant's favourite haunts in Paris. Lunch-time there drew all his old journalistic cronies. He could take instantaneously the Paris pulse and the news of the moment. It was true he was to have had lunch at the Elysée Palace but that had been cancelled at the last minute. The date was now for the following day.
Lunch turned out to be a heated but amusing affair. Grant could not resist baiting the Israeli Minister. It was doubly enjoyable because, for the first time, he had met a CIA agent with a wicked sense of humour. The man, Ben Johnson, dissolved them all into laughter with his up-to-the-minute political one-liners. His timing was perfect. The meeting must have ended well because, after their boozy lunch, they all shook hands, and before they dispersed they agreed to meet sometime around eleven that evening at Harry's Bar on the Rue Dannou.

Over the years, Grant and Irving had stayed in touch by telephone, tele-gram, and letter, but it came as a great surprise to both of them to realise that it had been more than ten years since they had last met in Cairo. Grant had an unexpected free afternoon. He had decided to stroll from the Crillon across the Seine, and spend the afternoon wandering around Saint Germain des Prés. The two men walked together as far as Irving's offices on the Rue de Rivoli, where he insisted Grant come up to see them.

Irving Kirshner was now the number-one art detective in the world. Madigan was a respected writer on geo-political wars, a political journalist, and a TV interviewer of international men of the moment. Both men had success and reputation to spare.

Over the years Irving had bombarded Grant's New York office with brown-envelope packets of photographs. They showed missing paintings. Irving always lived in hopes that one day Grant or someone else in the office might recognise the lost works of art that might give him a lead. More than ten years of packets, and never a word about them. Not that Grant had not given them his attention. He had simply never recognised anything in the photographs that could help Irving.

They were discussing this as they climbed the stairs to the first-floor offices overlooking the Tuileries gardens. Introductions were made among the staff. Irving decided to join Grant for the afternoon. Work could be put off until the following day.

While Grant waited for Irving to make two phone calls, he lit a cigar and studied the display of photographs opposite Irving's desk. A mélange of photos in both black and white and in colour: all sizes, any shape, all attached to the cork wall by glass drawing-pins. Written diagonally along the upper left-hand corner of each were different notations: Cracow 1939, Paris 1941, Warsaw 1940, Prague 1941, Budapest, 1939 and 1941. They were camera shots of paintings, sculptures, rare manuscripts and books, the odd photograph of a man or woman.

Slowly, Grant paced beside the wall puffing on his cigar and examining the photographs. Irving put his hand over the telephone, and called across the room to him, 'My failures. These are my mysteries yet to be solved. My magnificent obsession continues.'

'No wall of successes?' called back Grant over his shoulder.

'Naw. Successes we file away. But keeping my failures up front sharp-ens my wits. I hate having failures. It makes me feel guilty.'

Grant turned around to face Irving, smiling. 'That's very Jewish.'

'What can I tell you? I *am* Jewish.'

Grant turned back to the wall, saying, 'Never mind, Irving, I know how you feel about failures. They don't sit too well with me either. But I'm more blessed about them than you are. I forget them, just like that.' He snapped his fingers, and was about to add, 'And they don't come back to haunt me either,' when, amazingly, he did recognise one of the black and white blow-ups. Written in wide, red felt-tip on an angle it read, 'Who is this woman?' Grant pulled the glass drawing-pin from the photograph and plucked it from the celluloid montage. He placed it on the desk in front of Irving. He looked at it and then at Grant. Immediately he announced to the man on the other end of the telephone,' Got to go, Sam. Something's just come up. Call you tomorrow. Yeah, Sam, yeah. I promise, tomorrow.' He hung up.

'You recognize her?'

'Yes. Why is she on your wall?'

Irving turned the photograph over. He found some numbers written on the back of the picture, and called for the file through his intercom. Then switching it off, he leaned forward and asked Grant, 'What do you know about her?'

'You tell me what you know about her first, Irving.'

Grant sat down in the chair opposite his friend. While Irving spoke, he pulled out the bottom drawer of his desk and took out two squat glasses and a bottle of Calvados. He poured two fingers-worth in each glass and handed one to Grant.

'Not much. Pretty lady, as you obviously know. She turns up in some fairly odd places around the world which we have under surveillance. She surfaces in two interesting files, MOSSAD's and the CIA's.'

'Two secret intelligence files. I don't believe this! Israel and the US interested in her activities? That's rich.'

'Then you do know her?'

'Yes, I know her.'

'OK, at last we're getting someplace with this lost babe. I'll tell you all we've got. Several photographs of her coming and going at the houses of some top Nazi criminals still on the loose whom the Israelis are trying to snatch to justice. We're talking the last of the real big guys, Grant. We're not talking little *pishers* here. The front-rank war-criminals left. A few second-rankers. She has some pretty dicey friends. The closest we have been able to get is what you see. This photo, and these.'

Irving removed several other glossy snaps of Cheyney and handed them to him. Pictures of her with several different men. Nothing at all compromising.

'We know she's American, wealthy and interested in the arts. We've been trying to locate her for years. Every time we come near, we lose her again. Wait a minute . . . there's two people you know now connected with these bums.'

'What are you talking about, Irving?'

'It's coming back to me now. Remember when I asked you to help me the last time we met in Egypt? That guy . . . we had a picture of you with that guy.' Irving took a long swig of his drink, then banged his hand on the desk, 'Got it, goddamm it! I got it. Austrian, handsome, suave type. Walbrook, that's the dude's name, Kurt Walbrook. He was there again at the Albert Semanan birthday-bash you went to with your friend the prince, and Otto Furtwangler. It's all coming back to me. It was the night Kennedy was shot. You remember. Nobody forgets where he was that day.'

Irving was now padding around his office: a blood hound about to locate its prey. He found a photograph of Kurt Walbrook in a file marked 'Grant Madigan'. Grant didn't care for being in a file all his own in Irving's office; he knew what that meant. Irving laid the picture of Kurt next to Cheyney's on the desk in front of Grant. He had checked the writing on the back. He sank into his chair and tilted it against the wall, and took another swallow of the Calvados.

'OK. Now here we've got two people, one who you've been seen with at one of those big Nazi do's, the man Kurt Walbrook. Now you know this woman, who has been seen with people of a similar persuasion. We know she deals in art, we know Walbrook is a famous collector, and so was his family, going way-back. I've tried to get something going on him. Not a thing, he's squeaky clean. But I keep thinking he shouldn't be. He's either a sympathiser or is laundering dirty paintings instead of dirty money for those bastards. None of which we can prove. The guy is thick with those miserable low-lifes, but clean as a whistle himself. So was his father. I don't know how they did it. Even the mother, the Baroness, the worse thing we can get on her is that Hitler worshipped the ground she trod on. That's if you believe Hitler worshipped anything other than his own gorey visions. She received them all – Himmler, Speer, Eichmann, Hess, Goering, Bormann, Mengele – all the ghouls from Death Row – and we were never able to pin a thing on her. I know, as sure as I'm sitting here with you, the Walbrook art treasures include plenty of stolen works. Can I prove it? Not on your life. I need a break, maybe the lady is it. Who is she?'

Grant finished his drink and placed the glass on the desk. 'Jesus, Irving, you're some detective agency. Her name is Cheyney Fox.'

'Cheyney Fox – great name.'

'Yeah, and a terrific lady.'

'You know her!'

'Yes, I guess you could say that. And she's married – wait for it, Irving – to Kurt Walbrook. And I can tell you one thing for sure: that lady could not possibly have anything to do with stolen works of art. Not knowingly, anyway. And especially if it was Nazi loot from the war. If she's dancing at their parties, you can be sure she's not dancing there by choice. That might be the break you're looking for.'

'How the fuck do *you* know all this, and *we* couldn't get to first base on information on her? How did we miss it? It's goddam obvious there might have been a connection between the two.' He threw the switch on the intercom and barked into the receiver. 'George, Ruth, get the fuck in here.'

'Grant, how do you know all this? Are you still in touch with her?'

'No. Haven't seen or heard from her in years. A lot of years. How do I know it? Because, as patrons of the arts, his name occasionally crops up, hers too, in the New York art-scene, or in some esoteric article on contemporary art.'

'What about our news-clipping service? How did they miss her? We haven't been able to get a name on her.'

'Simple. It's so simple you're going to hate yourself, Irving. Though she's married to Walbrook, she never uses his name. She has retained the name Cheyney Fox. She's rarely photographed. In fact this is the first photograph I've ever seen of her. She slips in and out of art circles and is rarely in the public eye. I would say, if you're looking for a break, I know this woman's character: if you're more than usually sensitive with her and really tread softly, she might be it. But, whatever you do, leave my name out of it. I want your word on that. No questions asked.'

'Ah, it was personal.'

'Yes, very personal.'

'OK, you've got my word on that. But I gotta tell you, old buddy, I'm really grateful to you for this. It may be a terrific lead. I owe you one.'

'Just remember, Irving, I'm out of it. I don't want to know. I have no interest in the lady or anything she does.'

276

Chapter 30

Bitter chill: cold rain sheeting down. Gusts of it, driven by a fierce wind coming off the Seine, whipped round Chelsea's ankles and beat against her legs. Finally, three doors from her destination, the restaurant where she was going to meet Roberto, it snatched the umbrella from her hand. She watched it soar towards the grey sky in a series of upward somersaults as it flapped away above the wet tarmac.

Just inside the restaurant Cheyney found an anxious Roberto. He apologised profusely. It was a dreadful to have dragged her here. He and the maître d' helped her out of her wet things. She went dripping to the ladies' room to dry herself off as best she could with the help of the maid. She returned to a whisky and Roberto.

It was always a joy to see him. That special kind of goodness of his was always warming. His Giacometti figure – so gaunt and slender, so proud and princely – was never less than impressive, no matter how well you knew him and all his human flaws.

'Much as I love you, Roberto – thrilled as I am to have this clandestine lunch with you – what is this all about?' she teased.

There had been a phone call from him three days before. He had seemed nervous, but came right to the point. Could Cheyney meet him in Paris for a day, without Kurt knowing? Above all, Lala was not to know either. They had fixed the date, the place, and the time. If she could not make it, she was not to call him back. Just a message at the restaurant. Irresistibly mysterious.

Cheyney took a chance on her getaway. She simply announced to Kurt and Taggart that evening that she wanted to go clothes-shopping in Paris. It was a calculated risk: either of her two men might want to join her. Taggart loved to hunt down tin soldiers for his collection. He and Kurt had assembled a roomful of battlefields, all authentic period pieces. They were currently re-creating Napoleon's march through Egypt. Taggart knew every corner of Paris where he might acquire more metal recruits for the campaign. As for Kurt, he liked nothing better than to take Cheyney on a shopping-spree through the haute couture salons. But she also knew they had other passions.

'Oh no, Pa, not shopping in Paris! Couldn't we go skiing instead?'

They were both top-class off-piste skiers, which Cheyney was not. A gleam in their eyes, and she knew she was safely booked in for her secret *rendezvous* with Roberto.

'Come on, Roberto. Relax, old friend, I'm here. Now tell me all about it.'

'There's someone who wants to meet you. And someone I would like you to meet and help. If you can – without compromising yourself. I don't know really how to put this properly, Cheyney. You know that I am devoted to both of you. It's thanks to having worked with you and Kurt that Lala and I will be able, if we are careful, to live comfortably for the rest of our lives. And we are friends, after all. But this contact of mine, he is a good man. He's doing good work, I think it best for him to tell you what all this is about.'

'Well, where is he? I'm starved.'

Roberto looked relieved. She was nicely relaxed about it all. They were shown to a small seventeenth-century panelled room overlooking the river, a private dining room. It was here that Cheyney got to meet Irving Kirshner.

The next four hours in that room with Roberto and Kirshner blew a whole cluster of cobwebs from Cheyney's mind. Self-interest and loyalty to her husband and child could not simply be sloughed off. When she was assured by Irving Kirshner that even a zealot could not pin on Kurt Walbrook a Nazi past, she felt all sorts of relief. His only crime, so far as they could prove, was that his magnificent obsession for art and beauty had made him a lot of rotten friends.

All Irving wanted from Cheyney was to identify photographs of works of art. Tell him where she might have seen them. She could leave the rest to them. Here was an opportunity to leak information to government agencies if she got a whiff of criminal deals in war-loot being set up by her husband's contacts. She could off-load guilt at having turned a blind eye – as Kurt had done all his life – to what she knew was wrong.

'If you should want to help us, you had better know that this is no lark. Even though all I will ask you to do is meet occasionally with myself or a colleague to identify photographs and tell us, if you can, where you have seen them. No more than that. I will never contact you directly, always through Roberto. Otherwise you will call me, on a certain date each month. Or at any time you need me. We'll have to keep it sneaky like that for your own safety. You know some pretty ruthless killers. I can more or less guarantee you and your family will be safe, so long as you are discreet. But if you want to walk away now, and forget we ever met – well, it'll be a disappointment to me, but I can live with it. My work will go on anyway.'

278

Cheyney agreed to think about it. She would meet Irving Kirshner the next evening for dinner in her suite of rooms at the Plaza Atheneé. Some quick-fire soul-searching ensued. Cheyney made her decision. If Kurt chose to remain indifferent to everything he knew about these people and their treasures, that was his privilege. She had her own conscience to think about. She chose to halt her slide into corruption, at least in the art world. What she did, she did for herself and her son and Kurt. He would benefit because she would have resolved her problem about his 'friends', that bone of contention in their relationship.

For a time she had glimpses into the furtive and dangerous world of espionage. A world where Israeli, Russian, or French agents – and which of them was she to trust? Which of them was not using the past to gain some present goal remote from righting the wrongs done in the last war? – vied with each other for the scant information she might supply.

Irving Kirshner and Cheyney Fox met five times in various parts of the world. Their clandestine meetings were eventually to result in the return to the French government of a valuable Delacroix, one of the pictures that disappeared from sight during the occupation of France. A Caravaggio to the estate of a Count Piotrowski of Cracow, who had died valiantly trying with his brigade to halt the march of Germany into Poland. Two Renoirs and three Rubens to a Walter Rothstein, formerly of Berlin, residing since his release from Auschwitz in London.

But it was their fifth and last meeting that was to put an end to her little game of I-spy For Art. Irving and the American and Israeli agents she became embroiled with that day pledged that when she quit, her role would be officially forgotten. A one-off involvement for her. No repeats.

It had to be that way. With secrecy assured, Cheyney was about to enable Irving to trap Albert Semanan, and net his entire collection.

Had she ever set out to do this? For years she had tolerated Albert because Kurt was devoted to him. But what was behind Kurt's devotion? Then it was spelled out for her by Albert himself. It happened, as is often the way, by chance. A word let slip, and then too many more added. Once that happened, Cheyney had to rid herself and her family of Albert Semanan forever. And only Irving Kirshner could make that happen.

The three Walbrooks were on a visit to Semanan's kingdom in the desert. These visits strained Cheyney and Kurt's relationship. The place and Semanan's cronies brought out the dark side of Kurt's nature.

It was just before dawn, and there was no sleep in Cheyney. He had made love to her, particularly tender and sweet sex, had spoiled her with it, wanting all through the night to pleasure her, until she begged him to stop. That was not unusual, except when they were staying with Semanan. At those times he might make sexual demands of her that were outrageous, akin to sadistic.

She watched him sleeping. So many years, and still he was an enigma to her. Yet, he possessed her, and she loved him. She kissed his cheek, ever so lightly, sad that, love her husband as she might, she still yearned for a kind of love from him he could never give. Where was it to be found in him? She slid out of bed and covered her nakedness with a silver sheer silk dressing-gown. Barefoot, she slipped noiselessly through the French doors. A bright white half moon led her through the garden towards the Nile. Fortunately, she heard Otto and Semanan talking long before she saw them, which gave her a chance to slip behind a hibiscus bush. Her intention was not to listen but to hide. But she stayed hidden and listened after she heard Otto say, 'He will never do it, Semanan. He might have if his mother were still alive, but I know him. With her dead, he no longer believes as once he did in our cause.'

'It is quite simple, Otto. He will do as I want him to or he and his family will be disposed of. I intend to sink a billion dollars into Germany. I mean to re-create the kind of political machine that will put the old guard – with some new faces – back in power. We need his money and his reputation to help do it. I have no intention of withering away here in the desert with my art collection. In five years I expect to be home in Germany. Our dream will be fulfilled. I want five hundred million dollars from Kurt as his personal contribution. I can assure you he will give me his word on that before we return from our cruise up the Nile.'

'You seem so sure, Semanan.'

'Oh, I am. With his wife and son under guard here, as my insurance policy, why should I not be? You worry too much, Otto. I always get what I want.'

More was said, but Cheyney registered none of it. She was too trau-matised by what she had already heard to listen properly. She had no idea how much time had passed before they continued their walk through the garden, before she felt strong enough to make her way back to the house and her bedroom. Back in bed, she felt safe next to Kurt. But was she? Were they? It was all too fantastic. Had she misunderstood what they were saying? No, of course she hadn't. Had she misinterpreted it? She placed her hand on Kurt's shoulder, about to shake him. It came to her suddenly that he would not believe her. He would assume she had been dreaming. She let her husband sleep on.

'I want to go home, Kurt. Today,' was her morning greeting to her husband.

'Don't be ridiculous, Cheyney. We have only just arrived, and Taggart is looking forward to our trek into the desert. Albert has just given him an Arab stallion. Aren't you going to let him ride it?'

As if on cue, there was a knock on the door. Taggart looked princely in

280

his riding clothes. He was obviously keen to get started. They were behaving as if nothing out of the normal could happen. She wanted to shout it all out to them, to sweep them up, to get away. She knew they would think her mad. She felt more confused than ever. They kissed her, made a fuss over her, the two men she loved, and were gone, promising to be home by dark.

She dressed hurriedly and dashed through the palace rooms. From the courtyard she waved them and their party of ten other riders goodbye. Cheyney walked with Semanan, who was overseeing their departure, to the edge of the parkland. They watched the party disappear into the desert. When Cheyney and Semanan turned back towards the palace, he placed an arm around her shoulder and said, 'And have you made plans for your day, Cheyney? Or will you allow *me* to amuse you?'

The innuendo was there: in his voice, in the way he raised her hand to kiss it, deliberately grazing the side of her breast with his arm. A habit he practised whenever they were alone. It always annoyed her intensely. No coldness from her had ever curtailed the unwelcome gesture. This time she ignored it because she was distracted by the ice in his eyes. His words were all warmth. Hot and honeyed. They shocked her into action. Her mind kept telling her, 'Irving Kirshner. Find Irving. Get out of here. Find him and tell *him* what you heard.'

She replied, with the first thing that came into her head: 'I wondered if you would lend me the sea-plane for the day? I'd like to go into Cairo for a few hours. The hairdresser. And the dealer Mahmud claims he has the most perfect Pharaonic gold necklace for me.'

She saw greed sparkle in his eyes. Pharaoh's gold. It was a good ruse to get away. He could not resist seeing the piece, and there would be no other way unless it was brought to him. Cairo was still too dangerous for him: a city that housed his potential avengers. He agreed at once, on condition that, if she rejected the necklace, she would bring it to him on approval. Then he insisted, 'At least have breakfast with me before you go.'

Any qualms Cheyney had about drawing Irving into this problem were dispelled when she entered the breakfast room and confronted Otto and the man she had met in Paraguay. Otto, especially, seemed embarrassed by her presence. That was proof enough for Cheyney. The ominous things she had heard were no figments of her imagination. Until she sat across the table from him that morning, she had felt the least uncomfortable with Otto of all Kurt's old-guard Nazi acquaintances.

Soon after their arrival, the two men made excuses and left the table. Cheyney had no idea from where she was gathering her strength, but gather it she did. Breakfast was fresh mango juice and Roederer Cristal champagne, served to them both in seventeenth-century rock-crystal goblets; a soufflé flavoured with truffles, and slivers of parma ham hardly thicker than a piece of darning thread; hot, crisp slices of toasted brioche, and cups of steaming hot Fortnum's Royal Blend Tea. Thus fortified she took command.

Always keeping her eyes on the white silk organza tablecloth, its embroidered white flowers, the Haviland china – anything, so as not to make eye-contact with Semanan – she composed herself. She was half-afraid he would catch in her eyes her loathing for him. She made conversation. Might he be inept enough to let slip more of his plans? Something that she might use to extricate herself, her son and husband from his clutches: she was certain that Semanan the political fantasist was capable of murder.

'I do believe that, in all the years I've known you, this is the first time you and I have ever been alone over a meal together.'

'Your choice, more than mine, Cheyney. I am all the more honoured and delighted.'

An awkward silence followed. She felt he was waiting for her to say something. She didn't know what. Working on instinct alone, which had at least gotten her free from him and the estate for a day – no mean feat, since he was so paranoid about the comings and goings of people in his fortified desert abode – yet again she blurted out the first thing that came into her head.

'I have always been a little afraid of you.'

'How flattering. May I ask why?'

'Because I have never been able to understand the close relationship you have with Kurt, the bond that links you.'

'Then should you not have asked your husband?'

' "Friendship, a deep and abiding friendship never to be broken." Kurt's very words.'

'True enough.'

Cheyney had to muster all the control she could find within herself not to shout, 'Liar! What about the plan I overheard in the garden? Liar, liar!' Instead she claimed, 'I am here breakfasting with you because I think at last that I understand it. It is a friendship between men that doesn't really have a place for me in it. It's that and nothing more, isn't it, Albert?'

Again, silence lay heavily between them, only this time it sent a chill through Cheyney. She heard the meanness come into his voice. She stiffened herself to act a role she knew she had to play.

'I have always found you charming. Beautiful and charming, Cheyney. And intelligent. But I have never understood this elaborate pretence you make of not knowing that we are the last of the Nazi hierarchy. And that, although Kurt was never one of us, his mother was, and he was a Nazi sympathiser who chose to remain neutral in England and Portugal because it suited his and our purpose.'

'I didn't know. I guessed,' she answered, trying to appear calm.

'Don't you and your husband talk to each other, Cheyney?'

She ignored the question.

'Guessed, and have now accepted my husband's past as I accept yours. Which is why we are having breakfast together.'

'Ah, then this is a change of heart, a new beginning for our own relationship, Cheyney? Is that what you are trying to tell me?'

'Yes. In a rather awkward way, it seems.'

Semanan rose from his chair and came around the table to sit down in the empty chair next to hers. He raised her hand and kissed it, stroked her hair. Cheyney had to fight the inclination to be sick.

'What has brought on this extraordinary change of heart, my dear, beautiful Cheyney?'

'Time, and loving my husband and son more than anything in this world.' She gave him a hard stare and pressed her advantage. 'Time . . . Oh, just look at the time! I want to leave now, Albert.'

He threw back his head and laughed. 'You are embarrassed. How charming. Never mind, Cheyney. I have waited a long time for you to appreciate us. Now I can wait a little longer for you to appreciate me.'

The meaningful looks, the squeeze of her hand. Yet again, the arm accidentally brushing against her breast as they rose from their chairs. Fortunately the sound of the sea-plane taxi-ing up to the dock was distraction enough for her to get away without having to say another word. She rushed to her room to change, his sinister laughter ringing in her ears. He was there on the dock to wave her off and tell her that a car and driver would be waiting to chauffeur her around Cairo. And she was gone, without once looking back to see him watching the plane taxi up the Nile and glide effortlessly into the air.

The plane skimmed the river up to the shore almost opposite the Hilton Hotel. Two men lashed the silver-winged beauty to its mooring, while the pilot helped Cheyney to disembark. She kept telling herself, Remember, nothing out of the ordinary. All must appear as normal. Pray you can find Irving.

She had never been naive about how powerful, wealthy, envied and admired Kurt was, nor the irrational behaviour men such as her husband might bring out in other men and women. So she had become quite used to bodyguards and cautious chauffeurs, without the kind of paranoia Semanan suffered from. She had always, when in Egypt, used his men as casually and easily as Kurt did. She had created a rapport with them over the years. Although she had to be cautious because she knew they reported everything back to Semanan, she was certain she could give them the slip if she had to. She was confident she would find Irving.

They greeted her enthusiastically at Costi and Taki's, the hairdressers in the Hilton. Yes, of course they could fit her in. She slipped into a gown. As soon as her hair had been washed, she called Semanan's bodyguard in from where he hovered in the hall. She asked him to save them time by going to fetch Mahmud the antique dealer and bring him to her. She would be at least two hours in the salon. Just enough time for him to get through the Cairo traffic to the other side of the city and back. For her, freedom from Semanan's spies.

Irving was not in Paris, but his office promised they could reach him and he would call her within the hour. He did, from Rome. The moment Cheyney heard Irving's voice she knew everything was going to be all right. Her relief was so great she broke down, blurting out all she had heard between dry sobs of anxiety. She was almost incoherent. Irving spent minutes trying to calm her. What finally did it was his saying, 'Cheyney, we take care of our own.'

'Yes, and that's what I'm trying to do, Irving,' she answered in a more controlled voice.

'Good, then let's proceed. First, hang up this telephone. I'll call you back in ten minutes and tell you where to go to meet two colleagues. They will help us work out what to do.'

The three-way conversation that took place between Cheyney on one telephone, Efram Sagar, a Mossad agent sitting next to her, on another, and Irving on his in Rome, was hardly necessary. Based on information they had received that Semanan was chancing a journey, Mossad had been plotting to lift him in a swoop on his motor-launch sometime during the trip up the Nile to Abu Simbel. They calculated it would be during the night of the second day. Efram was none too happy to receive Irving's call. He knew Irving would want the paintings, and to get into the palace. That was too complicated. Efram said all they wanted was Semanan, and there was no chance of getting into that fortress without a mini-war. Israel, because of diplomatic relations with Egypt, couldn't do it. The CIA would turn a blind eye to the operation, but not to a military raid that involved hundreds of people. Irving was furious and on his way to join them. Cheyney no longer knew what to do.

She pleaded, 'What about me, my family?'

'Listen to Efram. Do what he tells you. I'm leaving for the airport now. And Cheyney, Efram and John Collins will see to it you all walk away as if nothing happened. I have your word on that, Efram, don't I?'

Efram hesitated before he answered. Then looking at John Collins, he said, 'John, it was your tip, it's our ball game. If you can keep your informer safe, how about a countrywoman who can help us?'

'Has helped us!' shouted Irving down the telephone.

John Collins, who had taken it all in along with inhalations from a cigar, took the telephone from Efram. 'Irving, this'll cost you. You owe me one. Quit screaming, get in the air and jet your ass down here, or you'll miss the whole fucking show. Yes, Irving, yes.' He hung up.

'This is a nightmare,' said Cheyney.

'No, it's not. You think that way, lady, and it will be.'

John pulled up a chair next to her and poured two fingers of whiskey into a tumbler. He handed it to her. 'Belt this back, lady, and tell us everything you know. From the start, including how you became involved with Irving. We'll work it all out from there.'

Many things surfaced during their conversation, not least the answers to many of the questions Kurt had forbidden her even to raise. Relieved as she was to have confirmed the truth about her husband, she still resented the look in Efram's eyes that told her guilt by association was guilt enough. And the raised eyebrow, 'those-are-the-facts-lady' look in the CIA man's eye. His indifference towards Kurt when he had a criminal within his sights should have reassured her but somehow didn't.

They were all waiting on the dock for Cheyney on her return: Kurt, Taggart, Semanan, Otto. Smiling faces, waving arms. Never before had she felt guilty about helping Irving. Not once had she seen it as a betrayal of Kurt. But she had a twinge of that feeling now. For the first time she had agreed to participate actively in something she knew Kurt would never forgive her for.

When he placed his arms around her and kissed her, she wanted to blurt it all out. What she had overheard: the Israeli plan to catch Semanan, the most senior top Nazi war criminal still free and unpunished for his crimes against humanity. They had given her the proof of that, and more. Kurt Walbrook and his father had never joined the Nazi party. Their guilt lay in their attachment to the Baroness who had, and by association with the top people in the party. And in coming out of the war wealthy, their fortune intact, like so many other aristocratic, wealthy Germans. They couldn't even prove that Kurt Walbrook was an anti-semite, let alone a collaborator.

It was impossible for her to reveal anything there and then. But there was still time to talk to Kurt, give him a chance to explain his attachment to such a monster. He could make a clean breast of the past. She could tell him what she had overheard, and let him find a way out. They need never associate again with the likes of Albert Semanan.

When they were alone dressing for dinner she tried. He seemed never to take his eyes off her, wanting her, it was in every glance he gave her. She kept avoiding the erotic tension building between them. He was sitting on the edge of the bed, and finally, as she passed in front of him naked except for a diaphanous dressing-gown, he reached out and yanked her off her feet and into his arms. He opened the dressing gown and roughly shoved it off her shoulders. The moment his hands touched her skin, his lips hungrily sucking on her nipple, he felt her stiffen with anxiety and released her at once.

'What's wrong?'

'Nothing,' she answered, attempting to pull her dressing-gown closed.

'For the first time since I've known you, you are lying to me. Now, I'll ask you only one more time, what's wrong?'

She scrambled off the bed and walked to the wardrobe. She dropped her dressing-gown to the floor and slipped into a no less seductive one of powder blue silk moiré, with cuffs and lapels of a darker blue. A St Laurent robe he had bought her. It did at least cover her nakedness. She swung around to face him, visibly trembling as she tied the sash around her waist.

'I hate Albert. He is an evil man, and I don't know why you remain loyal to him. Why do you?'

'I told you, Cheyney. He's like family. Now leave it at that. I'd have thought you would have come to terms with that as a fact by now. It has nothing to do with us. Subject closed. I don't want to hear about it again.'

'Well, I am afraid the subject is not closed for me.'

The look of anger on Kurt's face frightened her. She had never seen him like that. He started towards her. She was terrified, but stood her ground. He grabbed her by the shoulders. His fingers dug into her flesh. Then the honeyed, sensuously husky voice, 'Sheyney.' He closed his eyes, that seductive emotional habit of his. Again, 'Sheyney,' he whispered, and the long lashes trembled. Slowly he opened his eyes. She felt herself slipping, slipping, under his spell. He possessed her entirely. She began to whimper as he pulled her tight into his arms and kissed her. Sucked hungrily on her lips until they parted and he was kissing her deeply, passionately. Slowly he released her, and stroked her hair and grazed her cheek with the back of his hand. And she broke down and began to weep. In between sobs she blurted it out, what she had heard in the garden in the dawn of that day.

Taking her by the hand, he led her to the bed, where they sat down together. He calmed her, and then made her repeat everything she had heard. She could tell nothing from his voice, the look on his face. He cradled her in his arms.

'It's unfortunate that you overheard that conversation.'

'Unfortunate? Is that all?'

'Put it out of your mind. Semanan can do nothing to harm us, I can assure you of that. Leave it with me. He has a dream which can never be, and that is all that this amounts to. I could always talk him around, and I will this time as well.'

She couldn't believe it. He was sympathising with Semanan! She was going to tell him about the plot to kidnap Semanan. That she now knew the truth, about him and the Walbrook family. But Kurt kissed her once more on the lips and sealed them forever from telling him about anything she had done for Irving in the past, or what she was about to do for Irving and for her family, her marriage. Because when he released her he said, 'You must forget you ever heard that conversation, Cheyney. Don't think about Albert. Just take him as a remarkable man who has amassed one of the finest collections of art and artefacts the world has ever seen. And remember that one day it might belong to me, or to Taggart. And, if that happens, then ultimately the collection is not just for private eyes but for the world to see. I have spent a life-time on this, Cheyney, and it would be best if you kept that in mind. That and the fact that I love you just as much today as the first time we met. Only now, my Sheyney, I adore you as well.'

Was it the greed within his magnificent obsession that blinded Kurt? She was once again swayed by his almost mesmerising charm. Her husband was still the consummate spellbinder. What surfaced this time for Cheyney was the realisation that he was a far more tough and ruthless spellbinder than she had ever allowed herself to acknowledge. He did what he had to do. She would do the same.

The person involved in the snatch (John Collins' term for the Israeli operation 'Killer One') who suffered the most anxiety over the affair was Irving Kirshner. Not allowed to participate, unable to see and help Cheyney with her small but crucial part in the affair, and with no way in to do a bit of snatching, on his own account, of art treasures, there was nothing for him to do but to await the outcome.

Cheyney's role had been simplicity itself. The only risk she ran was of not being convincing with her husband and Semanan.

An hour before he was to embark with Otto and Semanan on their cruise up the Nile, Cheyney persuaded Kurt to change places with her. He would take her place on a three-day camel safari in the vicinity of Luxor, with Taggart and four chums who were at that very moment on their way in from Cairo. That had been the easy part. The look on Semanan's face when she and her luggage appeared on the launch and Kurt explained the change of plan was black but controlled. Then Kurt announced that he and Cheyney would change places in Luxor, and she would ride back down the other side of the Nile and home with the boys, while he would complete the trip with Semanan and Otto to Abu Simbel. A modicum of Semanan's anger subsided at this.

Kurt seemed unaware of the tension the change had caused. Not so

Cheyney. Her blood chilled when Semanan said, in his most charming but decidedly cold manner, 'Enchanted as I am by this change, I wish you had consulted me on it. I am loath to change plans already established. You both know that. It always puts me on guard, makes me suspicious. This once, but please, never again.'

Cheyney thought her knees were going to buckle. His words made her anxious. The suspicious look in his eye, his moist fleshy lips on her fingers when he kissed her hand and raised his head and gazed at her. It was easy to read vengeance into that look.

They proceeded up the Nile. Always keeping in the centre of the river, and flanked by two open speed-boats, six armed men in each, patrolling between the cruiser and the shore. The *Cosima*, a fast motor-launch, was a sleek white beauty with six double master-suites of rooms. A thoroughbred that brought out the villagers along the river to admire and cheer them on. Women robed and draped in black, the occasional sparkle of silver jewellery in the sun, and men in their shabby robes and turbans. Children danced and played and bathed. Semanan was an excellent host and they were traversing the river at a relaxed speed. It was a chance to savour the flora and fauna on both banks.

That evening they dressed for dinner, and dined on sumptuous fare: caviar, tiny song-birds roasted in honey, and lobster and fresh salmon. They drank cold champagne, Roederer Cristal, and listened to *Lohengrin*. And at every moment Cheyney thought the fear in her heart would overwhelm her and all would be lost. Albert Semanan would discover her treacherous soul. He saw her to her room. She closed the door behind her, locked and leaned against it, actually sobbing with relief. Only then did she allow herself to whisper in the darkness, 'So far, so good.'

The snatch went like a typical Israeli operation. Perfectly. Except for one thing. Semanan cheated them out of a great show trial and a noose.

On the second evening out on the river, Cheyney, Otto and Semanan went ashore to visit by moonlight a small, relatively unknown temple, at her request. It seemed to be working too easily. She got him at the right time to the right place, and with only two bodyguards. Semanan seemed particularly charmed by the place. It was he who asked Otto and the two men to return to the *Cosima* for champagne, glasses and a butler, and to hurry back.

Otto and the men had hardly pushed off from the shore when he said, 'They often say that love and hate are twins. I can only assume we are alone here together, Cheyney, because your feelings for me are changing.'

There was a rustling in the tall grasses between them and the Nile as it lazily lapped the shore. He stood up. They heard the sound again from another direction. The moon was not full, but extremely bright. Each

288

could see perfectly the other's face. Cheyney was terrified inside but outwardly controlled. The sound came again from yet another direction. She watched the change in his expression which became more pompous and evil than ever she had seen it.

'It would seem that I am mistaken.' With that he slapped Cheyney hard across the face. He caught her before she went down and held her by an iron grip around her throat. His last words to her were, 'Answer me, madam.'

She saw the two men behind him. The cold black steel of a magnum shoved into the back of his neck. She could hear the other men, shadows in the dark.

She rasped out, 'You would have killed us.'

He snatched the three-thousand-year-old gold necklace that she had bought from around her neck. There was neither fear nor remorse in his eyes. He exuded a stench of hatred and evil when he raised his arm, attempting the Nazi salute, the gold necklace dangling from his clenched fist. A hand from his captor yanked at it to twist it behind Semanan's back. A short violent shudder, eyes still glaring at Cheyney, and he keeled over. He had bitten a cyanide capsule under a capped tooth.

The next four years were almost ominously happy for Kurt Walbrook. He had everything he ever wanted. He and Otto inherited the entire Semanan estate. He had a son and heir whom he adored and who loved and looked up to him; a wife he had extendedly wooed, with whom he was still besotted, and who still contrived to stir and satisfy his complex sexual needs. For the first time in his life, his 'magnificent obsession' (as Cheyney thought of his passion for rare works of art) came second to them. Every year with the help of Irving Kirshner, to whom he was introduced by Roberto, he returned to the world missing art treasures, but only after their provenance was substantiated. Three museums were being designed to contain the remainder of the Semanan Collection.

He never learned the true circumstances of Semanan's death. He was never to know of Cheyney's involvement with Irving Kirshner. A young Japanese friend, Takashi Ishiguro, became an even more intimate part of their family life, variously a companion to all three of them. The Walbrook Collections kept expanding, and Kurt remained loyal to the very friends Cheyney detested. He would never at any time allow Semanan's name to be discredited by Cheyney or anyone else.

They were in Venice, Kurt, Cheyney and Taggart, for the annual meeting of the Walbrook curators. All business completed, all house guests gone (except for two of Taggart's school friends from Austria, who were staying with them). Kurt declared it was strictly fun-time. He took the boys off to explore Venice. They returned in the motor launch for Cheyney and set off to Torcello for lunch. After a splendid meal and an extra treat – allowing the boys to drink wine – they walked over the island picking armfuls of wild flowers from the fields. They placed them in make-shift vases in the ruins of the basilica.

Teased by Taggart and the other two boys, who thought it incredible that Taggart's mother and father had been married in an ancient ruin, Cheyney and Kurt re-enacted their wedding ceremony with the boys as guests. But only after the boys undid her hair and made wreaths of flowers for a head-dress. Kurt and Cheyney stood exactly where they had done nearly thirteen years before and ad-libbed a ceremony and their vows for the romantic, tipsy twelve-year olds. But the ones most affected by their wedding were Kurt and Cheyney themselves. Walking down the path alongside the canal to the boat that waited to whisk them back to Venice, Kurt whispered, 'We must do it again in another thirteen years.'

A dinner that evening for a few Venetian friends confirmed to Cheyney how happy Kurt seemed to be. She revelled in his happiness. In bed that night he was fiercely passionate in his love-making. His sexual ardour seemed to burn brighter than ever for her. No matter how many orgasms she had, he induced more and more from her. It was as if he sought to drown in pleasure.

They were still under the spell of Eros long after dawn rose over the domes, towers and roof-tops of Venice. Though exhausted, there seemed to be no sleep for Kurt and Cheyney. Instead they lay quietly in each other's arms, in one of the most splendid and luxurious bedrooms in the world, just absorbing the power and beauty of Botticelli paintings and drawings, seventeenth-century silks and damasks, furniture and mirrors, and tapestries so fine as to look like worn paintings, romantic enough to soften the hardest heart.

At seven o'clock, they recognised Taggart's knock at the door. They smiled at each other. Cheyney rose from the bed and slipped into her dressing-gown. She unlocked the door to the three pubescent youths in pyjamas.

'Mom, can we have breakfast here in your room with you and Pa?'

Before she could reply, Kurt called out, 'Yes,' and she opened the door and waved them in. Breakfast was strawberries, raspberries, fresh peaches, ogen melon, parma ham, a stack of sausage patties and scrambled eggs, hot bread and honey, and black coffee served with hot milk. The lapis lazuli table was set in front of the windows. They made their plans for the day. Taggart's two friends disappeared to bathe and dress, and Kurt surprised them by going back to bed.

Cheyney and Taggart slipped into bed on either side of him, and made a fuss of Kurt, plumping cushions. Taggart smoothed back his father's hair with his fingers. The sun streaming in seemed to cast a special light on the Botticelli painting confronting them from across the room. Kurt seemed unusually quiet, very still.

'It's your favourite painting of them all, isn't it, Pa?'

'Yes, it's the one that I coveted the most, my favourite. But not the one I am most proud of owning.' He placed an arm around Cheyney's shoulders and said, 'I think the proudest moment in all my art life was when we were at the opening of my gallery for Acton Pace paintings. And as I get older, it's those paintings, the abstract expressions of oblivion, that excite me the most. Maybe one day I might get to love them more than my Botticelli. And that, Taggart, is all thanks to your mother.'

He kissed Cheyney on the shoulder and asked Taggart to fetch him another cup of coffee. Still with his arm around Cheyney, Kurt leaned back against the pillows. Before he closed his eyes Cheyney saw him look up at the Botticelli and smile, then at Taggart, graceful as a painting, carefully carrying the cup and saucer to his father. Their eyes met. Taggart smiled back at him and quickened his step.

Slowly Kurt closed his eyes, in that way that still made Cheyney's heart flutter. Taggart crawled on to the bed and snuggled next to his father, still balancing the cup and saucer. Kurt Walbrook placed his other arm around his son, then laid his head back against the pillows, a faint smile upon his lips. Taggart sipped from his father's cup before offering it to him. There was no response. Kurt's long thick lashes were moist. A single tear lodged at the corner of his eye slowly trickled down his cheek. Cheyney felt her heart would break.

'Mom,' an alarmed Taggart exclaimed, just barely above a whisper.

Cheyney took the cup and saucer from the boy's trembling hands. Tears filled Taggart's eyes, his face turned ashen. 'Papa, I don't know why you're crying.' He bent over his father and kissed his tear-stained cheek. And Kurt slumped over dead against his son.

NEW YORK . ETON
COLLEGE . GARMISCH-
KONIGSBERG . ORLEANS.
1988

Chapter 31

The restaurant was New York chic. Up-to-the-minute decoration, fashionable food, finest wine, promptest service. The location was right, and the right people were on display there.

Before the three sat down at their table they met at the bar. Archy Head had been the first to arrive. He made his entrance the way that wealthy, celebrated people feel they must. The slap on the back to the maître d', the friendly chat about their respective families, how business was, how happy they were to see one another. The maître d' would tell the chef Mr Head was there, Mr Head told the maître d' about his latest cache of rare wine, until finally the maître d' dematerialised to renew his act with the next celebrity.

Archy Head was sipping his martini when Nelson Quirlan, the tall elegant museum director, came up to him at the bar.

'Really, Archy, who ever heard of meeting for lunch at 11.45?'

'Cheyney Fox, that's who, and she's late. It was this time or no time. She has to make the afternoon Concorde to London. Lunch, brunch, call it what you will, so long as I feed you and we have this meeting.'

'She'll be hard pressed to make it, even with a helicopter from here.'

'No problem, she'll make it. And she always has her Washington Senator's name to drop. They'll hold Concorde for her without blinking an eye. What will you drink, Nelson?'

'A dry martini with a twist of lemon.'

'Alfredo, make that two of the same.'

'How are you, Archy? It's a pleasure to have a meal with you and Cheyney today. It must be six months since the last time we three dined together. How is the lovely Liz?'

'Let's just dispense with all the right things to say, Nelson, and get down to the nitty-shitty of this meeting.'

'Meeting? I wasn't aware that we were having a meeting. I thought this was a social event. Well, Archy, why are we having this meeting today, instead of the special-occasion lunch party I thought we were having?'

'Cut the bullshit, Nelson. You know damn well what this meeting is all about. You and Cheyney Fox are in trouble, and I stand to be the big loser and to look a fool. I won't have it. You're a cool one. Playing coy, the sophisticated smooth museum director, about to go down the drain for backing Mike Cooli and Neo-Abstract Pop Art.

'I stuck all this motherfuckin' art on my walls on your expert say-so and Cheyney Fox's knowledge of the market! And what do I find? I have been gently frog-marched down the garden path. That it's all a fraud, a fucking fraud. That there is a chance that the twelve million dollars I have invested might be worth chicken-shit.

'I promise you, you clever closet-queen, that if Mike Cooli and the goddam Neo-Abstract Pop Art movement and its ranking in the international art market collapse, so's I can't off-load my collection on the museums as a substantial tax-benefit, you go down with me. I will sue you personally, the museum, and that sleazy con-woman, Cheyney Fox.'

Before Nelson could take in Archy's tirade, Cheyney Fox came in and stood between them. Archy began to bristle at the very sight of her. Everything about her was an affront: the subtly regal sweep across the room under admiring eyes, the undeniable chic of her red, slipper satin bias-cut skirt and long-sleeved black cashmere military-style jacket, fitting like a second skin on her much too sexy body. She looked too good, too sexy, too damned intelligent. He was even offended by the way she had dressed her hair – pulled back off her face with combs, its long, loose tresses shining like black silk down her back to her waist – such a feminine contrast to the tight-fitting jacket that finished above her hips.

'Hello, Nelson. Archy, you're showing yourself up like the common Brooklyn thug people take you for. I thought you'd lost that when you turned patron of the arts. I suggest you lower your voice and cut out this crass behaviour. That is, if you'd care for me to join you for what looks set to be a distasteful but necessary meal.'

She then turned to Nelson. 'You look as pale as a Marin water-colour. Why don't you finish that drink and have another? And, as for you, Archy, do you think you can handle another, and this meal, without becoming belligerent?'

He began to look belligerent before he had decided what it meant. To the barman Cheyney said, 'Alfredo, please send to our table two of the same for the gentlemen, and a Dubonnet for me.'

So three prominent New York City art-world figures sipped their drinks in silence, eyeing each other in turn, and occasionally the peach-coloured rose in the centre of the table. Archy Head had recovered himself sufficiently to order for his guests. Anger still lingered in his eyes.

The eyes of Nelson Quirlan were opaque with hurt. Those of Cheyney Fox were clear and cold.

Nelson broke the silence. He had his piece to present to the other two about the position he intended to take *vis-à-vis* Mike Cooli.

'Archy, you are not the only collector to panic over the state of the American art market, but you are the only collector who has threatened me. I wouldn't like you to do that again. No, please, don't interrupt me. I owe you no explanation for anything that I do in my life but I want to state my position to you now, once and for all.

'As a museum director the only obligation I have is to the museum and my board of directors. If ever the time comes when I am not doing my job, no doubt I will be fired. Not something I anticipate right now. Our museum is packed out each day. It's doing better than it has in its entire history.

'I have supported Mike Cooli and Neo-Abstract Pop Art since it became a movement. It took off. It has proved itself as art of our time. We are a modern museum dealing with just that, the art of our time. The point is that Mike Cooli paints a culture, a set of tribal tastes and customs, which embodies what life is today. Just as Andy Warhol did in the sixties and seventies, and any number of artists before him. A museum director's job is roughly equivalent to that of a cultural anthropologist.

'Oh, and one thing further – we've never bought on the say-so of just one man. Always the acquisitions board. If the board ever thinks they have too many Mike Coolis, they will auction them off at the best price they can. I am governed by the board.

'Archy, your cheap threats are up against art history. Mike Cooli is part of it. That alone will save my job. It will also prove that museums are not into art just for investment. Yes, I know why you are upset. You have made millions of dollars by donating to museums all over the country. And the Internal Revenue Department can be a real bother. Not to mention that your gravy train might be derailed if Neo-Abstract Pop goes out of fashion.'

He turned to Cheyney. Putting Archy straight had raised his spirits. 'I suppose he behaved as badly, screaming fraud and suits on you, Cheyney, when you surfaced three years ago to put the Pop Art World into a spin with your revelations about your role in Pop Art and Andy Warhol? Although, I wonder, did he get to call you a closet-dyke?' A raised eyebrow, a slight twist to his lip.

Archy Head reached across the table to grab him. Nelson Quirlan immediately jumped up. Cheyney took a firm grip on Archy's arm, stopping him but not his mouth. It loosed a spray of tired obscenities that reached as far as 'cock-sucker' before drying up. At low volume, his voice held a venom worse than if he had shouted. His angry eyes were pink-veined.

The waiter brought a pale golden soufflé to the table. That gave Nelson his exit line. He placed his napkin on the table and, looking at the other two, said, 'Excuse me. I am sorry, but as you can see, luncheon is impossible.' He walked away.

Archy Head turned to the waiter and instructed, 'Arthur, Mr Quirlan finds that he is unable to lunch with us. Remove his place-setting before you serve the soufflé.'

The two remaining diners were served. The steward poured an excellent, perfectly chilled Chablis. Both of them remained silent, deep into private thought, while they ate.

Cheyney's thoughts were understandably still focused on her nomination and her meeting with David Rosewarne. Would he, wouldn't he, represent her? Should she, shouldn't she, go for the position offered her by the President? Taggart . . . How, if at all, would this job affect her son? And, not least, how proud Kurt would have been of what she had accomplished since his death.

Coffee was served, a glass of Calvados put before each of them. Cheyney pushed hers aside. Archy chose a cigar, prepared it with great care, and lit it. Both sat back and appeared to relax before broaching the business in hand: what to do about the Archy Head collection.

'Cheyney, I hope you have some very clever plan, some good answers. At least as good as the ones you had for me to invest my money and my name in the works of that cock-sucker con-man you called a great painter! We both know that what I do with my collection of Cooli paintings will make or break me, you, and the whole Neo-Abstract Pop movement. We made a fortune manipulating his paintings. We want to keep that fortune, even if it is on paper. Or canvas. Whether we like it or not, we are in this together. That little speech of Quirlan's only shows how fast we gotta work. If he's now taking that holier than thou position, then so will the other museum directors.'

Cheyney Fox remained silent. She plucked the full blown peach-coloured rose from the silver bowl in the centre of the table. She placed it in the palm of her hand for a moment, marvelling at its fragile beauty. With her finger she stroked the velvet of several of its petals, and then raised it close to her face where she gathered its exquisite scent into herself. She looked over the rose into Archy's eyes, and then very carefully replaced the rose in the bowl.

'How long is it, Archy, that we've known one another? Two, three years? Certainly long enough for you to know that I have never pretended to be anything other than an art-dealer. The job of a dealer is to sell works of art. I have been an excellent dealer for you. You were getting more than just works of art. You were getting another lifestyle. Your paintings began to be borrowed for museum exhibitions. You saw your name in catalogues.

And then the accountants were brought in. Donations to museums as a tax-dodge became a secret, lucrative business. More fun than manufacturing men's string vests. The more you invested and donated, the more the value of your paintings appreciated. One day you woke up and found you were a great patron of the arts. You felt yourself more important than the artist, or his representative. The dealer suddenly became nothing but a salesman to you. Then, suddenly, the value of your collection is questioned, and your dealer turned salesman is a con-man. *En plus*, he is a partner in the crime of over-valuing your collection. You've conveniently forgotten the profit of many millions of dollars in tax-deductions which your art foray made for you.'

'Prove it, Cheyney.'

'The only thing I intend to prove, Archy, is what the educated world knows: that I own extraordinary art galleries that are internationally respected.

'Now, as you are one of my best clients, I will of course keep you fully advised of our forthcoming exhibitions and any important paintings that come up for sale. As to what *I* am going to do about Mike Cooli, Archy? Nothing, not one thing, old chum. I don't have to. I don't own any. The gallery doesn't own any. We sold our entire stock at top prices in London, Geneva, Rome and San Francisco eleven months ago. I am very interested in several new painters, and we are committing ourselves heavily to them. You see, Archy, that's the difference between an art-dealer and a salesman.'

She rose from her chair. Raising her chin just a little bit higher and tilting her head at a slight angle, a gesture of hers that positively infuriated him whenever she did it, Cheyney said, 'You don't listen, Archy. I never could figure out whether it is your ego or your greed that blocks your ears. So I repeat what I have told you on countless other occasions: always buy a painting because you like it, because it adds something to your life. No other reason for buying a work of art counts. If it turns out to be an excellent investment, you win twice.'

She picked up her handbag and turned to walk away. Archy rose from his seat and, grabbing her roughly by the wrist, said in a whisper filled with venom, 'I'll ruin you, you bitch.'

'You can try, Archy. But you won't succeed. Now, please let go of me.'

There was something in her eyes as hard as steel. It took him off guard, shocked him even. He saw that she was right: he would not succeed. He removed his hand and swore to himself, But I'll damn well give it one helluva try.

Cheyney's plum-coloured Rolls-Royce was waiting at the kerb when she stepped out of the East Fifty-Fifth Street restaurant. On sighting her

Gibson, the driver, sprang immediately from behind the wheel. He opened the rear door, and she slipped into the seat next to Kathy Spreckles, her assistant, there to hand over tickets, passport, and a chic, slim shoulder-bag containing a change of clothes. The car swung into Fifth Avenue and they headed for the Heliport and the helicopter revving up to take her to Kennedy Airport and the mysteriously delayed Concorde flight to London.

Chapter 32

Eton still filled her with awe. It was just the name of a small town in south-east England merging with Windsor on the river Thames. But it was synonymous with a great school. For some English people, it was unthinkable that a son of theirs should attend any other. She wasn't one of them. Usually by the time she arrived at the College she had to gear herself up not to be overwhelmed by it. She always wanted to be blasé about the school, and gave herself stern little lectures as a means of achieving this. 'You are acting like an American tourist, which you are not. You have a son who studies here. A husband who was a generous benefactor to the school. You yourself have been a benefactress. So what if these hallowed walls go back to the 1440s when Henry the Something founded the school? You don't go all wobbly when you walk through Harvard Yard, or get an eyeful of ivy-covered wall at Yale.' The lecture rarely worked.

Her next ploy was always rationalisation. That never worked either. How can you rationalise an ambience that has developed over more than five hundred years? An atmosphere of time and place, of education, of the moulding of young boys into young men. The hundreds of now-silent voices that once echoed through the halls, across the playing fields. The long gone boys in their black tails and stiff collars whose whole lives were formed within these ancient walls, the ghosts of old Etonians, were a force all on their own. The famous scholars and robbers, cads and cowards, heroes, aristocrats and gentlemen, were in the very patina of the stone and wood that Cheyney saw in the Houses of Eton College. The ambience simply was not going to let itself be rationalised away. Only being a boy and attending the school, like her son Taggart, was ever going to stifle the mystique. A mere parent hadn't a hope.

Privilege. From outside, it simply reeked of class and privilege. That always managed to be awe-inspiring. One day her son might be bound forever to his former schoolmates, as one of an exclusive group of men who made up 'the old-boy network' to end all such networks, famed for taking care of its own.

Cheyney had missed that in her life, had always felt the outsider, the loner. Although it had never been a problem for her, she was subtly aware that she had missed the bond of old school friendships and the lessons that they taught, something that a fine public school education used to offer. More than that was the basic academic education that could open up doors for him to Oxford, Cambridge, Yale, Harvard, Princeton, the best universities in the world. The disciplines of school games and of simply living communally with his fellow man that Eton was thought to be furnishing: they might mould the character of Cheyney's boy as she or Kurt could never do. They loved him too much not to make him go to Eton. But, at what a sacrifice! A sacrifice Cheyney had in the end to make alone, because of Kurt's sudden death a few months before the boy was to leave for England and school. But bravely both mother and son followed through, because it had been Kurt Walbrook's fervent wish – since the day Taggart was born, and he had promptly entered his name for the school – that Taggart Fox become an Eton boy.

Torture for Cheyney when the moment had come to send Taggart away to boarding school. He was a mature thirteen year-old, well-travelled, intelligent, sophisticated even, for a boy his age, a natural athlete, a likeable lad and leader among his childhood friends. But to Cheyney that day three years before when he had started his first half, he was still the little boy she had to give up so he could become a man.

About the only thing that did place Eton's awesome presence in reassuring perspective for Cheyney was when she remembered, as she did now, that Taggart (called TG by the boys in his House; initials were currently chic) had taken an instant liking to the school. Insofar as you could measure such things, the boys and the school seemed to take a liking to him. Eton became for both Cheyney and TG a happy and secure experience, a part of their lives.

Taggart's life in school was ruled less by the Head Master than by the man in charge of the House he belonged to. She contacted Taggart's Housemaster and explained about the possibility of her taking on a public office in the States which might cause some interest in the press who could trace her son to the school. She wanted the school to ignore it, and carry on with their policy of giving out no information on their pupils. The Housemaster was loftily reassuring, like one who had been shielding the offspring of princelings and property magnates from importunate newshounds for years. Taggart would not be troubled if he did not want to be. She left the Housemaster, declining his invitation to use his reception room, and went to wait for Taggart at the boys' entrance.

She stood by the pigeon-holes and watched several boys dart in and out of the boys' entrance hall, picking up their post, a book, a sock, a cricket hat, a glove, all sorts of odd things, from the open boxes. She heard them calling Taggart. 'Fox, Fox, Fox,' reverberated through the corridors and down the staircase.

'That sexy mother of yours is here, TG,' she heard one of the older boys say louder than he meant to. He had passed her at the foot of the stairs, and given her a less than filial glance. He had bounded up the stairs in rampant leaps, three at a time, all but flexing his muscles.

'Fox, you really are a lucky bastard!' she heard him say to her son.

'I tell myself that quite a lot, Andrew.' She recognised the gaiety of Taggart's voice before she saw him come skipping down the stairs.

'Hi, Mom.'

'Hi, TG.' They hugged each other.

'How did you manage this?'

'With difficulty.'

'I'll bet,' he said, smiling. 'But not with too much difficulty, if I know my mom.'

She put her arm around her son's shoulders and asked, 'A picnic somewhere? Or the Italian restaurant – you know, The House On The Bridge? If we go Italian, then you and the boys in your House get the Fortnum's de luxe picnic-hamper. If we go on the picnic you get what's left of the hamper. Before you answer, I might add the picnic I had made up is for eight ravenous boys, condemned by their parents to public school food, plus one adult. That should leave sufficient for you to make an unbiased decision.'

'You think of everything, Mom. Tricky decision. I dunno . . . How serious is this visit? If it's real privacy we need, then it has to be the picnic.'

'Good thinking, TG. But where?'

They both looked out the window and up at the sky at the same time. 'English spring, and picnic. The perfect equation for rain. Some place with shelter close by has to be the solution,' said Cheyney.

'I know just the place. Down by the river. Only fifteen minutes from here.'

'Sounds OK. Oh, I'm so happy to see you, TG.'

'Me, too, Mom. How long are you here for?'

'Just long enough to have lunch with you and give you some news, and make an evening flight to the Schloss.'

'For the official opening of the Museum?'

'Yes.'

'I wish I could be there.' He held up his hand as if to silence his mother before she said a word. 'I know, school, and we agreed it would be more fun for me to go with my friends at half term. Is it good news or bad news, Mom?'

'It may be no news at all, TG. An interesting situation has developed, and I have come to talk to you about it.' Cheyney felt suddenly edgy and looked around her. 'What are we doing standing around here?' Mother and son looked up the stair-well. Half a dozen adolescent, pimply, but well-groomed faces drew back from the banisters above them.

Arm in arm they walked from the House to Cheyney's grey-green Aston Martin. Taggart's eyes shone when he saw it. 'Phew!'

'Does that mean I chose the right car or the right colour?'

'Let's just say you didn't get it wrong, Mom.'

Cheyney slipped into the cream-coloured, glove-leather seat behind the wheel. She turned the key, and the car didn't spring but purred into life. She eased the gears into first. The car rolled seductively into motion.

She gave her son a sidelong glance, seeking reassurance that neither her presence nor her new car was exposing him to ridicule. Wealth was better for being understated in these latitudes. She knew how boys were at that age: mother jetting in to talk to her son was bad enough. The only thing worse was if she sported a hat. Or didn't. It was difficult to know some-times. She breathed a sigh of relief. Hatless seemed to be right. And her hair was long and straight and loose, with the shorter sensual wisps at either side of her face, reaching to just above her shoulders. It related more to glamour and youth than another mother's Mayfair hairdo. Flash cars: red, electric blue, yellow; anything Japanese on four wheels that was sup-posed to be a sports coupé; Fords; could lose Taggart points in the boys' rating-system. Equally a wheelspin, a mother crunching the gears, could dog a boy's career at school for several weeks. Mothers were best if hardly seen and scarcely heard. Mother-love was better expressed tangibly through the food hamper. Invisibility was a virtue. Unless she contrived to look more like an erotic young goddess, an imagined sensual delight. Cheyney had something to offer here.

She could read nothing in Taggart's eyes or his expression. That was good. With Taggart that was a sign that things were as all right as they could be, given her appearance at the House at all. She followed her son's momentarily distracted gaze from his inspection of the car. She saw that a number of the windows of his House were half open. From each one, a clutch of impassive faces peered down at the car to watch them drive away. Supercilious? Admiring? There was such a thing as paying too much attention to adolescent susceptibility. But Cheyney was relieved that she had got it right, amused at the thought that all of them – son included – were waiting for her to fluff their exit. A toot of the horn, acknowledgment in any way that they had an audience, that would be enough. She changed into second, and looked through the rear-view mir-ror. Several of them were hanging out of the window as she took the corner. She was delighted, fairly certain she had lost Taggart no points. She slid the gears into third, and they filtered into the traffic. Taggart turned to look at her. She stole a glance and they smiled conspiratorially at each other. Then she turned to concentrate on the traffic and his directions.

'How's school?' she asked.

'Great.'

'That's what your Housemaster says.'

'Anything else?'

'Interesting boy. Unusual boy. One of the best all-rounders the school has got. First class in athletics and classwork. Eton is *jolly* pleased with you, I almost regret to say,' she teased.

'OK, very funny, Mom.'

'Yes, but funny-good, Taggart. I mean that. I'm really pleased for you, and for me. Papa would have been pleased to know how happy you are here, and how well you're doing.'

'Do you still miss him a lot, Mom?'

Cheyney was surprised by the question. Taggart and his late step-father had been extraordinarily close, possibly even closer that they would have been had the boy and Kurt been natural father and son. But, although he talked about his 'papa' often, Taggart had never asked her that before. Indeed, never asked her about her relationship with Kurt. She wondered what prompted the question.

Taggart was twelve years old when his step-father died. He was shattered at having lost one of the two people he loved. The constant stream of mourners his father's death brought to the house didn't make it easier. Takashi, who was like an older brother for him, helped a great deal. But the intense loss was strangely eased by Taggart's awareness of having another father.

A year after Kurt's death, when Taggart was thirteen, he stayed, during the school holidays, at the country house of his best school friend, the son of a British Cabinet Minister, host in his own country house to a wide range of personalities. There, Taggart Fox and his school chum met and were befriended by another house-guest – Grant Madigan.

The two boys and the reporter hit it off together. Taggart's restrained hero-worship of the rugged, realistic, yet gentle and shrewd newsman grew alongside a gradual recognition that this man was probably his father: there could hardly be two Grant Madigans. He was actually confronting and coming to love his own father, without being able to tell the man. Gradually his need to conceal the truth grew into a desire for love, as Kurt had loved him, as father loves son.

In the two years that followed, while Taggart was at Eton and Cheyney Fox was re-establishing herself at the top of the New York art world, Taggart saw Grant Madigan several times, and a relationship began to develop between them. It had always been Taggart's intention to tell Cheyney he had met his father. But, not yet.

He heard his mother answer, 'No, not as much as when he died. Don't

305

think that I'm forgetting Papa. I could never do that. But, the day after tomorrow when we open the Schloss to the public, that part of my life when I was with your step-father is over, finished forever. I am building a new life without him now, Taggart. But try and understand this – he will always be a part of whatever I do. I'm sure you feel the same way.'

And, yet again, he savoured his secret, and put off telling her. Instead he asked, 'Did Takashi come over with you?'

Again she was surprised, not by the question, but by the abrupt change of subject. It would otherwise have been perfectly natural for Taggart to ask about Takashi. After Cheyney, Takashi was Taggart's best friend, and the boy knew that he and Cheyney often travelled together. He had known Takashi since he was five years old, and looked upon him with just a slight case of hero-worship. When he had understood, just over a year ago, that Takashi and his mother were lovers, the bond between the two grew even stronger. It had been Takashi who taught him the Japanese martial arts. From Takashi he acquired his love for motor bikes and motor racing, a subtler admiration for pretty girls, and his desire one day to be a great art-historian.

'No, he's in New York, but will be at the Schloss sometime tomorrow. He did, however, send you something. Look behind your seat.' The boy turned round and rummaged behind him. He came up with a squash racquet in a maroon-coloured, soft leather cover. He unzipped it and his face lit up.

'He did send a message. Oh dear, I do hope I remember it,' she teased. The boy rose to the bait.

'Mom, the racquet is smashing, so light, yet solid. It feels great in the hand, and the subtle change in the shape is really slick. I can't wait to see what it will do for my game. Oh, Mom, it's great! Don't tell me you forgot Takashi's message, you've got to remember. Think, Mom, think! What did he say about it?'

'Oh, something about the Rolls-Royce of squash racquets. Some such thing. That this is the prototype, the original, and signed by the designer or someone special. I simply don't see how the pair of you can get so excited about a squash racquet. But he did say to call him collect, if I was going to be all vague about the thing.'

She smiled at her son's enthusiasm, and turning to face him for a moment, said, 'Call him, Taggart, collect. Actually I think he misses having you around.' The boy beamed, and then issued more road directions.

On the outskirts of Windsor they took a narrow paved road, and then, where it forked, an even narrower dirt path. It ended abruptly in front of an old weather-worn boat-house with peeling grey paint, its roof partially

306

caved in. It was standing among tall grass and wild flowers. Its first-floor porch hung drunkenly over the river.

'This car does go in reverse, doesn't it?' His turn to tease. Cheyney blushed, and Taggart began to laugh uproariously. 'Mom, I don't believe it! You've never even had it in reverse.'

'Well, I haven't exactly had time. I only drove it out of the showroom this morning. Now, you won't go telling the boys at school, will you, Taggart? If you do, I shall feel such a fool.'

'So would I, Mom.

He reached into the glove compartment and took out the manual before he opened the car door. Then, looking at his mother with a twinkle in his eye, he said, 'I'm starved. You do know how to open the boot, don't you?'

'I'm not entirely a fool, dear.' She rather smugly reached under the dashboard and pulled a small lever. The steering wheel dropped neatly to its second position. Taggart didn't even laugh. He turned his head from side to side in disbelief. Cheyney's face was hot and flushed. Her son leaned against her and, for the first time since mother and son had met that day, kissed her. He put his arms around her and gave her a loving hug.

'Yes you are, Mom, when it comes to anything with a motor in it.' He opened the manual, and concentrated on finding out where the release-lever was for the boot, if indeed there was one at all. His kiss, Taggart's affection, touched her heart as her son's love for her always did. Cheyney had to fight back tears. Time was short this visit.

The dock was partially collapsed into the Thames. What was left at least stood firm. Taggart heaved himself on to the rickety boards, and then helped Cheyney up. 'How did you find this place?' she asked.

'Better not to ask, Mom. And it would be better if you don't tell anybody in my House where we picnicked.'

'I think I understand,' said Cheyney, trying to look disapproving. They sat down on white, calfskin-covered cushions Taggart found in the boot of the car, and together opened the Fortnum & Mason basket. Cheyney shook out a light-blue linen cloth with a border of navy blue stripes, and checks of a bright red and white, five inches deep all around it. It turned the drab berth into a gay and happy place. Especially so when she had laid out the linen napkins, an all-over pattern of full-blown, bright red roses with a border the same as the cloth's.

The Waterford crystal goblets and white Limoges plates, with a band of blue and red around them, sparkled under the warm sun. 'Flowers. What we need are a few flowers,' said Cheyney, looking hopefully at her son. He good-naturedly hopped off the dock and set off to find some, calling back over his shoulder, 'Well, if you're gonna die without them . . .'

307

'A few would be fine, Taggart. No need to cause an ecological disaster,' she called back. Happy just to be there with him. It was reminiscent of the scores of picnics they had had together in some of the loveliest places in the world. She listened to the lap of the river against the shore, the song of small birds, felt the warmth of the sun on her shoulders, and gave a silent prayer of thanks for having Taggart. The rest of her existence paled next to the delight of being with her son.

She finished laying out the Fortnum's feast. Cold vichyssoise, Taggart's favourite, with snips of fresh chives floating on the surface of the rich cream soup greeted him when he sloped back on to the platform, a handful of wild flowers, bluebells mostly, and lovely unusual grasses, shoved into a broken whisky bottle filled with Thames water.

Taggart's eyes viewed the feast greedily. There laid before him was a *soupçon*, a portion just large enough to give a mid-term taste, of each of his favourite things:avocado stuffed with prawns, lobster tails, quail's eggs, sausages wrapped in bacon and filo pastry, southern fried chicken, a green salad, a potato salad, a bean-and-celery salad, hot ham and chicken cider pie. He watched the bubbles rise in the goblet he held in his hand as his mother poured chilled apple juice. He tried to take his mind off the puddings: chocolate mousse, wild strawberries and fresh cream, mangoes and peaches and luscious black grapes, Stilton. Thirsty, he took a long drink, and Cheyney refilled his glass.

He dispensed with the soup spoon and drank from the bowl. Looking over the rim, he watched his mother follow suit. He selected a southern fried chicken drumstick and took a bite out of it. With mouth full, he said, 'Not a bad banquet, Mom. This is great, but what are we doing here? What's going on?'

A wave of anxiety washed over her. She couldn't quite understand why. She stopped thinking and plunged in. 'I have been offered an appointment, one that could be controversial. And I have a good chance of getting it.'

'That's great. Sounds all right. Just for the States, or for the world.'

'Just for the States. The world next time!'

'Oh, you'll win. You'll wipe out the opposition, Mom. Is that what this is all about? What're you so worried about?'

Taggart picked up a large silver spoon and plunged it into the hot ham and chicken cider pie, schoolboyishly careful to serve his mother before himself. Cheyney explained the position on offer to her, the politics involved. 'Well, what do you think?'

'What am I meant to think? And why are you so nervous? You're already a big shot in the art world. It's got through to the odd boy at school. Even some of their parents know who you are. I don't know another boy at Eton

308

with a mater as clever and famous as you are. Not one of them has the power or influence in the arts that you already have, the world over. I think this job is one you deserve, and should have. I don't know what you thought I was going to say, but what I do say is, go for it, Mom, go for it.'

The immense relief Cheyney felt hearing her son encourage her this way made her almost dizzy. For most of his life she had stayed completely out of the limelight. Taggart had known her as nothing more than his mom, whom he could depend on to be there always. In the three years of her climbing back to the top of the art-world ladder, he had appeared to enjoy her new role in life, taking every opportunity he could to be around the artists in their studios, the galleries and museums, always interested in every new painter and painting she came up with. She credited that to the love of art he had shown since he was a small child. Here, picnicking by the river, was one of the rare times he expressed his feeling about her and her profession.

Suddenly she was ravenous. She picked up a large knife and cut into a cold game pie. Leaving the end slice thick with pastry on the plate, she sliced two pieces rich with pheasant and quail and woodcock and placed the first slice on Taggart's plate, the other on her own. 'Wait a minute, Taggart. "Going for it" may not be that easy. Not for either of us.'

She had said it, and there was no turning back. She would have to warn him that, when an investigation began, the knives would be out.

'Why not? And what's it got to do with me?'

She explained about the procedure, the official probing that might rake up things from her past, things that might lose her the appointment unless she faced them and fought them. As she spoke, she watched his face intently for a sign of disapproval, anxiety over the invasion of her life and his own. She could read nothing in his face. During the telling, he had gone through one lobster-tail, most of the potato salad, and four gherkins. He was slicing into the stilton. She suddenly wanted to cry. He was so sweet and so innocent. Why should he have to confront the dark side of his mother's life? Possibly learn things about Kurt that might shock him? For Taggart had thought his step-father perfect. Cheyney had gone to great lengths to make certain of that.

'Mom, we can handle it.'

'I'm not so sure I want you to have to handle it, Taggart.'

'I thought you were here because you wanted to give me that choice, Mom? You and I have equal votes always, don't we?'

He's got me, she thought. 'Yes, that is why I'm here. And that's true, we do have equal voting-power. But, before you cast your vote, I have to be honest with you. Facts are almost certain to be revealed about me. I would never have concealed them from you, but I would be happier if they never surfaced in public.'

'For example?'

That caught Cheyney offguard, but she refused to shy off now. She answered: 'OK, a perfect example, and this is only one. I was once mixed up with some probable Nazi war criminals, Israel, and the CIA. It was to do with paintings. I don't want to spoil your lunch with all the ins and outs of it. It's something I'll have to recall in detail when the investigation gets going. I can explain it all then. If it gets out and the press takes it up, a distorted picture of the facts might come across. My involvement may not be well received. It's always hot stuff if Nazis can be dug up. Everyone has a moral freebie. But the point for us is the total invasion of our privacy. Domestic *blitzkrieg*!' She looked for a sign of shock at this news. She could see none in his boyish face. Did he think he was just part of a movie?

The boy wiped his hands on his napkin and tossed back his head. He ran his fingers through the shock of dirty-blond hair that fell to one side of his forehead. He looked into his mother's face with his large dark brown eyes, and asked, 'Mom, did you ever kill anyone? Deliberately take a life.'

'What a question, Taggart! Of course not. I may have made some stupid mistakes in my life, but I never got around to killing anybody. Are you serious?'

'I thought you and I decided that the one great evil was to take a human life. Next was not to do all you can to make the most of life. I don't think you are guilty of either one of those things so I don't see that I have any choice but to vote in favour of your accepting the appointment. And frankly, Mom, I don't think you do either.' He emptied his goblet yet again, and smiling at Cheyney, reached for the chocolate mousse. So far complexities were weighing light on him.

She looked at her son with some pride. Maybe he was the remarkable fifteen-year-old the Housemaster took him for. She managed a forkful of the game pie, and said, 'You know Taggart, sometimes I think you're fifteen going on forty.'

'I don't want to be rude, but sometimes I think you're an over-forty going on fifteen! How could you even think we couldn't cope with this thing?'

And then, before they realised what was happening, they were in each other's arms and kissing each other excited about Cheyney calling the White House to accept the appointment.

Now it was Taggart's turn to watch his mother delve into the food. Between spoonfuls of chocolate mousse, he spoke to her, 'Mom, have you a plan? A campaign of how you are going to handle this thing to win?'

'No, not exactly. I have two lawyers, well one and a half actually. You know Judd Wyatt. The other is a man called Rosewarne, he's the half because I have yet to confirm he's working for me. He was my legal adviser way back before you were born, at the time I had all my troubles in the sixties, in the Andy Warhol days. I think between the two of them they can handle any problems that might arise from my speaking directly to the press, or any investigation committee. An investigation is inevitable, by the way, TG, the norm in the case of an appointment like mine. I have sort of gathered my generals together. But no, I have no real campaign planned. Both lawyers and Takashi agree it should not look as if I am soliciting this job. And there seemed no point in thinking any further about a campaign to win until I had seen you. Why, what do you think?'

'Well, Mom, the way I see it, you've got some critics and some enemies. We know that from when you came out with your Andy Warhol story, three years ago. They're sure to rally round again for an attack.

'If it's anything like school, I know just what will happen. Soon as your name comes up for captain of this or head of that, they're on to you, all the people who think they ought to have the post. Everyone remembers everything bad they ever knew about you.

'I think you just have to face them. If you back off it makes you look guilty. You have to tell the truth, put the record straight. If people don't believe you – well, there's not much point in your getting the post anyway, because you won't have any authority when you've got it. That's how it works at school, at least . . .'

Cheyney began to think that school sounded pretty much like the world in general. The same bitching, the same ground rules. Her son's advice was in tune with her own instincts.

'Agreed then?' he insisted.

'Agreed.'

'Now listen, Mom, I'm going to be over here, wallowing in the old Etonian traditions, while you're out there having fun battling the real world. You've got to promise you will call and tell me all about it, if there is anything I can help with, anything I should know even if things get rough. You've got to have trust in me, Mom, to know that whatever does get through to me here, no matter how good or bad it is, we have made our resolve and I can handle it. Mom, do you think it would be too piggish of us to open a mango?'

Cheyney began to laugh, mostly from relief and answered, 'Why not?' Then as she cut into the mango, 'You're quite a boy, Taggart. I'm always throwing things to you from left field, and you're always catching them, and turning them into victories.'

She recognised a sheepish look that on rare occasions came into Taggart's eyes. He said, 'Mom, you're going to have to learn to play cricket. It's full of surprises. You ought to find out about it. Just in case you think baseball is the name of the game and wake up one day and find I've been playing cricket all along.'

Now what was he getting at? Not for the first time that day he seemed to have abruptly shifted the ground of their conversation, as if he had something on his mind. 'Is there something I need to know right now about . . . cricket?' she asked.

He almost told her about Grant Madigan, right then and there. But the moment passed. He sensed bad timing, so he answered, 'No, not at the moment. Everything is just fine. How much do you want this job, Mom? I'm thinking you really want it a lot.'

'You would be thinking correctly. I really do want it. But, I repeat, it isn't going to be easy. Appointments like this never are. Now you have one last chance for us to change our decision to "go for it". One word from you . . .'

'Just slice the mango, mom.'

For the next twenty minutes they talked and laughed, and suddenly he had reverted from the half boy, half man, back to the young boy, who could at times be even a little childish. When they were packing up to go back to Eton, he playfully tied several of the wild flowers in her hair. He began to recite:

> Here's flowers for you:
> Hot lavender, mints, savory, marjoram;
> The marigold, that goes to bed with the sun,
> And with him rises weeping; these are flowers
> Of middle summer, and I think they are given
> To those of middle age . . .

'And I think,' said Cheyney firmly, 'that Shakespeare wrote "given to *Men* of middle age". So keep your middle-aged flowers for whoever's teaching you English Literature, if you don't mind. Spare your mother, who is trying to look young and sassy.'

Then Taggart looked at his watch. 'I'm due back at school, Mom. Cricket practice, you know. I shouldn't let the team down.'

'And I have to call Washington, get the car back to the Gallery in Mayfair. Alex has to drive me to the airport, so I can make my flight, and the car to the air-freight office. I actually bought it to have in the States.'

Once the car was packed, they took their seats. After clicking his seatbelt on, Taggart looked at his mother mischievously. She kept her eyes on him. Their eyebrows did the talking. She shot the car into reverse. The wild flowers and grasses became a blur, sand and dust clouded up around the revving sports car. Taggart nodded silent congratulation: his mother could reverse an Aston Martin after all. At the fork in the road she spun the car round and pressed the accelerator to the floor. Until the traffic closed in on

312

them, she drove like a racing-driver. Between excited laughs, Taggart shouted navigational instructions: 'Police trap on the left. Lorry on our tail. Christ in heaven, Cheyney! You almost hit that woman. What a way to take a corner! Change down, change down. Oh *no*, Mom, Mom, you'll never make it! Power, it needs more power.'

'Don't give me that, Taggart. How's this for power?' She pulled out as soon as she saw a gap. With a trans-continental lorry bearing down on them, she passed three cars and slid safely into an opening between two more.

Taggart watched her every move, the way she revved the motors, managed the gears and the brakes. They were in Windsor. She was forced to slow down and flow with the traffic. Taggart favoured her with a schoolboy's back-handed compliment: 'Mom, you're the best non-professional, *almost*-reckless driver I know.'

Taggart gave in, and allowed himself the luxury of adoring his mother. This was the way he loved her best, just the way she was being right now. Young, carefree and naughty, with child-like qualities. He wondered, if Grant Madigan saw Cheyney again, just like she was now, would he fall in love with her? How could he not? 'Mom, stop the car.'

She pulled the Aston Martin over to the kerb, cut the engine and turned to look at her son. They both laughed and she said, 'Got you, didn't I? Admit it, you were chicken when I passed those cars on the slope!'

'Never.'

'Really, never?' she teased.

'Yes, Mom, really never.'

The pair of them sat there allowing their laughter to die away, and putting on their more serious faces. Cheyney brushed her hair while Taggart held a mirror for her. Almost unconsciously the boy stroked the length of it down to the middle of her back. He loved his mother's waist-length hair, always had, since he was a child. Cheyney took the mirror and returned it with her brush to her handbag, and said, 'Well, I guess this is it TG. Back to Eton.'

'Mom, you know what would be a gas?'

'No, TG, what would be a gas?'

'If you called the President of the United States from a public call-box.' They both burst out laughing.

'You've got a great sense of style. You're right, that would be a gas. I've got a credit card. I could do it.'

'Then let's, Mom. From a telephone near Windsor Castle. I know where there is one. It's only about three blocks away.'

'You know, Taggart, I may not get to speak to the President. He may be busy with other things like Russia, Central America, the national deficit.

You may have to settle for me speaking to the White House and his secretary.'

'That'll do.'

A few minutes later, Cheyney was squeezed into a telephone box looking up a curve of busy street at the looming stoniness of Windsor Castle. She was supplying her credit card number to the operator, then the telephone number given to her specifically for the call she was making. Taggart was leaning against the open box listening. He quickly drew away when he saw several Etonians, not in their unmistakeable garb, walking towards them. Why now? Here? Weren't they off-limits, anyway? When they saw Taggart, they called out and joined him.

Cheyney was waiting to be put through to the President when she heard one of them say, 'Your mater sending for the break-down service?' All the boys laughed.

'No, Westerly. Just calling to say hello to . . . someone.'

Cheyney made her second long distance call to Judd Whyatt to tell him her news and how pleased the President was. The thought of making a third call to David Rosewarne never crossed her mind. Several minutes later, she watched the boys, Taggart one of them now, walk away, swinging the Fortnum's hamper between them. All of them were chattering at once. There had been no chance for a sentimental goodbye after Taggart agreed to join them on some mysterious errand. Just a quick look of mutual approval between mother and son, while the boys tried out their charm on Cheyney.

Chapter 33

'She never loved him.'

The whisper was more like a hiss in Cheyney Fox's ear. She tried to ignore what she heard, but how can you ignore the truth? Especially a truth that you thought had been your own well-kept secret, rarely admitted even to yourself, suddenly revealed in a stage whisper to a gathering of strangers.

'He knew it, and didn't care. Kurt was never a man much interested in love. His appetites lay elsewhere, and she satisfied them all. The bitch, the whore!'

The woman's venomous words pierced Cheyney's consciousness like a viper's darting tongue. The voice stung again.

'Kurt Walbrook's widow – Cheyney Fox – who thinks she has buried their secrets. All those mysteries and memories, the lies they lived, prospered and became famous on, shovelled into a grave under this monument to his memory. And now, this baronial home of his opening to the public as a Museum of Contemporary Art. Does she think that'll silence the ghosts that stalked their lives? One day those ghosts will speak the truth. Then all her illusions about herself will explode in her face and shatter her smug little life. She will be made to understand that she is what Kurt Walbrook moulded her into. Nothing more. Just another whore with ambition and a bit more knowledge than most, who chose the art world to hustle.

'All that lust, ambition, greed; those failures and weaknesses – they never deceived Kurt. He used them, made capital of them. Played with them, and her, to satisfy his own hungers. He was always protecting her from the outside world right from the time he scooped her out of the gutter. He possessed her, enslaved her by the one real truth of their life together: his love for her son. So long as he was alive that was what ruled her. The family relationship between the three of them – mother, son, step-father – was the only perfect and honest thing Kurt Walbrook and Cheyney Fox ever shared.'

Cheyney, riveted by the intensity of the hushed voice behind her, forced herself to remain calm. Distractedly she heard the Austrian Minister intone his country's gratitude to her for endowing the private museum they were about to open to the public. There would be two exhibitions a year of contemporary painting and sculpture. Her generosity would ensure that this was the pattern for the next seven years.

But to listen was not easy. The woman behind her simply would not let up. Several people sitting close to Cheyney began to fidget with embarrassment for her. One man tried to silence the woman with a loud 'Shush!' This merely released a buzz of whispers from those around them. They were still hearing the woman's slurs. Suddenly, Cheyney had had enough. She sprang out of her chair to confront the speaker. A hand restrained her, gripping her slender wrist.

'Not a good idea, making a scene.'

Cheyney looked down at the man sitting next to her. She glared at him, determinedly peeled his fingers from around her wrist. 'You should know by now, Senator, I never make scenes.' Instead, she approached the lectern, took the Minister by the hand, announcing with a forceful exhibition of charm, 'Please, sir, you are more kind than I deserve. I cannot allow you to go on.'

He was cut off from his prepared text. Cheyney Fox, the American art-dealer, could upstage even an Austrian Minister. She deftly snipped the white satin ribbon. It fluttered up, rippled on the gust of an early spring breeze and then lazily trembled on its way to the ground, declaring the Museum open.

The hundred-odd guests rose from their gilded, red silk velvet music-room chairs to give a standing ovation in recognition of the occasion. Cheyney had not made a scene, but she had made something happen. She now zeroed in on her quarry, the malicious woman seated behind her. How could someone be so deranged, so full of hatred for her?

The ceremony was taking place outside, under a marquee of white canvas, open on all sides to the beauty of the Austrian wood rising dramatically over steep ridges above the Schloss. It billowed over a section of the cobbled road that formed a mile-long avenue between aged chestnut trees in fullest bud. Here the trees yielded to an impressive stone bridge spanning the wide, deep moat that circled a many-roomed hunting-lodge of white stone, with dark blue shutters and a crown of turrets.

The sound of applause drifted away as the crowd milled across Persian carpets laid over the cobblestones. Programmes in hand, the chattering mass crossed the bridge to the sound of racing water, each person anxious to be the first to see Kurt Walbrook's collection of Old Masters and Impressionist paintings in their setting, the deceased Baron's fifteenth-century home, together with the Fox Collection of Contemporary Art.

Cheyney smiled and shook hands and fought her way against the stream of people. She reached the place where she had been seated. The chair behind hers was empty. An exhibition brochure lay across the seat. Each page had been deliberately torn out, and then torn again once, from top to bottom, corner to corner. A ragged, diagonal mutilation fuelled by hatred. A breeze blew under the empty marquee. It swept several of the torn coloured photographs up into the air. Cheyney watched. Somehow, this dismembering of that Museum's commemorative catalogue was far more disconcerting than the hissing sound of the woman's venomous voice.

Yet how she had detested that woman's German. The language too coarse and guttural for her ear. Although fluent, Cheyney only spoke German herself when absolutely necessary. She had made English or French the first language spoken in their home. German was only for when they were in residence here at the Schloss Garmisch-Konigsberg.

Scraps of a Miro and a Motherwell, a Rothko, and a Campbell's soup can fluttered, almost tauntingly, in front of her on a current of air. She reached out to grab them, but they eluded her and danced away like snowflakes under the elegant marquee. Cheyney reached down to gather up the remaining pages from the red velvet seat of the woman's chair. Before her associate and lover Takashi Ishiguro could say a word, she plunked them in his hands, saying, 'Please get rid of this mess,' and walked away. She had taken only a few steps when she turned around and said, 'I'm so sorry, Takashi, I was distracted. Did you want me for something?' At that moment a torn page reproducing an Andy Warhol painting of a Campbell's soup can with a torn open lid, went into a gentle tail spin and alighted on her bosom.

Cheyney Fox was taken by surprise. She recoiled for a split second, and then, picking it off her chest and looking at it, burst into laughter.

'Andy would have loved today. All the glamour and elegance of the occasion, the galaxy of art-world celebrities, famous collectors, Austrian dignitaries. And he would have been in awe of the museum and the collection. Without letting on, though. Do you think this is his way of telling me? Andy reaching back from the grave and saying, "Gee, oh gosh, well, ugh. *Terrific*! You're fabulous," the way he might have, half a lifetime ago?'

She began to laugh again, and handed him the coloured scrap. The breeze that had sprung up had now died away. The sparkle of beautiful people was nearly gone from under the marquee. She and Takashi walked together slowly, joining the tail-end of the procession of invited guests crossing the bridge and flowing into the museum. Cheyney tossed back her head and laughed again.

Slipping her arm through his, she announced, 'Oh, God, is it ever good to be back in the art world, and at the top! I feel born again, alive again, as I have not been since I slunk away from it. I had no idea how dead my life was, without the thrill of working and dealing out there in the open, in front of the world. Granted not all the time, but most of it. But for Kurt, I wonder if I would be where I am today. And my boy, Taggart. How could I have survived at all, had I not had my love-child?'

'Where do you go from here, Cheyney?'

'Higher, just a little higher. To the top, maybe, and then . . . over the rainbow.'

'Where does it come from, this scent you have for discovery, your eye for abstract beauty, your constant passion for great painters and paintings?'

'Who knows? Eye? Scent? It feels more like a heavy cross that I have carried for as long as I can remember. It has never been easy. I have loved and I have hated, and I have given up my passion for art and the art world. Now that I've reclaimed it, you can be sure I don't take it for granted. And there is something else. Who wouldn't like being a powerful force in the art world? It gives me a chance to balance out my past failures.'

To herself she added, 'Would that I could balance out my past loves, most especially the great love, the grand passion shared with another soul I yearn for, even now.' Then she chastised herself for still loving, still wanting, the impossible. Grant Madigan. The very idea embarrassed her. She put him, as she had so many times in her life, out of her mind.

Cheyney and Takashi stopped for a minute and listened to the sound of the water rushing far below under their feet. They remained silent, letting her words dissolve on the light warm spring breeze, and race away with the water below. They looked into each other's eyes. There was emotion there for the monumental accomplishments of the day. For seeing the fruits of years of work together. Far from jaded, they could still react in anticipation of the thrill awaiting them. The power of beauty, peace; the tranquillity a museum of art can cast upon the soul. The inspiration that great works of art can stir in the mind and heart. And for the couple standing on the bridge, especially this museum, created by Cheyney Fox. Their hearts were singing in their eyes. But there was something else there too. Another kind of emotion, more sensual, that flared up and smouldered.

The tall, slender Japanese smiled, bowed respectfully, and taking her hand in his kissed it. The touch of his lips upon her fingers ignited a passion in her she had not expected to feel on this momentous day. But it was there, warm and rich, like an early morning sunshine that dissolves the dew. She smiled back at him, grateful for their multi-levelled, ten-year-old association, and placed her hand on his shoulder. They were still looking into each other's eyes. The warmth of their feelings expressed itself in a slow smile. Arm in arm, they continued across the bridge to the entrance of the museum.

They walked in silence, in bright sunlight, enveloped by the sound of roaring water in the moat below and the hum of conversation from the crowd surging with them towards the huge open wooden doors decorated with ancient Persian bronze studs in animal forms. Occasionally someone tapped Cheyney on the shoulder to congratulate her on the occasion of the museum's debut, others on her nomination, already in the news. She responded graciously before turning back to Takashi.

'Did you come to find me for anything special? I was distracted by that sick woman who was saying such vile things about me. To think it has already begun, the scandal and gossip! I was upset at the thought of having to call David Rosewarne and tell all. Who in their right mind wants to review their past, relive what is already behind them, and worse, make it public? It does rankle. But none of that seems to matter one bit now.'

She stopped and, lowering her voice so that her words were only for him, told him, 'It was the feel of your lips upon my skin. It woke me, swept me away from the ugliness. Your lips, as always, put me in touch with the core of myself, reminded me that only I know the truth and falsehoods of my life.'

Such directness could have made Takashi Ishiguro feel embarrassed, but only until he felt her press a key into his hand. No words were needed. They wanted each other, could actually feel sensual excitement stirring within, in anticipation of the erotic interlude that was to come. The shared invisible lust vibrated now between them.

'I had come to ask you if you were returning to Washington on the State Department jet with the Senator and Judd, or if you wanted me to make alternative arrangements. But now that question is redundant.'

They entered the museum together and were immediately swept into its light and airiness. An unearthly delicacy of substance or character dropped like some invisible net, enveloping in a special world all who entered.

There was something remarkable in the way the chatter of the people stepping into the central gallery abruptly turned to silence. Even the expression on their faces altered. It was as if all that was superficial and trite had been left outside the museum, like unnecessary baggage.

The crisp whiteness and polished satin look of the Carrara marble floor, the ramp as wide as a room, and the broad hand-rail sweeping four storeys up in an elegant snail's spiral, were pure architectural perfection. The natural sunlight pouring through the glass roof at the top filtered down through the open centre of the spiral, changing architectural perfection to sculpture. The infinitely gradual incline of the cantilevered ramp functioned as a floor from which one viewed the works of art. The curving wall from the ground to the top floor, twelve feet back from the balustrade of clear glass below the marble hand-rail, was where the Fox Collection of contemporary paintings hung. Each canvas was lit within its frame, so that every painting, though hung in an open gallery, shone singularly to every pair of eyes viewing it.

Dozens of waiters in white jackets offered Czechoslovakian crystal flutes, hand-decorated with gold arabesques and rims, filled with fresh strawberries and champagne. People trailing up the spiralling ramp, glass in hand, faces glowing with excitement. Absorbed in the great paintings, they charged the atmosphere, making it electric.

To have transformed what had once been the open courtyard of the Schloss into the main gallery was absolutely the correct thing to have done. Cheyney had then been able to keep the remainder of the miniature Austrian palace, really a hunting lodge, relatively intact, and, as such, many of the rooms were used for exhibiting purposes. A museum stunningly conceived as individual galleries, exhibiting works of art from ancient times to the present, all linked together under one roof. The overall design flashed through her mind and was quickly dispelled, as was all else about the day, in the wake of viewing the exquisite paintings and sculptures in the main gallery. They sang to her. No, they were an orchestra. For they hung together, each attuned to the other, a visual symphony of art. They set her heart to a faster beat by the sheer power and beauty they exuded. Combined with her inner sensual feelings, triggered by an exquisite kiss from Takashi, she felt her very soul about to flower.

There was something else Cheyney was experiencing: an extraordinary sense of freedom. With this day behind her, and her name flashed around the world as a candidate for America's first lady of the arts, Cheyney Fox was through, finished forever with that part of her life that had for so long belonged to Kurt Walbrook, and to Austria. She had, for years, been executing a secret plan. This day was the culmination of it.

In the morning she would be gone from Austria, to return only for the odd visit to the museum, a concert in Salzburg, to ski on Walbrook mountain with her son. An American in transit, who could say and do as she pleased, without fear of offending her husband and his friends, his country. No longer would she have to pretend that *Anschluss*, the union with Nazi Germany that took place in March 1938, never happened. The old Austrian aristocracy – friends and relations of Kurt who had welcomed Hitler's armies, and still, behind closed doors, asserted that they had been right to do so; men and women who still mourned the passing of their Führer – would never be a part of her life again.

Cheyney and Takashi allowed themselves meaningful smiles before they parted. 'Shall we say, as soon as you are able to get away?' he asked. She raised her glass, and, to a seductive nod of her head and a twinkle in her eyes, they parted.

*   *   *

Senator Harvey Wigan, known at home along the rugged northern Atlantic coastal state he represented and in Washington as 'Harve', finally extricated himself from the gaggle of attractive women fluttering around him. Spotting Cheyney about a third of the way up the ramp was his incentive. He made his way towards her as quickly as his long legs would carry him without making his pursuit too obvious.

Eyes fixed on her, he took in every nuance of beauty in the woman he had been wooing for the past few years. The Senator was a stoic New Englander, a typical native son, whose philosophy of virtue as the highest good had served him well. It had made him one of the most respected men in the Republican Party. He could hope to have the White House in his sights, in four years or maybe eight. He was a handsome widower who served his state and his country well because he was ruled by the highest ethics and, as required, could control his passions, indifferent to passing pleasure or pain in himself or in the people he represented. In short, a person of great self-control and fortitude, able to live austerely when he had to. But inside that crusty façade lived another man who could and did let go, so long as it never challenged his ethics. A pussycat of a man, as soft as he was hard. A man with an appetite for sex who exercised it in lovemaking rather than whoring, and who effortlessly attracted the most exciting available women on the political circuit.

He hardly took his eyes off Cheyney as he walked towards her. The tall, slim-hipped woman, with her long back and exquisitely rounded buttocks and breasts, satisfied his every sexual fantasy. The intelligent, creative mind excited his admiration. The sensitive loving mother who, against all odds, was able to understand and practise real and constructive family love. From her he had learned what a truly loving family relationship could mean. This fascinating and complex woman, whom he meant one day to make his wife, was unaware of him, lost in a painting, yet drew him magnetically towards her.

How beautiful she looked to him, dressed as she was, all in black. Cheyney had chosen very carefully what she would wear that day. A dress of silk crêpe de chine with a deep V neckline that plunged to below her breasts to accentuate a sliver of exposed creamy flesh, attracting, even titillating, without being vulgar. Its skin-fitting bodice eased itself into a skirt, cut on the bias, that fell to just above her knees. When she walked it moved gracefully, sometimes swirling, at other times clinging to the curves of her strong sensual body. The sleeves, by contrast, were lusciously ballooned, and the crêpe de chine, black on black, damask pattern of full-blown roses finished tight to the wrists. Black stockings and high-heeled black alligator pumps encased legs that seemed to go on forever, and feet which were slender, long and elegant.

321

He was no more than five feet away from her. He stopped and studied Cheyney's face under the elegant, wide-brimmed hat, a sombrero shape of finely woven straw lacquered black. Under it her long, shiny, coal-black hair was pulled back in an intricate, pretzel-like twist at the nape of the neck.

Her large, violet-coloured eyes danced with excitement as she stood engrossed in the De Kooning painting from his 'women' series. She had eyes for nothing else. What of herself was she seeing in this volatile, sexual, cruel, big-breasted figure by De Kooning? The good Senator studied the painting's slashes of colour: red flesh, big frightening black eyes, the devouring mouth – all so powerfully female and aggressive, they nearly jumped off the canvas. He sensed that, if she could, the woman would eat him alive. She was depraved sexual madness, gloriously female, gloriously cunt. The woman, all paint and canvas, sucked him into herself, and his heart skipped a beat for the ecstasy of her, and the genius who created her.

Someone grazed his arm and, in excusing himself, he broke the spell of the moment. He turned his attention back to Cheyney's face. So pale and flawless a skin, he thought. He imagined the feel of the high cheek-bones, the jaw-line, and the shape of the chin in his hands, familiar to him from the many times he had held her face and caressed it, made love to it. How many times his finger had traced the long straight slope of her nose, a perfect nose such as might have graced the Venus de Milo. Those moments were enshrined in life now.

He focused on her lips and her mouth, so sensually perfect and alive. Mouth and lips that had mastered the art of erotic lovemaking. Today covered in perfect red. He sighed, dazzled as he always was by her beauty and her style.

Still she hadn't seen him, not even when he went to her and placed a hand gently on her shoulder. Only when he spoke did he gain her attention.

'Cheyney, what a great achievement. We'll be leaving, all the Washington crowd, directly after lunch. If you like we can . . .' She stopped him by placing a finger gently over his lips.

'I won't be going with you, Harve. A change of plan. I hope you don't mind.'

Of course he did. But there was something, a tone in her voice, a look in her eye, that proscribed his showing it. Harve was a shrewd politician, a careful man who knew the danger of pushing or pulling when the time was not right. He took her face in both his hands and with great affection kissed her on the lips. He smiled, then without a word, slowly turned on his heel. Before he even took a step, Cheyney placed a hand on his shoulder, 'Lunch? We can at least have that together.'

322

He hesitated for a few seconds and then turned back to face her. He was encouraged by the look of relief in her eyes, more so when she said, 'Oh, good. There is a sumptuous buffet for my guests. You will love the food, and for you and me, the Austrian Minister, two princes, three great painters and a sculptor, two museum directors, and four of your Washington big-wigs—' she had the good grace to take a deep breath and laugh at herself before she continued – 'a table set in the sun where we can watch the black swans in the moat, and have a perfect view of the white marble sculpture garden and the tree-covered mountains beyond. If you had said no, I should have despaired.'

The words were all the right ones, but the eyes – he saw nothing of what he wanted to see in the eyes. Desire. Flickers of her carnal nature. Love. Passion. Those emotions she sometimes had for him. Not there today. Today's message was, friend, affection. He settled for that.

Chapter 34

It was late afternoon. Takashi was waiting for her. The baroque splendour of the eighteenth-century room was bathed in the golden light of a sun that was dropping fast now in a still clear and bright blue sky. She pushed the pair of twenty-foot high doors open and burst into the bedroom once reserved for the visiting royalty of Europe. He was standing by the window, the light a frame behind his body. She saw him, and calm entered her soul where moments before all had been fragmented and confused.

Takashi's naked beauty, his fiercely masculine and yet soft and tender sensual looks, instilled in her a sensation of quiet that could leave her open and vulnerable on the one hand, and, on the other, bring all her quiescent sexual passion wide awake. Her need for intimate physical contact became acute. He was, when lust was all important to them, as it was now, fire and ice for her.

The body . . . such perfect young flesh. The skin the colour of bronze and so smooth and silky, with the texture of fine polished marble. Unbroken by a blemish or a single hair except for the mass of black covering his pubis and accentuating a formidable penis that, like the licentiousness in his dark and smouldering oriental eyes, his voluptuous lips and exquisite mouth, promised ecstasy and always delivered more. Instantly captivated, Cheyney was disarmed of her need to be in control. She was mesmerised by him, and their mutual lust for each other.

He ran his fingers through his straight black hair. She watched his every movement as he walked towards her. Her anticipation was heightened even more by the need she recognised in his eyes, the passion, the love she saw in them.

Scent of freshly cut lilacs; deafening silence mingling with the golden light to envelop their senses. Her heart beat faster as he reached out and slowly pulled the long pin from her hat. She watched him remove it, riveted by this simple action that, to her eyes, appeared as slow motion. He placed it on the Louis XIV commode next to her.

It was their eyes that spoke, and what they said sent a shiver down her spine. He unbuttoned the sleeve fastened tight around her wrist, and then turned her hand palm up and licked a small spot in its centre with the tip of his tongue, then sealed it with a kiss. Again, he tasted the flesh from the palm of her other hand. The taste of her was always an aphrodisiac for him. He felt her tremor of bliss, her sigh of nervous passion. She lowered her long and luscious lashes and took a deep breath. Takashi stepped behind her and opened, one by one, the tiny concealed fastenings at the back of her dress, and then slowly eased it off her shoulders and let it slip to the carpet. He lowered his head and placed a kiss upon her shoulder.

Facing her once more he saw a tear poised in the corner of each eye. Her breasts tantalised him. The already erect nipples and pale pink nimbus, the weight and superb roundness in his hands, ignited the flame that always smouldered within him for her. He ran his hands from the sides of her breasts down her body, and with the tip of his tongue he licked away first one tear and then the other, as he broke the thin cords of her panties from her hips and slowly slid the patch of black silk from between her legs.

The mood suddenly changed. Not that he became less tender. More that the sight of her standing in black high-heeled shoes, naked but for provocative dark stockings held in place by long garters attached to a belt of matching black lace, signalled sex. It triggered the animal passion they shared, their desire to feel the thrill of hot, molten sexual bliss.

In one swift action Takashi swung Cheyney off her feet. He cradled her in one arm, and wrapping one of her legs over his hip, his adept fingers teased her more intimate lips, opening a floodgate of pleasure for her. Her heartbeat racing, she bit hard on the soft inside of her mouth, trying to quell the sensation that she was dissolving. He burst into her with one swift, sharp thrust. She gasped, and again and again called out his name. He silenced her with a kiss that she hungrily responded to while she clung to him, arms around his neck. And then, slowly and determinedly, he made love to her with his raging penis, so that they both might feel every excitement their coupling generated. At the same time, he buried his face in her breasts and grazed and sucked her rigid, needy nipples with his lips.

In a passion of pleasure, she encouraged him for more. She was helpless to do otherwise, because with his every exquisite thrust, she longed to give a little more of herself to him. He carried her to the large, canopied bed, draped in black silk damask. There Takashi and she revelled in his sexual possession of her. She took him not with passive resistance but with active receptiveness that stirred their sexual lechery. They fucked as one being with two souls.

While their bodies eagerly submitted to the sexual rhythm of passionate intercourse, he whispered to her, 'Oh, how good wanton love can be when both say yes to it. No substitute for this.'

His words inflamed Cheyney. She could bear no more, and came in such a violent passion that she called out, 'Yes, oh yes!' before she silenced his words and all their thoughts with a kiss where mouths opened and tongues met and made love as well.

Takashi now, having achieved sexual release and his own private ecstasy, continued to make exciting and imaginative love to her. Every orgasm Cheyney had was now enjoyed passively by Takashi. Eventually with gentle kisses and caresses he finally calmed Cheyney's sexual passion.

In bed, between sexual trysts, they drank chilled champagne and dozed in each other's arms. Finally Cheyney spoke. They were lying on their sides, facing each other, against large soft pillows covered in white linen and ecru-coloured chantilly lace. Pools of soft warm light filtered through the silk lampshade, casting an erotic glow over the bed.

'You make the world stop and let me get off. When we make love, it's a deep and abiding erotic love, all-consuming. That it should have happened once seems a miracle to me. That it should happen, as it does, every time, an even greater one.'

While she spoke, he stroked her hair. Then he raised her from the cushions. They sat opposite each other, resting on their haunches in the middle of the bed, holding hands and gazing into each other's eyes. He placed her hands one on each of her thighs, and did the same on himself. Then he bowed his head and remained that way for several minutes. A silence descended upon them. A deep, spiritual, soul-searching kind of silence, cleansing, healing, rejuvenating.

When Takashi finally raised his head and looked once again into Cheyney's eyes, he was able to see another kind of woman in them. He reached around her and slowly pulled the pins from her hair, unbound the twist at the nape of her neck and watched her waist-length hair tumble down around her shoulders. He brushed out the long and lustrous tresses and arranged them most carefully off her face and down her back. 'Don't move,' was his gentle injunction, more compelling than any command.

When he returned to her, he sat on his knees before her once again. He took some of her hair from either side of her face and draped it into shoulder-length pieces, brushing them until they shone like silk. He sat back and viewed his work with great pleasure. She was magnificent in her nakedness, veiled only by her long, straight, black hair, the wisps at the sides framing her face.

He dressed her in a splendid eighteenth-century white kimono, heavily embroidered in burnished gold. The pattern of chrysanthemums danced in the lamplight. He was meticulous in arranging every fold around her. When he had finished, he held a hand mirror for her to look at herself. Tears came to her eyes. She never imagined that she could still look pure, that there might still remain a vestige of innocence in her soul. But there was, and Takashi knew how to read it. He took her in his arms and they made love again. This time their intercourse was as if she were a young girl again, a virgin. They allowed themselves the pleasure of letting their passion build slowly, very slowly, into a frenzy of lust, and from there into the secret twilight zone of depravity.

When he awoke she was gone.

Cheyney moved quietly through the deep seclusion of the wood, trying not to disturb the things around her. It was still dawn.

As the sun rose, the path flattened out and she came to the edge of the village. Cheyney began to hum to the rhythm of her shoes on the cobblestones. She felt on top of the world.

The village streets at that hour in the morning were almost deserted. The only sign of life, the milkman, whom she didn't know, the butcher, whom she did, hanging up a whole pig, between hooks heavy with fat and sassy-looking links of sausage, a whole calf's liver. She said hello to the milkman, who doffed his hat, and she waved to the butcher and walked on in the direction of the bakery.

She walked down a short road of uneven stones that ended in a *cul de sac*, pretty for its hanging baskets of spring flowers and eighteenth-century crooked houses. The scent of daffodils, hyacinth and tulips mingling with that of freshly baked bread, cinnamon and vanilla, was as dizzying as a heady perfume. She walked through the open back doors of the bakery and into the kitchen. The clink and clang of bread pans, cake tins, baking sheets, the whirring of heavy-duty mixers, the hissing of the gas jets of the huge ovens greeted her, as did Gunther the baker and Gerta his wife. Klaus and Heinrich, their helper sons, accorded her a nod.

She was famished, her mouth watered for the hot rolls and fresh butter, the taste of rye and caraway seed, the bowl of hot black coffee that was being rushed to the long oak table, white from years of scrubbing and ingrained flour, where she sat. The other chairs at the table remained empty. They all knew the drill expected when Kurt Walbrook's wife, or her son, visited the kitchen. A greeting, the old black coffee-pot on the table, then back to the baking. Except for the dash to the table with samples just out of the ovens, until one of them cried out enough. They especially liked having her there, the way she sat quietly and took in the theatre of the baker's kitchen, hungrily ate all their creations set before her, but let them get on with their work.

Cheyney ate two rolls, dripping with butter, and drank half a bowl of coffee before she reached for the telephone Klaus had placed on the table near her, all part of the drill. She always asked if she could use it to call the Schloss for someone to pick her up. She dialled, the telephone rang several times.

327

'Hello.'

'Hi, it's me.'

'Hello, you,' he said.

His voice warmed her, and for a second she thought that she might love him more than she realised or wanted to. 'This is not the way I meant to wake you, I had something more exotic in mind, something more intimate,' she said provocatively.

'Promises, promises. Are you all right?'

'Never better. Yesterday was marvellous. Last night with you, sublime, more than sublime. And, I have started today with the dawn on the mountain. Come and have breakfast with me.'

'Then you're at the bakery in the village?'

'Right.'

'I'll be there as fast as I can. Bye.'

Her reaction was quick: 'No, Takashi, don't hang up. Are you there?' she asked somewhat anxiously.

'Yes.'

There was a moment of silence while Cheyney recovered from her surprise. Her reluctance to let him go; the relief she felt, when she heard his voice still there on the other end of the telephone. She could hardly credit the impulse that now made her say, 'Takashi', with lowered voice and back turned to the busy kitchen. Looking out of the window and up towards the mountain, she whispered,

'I love you.'

'Yes, I know that.'

'In such a powerful and special way, that I never think to tell you.' Again there was silence between them.

'Takashi.'

'I'm still here.'

'We've been blessed by the gods.'

'They show taste. I'm on my way.' The telephone clicked and the dial-tone whined in Cheyney's ear. She replaced the receiver. Smiling and feeling outrageously happy, she turned back to her super-calorie breakfast.

She refilled her blue and white glazed pottery coffee bowl and, holding it in both hands, lifted it to her lips and sipped. She liked the heat warming her palms, the steam teasing the tip of her nose. Gunther carried over to her a huge wooden paddle with a long handle that he used to feed the bread in and out of the old-fashioned deep oven. He gently shook a delectable-looking twisted roll of sweetened dough filled with a delicious poppyseed paste. She set about trying to detach a piece of it. But it was so hot it burned her finger-tips. She fanned it with her hand impatiently and thought about Takashi.

Several samplings later, she heard the Harley Davidson motor-cycle echoing hollowly through the still-deserted village streets, and smiled to herself. Then it roared into the cul de sac. She turned to face the rear entrance of the bakery and watched him walk through the door. How handsome and sexy her lover looked in his brindle-brown tweed trousers, his white, crew-neck cotton tee-shirt showing through his open, black-leather Armani jacket. The unbearably sensuous oriental face.

Their eyes met at once. She watched him reluctantly divert his gaze to greet Gunther and hand him a box of Havana cigars, toss a rolled-up parcel of motor magazines to Heinrich, and kiss a giggling Gerta's flour-covered hand. Pink with delighted embarrassment, the baker's wife handed him a coffee bowl and he walked towards the old oak table, and the woman he loved.

Takashi sat in the chair next to Cheyney. She poured him a cup of coffee, and watched him slice a small round wholemeal roll and spread it thick with butter, cut it in half and place her share on the plate in front of her, while he bit into his, with strong, perfect, white teeth.

'Even your teeth look young,' she said, teasingly. He laughed.

'Never mind my being young in the tooth. Those were pretty nice things you said to me on the telephone. Would you care to expand on that theme? Or shall I just say thank you for last night and my life with you?'

'We're getting too sentimental.'

'Possibly.'

'Well, I am. I have done nothing since I called you but think back, remembering the day we met. It was ten years ago, just about this time of year.'

'No, Cheyney, not just about this time of year, exactly ten years ago today. I have your anniversary present in the inside pocket of my jacket, but discretion forbids me to give it to you here. Outside, later.'

Cheyney reached under the table and found his hand and squeezed it. 'You're so good, you never forget the extra special days in my life.' She deliberately switched back to memory, wanting to fudge what was fast becoming an emotional moment for them both. 'You were so very young, practically a boy. Handsome and so full of surprises. In that you have not changed one bit. It was at Christie's auction-house in London. I was with Kurt, you were alone, seated next to me.'

Gunther arrived with his paddle and eased four *schnekken* – a tricorn bit of buttery pastry, spread with cinnamon, sultanas and walnuts, rolled over itself several times and turned in on the corners in the fashion of a croissant – on to the oak table to cool. Their pungent scent smothered reminiscence. What sweet perfume. Cheyney and Takashi remained silent while Cheyney broke off chunks of onion bread and buttered them. They ate, and drank their strong black coffee with gusto, each thinking about that day and how their relationship had come to be as strong and uncomplicated as it seemed on this anniversary.

They had both been bidding on the same picture, a Jim Dine. Not for the first time that day had they been competing against each other for a work of art. After they had outbid several other dealers, they had fought it out between themselves for a 1962 Andy Warhol, Soup Cans, oil on canvas. Takashi got that after Cheyney had reluctantly dropped out. She ran him aground and paid a record price for a Hans Hoffman and a Motherwell. But she lost a 1960 Jasper Johns to him and a Roy Lichtenstein she had sorely wanted. He was buying up the American icons of the sixties, just what she was after. She was tense and angry, losing them to him. She bid again, determined that the Jim Dine painting would be hers. Then Kurt bent forward and across her and tapped the young man on the sleeve, for his attention, and addressed them both.

'Don't you think you are both being just a little short-sighted? Would it not be to your mutual advantage to become partners now and sort the details out later?'

It was then that Cheyney Fox and Takashi Ishiguro looked at each other for the first time. She was angry with Kurt, for interfering, and being so right. And clever. And even more angry with her opponent when he turned out to be not a shrewd dealer, but a slip of a lad with an inscrutable, passive, oriental beauty, a boy no more than eighteen years old, clever and determined beyond his years.

The auctioneer was pushing on, working the crowd and the telephone bidders to enter into the action, looking for another record price. The tension in the room was augmented by the temporary silence of the two top bidders But it was more than the pressure of having to make a decision quickly, before the gavel fell and the painting was knocked down, or having the entire room of world-famous dealers, collectors, museum directors watching the two relatively unknown private collectors battling it out that made Cheyney raise her hand ready to shake Takashi's in a silent agreement. It had been something quite inexplicable, an inner sense of rightness. And when he respectfully bowed his head to her she had no doubts that she had met a most extraordinary young man, who would be an admirable partner.

'Shall you complete our first transaction? I will take on the next one, if there is to be a next one this afternoon,' were his first words to her.

That evening the three of them celebrated their unorthodox purchase of nine paintings and their partnership, by dining in Claridges, where both the Walbrooks and Takashi Ishiguro were staying. They agreed to remain partners rather than divide their purchases, and for each to take possession of half. Every year to exchange them. They would leave the partnership details to their respective lawyers.

Other than that they learned little about each other that evening: Kurt and Cheyney that Takashi Ishiguro was indeed eighteen years old. The son of one of Japan's wealthier industrialists, who was also a renowned collector of art and artefacts. That the Ishiguros were direct descendants of the Shoguns that had ruled Japan in the fifteenth, sixteenth and seventeenth centuries. That Takashi was a Harvard University student of art history, with a passion for contemporary paintings, which his father unquestioningly financed, fast motor bikes, which his father did not, and an infatuation with Paris and New York, parts of which his father owned.

Takashi, for his part, learned that the couple he met at the auction were the usually reclusive private collectors Kurt Walbrook and his wife, Cheyney Fox. Only that, and the miracle of falling in love.

'A slow love lasts longer. That's what I kept telling myself, as I walked away from you and Kurt after we had dinner together that night,' said Takashi, standing up and exchanging the empty coffee pot for another from the stove behind Cheyney.

He poured some of the steaming liquid into Cheyney's bowl, and, seeing everyone in the kitchen preoccupied he placed a hand on her shoulder and squeezed it for a brief moment before he walked behind her and took his seat. 'During the following two years, when I stayed away from you, and the five years subsequent to that, when I decided that it was better to love both you and Kurt than not to be near you at all, that thought became a philosophy. And not a bad one.

'Of course, I never stopped wanting you in the erotic way I knew Kurt had you. But knowing that was impossible, I had made up my mind never to suffer for it. That decision only honed my desire for you to an even finer edge. Kurt was aware of how much I loved you both. I always suspected that he knew as well how much I wanted you in the way we are together now. But I was certain of it when, as the years passed and the three of us became almost inseparable, you learned to love me and want me. There were times when it showed in your eyes.'

'Don't. Stop. No more.'

'Why? It's been a long love and a good love, and we have every reason to be pleased with ourselves for it. We were never unfaithful to Kurt. And now, if you're *sure* you've had enough to eat, it's time to go.'

He stood up and she followed, laughing. She whispered, 'No wonder we love each other, we know how much our roles mean to us, and, more important, bless each other for them.'

Chapter 35

Cheyney arrived from the triumphant opening of the Museum Schloss Garmisch-Konigsberg with high hopes of success in becoming America's first Secretary of State for Art. The last two years had taught her how to live with the sudden incursion of fame into her life – fame in the world of art, that is. But she certainly was not prepared for the unimaginable euphoria generated by the support her nomination was receiving.

Cables arrived from all over the world, dozens of them every day. Her gallery's telephone was besieged. The exhibition of Four New Painters on the first floor of the multi-floored gallery was packed with people. Every work of art sold on the first day, following the news of her nomination being broken by the press.

Gallery Two, on the second floor, had a showing of Abstract Expressionist paintings. It included Rothkos, Motherwells, Franz Klines, several by Acton Pace never seen before, Clifford Stills. The queues pressed all day at the door. It was the same in the Cheyney Fox Gallery Three, to see the sculptures of Calder, Henry Moore and Pablo Picasso.

Cheyney herself was surrounded by the sycophants of the art world, hundreds of instant friends, associates, colleagues. She was watched closely by David Rosewarne, whom she had gone to see immediately on her return from Austria, and to whom she had supplied a detailed resumé of her life and work, anything she thought relevant to his job of protecting her. It had not been an easy few hours but as he pointed out, 'Your life, from the day you accepted the nomination, has become an open book. If you can't stand the heat, get out of the kitchen, right now.'

The memory of Taggart's face suddenly loomed up in front of her: Eton, and their picnic only a few days before. They had taken a family vote, and she wouldn't dream of letting her son or herself down. 'Go for it, Mom,' rang in her ears. She had smiled at David and said, 'I've got all my pots bubbling on the burners. Some may boil over and mess the stove, and it may be hotter than I may like, but I'm not about to run away from it.'

From a distance, Harve also kept a close watch on Cheyney's progress, lobbying whenever and wherever he could discreetly influence. And Judd Whyatt, whose determination that she should win was prompted solely by a belief that she was right for the job, with his influence and quick, clever mind, played guardian more effectively than anyone. He was their key trouble-shooter. He knew not only the law, and the real power-brokers in Washington and Europe, but also how best to work the media to his client's advantage.

While Washington was making discreet inquiries as to her worthiness, the media, during that first week, fell in love with Cheyney Fox – her wealth, glamour, beauty, success. They revived, of course, the old Warhol connection and made the most of that. They loved her because she was portrayed as a winner, one who had made it from back field. Women wanted to look like her, men wanted to capture her. Suddenly everyone wanted her style, to know whose clothes she wore, who dressed her hair, how she managed her life, her loves. How she combined an erotic charisma with being an enormously successful businesswoman. That lasted a week. But a week is a long time in the history of hero-worship.

Suddenly everyone felt cheated. Her critics multiplied. When Takashi sent her a bodyguard, she thought he was over-reacting. Her objections faded after a rather messy encounter with an unsuccessful painter and a can of luminous yellow paint. The art gossips said that Acton Pace's widow was preparing a legal action against her that would scream 'Fraud, cheat, thief!' Reha was blabbing to anyone who would listen.

The winds began to blow against Cheyney. The press was suddenly filled with the story of the widow's claim that Cheyney Fox had manipulated Pace and the prices of his paintings. That she had stolen them from the man when he was mentally unbalanced. That was bad, but there was worse to come. Reha Pace announced to the press that she would sue for restitution of the paintings Cheyney owned, which daily grew in value. She even went on television to insinuate in an interview that Cheyney Fox had been instrumental in driving Acton Pace over the edge. His grisly suicide was raked back into brief media life.

Cheyney managed to remain calm. David Rosewarne and Judd Whyatt were fielding the nastier accusations. When Washington blew cold, Judd Whyatt got on the telephone and spoke with them. He did not tell Cheyney what was said, but Washington ignored the press and stuck by her. They continued to pursue their own investigation into her affairs.

Andrew Schwartzkopf, an influential New York critic, came out against her. He claimed there were others better qualified in the arts to hold such a position. Then there was a less important but more commercial critic, the sort who get to the non-intellectuals, a ladies' glossy-magazine journalist called Anya Hour. She managed to mix being very dumb with being very powerful. She got lots of coverage by innuendo about how Cheyney Fox had got to where she was, through her dazzling looks and masculine backers.

The top art critic in the United States, Richard Windus, wrote an article for *Time* entitled:

WHY CHEYNEY FOX HAS GOT MY VOTE

Yes. Because I believe in Art, but not the art world. And so does Cheyney Fox, even though she is part of that establishment. Yes. Because I believe in the artist, in the act of creativity, and that, once the act of creating a work of art is completed, the object then speaks for itself. Cheyney Fox believes that too. My many other reasons for saying 'yes' for Cheyney Fox are all minor beside those two essential beliefs. She has my vote, and my admiration.

During the several weeks that followed controversy raged. Cheyney stayed quiet and held on tight. But, she thought, the worst was yet to come: when the media latched on to the past of her husband Kurt, and the terms of his will whereby she and her son were enriched at a terrible price. The ill-gotten gains of her husband's life had become hers: treasures, among which she could not distinguish those that were marked by blood and violence from those honestly acquired.

The passage of time might seem to have conferred respectability on her husband and his collection. Here she was, his heir, about to be honoured. Yet her very prominence in the world of art might be based on that great rape and murder of all the values of civilisation by the Third Reich. Her husband had dealt with the supporters, heroes and profiteers of the crumbling Reich, men who were still unrepentant Nazis amid the comforts of a civilisation rescued from Nazism, and now the world might get to know that.

What a field-day her enemies and the press would have with that. How could she unravel it all? Yet if she did not unravel it, there were others who would do so. Cheyney felt herself spiralling towards some kind of disaster.

How many times during those weeks had she thought of Kurt? He seemed to be at her side all through the controversy. He and Taggart. It was their spirit, combining with her own, that made her strong and tall, and able never once to flinch. Their love had made her a woman rich in more things than wealth.

During her darkest days in the sixties, she had often wondered what she would do if she ever came face to face with Tony Caletti, the bookkeeper who had actually ruined her. When he appeared at the gallery, she didn't even recognise him.

Takashi, newly arrived in New York, was at her side when Katie said there was a scruffy man who insisted on seeing her, and gave his name.

334

Cheyney felt nothing. She just urgently wanted him off her premises. He insisted on coming in to her office.

'I always said you'd make it big one day. I guess you're surprised to see me. Aren't you even gonna ask me to sit down?'

'No. What do you want?'

'Maybe I don't want anything.'

'Good, then leave.' She buzzed and asked for Bob and Ray to come in. The two bodyguards were in the room before she even put down the receiver.

'Mr Caletti is leaving. Would you be kind enough to see him out of the building?'

'Hey, wait a minute. I wanna have a chat with you. Maybe you oughta have a talk with me,' he said menacingly.

'We've done this scene before, I don't intend to do it again. And if you are even thinking of blackmail, or selling your true confessions, you would do well to remember that this time I have enough money to prosecute you. You could find yourself behind bars for a fair slice of the remainder of your life. Now, out.'

Takashi moved menacingly towards Tony Caletti who fled, Bob and Ray behind him.

Cheyney sat down and laughed until tears appeared in her eyes. Eyes that were not laughing at all. She wondered what other skeleton was going to come rattling out of the closet.

The next was a six-footer. It turned out to be Christopher Corbyn's. Although they had not seen each other for years, they had parted on friendly terms. When he appeared at the gallery to ask if they could have lunch together, she should have guessed something was amiss. She could not remember his ever taking her to lunch when they were in love. He was ill at ease from the moment they met in one of his upper-Fifth Avenue dowager-duchess's apartments.

She was prompted to ask almost immediately, 'Christopher, out with it. What's wrong? Why are you so nervous with me?'

He confessed at once, 'I've made the most terrible blunder. I feel I have to warn you about it.'

Cheyney felt a sickness right in the pit of her stomach. 'What do you mean, Christopher?'

'I told the Heads we would have had a grown-up son by now if you hadn't chosen to have an abortion. I'm sorry, Cheyney. He especially kept asking about you. What you were like when we were together. It just slipped out.'

'Just slipped out? You shit! Things like that don't just slip out. How many paintings did he buy, Christopher? Four? Five?'

'Three, actually.'

'You pig! For once you weren't piggish enough. He'd have bought seven for the news you just gave him. Congress will just love ratifying the nomination of a woman who had an abortion. How ironic that you should talk about it now. Why didn't you have the guts to talk to me about it when it mattered?' Without another word she walked out. She went straight to warn David Rosewarne what was about to surface against her.

But, whatever was thrown at her, Cheyney would not talk to the press, and she maintained her low profile. There was just one person she would have to warn about what might be said: Taggart. She would not do that until she could sit him down and tell him her whole Christopher love-story. She wanted him to have the truth about the abortion.

Judd arrived at the gallery just after it closed. The semi-darkness gave it an eerie and sensual feeling. He called out her name as he walked through Gallery One to her office. There he found her still working with Takashi and Katie Spreckles, third in line in the gallery's hierarchy. All three looked up in surprise.

'Judd, I didn't expect you. Come in.'

'I know. I took a chance that you would be here. Is it awkward?'

'No, of course not.'

He and Takashi shook hands. Katie received a friendly peck on the cheek, then began to gather up papers.

'No, Katie, do stay, I want to get your view on this, along with Cheyney's and Takashi's.'

The three sat down in Barcelona chairs of tobacco-coloured leather and steel around Cheyney's glass desk. At times Judd could not help looking on Cheyney less as a client and friend, more as an erotically desirable woman. This was one of those times. There are certain women who are provoca-tively sexual without even trying. Cheyney Fox was one such. It was manifest in her every little gesture. She was just as sensual, exciting and provocative as she had been when they first met way back in the sixties.

'Archibald Head has just had an interview with a reporter from the *Times*. The reporter is a good friend. He says we'd better be prepared for a full frontal attack from Head. He suggests anyone who's been bankrupt can't run a business, and is obviously unfit for large-scale responsibility for the country's art and artefacts. Not to mention the huge sums of money that will be passing through the offices of the Secretary of Art. I thought I should put you in the picture, so to speak. Ultimately it doesn't mean much. Just another guy hankering after the job and shooting his big mouth off.

'But what really does mean something is how Washington evaluates the discretion and calm you are showing in front of all the shit that's in the fan. And most especially the way you have managed to stay out of the media, and not let yourself be dragged into sensational interviews.

'Gore Kern – he's lobbying for you in Washington – asked me if we had any strategy for when the heat is really on. Which it will be, because your personal position is not improved by your being at the centre of a political issue. There's a massive controversy building in the media about the very creation of a Secretariat of Art. To say nothing of a Federal subsidy for it.

'It just came to me out of nowhere that we do have a strategy, only none of us knew it. What we've been doing so far was right – protecting you, Cheyney, by speaking for you. But we can't go on this way forever. A time comes when silence starts to look like guilt. The answer, of course is that we announce – at the right moment, mind you – that Cheyney Fox will give no press conferences until after her appointment has been ratified. Then she will give one in-depth, hour-long interview with some guy like Madigan. Grant Madigan. He's the sort with the right media-impact and status to swing it our way. Do an interview with some hot-shot like him, and it could put you in Washington. He's good enough to persuade America who and what Cheyney Fox really is. Whether she's right for the job on offer.'

Takashi and Katie enthused simultaneously, faces beaming. All Cheyney could think of was fifteen, nearly sixteen years ago. A long time to have loved so completely, and lost so utterly, and have killed so deliberately all feelings for a man. She felt nothing at the sound of his name. No more than she did when she watched him on TV, which had only been once, or read something of his, which had not been often. Or when her son asked anything about his natural father. For years Cheyney had trained herself to feel nothing for Grant Madigan. But she did still feel the loss of her one and only great love affair. Taggart, the fruit she reaped from it, was living proof of how divine it was to have had even a taste of real love and Grant Madigan.

She smiled at her three friends and said, 'You are clever, Judd. And I agree your plan has got possibilities. Go get Grant Madigan.'

Chapter 36

Cheyney was not so much nervous as confused. Was it after all such a good idea to submit to a grilling for TV by Grant Madigan? What bravado on her part: 'Go get Grant Madigan'! Really, what a way for a gal to talk. Movie-script stuff. For God's sake, she was meeting Taggart's natural father. Her son would have to be told. What then? Suddenly Cheyney felt this meeting was fraught with danger.

Setting it up had not been easy. Judd had had to agree that the two of them should meet in a private place, and alone, for their preliminary meeting, because if the TV interview did happen, Madigan would insist on secrecy. No leaks to the press. His own network and publicity machine would want to handle everything. There was no getting out of the preliminaries. Cheyney would have to show up.

Madigan's first reaction to Judd Whyatt's suggestion that he interview Cheyney was "Impossible!" Not for any feelings he had about Cheyney. There were none left. He had killed them off when he walked out on her those many years ago.

No, tempting as it was professionally, it was impossible simply because of the timing. Madigan's schedule was already top heavy. Whyatt continued to plead. What he was offering was an exclusive interview with a potential superstar. A real scoop.

Reluctantly, Madigan reviewed his own knowledge of Cheyney Fox. He was certain that his audiences would be no less fascinated than he to hear her version of her rise to fame and fortune, and what she would say about the supposed Nazi loot said to have become the foundation of the Walbrook Collection.

He would, of course, like the story of what real spy-games she had to play with the CIA and the Israelis to grab the Nazi treasures they wanted. How she managed to get access to the highest levels in the White House, the Kremlin, the Elysée Palace. And what of the secret CIA photos of her on the arm of a former Nazi general, or others, in palatial South American residences, marked, 'Woman, North American, Unidentified'? Fakes to set her up as some kind of a modern-day Mata Hari? Of such stuff were headlines made. The papers weren't billing her as Ms Clean. And what had she done for Irving Kirshner? Had she helped him? He had seen Irving many times since that day in Paris when Grant gave him Cheyney's name. But, at Grant's request, Irving had said no word about her.

As soon as he had finished his conversation with Judd Whyatt, Grant called his research department to pull everything they could find on Cheyney Fox. What they came up with intrigued him more every minute.

Mega-rich Japanese industrialists took heed of her advice in art and architecture. One at least was committed to her in devoted friendship. Why her? What made her capable of beating out other dealers? What did she have, and what did she give, above and beyond her expertise? Sexual services? CIA services? Either was a possibility: both were rumoured. Middle Eastern sheiks and princes, two of whom Grant knew well, were said to be besotted by her. They heaped spectacularly generous gifts upon her. Why?

What made a woman like Cheyney Fox tick? One with as many powerful enemies in the art world determined to destroy her, no matter how, as she had admirers. Those enemies she'd made after she broke a silence over American Pop Art and her contribution to it through Warhol. The Campbell's soup cans. A can of worms there, maybe, Madigan mused. What kind of power did this woman have, to be able to turn the art world of the sixties upside down with a single absurd idea?

And there was, too, the glamour-aspect of her life. Happily married to a wealthy European dilettante until his death, a man no other woman had been able to lure into wedlock. A ravishing wife to him; a world-hopping mother, devoted to her son; a career woman. All pretty good material. It suddenly seemed less impossible. He called in his assistant. They tried to work out the changes that would have to be made in schedules. How, where, and when it could be done.

It was just a short walk away from Cheyney's Central Park South, twenty-room penthouse apartment to the Plaza Hotel. She was quite looking forward now to meeting Grant Madigan, and persuading him to do the in-depth interview. That was after she had screwed up her courage to call Taggart. She was relieved to find that the hurtful gossip and innuendoes in the media had not as yet penetrated the ivy-covered walls of Eton. Boys had more pressing concerns than the state of American art.

'Mom, stop worrying about me. You simply have no idea how insulated we are here from the hard real world. Ain't heard nothing yet. When and if I do, I can cope. Do you think you are the only mother whose son goes to Eton who has been involved in scandal? Sometimes you're awfully naive, Mom. Forget it. We're primed here to handle whatever is thrown at us. It's what you pay for every Eton term.'

'You sound just like your father.'

339

'Well, yeah. If he was still alive, Mom, he'd say, "Sheyney, my dear, do get on with it." And them's my sentiments too.'

Tears had come to her eyes: Taggart mimicked Kurt's Viennese accent perfectly.

Cheyney found what a healer time really is. She could hardly equate Grant Madigan, this media-personality, honoured by so many remarkable men around the world for his relatively unbiased journalism, with a lover who so ruthlessly abandoned her, a lifetime ago.

She felt the meeting was going to be comparatively easy after the day she had already had. A morning at the gallery where 'business as usual' was more fraught than usual. Two museums wanting the same Clifford Still. One of the best architects in the States having a tug of war with his client: should they go for a two-million dollar Henry Moore sculpture, or commission Oldenberg to create a piece for the atrium of a business-complex in San Diego, California? Cheyney had been burdened with the casting vote in the matter.

Lunch with Harvey Wigan. The good Senator had flown in from Washington just to see Cheyney. She still had no idea what had induced her to behave as she did when he demanded, 'I insist you become Mrs Harvey Wigan before you take office. Cheyney Wigan: it suits you, you know.' Suddenly the very idea of being Senator Wigan's wife appalled her. Harvey, who had been so good to her, who had been such an exciting companion. Attractive, interesting Harvey, imaginatively sexy out from under the Capitol's rotunda. Harvey, who could give her the family life she missed, be the husband she liked having. She found herself aghast at the very idea of it!

Whatever had impelled her to reply as she had done when he playfully nudged the open jeweller's box across the damask cloth towards her, the fat diamond sparkling in the restaurant's designer lighting? 'Harvey, much as I like you, I don't want to be Senator Harvey Wigan's wife. I'm sorry, I'm flattered, and believe me I wish and have wished all along that it could be so. But I simply don't love you. And please, Harve, don't ask me again.'

'But you always knew that it was on the cards!'

'On the cards, Harvey, and in my head. But not in my heart. I suppose you will hate it if I tell you we must call this romance a day and remain good friends.'

'Of course I will hate it! I've settled for "good friends" for too long as it is. And, Cheyney, time is running out. I want a wife.'

'I know, Harvey. That's the problem. You want a wife, and I'm not the woman to fill that bill. I think I'd better leave.' Cheyney closed the ring-box and pressed it into his hand. She kissed him gently on the lips and whispered in his ear, 'Forgive me.'

He looked quite shocked. What man expects such summary rejection? He asked, 'It's another man, isn't it?' His tone told her he would find the rejection more acceptable if that were the case. A bed already full was more palatable than a brusque brush-off. Not want to be Senator Wigan's wife? But Cheyney couldn't even manage a little white lie. All generosity gone, she couldn't even give him that. She felt a bitch when she said, 'No, Harvey, I'm not refusing because of another man.'

She had risen from her chair. He had held on tightly to her hand. Choked with disappointment, he could still play the good guy. 'I won't, of course, withdraw my support for you. That will always be there. But you will understand if I don't stay in touch.' Ever the gentleman, Senator Harve, thought Cheyney. She made a bet with herself as she walked away from him through the restaurant: He'll have a wife within sixty days. She felt less of a bitch for turning him down. More high-as-a-kite with relief that she had. It was time for self-preservation.

Judd Whyatt's comment, when they spoke on the telephone that afternoon and she told him about the Senator, was, 'You do pick your moments, Cheyney.'

'He picked it. I didn't.'

'The Senator took a gamble and lost. I hope you haven't.'

'Did you seriously think I could marry a man like Harvey Wigan after being married to someone like Kurt? I only pretended to myself that I could. You might have warned me, Judd.'

'Would you have listened? Never mind all that now. Cheyney, you must get Grant Madigan.'

'I will.'

Walking up the Plaza steps, Cheyney nodded to the doorman, but was thinking of her lover, Takashi. His young flesh, his virility, still warmed her from their afternoon of lovemaking. What an agreeable minor miracle that sex for Cheyney was still such an uninhibited pleasure. It was not unknown at her age for its attraction to be on the wane. She owed her continuing interest and aptitude to Takashi and their rich and full erotic life together. She had been so lucky in her sexual life, to have been able to replace the loss of her libertine-lover husband with the equally exciting Takashi. They had loved each other for a very long time. Had she not been more than twenty years older than her lover it might – who knows? – have led to marriage. Women had done stranger things.

What a day, she thought, while standing in front of the door of Suite 2612, her fist poised to knock on it. She realised she felt not frazzled but excited. As if ridding herself of Harve had set her free, and sex in the afternoon made her young. She tapped on the door.

Grant opened it. They shook hands. Here, standing before her, was not the TV celebrity, the star author that she had come to meet. Here was

Grant Madigan, off-screen and in the flesh. Still the man she had loved more intensely than any other. The father of her only child. Cheyney was disappointed and disconcerted – she half-preferred the glossy media image. The man was something too real she might have to deal with.

'Come in.' His smile was as winning as she remembered it. 'The years have been good to you, Cheyney.'

'Hello, Grant. I do appreciate your seeing me at such short notice.'

'Something to drink?'

Banalities. Small talk. The view over Central Park. What a handsome drawing-room he had. How he still enjoyed living in hotels.

Unworthy of both of them, their conversation managed to create a nervous tension between them that had not been there when Cheyney had arrived. She felt her self-control slipping from her.

Cheyney turned away from the window to face Grant. She caught him taking a long intense look at her. The erotic feelings he had for her were still there. His eyes said it all. She hoped he didn't recognise the same in hers. What was obvious to both of them was the mutual respect they had for each other. Success appreciates success. Travellers on the same rough road.

Both still bore the scars of wounds inflicted during their last encounter, though they had healed long ago. They made an effort to ignore the past, which was more difficult for Cheyney. She was carrying a huge secret, a son conceived from their last violent, romantic interlude.

'I can't stand this small talk. Can't we just drop it? Or do you think we've changed so much?'

'We couldn't be where we are today without changing.'

She sensed his antagonism. The way that they looked at each other, the movement of their bodies, indicated a residue of bitterness still lying under the layers of forgetfulness, jangling reminders of infatuation and intense erotic feeling.

Grant broke the silence. 'This isn't going to work, Cheyney.'

'No, I guess it isn't.'

'Let me finish what I started to say. It isn't going to work unless we drop this ridiculous antagonism between us. There shouldn't be any. We must throw out this emotional discontent we feel with each other if there is to be any hope of our working together on an interview.'

Cheyney finished her drink and held out her glass. Grant took it in one hand while he downed his own drink, and then went to the table he used as a bar. He refilled their glasses.

For a moment her defences crumbled. She confessed, 'Oh, Grant, I don't understand. I promise you, until I stepped into this room, I had forgotten about us years ago.'

'OK, Cheyney, maybe it is a kind of defence mechanism against any desire we still might feel for each other. Why don't we begin this meeting again? Try less hard to defend our own position. Our war was over long ago. Let's just be ourselves. See where we can get to from there.'

'That sounds right to me, Grant.'

She rose from her chair and they walked towards each other and touched the rims of their glasses in a mute toast. New beginnings echoed in the chime of the glass. Relief flowed through Cheyney. She sensed that every-thing was going to be all right. They smiled, and Grant led her to the grey, damask-covered Queen Anne sofa where she sat down. The large ottoman was covered in an Aubusson tapestry depicting a hunt through a wood, all dark rich greys and green leaves, and a deer in full leap. He pushed it up close to her feet and then sat down on it, facing her. He smiled. A smile that felt good to her: she was able to return it.

'Now look, let's forget about us, all the niceties we might ask about each other's lives and how we spent them. We're not here to catch up with each other, we are here to see whether we can put together an in-depth inter-view with you. A prime-time television show that will beam across the States. First of all, I must know how you feel about this, Cheyney. That's basic.

'There are things you must be made aware of. Like, there is nothing more merciless than the eye of the media. I'm sure you've figured that out in the last few weeks. But still, you have haven't seen the claws on the beast yet. That's because you've kept silent. Not given the media anything to punch you out on. A clever move.

'My researchers have been working since Judd called me. I've been reading what data we could find on you. Had to decide whether you are in fact good enough material for us to work with. I believe you are. Up to a point, anyway. Whether the camera likes you is another matter. For what it's worth, I think it will. What that means in layman's terms is that I think you will come across very well on television.

'You must realise that the publicity machine behind my show is enor-mous. And we have a tremendous audience. An interview with you will not be beamed across North America exclusively. We have contracts world-wide. You have to be happy with that. So far so good?' he asked, patting her on the knee. Not a provocative pat but one aimed to comfort, put her at her ease. And she was comforted by it, duly appreciative of his efforts.

'Yes, so far, I think.'

'Good. Listen, what they say about me is that Grant Madigan is a notably tough investigative journalist. It's true enough, I am. I'm also honest, direct in my approach, I don't cheat or manipulate the men and women I interview. I play quick and clever. I'll know how to make you open up to me, in front of millions of people. I'll get you to say things you have held hidden all your life. You'll be surprised at some of the things you will defend, ignore, attack. Your life will unfold on the screen. And it may turn out to be a life you have had a distorted vision of until now. We are all guilty of living with illusions about who and what we are. It's a helluva lot to take on, Cheyney. Are you up to it? Is it really what you want? This show could just as easily lose you the position in Washington as win it for you. It's a turkey-shoot, kid.

'There's more you should know about me. I don't skirt around issues. There will be questions that you may not want to answer. Let me give you an example. I might ask, "Miss Fox, one of the more unpleasant accusations against you is that you have accumulated art treasures from European sources with questionable wartime records. Can you tell me about that?" '

'Grant, my conscience is clear. I don't care what the public deduces from my life, but I can't be certain that some of those closest to me in the days when I was married to Kurt Walbrook could survive the kind of questioning that makes exciting television. I don't want to cause the dead who were dear to me to be implicated, even by association, in the heartless plundering of a war-ravaged Europe. And that could easily happen. It would make me cautious in my answers, unless you know how to lead the questions so that I can be open and honest and not hurt anyone.

'I know myself very well, Grant. I can give you the interview you want. But only if I am relaxed enough to follow your leading questions with spontaneous answers to whatever you throw at me. I trust you. We're dealing here with the pride of two professionals. Your life's work and mine are too important to us to make this interview anything but the best. The public can conclude what it likes. I don't think either of us has come this far not to stay brave.

'I am not going on that box to bare my soul for reasons of vanity. I am going out there to give a picture of myself to the American people. So they know who they're going to get as a Secretary of Art. Because I deserve to win. I don't see how you can take advantage of that. There's some who will want me and others who will not. And that's OK with me.

'I'm nervous about just one thing. I have a son, a most handsome, bright and good boy. A remarkable son – just like every mother's son. The most important thing in my life. If he knew that I were here with you tonight, he would be thrilled to think we might work together. He would say, "Mom, let it rip, go for it, tell all. So long as you didn't murder anyone, I can cope." But, Grant, I don't want to test his stamina. Yet I know my son is right. I *should* let it rip. I owe it to many people to give it my best shot. A dead husband who gave me everything. A son who loves me and is proud of everything I am. Friends who have stood by me, who know my worth.'

'I hear you, Cheyney, and I like what I hear. We will have to drop everything, get to work within the next day or two, if this is to be of any benefit to you in swinging public opinion your way. Let's have dinner.' He looked at his watch. 'I hope you don't mind, I have asked two of my associates to join us? My first assistant and my producer. There is a great deal more to this than just sitting opposite each other, me with a fat cigar in my hand and you answering questions. I would like to bounce off them some ideas on how we can handle an interview with you. I know, for example, just from this meeting, that we cannot do it live from a studio. We still have to tape for two or three days, maybe even more, and edit. Have you ever been on camera?'

'No.'

'Are you going to like being on camera?'

'No, I know I will hate it. Most days of the week I'd rather dangle from a meat hook. I'll be very uncomfortable.'

'Well, we'll have to work on that then. Oh, there's the doorbell. Think about this while I get it – your life from *your* point of view. We've been treated to an awful lot about you from everyone else's. That wall of silence you've put up against the media can work for you now. This can be *your* chance to tell your story the way it really is. A – forgive the cliché – success story, rags to riches, a passion-for-art story. On a sophisticated level, of course. If you can tell it to me, we will know how to peel off the gloss, get under your skin and show the world who and what you really are, and what you have accomplished. Maybe even what you can do as Secretary of Art for this country.' There was another ring on the doorbell. 'Think about what I've just said. A casual dinner with the three of us to see how we get on and what we can do, and we'll take it from there. Trust me.'

'She's one terrific lady. She will be the best woman he's ever had on the show. I had no idea she was so glamorous and sexy. Don't you think so, Bob?'

'I'll say! Sexy *and* fascinating. She has led some life. I can't remember the last time I enjoyed myself at a business dinner as I did tonight. She's alive, this lady, and clever. More amusing than I thought she would be. She's quite a combination: fifty per cent a sophisticated European, a smidgeon of New York street-fighter, and yet, for all the years she lived abroad as an expatriate, still very apple pie and ice cream American.'

They waited for Grant to say something. He remained silent, contemplative. Bob asked, 'You're not saying much, Grant. You're not still unsure, are you?'

'No. But listening to you guys only confirms to me how difficult it's going to be to peel off those layers of chic and get down to the real woman.'

'We'll do it in the country. She's bound to have a house in the country.'

'Let me sleep on it. We'll talk first thing in the morning.'

Bob and Sara exchanged puzzled looks. Why the hesitation? She was too good to miss.

Chapter 37

Taggart's ears caught the sound of the Harley Davidson's motor. Now it was idling. The motorbike was waiting in the street opposite. He listened to its motor rev, could recognise the pattern of the sound. It could only be Takashi! That was the signal they used to say, 'Come on, I'm waiting, we're going to hit the road.'

He raced from his desk to the window and flung it open. Takashi waved, pulled his black helmet off and beamed up at Taggart. 'Come on, we'll take a ride and go for lunch.'

He raced down the stairs four at a time and all but crash-landed into the Housemaster waiting for him.

'Fox, Fox, this will not do. Try walking. Back in four hours, Mr Ishiguro has assured me of that. Understood?'

'Understood, sir.'

The Housemaster walked him to the bike, looking only half-disapprovingly at the pair of them and the motorbike. Two of the other boys who knew Takashi from his other visits to Taggart were standing and talking to him, envy oozing from their eyes. Handsome, privileged young men in their tails and stiff collars, their establishment image so incongruous against the Harley Davidson, symbol of the sleek machine, the easy rider, the fast, free life of the open road. Takashi, himself an old boy of the school, was usually well received by masters and Taggart's friends alike. The machines he rode in on evoked envy and disdain in about equal measure. You could try too hard.

Taggart and Takashi shook hands. Takashi tossed the boy the spare helmet he had brought for him. Taggart slung a leg over the bike and sat down. He pushed the helmet down over his head. He was ready to ride pillion away from the school in search of the open road. The Housemaster and the boys languidly watched them disappear around a corner. They knew how little open road there was thereabouts.

Takashi found a place to stop not very far from Eton. A quiet space of green grass that undulated down to the river. The pair dismounted and gave each other a proper hug out of the sight of strangers. They collapsed on to the grass and both started talking at once. Takashi gave the boy right of way. 'You go first.'

347

'What are you doing here? I couldn't believe it when I was speaking to Mom this morning and she told me you were on your way here to take me to lunch. Can you stay for the cricket? And the Harley – where'd you get it? Did you just buy it? I don't recognise it as one of yours. Did you see my Housemaster's face? For a minute I thought he was going to forbid me to ride. Listen, that squash racquet's terrific. Taka, I'm really gone on a painting I saw in the Christie's catalogue. A Mirandi. I'd like to buy it. What do you think? Oh, before I forget, will you tell Mom I need some socks.'

'Hey, take a breath. How's school?'

'OK, school's OK. I'm their great white hope this year for cricket and rugby. I'm having a real good year. Hey, how come you're here?'

'I'm Mercury, with a message from on high.'

'Mom.'

'Right.'

Takashi unbuttoned his black leather jacket to remove a letter from the inside pocket. He handed it to Taggart while the boy was enthusing, 'What a great jacket.' He touched the leather trousers and added, 'Takashi, some riding-gear! I haven't seen that before.'

He laughed. 'And I've got two of these suits.'

'Greed is a dreadful sin. Not like you at all. Repent. You could save yourself if you gave one of them to me.'

'Hell for leather, eh? I suppose I had better let you save me from myself. One *is* for you.'

'You're kidding me?'

'No, I bought them when we were in Milan and your mother was having a splurge at Armani. Not a word to her. She says I spoil you worse than she does.'

'You do. And I for one think it's a good thing! Thanks, Taka, you really are an improvement on an older brother. You don't give me half the trouble a brother would.'

Takashi pointed to the leather storage-bags on the motor-cycle. Taggart jumped up, pulled out the leather biker's jacket and enthused about it. He stripped himself of his and put the new one on, all in one movement. Then he went for the trousers and found a small bush to change behind. He would get back into th: clothes the boys called 'standard change' before heading for school again.

'How's Mom? Is she coping all right?'

'Admirably. You've heard nothing here?'

'No, nothing. And so what if we do? I know it all anyway. I wish she would realise I'm no longer a baby. God, if she only knew that I'm one of the few boys in my year that's not a virgin, maybe she'd be less worried about me.'

'Good God, Taggart, this is not the time for true confessions! She would never stop worrying about you. Or forgive Kurt and me for helping you over your first sex-hurdle without her permission.' They both began to laugh. Memories were made of this.

The boy suddenly looked pensive. He said, 'You know, when I see some of the other fellows' fathers at school, I think of Papa. I miss him a lot. But I'm never sad, because we had such good times together. Mom really picked a good dad for me. Tell her not to worry about me, Takashi. I've got it together. That's the way they brought me up. That's the way I am.'

'Than I can reassure her that you are not worrying about anything?'

'Not a thing. I think about my mom and hope she's being tough and cool about things, but that's all. I don't even worry about my Latin or my Greek. Well, I wouldn't, would I? I expect the top mark of my division. I keep telling her she'll either win or she won't win, but she will have given her best shot. Just like if you're in Field at school.'

He tore open the envelope and began reading Cheyney's letter. Takashi sensed an unusual quiet come over the boy after he had finished reading. He watched Taggart place the letter in his pocket. They remounted and rode across the English countryside to Le Manoir Aux Quat' Saisons for one of Monsieur Blanc's gourmet lunches. Kurt Walbrook had imparted to his son his appreciation of fine French cuisine. The boy had a cultivated palate, which made school meals a torture to him. A pub-lunch wouldn't do if he was out of school.

After a sumptuous meal Takashi and Taggart lay on the grass under a spring sun. Several minutes went by before Takashi said in his usual gentle manner, 'You can tell me what's wrong, you know.'

'How do you know anything is?'

'Well, I have known you since you were a little fella, Taggart. You are not an anxious boy, but today I feel an air of strain around you. Only since you saw your mother's letter. So something in it has disturbed you.'

They lay there with their eyes closed and let the sun warm them. After several minutes he passed the letter over to Takashi. It was a natural thing for the boy to do. There was nothing in it that he didn't already know.

Cheyney had written to Taggart that she had seen Grant Madigan. That his natural father and she were going to do a 'Grant Madigan Talks To' show. She wanted Taggart to hear the news from her. She did not intend to tell Grant about his having a son, not until Taggart wanted her to, and the boy wanted to meet his father. That had always been their plan. She was still abiding by it. Nothing had changed, there was no rush for him to do anything. The letter was only to put him in the picture. If he wanted to talk to her about it, she had arranged for him to use the Housemaster's private telephone.

There were, since Kurt Walbrook's death, only three people who knew

349

that Grant Madigan had fathered Taggart Fox: Cheyney, Taggart and Takashi. Now, just as when Kurt had been alive, none of them had any qualms about talking openly about Grant. Takashi could not understand why anything in the letter about Grant and Cheyney meeting should cause Taggart to become suddenly anxious.

'Takashi, I've got a secret. I've never had a serious secret that I've kept all to myself before. One that I have not told to another living soul. I've always shared them with either you, Papa or Mom. Most of the time all of you. Of course I've had childhood secrets, I've kept to myself some things I've done, like all boys, but . . .'

'Hey, Taggart, that's OK. You're entitled to have your own private world, we all do. I'm just here if . . .'

'Takashi, I'd better tell you. I know I'll feel better for it. It's not causing me anxiety exactly. It's more like not knowing which piece on the chessboard to play next. I'm going to win, no matter what. It's a matter of which move to make next. A chap does want to play the game correctly.'

Man and boy were now sitting up and facing each other. Takashi was thinking about all the little scrapes he had gotten this young man out of since he was a five-year-old. He instinctively felt this was one the boy would have to get out of himself. He was, however, ready to listen and help if he could.

'You're not upset about Grant and your mom meeting, are you, Taggart?'

'No, not exactly. It's just that Mom is being so cagey about *my* meeting him.'

'You want to, don't you?'

'That's the problem. I *have* met him.'

That really took him by surprise. They looked at each other. Takashi could see the immediate relief in the boy's face at having told his secret. 'Maybe you had better tell me about it.'

'He doesn't know I'm his son. I didn't tell him. Talk about a lucky accidental meeting! When Papa died, the thing that helped the most to take away the pain of losing him was that I knew that I still had a father. Another father. After Papa's death, I started thinking about that other father more.

'About a year later, when I was thirteen, during a long leave, I went to stay at my best friend Puggy's country house. You know his dad is a Cabinet Minister, and his mom writes. And his grandfather – well, you know his grandfather the art historian.

'It's great to go there. They've always got lots of famous people staying, coming and going, in and out of the house. Fate, or my good luck, or whatever you want to call it, decreed that Puggy and I should meet and pal up with – guess who? – Grant Madigan. I never knew until then that he was a great friend of Puggy's father. Gee, Takashi, was I surprised. I sort of didn't have a chance to get all emotional about it right then and there because there were so many people in the room. I had to admit that he was so terrific, right off the bat, so I just sort of kept studying him.

'He's like a character out of one of the comic strips some of the fellows at school like to read. Adventure-comic strips. He's like a soldier of fortune. I thought about Mom and what they'd been like together. I couldn't exactly imagine it, but I guessed it must have been terrific. There was something else – the way the women reacted to him. Boy, I thought, my papa was a lady-killer. But this guy . . . I'm his son and one day I'm going to be a free agent and dazzle women like that!

'I was going to tell Mom about meeting him, but I didn't. I don't even know why. She was busy making the big move on New York and getting back into the commercial art world, trying to get established. And then she was getting all that publicity about her and Andy Warhol, and when I was with her in those days it was always so new and exciting, all the things we were doing. New York, getting to know it, the artists, the museums, the studios we visited. I sort of got distracted, and didn't feel like getting into a scene where, if I told Mom, she might get all emotional about it. So I sort of left it alone.

'Then, during the next two years, while Mom was shooting for the top, I spent more time with Puggy and his family, and Grant Madigan was there a great deal because he was working on three programmes that included Puggy's dad, his grand-dad, and the former Prime Minister, Ted Heath. He was good to us, let us watch the way the programmes were shot, and he seemed to take a lot of trouble with us. He really liked us. He took us out fishing a couple of times. Once he flew us to Scotland, another time we went to Paris with him. He couldn't get over how well I knew Paris, or my French. Once he hugged me, gosh it felt good, Takashi. Like coming home.

'I began to realise that I was actually coming to love my own father. And I wasn't able to tell the man. Gradually I began to understand that I was concealing it from him because I have this desire to be loved by him for what I am, me, Taggart, before I make any claim on him to love me as a son. You can understand that, can't you, Takashi?

'Yes, of course I can. The important thing is that you should not worry yourself into thinking you've lied to anyone, because you haven't. Your mom and Kurt, for as long as I can remember, have always told you: when you're ready, when it's what you want. And how you do it is up to you.'

'I hadn't thought of it that way.'

'Well, think about it that way, and be proud of yourself and your secret.'

351

In a burst of relief and gratitude, the boy threw himself at Takashi and gave him a hug. Takashi pulled him up to his feet. They were both all smiles and happy again.

For a brief moment, sadness killed the light in the boy's eyes. He sighed and said, 'Don't think I'll ever love Papa any the less because I've met my dad, I could never do that.'

'It never crossed my mind.' He tapped his watch with his index finger and announced. 'I don't dare to bring you back late. We have to ride, boy.'

Taggart threw an arm across Takashi's shoulder and said, 'I'm so much like my papa. He taught me so well, how to live and laugh, and not to fret. He used to always say, "Spare yourself the agonising over life, Taggart. You have better things to do and live for."'

'Kurt was right about most things, and in many ways you are like him,' said Takashi as he mounted the Harley.

'My dad and my mom, together after all these years,' mused Taggart. 'Is it too wild, too crazy to think . . . Oh never mind.'

'To think what Taggart?'

'Nothing. It's just that they're both so great, I don't see how they can't fall in love again. Well I suppose at their age that doesn't happen any more.'

The boy shrugged his shoulders, and Takashi laughed over the arrogance of youth. Was it a possibility? he wondered.

'I don't suppose we could get a doggie-bag of Raymond Blanc's gourmet tit-bits to take back to school.' A big smile broke across Taggart's face. He was fully himself again. The anxiety was gone. Takashi cut the motor and together they convinced the kitchen that it was essential that an Eton boy-bag be prepared since a doggie-bag was out.

Takashi thought a great deal about Kurt and Cheyney on his ride back to London. How they had got it so right for their boy. He only wished that Kurt could have seen what he had that day: a boy metamorphose into a young man. A fifteen year old, mature way beyond his years, the heir to one of the greatest art collections in the world and a great fortune, who had a foundation secure and stable enough to take him out into the world. It might have been more 'interesting' to be like Hamlet, who made a mess of having two fathers, but Taggart's way was more practical.

He found it mildly ironic that mother and son, without their knowing it, had jointly resolved to face whatever they must now that the spotlight was to be put upon them.

Chapter 38

'Help me, help me! Don't leave me. Not like this. I knew nothing about it.'

'Cheyney, wake up. Wake up, Cheyney. It's all right. You're safe. Just a nightmare. Sara, go get her a drink. Bob, call her maid. Cheyney.'

She woke from her ordeal with a start. She sat bolt upright, trying to catch her breath. Grant Madigan took her in his arms and tried to calm her. 'It's just a nightmare.'

Still lost somewhere in her dream, she pounded her fists against his chest: 'No, no.'

Grant pushed her away from him. He shook her as hard as he could, 'It's a dream, Cheyney. You're OK, safe here with friends. Now snap out of it.'

The fright disappeared. She was out of her dream, and collapsed against Grant's chest. 'It was that horrible dream again. Will it ever stop?'

She felt the beat of his heart against her ear, the comfort of his arms, and raised herself just enough to gaze into his eyes. Her face was ashen, still full of fright. He couldn't bear to see her like that. He crushed her to him in his arms and kissed her, wanting to protect her from her dreams, drive out all her inner demons, the devils that were haunting her.

His kiss brought her back to reality. She gently extricated herself from his arms. 'I am so embarrassed. Please, I'm all right. I'll be fine in a few minutes. It's a recurring dream. When it comes, it always horrifies me.' She looked up. Bob and her maid were hovering over her. Sara handed her a glass of water, her maid rushed forward with a shawl. Cheyney covered her eyes with her hands for a few moments. She could only apologise. She noticed Sara and Bob watching Grant Madigan, faintly puzzled. He did look concerned and embarrassed. That kiss, maybe?

Back in control, she tried to make light of the nightmare. 'It's a lurid recurring dream. I've lived with it for years, and it never gets better. Sometimes it's about Barry Sole. Sometimes the star is Andy Warhol. Always about the art world gone crazy. Me getting murdered, a different way in every dream. I am sorry to inflict it on you. It haunts me like some spectre from my past. It's always so vivid. Too real. It always upsets me beyond reason. Like a child's first horror picture.'

Cheyney downed her water in one swallow. Instant revival. She turned to Grant. Only half aware of what she was doing, she reached for his hand, held it and said, 'I think we could all use a drink. Will it interfere with the filming? Have you got your lighting reorganised?'

'No. But a drink would be great,' he answered, extricating his hand from hers as unobtrusively as possible.

Cheyney told the maid to bring champagne and a jug of fresh peach-juice. The camera and sound men joined them on the terrace. They were ready to continue filming. Grant explained the delay. There would be a short break. It was up to Cheyney and how she felt, whether they would resume work.

They were in Orleans, Massachusetts, in her twelve-bedroomed rambling Cape Cod cottage that clung to the side of a hill and overlooked the blue crescent of the bay. A spectacular view, a haven of calm water, and beyond were the crashing waves and white caps of the Atlantic Ocean. A rugged coastline stretched away to left and right of her property. It was secluded, the right setting for their interview. There was even a private funicular that ran from the lowest terrace of the house through the scrubby, wind-swept pines, mountain laurel and other New England flora, down to the beach and into the boathouse.

The quiet and isolation, away from her active working life, distanced her from the day-to-day progress of the investigation by the Washington people and from the media, who were by now printing anything they could unearth to keep the story alive. Seclusion was essential if Cheyney Fox was to relax and open up, reveal herself before their cameras.

A chill seemed to be blowing in off the ocean. Far out across the water, fog was gathering just above the wave-tops. They watched it slowly roll in towards the bay and change the seascape. They moved into the house.

The drawing-room was huge: two large stone fireplaces at either end of the room, and a sixty-foot wall of windows opening out on to the ocean view. It was comfortable and spaciously homey, yet supremely elegant. There was a concert-size grand piano, a half-dozen cosy sitting areas, each merging into the other to make one vast living-room of polished bare boards and scattered oriental carpets. Early American wing chairs and Queen Anne sofas and furniture mingled with deep, over-stuffed, floral chintz-covered chairs and settees. Imari pots, bases for lamps that issued soft warm light through large, cream-coloured silk shades. Over-sized bowls of other types of antique Japanese porcelain were filled with aromatic pot-pourris. Books lined walls otherwise punctuated with modern masters: Picasso, Clifford Still, Miro, Jasper Johns, Acton Pace, Hans Hoffman.

Two days' shooting so far. It was going well enough, but only just. It was not all Cheyney Fox's fault. Grant seemed to be having trouble getting into the stride of this interview. The crew gossiped about it; no one could quite put a finger on what was wrong. It seemed all there, but it wasn't – not yet, anyway. It needed something to make it take off . . . And then suddenly, while the house-man, Ahara, was pouring their drinks, they all sensed a change in the atmosphere. A gathering tension, as if before a storm. Just what was needed. The crew, Bob, Sara, and especially Grant Madigan, picked up on it at once. Only Cheyney seemed oblivious to it.

Grant and his team were old hands at this work. For more than a dozen years, they had travelled the world and shared some extraordinary times together. They were super-sensitive to that moment when mediocrity, the unacceptable, that is no good to anybody, dies and greatness is born. They said nothing, but put each other on the alert with their eyes.

Cheyney, still filled with anxiety after her nightmare, was putting up a front to cover her feelings. She felt rather exposed for having been caught in thrall to her bad dream. Restless, she kept wandering around the room. The delicious combination of champagne and peach juice took the edge off her unease. She took pleasure in seeing all her guests draped around the room, drinking and enjoying themselves. She was not unaware of how much they were trying to put her at her ease so she would come off well on camera.

She sat down at the opposite end of the Queen Anne sofa from Grant Madigan. She started talking, this time really talking to them as they had not heard her talk before.

'I really hate that dream. I hate being the captive of my past. And yet I know we all are. You Grant, Sara, Bob, all of us.

'I'm a woman with a past that will always stay imprinted on me. I used to wish that I could just shrug it off, like a snake sheds its skin. I'd always known, ever since I was a young woman, that what you are, what you do, how you live, ergo the identity you create for yourself, is what sticks to you. It never made me cautious, concerned about who I was or what I was, what I should or I shouldn't do. I guess I sensed a solid core within myself that knew the basics of right and wrong. I saw the world as a big wonderful place and life an adventure to be lived. Beauty and passion were out there ready to receive me. And so, out I went, though totally unprepared to face it. It was there, life, to be lived, and I was going to live it. Out of gratitude for the privilege of just being alive, I was going to make what contribution I could to life for all that it was giving me.

'The years roll by. Suddenly you have a past. An identity. When I was younger, before I met the man I married I used to think: I wish I could be like that snake, and wriggle out of that past and identity of mine. Now, I wouldn't want to, even if I could.'

355

She rose from the sofa to refill her glass and realised that the cameras had been rolling. The sound being recorded. She just looked at the crew, and smiled when they signalled thumbs up. She saw the look of approval in Grant's eyes and touched his shoulder – her first real sign of affection – as she walked past.

'Cheyney, something's happening. Just go with it. Keep on the way you're talking. Don't hold back now. We're beginning to know you. We will cut and edit, and you can have approval of the finished product before it goes on screen. But just keep opening up to us.'

She understood. He wanted her, or at least he made her feel he wanted her. His warmth, his enthusiasm, warmed her, gave her that same old one to one feeling she had yearned for with him for so long. She felt herself opening up to him. A flower blossoming in the sun.

Cheyney rose from her chair and went to look out the window across the bay. With her back to her guests, she said, 'That horrible dream, it's made me angry. I don't deserve such a nasty dream to be part of my life. I was a part of the downside of the art world in the sixties. I made my own special contribution to it, as you all well know and as the art-history books have recorded. And, whatever the reason, I don't seem to have resolved a certain conflict about my part in that world in those bad old days. And, believe me, they were bad for me twenty years ago. Not even after surfacing in the forefront of the art world, as I've had the luck to do these last few years, and telling my own version of the part I played in Andy Warhol's career, and my contribution to Pop Art – none of it appears to have done anything to still my recurrent me-and-the-art-world nightmare. One does not need to be a Carl Jung to figure out that conflict and guilt, no matter how many times slain, are still managing to surface, if nowhere else in my life, in those horrible nightmares.'

She turned back to face her guests. 'There are many upsides to that world that make it a positive and valuable one. I don't want you to think that there aren't. I just wish I dreamed about them. Art – the creative world – has been my life, my magnificent obsession, just as it was my husband's. Only I never admitted that to myself until after his death, when I returned to – as the media phrased it – "conquer" that world.'

'What was it that made you return?'

Ahara filled glasses again and Cheyney walked across the room and sat down opposite Grant. Something was sparking between them, if even just for the camera's eye. It was as if the other people in the room had vanished.

'Two things, actually. My magnificent obsession with art and dealing rose once again from the ashes of my husband's obsession, and Kurt's legacy to my son and me.

'When Kurt Walbrook died he left us everything. He had been setting

356

me up, strengthening me, hardening me to the world of business in art, long before I even knew about it. I owe him everything for grooming me to be the art-dealer I am today. He did it first for me, then for himself, and ultimately for us so that we could share his life to the fullest. He trusted me to do the right thing for him. To serve his passion for art. To serve those generations of collectors who formed the Walbrook Collections, when he was alive and after his death. He was a wealthy man who lived his whole life in a rich and beautiful world, and swept me and my son into it. He made our lives even more than that, exciting yet secure, and he loved us. We were a family rooted in his love for us.'

Grant Madigan was moved by the tremor of emotion in her voice. The look of love in her eyes for a dead husband who had obviously given her everything a woman could ever want from a man. His female audience would admire Cheyney Fox, if only because she had been loved and adored on a grand sale. But would they sense, as he did, that love Kurt as she might have, he had never been Cheyney Fox's *grande amour*? 'We were a family rooted in *his* love for us.' A dead giveaway. Another glance passed between Cheyney and Grant. In that flash of recognition that can pass between two people, he knew she had waited all those years for him. They were still in love. The realisation was a distraction he could ill afford on camera. He zeroed in on her words, trying, for the moment, to set his own emotions aside.

'And most of all he gave me my chance to be whole and strong and a vibrant, courageous human being. I grabbed that gift with both hands and have been running with it ever since.'

'Right to Washington?' asked Grant Madigan, composed now, and every inch the professional, a mischievous twinkle in his eye.

'If Washington will have me, that's where I'm going.'

'Your nomination seems to have caused turbulent reactions in the art world. You have been conspicuously silent about several serious accusations about you, your husband and your lifestyle until this interview. Why have you decided to speak out now?'

'Because I'm tired of being good and quiet and letting the world take its pot shot at me without my telling it the way it really was. I don't care what they say about me. I guess I do care what they say about my husband, and a brave young son whose first reaction to my nomination and our being exposed to the media world was, "Go for it, Mom."

'My husband was, even for me, a controversial kind of man. Someone I had to come to terms with. We had in our life together only one big difference of opinion: his befriending of former Nazis. But that did not make him an anti-semite, it did not make him a Nazi, it did not make him a thief or receiver of stolen art treasures. Nor does it mean that he condoned what they did. I can utterly refute these accusations made in or out of print about Kurt Walbrook in an attempt to besmirch his name and my character, because I was his wife. It won't do, you know. All this gutter press trying to smear me. The dirt won't stick because Kurt, quite simply, was a man who made no judgements on people. I was a woman who did, and especially on some of his powerful German and Austrian friends. Both of us made a constructive decision to agree to differ on the subject. During my married life, I remained civil to those people. Civil, and nothing more.

'A Rembrandt, two Renoirs, a Hellenistic bronze statue of Hercules photographed and catalogued in a Dutch museum brochure dated 1938, known to have disappeared during the German occupation of that country, were donated to a museum in Austria by Kurt Walbrook. Would you like to comment on that, Miss Fox?'

'No, Mr Madigan, don't ask me about that part of my husband's life. Nor about the paintings that were supposedly the foundation of my husband's collections. I know they're said to have been stolen from museums by the Nazis, the confiscated property of Jews put to death in concentration camps. You must take my word when I tell you I have had every one of them investigated. So have several foreign agencies: the CIA, Mossad, M15. There is no hard evidence of the truth of their origins. If ever any turns up, I will happily relinquish them to their former owners, in the name of my husband. But it will never happen. We must leave it at that, Mr Madigan. That is my first and last statement concerning the matter. Not because of any cover-up, but because I don't want my husband's reputation muddied with untruths and speculation. There's been enough of that.

'Kurt Walbrook was one of the great patrons of the arts of this century. His contributions all around the world were magnanimous, on a scale no other private person has ever matched. His museums, his travelling exhibitions, have greatly benefited the world. You might consider one day doing a posthumous profile of him. This one, however, is of me.'

'Cut. That was great, Cheyney, really great. Look, can I speak to you in private for a moment?' asked Grant as he propelled her across the room.

They withdrew into her sitting-room where he confided in her, 'I think I had better level with you, Cheyney. I know the secret reasons, as well as the obvious ones, why you are so well received in high places all over Europe as well as here in the States. Why you have powerful friends in the intelligence agencies. Why you're under the protection of some very grateful people, like my friend Irving Kirshner. I would like you to talk on camera about all those people you helped during the years you were married to your husband. All the Nazi treasures you did see, and did lead various agents to, that were eventually returned at least to the families of the original owners, or their country. Maybe you could say something about the several Nazis who have been convicted of crimes against humanity.'

'Impossible, Grant. Out of the question. It would be putting my own life and my son's in danger. My condition for helping was always that I should remain anonymous. The fact that you have that information frightens me. I would rather be called a Nazi sympathiser than have that information revealed.'

'It would be a brilliant character-reference for you. Win over lots of doubting Thomases.'

'Out of order. It could also get me killed. You must promise me never to reveal what you know, to anyone.'

Grant had to admire her courage. He, older and wiser himself, was moved by the life Cheyney had made for herself within her marriage. She had hinted there had been a dark side to it, though she gave nothing specific away as to what it was. Over the years Grant had heard about Kurt Walbrook from several of the man's former mistresses. Women still in love with the memory of Kurt Walbrook. He had woven a spell around them that had spoiled them for loving any other man. Grant sensed that was not the case with Cheyney. He could only assume she had risen to a sexual life that answered her husband's strong and bizarre erotic demands. The very idea of the carnal Cheyney with Walbrook excited desire for her in Grant. He placed his hands on her arms and drew her to him. He felt her tremble against him. Not taking her eyes from his, she firmly removed his hands and stepped back. There was no embarrassment, no anxiety involved. Just a firm gesture of retreat. He grazed her cheek with the back of his hand and said, 'OK, then, the subject is closed. I will do what I can to ensure the files are buried so deep in Washington you need not never worry again.'

They returned from the sitting-room. Cheyney went to stand by the fireplace. Grant stood a few feet away from her. She waved a hand at the camera man to let him know she was ready when he was. Then, turning back to Grant, she said, 'My husband picked me up out of the gutter, you know. Long before I even knew he was doing it. I only found out about it a year after his death. A friend confessed she had helped him help me.

'I haven't, until now, found it easy to talk to you on camera, Mr Madigan. But, as this interview has progressed, I have come to realise this is my only chance to speak out about how the circumstances and the environment of one's life can affect one's pattern of behaviour. How, for example, I got into the gutter. What it's like being there. What it took to get out.'

She told her story: her pathetic little successes, the failure of her gallery. She named Tony Caletti as her blackmailer. She told what was behind

Andy Warhol and his Campbell's soup can paintings. The horror of being down-and-out, penniless and broken-spirited, emotionally unbalanced, in New York City. About the extraordinary love of a man who could wait years for her to heal herself, solve her problems. Who could watch her begin her life again and grow secure within herself, and be able once more to leave her years of obscurity and move out into the world again. How his patience never wavered while he waited for her to choose to make a life with him.

Moved by her story, Grant Madigan could not but wonder at his former inability to involve himself with Cheyney Fox's life. All qualms about that were now gone. He found his way into her monologue. It became their dialogue. He was able to lead her on with the right questions and comments into riveting revelations about the art world and her place in it, her life as the wife of Kurt Walbrook, as a woman and mother of her time. Why she wanted the job the President had offered her.

The interview was going at a rocketing pace. Only once did it falter. Grant Madigan had begun a question, 'Miss Fox, you have had only one son, and he has retained your maiden name. Why did you . . . ?'

Cheyney interrupted him, 'That is not true. An oversight in your research, I am afraid.'

She spoke not unkindly. She surprised him not by the news that there had been another son, Andrew, but by the pain in her voice and in her eyes when she added, 'Even now, after all these years, the death of my baby son in a hideous accident is a loss that is still unbearable for me. In that, I am no different from any other mother who has lost a child. My children are the most precious thing in my life. Yes, even the boy who is dead, vanished from my world, still lives on in my heart. Please, leave me at least the privacy of my love for my children. Both of them.'

Grant Madigan had to take a break. Although she remained composed and in control, he felt her pain too acutely to go on. It grew dark. They lit the fires and turned on lamps, adjusted film-lighting. The pause was a brief one. Momentum must not be lost.

The cameras were rolling once again when, sitting opposite Grant Madigan, she admitted, 'I know I am a survivor on a grand scale. That I am a most unusual woman, even for these times. But I didn't start out wanting to be an unusual woman. Life made me that way. And now, by God, I love who I am and what life did to me.'

Grant Madigan had to fight back tears for this woman he had once abandoned so ruthlessly because he had been unable to love the old, vulnerable, failed Cheyney. He felt himself slipping into a new kind of love for the woman standing before him who had conquered adversity and come back a winner.

'And, Cheyney Fox, if you could wish for one thing, what would that be?' The deceptively benign probe, often inserted to close a Madigan interview.

The camera caught her pensive look and the slow breaking of a smile across her lips. 'To begin all over again. To call out, "Come back, Deanna Durbin, come back." ' She gave a brief laugh. 'I suppose that does call for some explanation.'

The camera panned away from Cheyney's face and in on Grant Madigan. It caught the glint of amusement on his lips, the controlled smile on the handsome rugged face.

'Oh, how I squirmed in my seat at the cinema as she sang her way into the hearts of dashing, world-weary heroes, who fell for her seductive voice and her pubescent sweetness and light. She could move mountains, bring off miracles, and always get her man with that voice and that innocence, all that dormant sexuality, reined in under girdles and bra, and pinched-in waist, and demure costumes topped off with a saucy hat here and a spikey heel there.

'That, Mr Madigan, was the stuff I was made of when we first met in a rainstorm many years ago. And, although I blush to think how shallow a woman I was in those days, there is still in me something that cries out, "Come back, Deanna Durbin. Remind me of your good celluloid self. Let me confess that what you stood for I never had."

'I want to tell her and the world how painful it is, how cruel and heartbreaking, to be not her but me. I know, too well, that it's better to be a winner than a loser, on top rather than under the heap. Because the crawl up the slippery slope is lonely and hurtful. Having done it twice, I should know.

'Mr Madigan, I can still watch her on the late-night movie and be reminded, forty years on, even with all my dreams and innocence lost, that to escape into one of her films and be shown how it might have been, still gives one a breather, a kind of hope. It took me a lifetime of pain and pleasure, a great deal of living, to forgive her her perfect, sugared little world – and myself for being intimidated by it.'

'Cheyney Fox, what you are telling us, then, is that your experiences have transformed what you claim was your ordinariness. Is that right?'

'Yes, I guess I am. Standing in the limelight, with all my mistakes showing, and having them fed back to me by the media, is a dreadful experience. But it makes me see that, all through my first foray into the art world, I lugged around all those old Hollywood values of mid-America, expectations of emotional comfort and success; the art-boy meets art-girl version of love. Recognition through experience of the dark side of the universe leaves me shattered by my own ignorance. It is grossly unfair for the media to use the woman of then against the Cheyney Fox of now.'

Cheyney's piquant speech to Grant Madigan induced an even stronger emotional truthfulness. It came over in combination with her beauty and sincerity to show her as someone overwhelmingly impressive. And that was all the public needed, all they wanted. Cheyney Fox, a star in her own right. For fifteen minutes? Longer, maybe.

Chapter 39

Grant Madigan, won over completely by her courage and inner strength, felt himself falling in love with her in a way he had never done before. The filming completed, he watched his crew crowd around her. He had only to see their reaction to her and the interview to know the public would take to Cheyney Fox. But he had his doubts about the establishment, the powers-that-be who vote on such matters. What might they think when viewing a powerful and fascinating personality such as hers? Might they find her in the end too sensational an individual, insufficiently stereotyped, to receive security clearance for the most prestigious position in the American art world? Grant had been around long enough, seen enough, to be concerned for Cheyney's chances of winning once their interview had gone out.

The team broke away from her to congratulate Grant. 'Dynamite,' said Harry, pumping his hand. Bob took longer over his enthusing. Sara told him they were great together, and, 'I'm wiped out by her "Come back, Deanna Durbin".' So was Grant. He intended to use that segment as his opening gambit in the television profile of Cheyney Fox and the art world.

At last they gave him a chance to say something to Cheyney. He went to her and, placing an arm around her shoulders, he lowered his head to kiss her with great tenderness. He told her how wonderful she was. How much he had learned, not only about her but about himself, in the last few days with her.

Every night while staying at the cottage they all dressed for dinner. Cheyney had surprised them when she suggested they bring dinner jackets. She explained that she was in the habit, no matter how busy or traumatic her day might have been, always to dress for dinner, even when she dined alone. A habit formed while living with Kurt Walbrook. Or a throwback to some English colonialist ancestor. She claimed it kept her civilised.

This was their last night in the Cape Cod House. They would all fly back to New York in the morning. The remainder of the work could be done there in the cutting-rooms. They were certain of what they had on the film. It was a Go, with a capital G. The publicity machine was to move into action first thing in the morning. In a week's time the public would have been brain-washed to stay home to meet Cheyney Fox with Grant Madigan. It would go out on prime-time TV across America, in England, and in several European countries.

There was cause for great celebration. Sara dressed to mark the successful completion of their filming in a short, cerise Halston evening dress. Cheyney wore a long black St Laurent tissue-thin cashmere dress, easy as a fine silk bathrobe – and twice as sensuous, because it opened half way up the thigh with every step she took. With it she wore dazzling Art Deco Cartier diamond earrings and bracelets. The men were handsome in their dinner jackets. The wind flowed, the food was delicious, they had music. The evening held the sweet enchantment of success.

Madigan watched, intrigued that his gentle probing had re-awakened in the woman he once briefly loved a sense of self. He was responding to the courage of her investigation of herself, to its emotional truthfulness. During the evening he watched her recognise that her dream had driven her away from loving men and women into using them. He listened to her alcohol-induced confession to Sara of how she once destroyed the love she felt for men, subtly but surely, by re-creating them in an image more suited to the needs of her own ego. He sensed a dimension emerging within her that had been missing in the younger woman he, for too short a time, enjoyed. Only now did he understand that their time together had not been enough. He wanted her, wanted again what they once had.

Talk off-camera had already informed Cheyney of Madigan's never having married, his sadness that he had never made time to have children, the unusual relationship he maintained with women, the desire for family life that he had never indulged: active, ambitious newsmen don't make good husbands.

He found Cheyney now to have those things once lacking in her. A re-kindling of the same erotic feelings he always had for her made it impossible this time round to restrain himself from falling back into love with her.

They were having one last brandy alone together. She watched him swish the Courvoisier around in its finely blown glass, and marvelled that she should love him still, and with no less passion. This man, the natural father of her only son . . . Here was a truth that she could not ignore. She watched him take great swallows of the golden liquid and shamelessly imagined herself absorbing his own luscious liquid. To have again from him those same powerful orgasms that she had experienced while creating the most perfect thing in her life: Taggart, their son.

It was Grant who broke the spell of the moment. 'Cheyney, we had to come a long way apart so as finally to come together. Does that make any sense to you?'

'More than I like to admit.'

She drained her glass. Without taking his gaze from hers, he removed the glass from her hand. The house was provocatively silent, the others having long since gone to bed. The sexual tension building between Cheyney and Grant had not been wasted on any of them.

Lost in their own emotions at so unexpectedly coming together, they chose to remain silent, not wanting anything to intrude on what was happening between them. Grant escorted Cheyney to her room. They made it easy for each other. There seemed no point in doing otherwise.

He opened the bedroom door for her. She took his hand and they stepped into the room together. Suddenly, to him, Cheyney Fox was like the other half of his soul.

For her, all those years without him vanished as if they had never been.

There remained still that same voracious carnal hunger they had always had for each other. Only this time there was to be more. They walked into the centre of the room, Cheyney switching on pools of soft sensuous light that seductively emanated through ivory silk lampshades. The light did nothing to dispel an erotic tension so acute as to be almost painful.

She walked to the foot of the white wolfskin-covered bed, Grant a few steps behind her. With deliberately slow, graceful movements she untied the sash of her cashmere evening dress and slipped it off her shoulders. Grant watched the soft, wickedly sensuous folds of the black, paper-thin woven wool fall seductively down her back, over her curvaceous bottom and to the floor around her feet. Naked save for the Art Deco diamond bracelets around her wrists, she raised her arms and pulled the combs from her hair. She dropped them on the floor.

Grant watched the long black tressses fall to her waist. A mass of silky threads. A voluptuous snare. He walked up to her and grazed his lips across her hair. Placed his cheek against the back of her head for a moment. Before he touched her any further, he begged her, 'Cheyney, love me. I never knew I could ever want anyone to love me as I want you to. This time around, my love for you will never waver. I promise. If we come together as I know we both want us to, I will never leave you. In the past I forced myself to run away from loving you.' He heard the catch in his voice and had to pause to clear it and gain control of his emotions before he could go on. 'We have both come a long way from the people we once were. I promise. I will never leave you again, ever.'

Only then did he place his hands on her naked shoulders. She raised her arms and held them straight out above her hips until they were level with her shoulders. He caressed them down to her diamond-covered wrists with his strong rough hands and the most soft and tender kisses. She trembled with expectation under his touch. Then, with one hand around her bare narrow waist, he pulled her roughly against him. The feel of her naked in

365

his arms spurred his need to possess her. Carnal love took possession of him. He sensed her need for him was as great.

Still in his arms, she made a tight, seductive turn-around to face him. Erotic love, sexual bliss, real love, all she felt for him at that moment, that she had felt for him in the past, all she would ever feel for him in the future, shone in her eyes.

He was overwhelmed by her love for him. He crushed her hard into his arms and kissed her. A hungry, thirsty kiss, as if he had been deprived of such real sustenance all his life, until that very minute. She pulled the jewels from her ears and dropped them on the bed. He kissed her again, deep, luscious kisses, where Cheyney and Grant lost themselves in the passion those kisses were generating. Now he licked and sucked one ear-lobe and then the other, her neck, her breasts; sexy, tantalising, erect nipples. Once again, mouths opened and tongues teased while she pulled his dinner jacket from his shoulders, undid the black satin bow tie and slid it from around his neck. Impatient to see him naked, feel his skin against hers, the taste of him in her mouth, she ripped open his shirt and fumbled with his trousers.

She wanted Grant, but found it impossible to tell him so when she could show him just how much. Acknowledge to him that she believed he loved her, now and forever. And so she took over. Together they undressed him, and they lay down on the soft, long-haired white fur. They spoke to each other with lips and tongues, caressing hands. No words. For them words would always be superfluous to feelings. Nothing could still their hearts, even though their animal passion for each other, their erotic extremes, blotted out all else in their need for sexual oblivion.

Sixteen years of sexual excesses, all erotic fantasies explored, of accepting the overt libertine in themselves, and offering sex to each other that enticed, thrilled, frightened, for the power that it wielded on each other, led them through orgasms and ecstasy all through the night. Nothing was held back. All was given and accepted in the name of sex and Eros and depravity. Pure carnal love.

Cheyney's eyes fluttered open against a tide pulling her down into warm luscious sleep. She heard herself whimper, and the unmistakable sound of a woman in the throes of sexual ecstasy. The short quick breaths and moans. He was holding her tight in his grasp, his body wrapped around her like a second skin. She felt the hugeness, hardness, of his penis as he slowly moved in and out of her. Long deep thrusts. She felt her vagina contract, sucking him into herself, then releasing him, with a rhythm of her own, still in a half-sleep. She raised her legs and wrapped them around his waist. She placed her arms around his neck and felt him even deeper, as if to the very core of her being. And she woke up.

Her first words to him were, 'I love you. I have always loved you.' And they kissed. 'I have never loved any man as I love you now. Nor belonged to any man as I belong to you.'

'Now and forever,' he whispered in her ear.

He felt her come in a sweeping orgasm, and held back, wanting only to continue to give her pleasure. Have her come again and again, until both were immersed in her sweet streams of pleasure. She called out his name in her throes of ecstasy, and he begged her, 'Say it. Cheyney, say it, "Now and forever." That you love me, now and forever.'

Unable to hold back another orgasm, Cheyney grabbed for Grant's hair with both her hands. She pulled his head back, the better to see his face. Then she kissed him with a wildness that dissolved them both this time. Only then did she say, 'Yes, now and forever.'

Cheyney and Grant recognised each other anew, as soul-mates able to share themselves wholly with each other. They rediscovered a love they had blanked out of their consciousness for sixteen years. And a new life together began for them.

Grant watched Cheyney sleeping, and felt there could not be a better way to live. That he had nothing more in his life to prove. That he was where he wanted to be. Doing what he wanted to do, which was to share his life with Cheyney Fox.

Always a man with goals, he realised they were no longer just for success. Now they were about living and loving with the woman lying next to him. The woman and her son. They were now about marriage, commitment, the norm. Having fun and feeling great and being happy.

Family, a ready-made son, were miraculously already a part of his life. It suddenly dawned on Grant that he knew few facts about the son Cheyney loved and cherished beyond all else. Not even the boy's name or age. What he looked like. Grant was too good a newsman not to sense there was more than just evasion here. He sat up and swung his legs over the side of the bed, curious.

He found the photograph. It was standing in a silver frame on the Queen Anne walnut desk in the sitting-room of the master suite where, after his shower, he chose to dress so as not to wake the still-sleeping Cheyney. He recognised himself in the boy at once. For a moment he thought it was the photograph of himself as a young boy that his mother had always kept by her bedside. Impossible.

Then reality surfaced and he understood. It was Cheyney's son. It was also the boy, Taggart Fox, whom he had become so fond of these last few years. Fox! How stupid he had been. It had never occurred to him that Taggart Fox was Cheyney's son. A newsman's mind was constantly inundated with facts. Some connections just did not get made. Perhaps he

367

had been meant not to make this link. Yet the boy had dropped enough hints. Grant had simply never picked them up. He walked towards the light of the large, many-paned window that overlooked the ocean. He was certain of it. Taggart Fox was his and Cheyney's son.

He felt her arms slip around his naked waist, her head rest upon his back, felt the warmth of her breath against his skin as she told him, 'No photograph does Taggart justice. He is more special than even that excellent photograph of him. And that's not just a mother's pride in her child. You will see when you meet him.'

Grant turned around to face her. She took the photograph from him and looked at it. He retied the terrycloth towel around his hips. Then she didn't know that he had already met their son. He wondered when she would tell him he was the boy's natural father. What the boy already knew. He actually hoped that Cheyney would say nothing for the moment. His feelings were too scrambled for him to respond carefully and correctly. He sensed that Cheyney's were no less so. Time, they needed some time to face this momentous news. All three of them.

Now, for the first time, Cheyney fully appreciated the cruelty she had inflicted upon Grant by denying him the right to choose whether to be a father to Taggart. She had made the mistake of appointing the older Walbrook to act as her son's protector from the best motives. She had always promised herself and the boy that, when the time seemed right, she would introduce father and son to each other. Let them choose whether to become friends. What was she to do about that promise now? Who could have guessed that Grant and Cheyney's love for each other would conquer all. Certainly not her when she denied him his son. She kept silent.

Takashi saw them as they entered the gallery. There was about Cheyney that something extra-special that he only saw in her in those fleeting moments when they were on the edge of oblivion during sex. She radiated that quality now. He felt one swift stab of pain for his loss, and then it was gone. It was only carnal loss. He felt they would love each other from afar. It had been that way before, when she had been married to Kurt Walbrook. It had been enough for him then: it would have to be enough for him now.

Cheyney introduced the two men to each other. Takashi sensed her concern for him. As soon as Grant had gone from the gallery, and they were alone, he put her at her ease. 'Don't say anything. It's obvious. I saw it the very moment you walked in with him. Believe me I am happy for you. I know you're in good hands. His reputation has preceded him. Be happy, Cheyney.'

'And you?'

'The thing about love, we both of us know, is that it lasts. You and I will always be special to one another. Maybe a trip around the world is in order for me. It's standard practice in these situations. I'll stay in touch. Tactfully, though.'

Cheyney wanted to ask him to stay, but she didn't have the heart to. When he kissed her goodbye, she could not hold back her tears. So many endings, so many new beginnings. Everything was changing yet again, and so fast.

For Cheyney and Grant, during the daytime it was business as usual. At night they surrendered themselves to carnal bliss. They discovered afresh a rich and beautiful love for each other. The days passed and Cheyney wanted to tell Grant about Taggart but simply could not find a way. She kept putting it off.

They watched a preview of the programme the day before it was to go out on the networks. Grant watched the woman he loved unreservedly grow pale as she watched, although she remained calm. They were silent with each other for several minutes after the video tape was finished.

'You are the most exciting woman I have ever interviewed. It's a wonderful programme. But I am prepared to withdraw it because I don't think it will help you get the votes of confidence you need to enable you to become the first Secretary of Art for the United States.'

Cheyney surprised him when she said, 'I had little idea, really, who I am, how much I have accomplished, how much I can still give the art world. Not till I saw our interview. I couldn't possibly think of asking you to withdraw it.'

The programme was a virtually unqualified success. It afforded Cheyney, for the first time since the public controversy over her began, some positive appraisal by the media. The telephones at the gallery were jammed with congratulations and offers of directorships and trusteeships of museums in the States and all over the world. Even one she had always coveted in Japan. Takashi rang through from Paris. They talked about it for an hour. Shortly after that call, Taggart rang. He had seen a copy of the tape which she had sent over by courier to the Housemaster. They spoke about it in between tears of pride and joy from her son, who thought both she and Grant were wonderful. At one moment Cheyney thought she would tell him about Grant and herself. But the moment passed, and Taggart was off the line before she could find another. They were both still stuck with their secrets.

The response was so positive, Cheyney and Judd were sure it was going to come off for her. Grant was still uncertain. Then another tremendous blow. A picture of Cheyney on a slime-magazine cover. A grainy photo taken straight off the TV screen. In block letters above: 'Is this woman a murderess because she had an abortion?' A publicised abortion was apparently meant automatically to disqualify any candidate from public office.

They had lost, they knew that. Even if they had not yet heard from Washington. Archibald Head had done his worst. He was a man of his word. Yet still the positive letters and phone-calls kept coming. Everyone marvelled at Cheyney's calm.

Grant could no longer bear not living with Cheyney. He kept his suite at the Plaza, but moved in with her. He refused to be separated from her in these last days of waiting. He gave her many opportunities to tell him about their son but it was something she seemed unable to deal with. As for him, though more than fond of the boy he had met first at a house-party, Grant had never in the past had much time to devote to puzzling out the possible reasons behind the friendship the boy seemed keen on perpetuating. Now, thinking about it, Grant was almost certain that the boy knew him to be his real father.

While looking at yet another photograph of the boy one evening, Grant suddenly recalled his laughter. He knew the sound as that of his own adolescent gaiety reborn. Why had Cheyney kept this from him? Was that the proper question now, or was it not rather: when would she tell him? And what did the boy himself know about his real parents' relationship?

The hard-bitten Madigan was awed by the strangeness of what was happening. Every day he allowed himself to fall a little more in love with this boy he already knew and liked. The moments of hope that Cheyney might volunteer her secret passed. At night, their renewed sexual passion for each other obliterated other considerations.

When she awoke one morning, Madigan was gone. There was a note. 'Stay brave. No worrying.' He would return within a few days to face with her the verdict of the Federal investigations. He loved her. Their lives were now to be led together.

The complications were more with the school than with the boy, because, of course, Taggart had been preparing for this moment secretly for almost two years. It was so reminiscent of how his father Kurt had plotted and waited for Cheyney. But Grant Madigan was not to know that as he stood at the window in the Head Master's office looking across the quadrangle at the tail-coated youths crisscrossing the patches of grass and gravel.

It had taken one cabinet minister, two ambassadors and a call made by the Head Master to Takashi – who, as it happened, was Taggart's guardian – Grant's own international fame, and his good standing with the school, for him to be accorded a meeting with the boy.

Only the thought of easing Cheyney's obvious dilemma kept Grant from bolting from the room. Nervously, he waited to confront the boy he

370

had become so attached to. Grant Madigan had ever known, until now, such emotional turmoil. And he didn't like it one bit.

'Hello, Mr Madigan.'

The sound of the boy's voice served to remind him of how clever, bright and mature Taggart was. Anxiety dissolved in an instant. Grant Madigan turned away from the window to face his son.

'How goes it, Taggart?'

'Great, Mr Madigan. You've met my mom. I could tell you liked her.'

'Yes, Taggart. I sure do like your mom.'

'I mean she's my mom, so I didn't think of her as this famous, glamorous, fascinating woman. Well, not until I saw that programme. I don't see how she can lose, Mr Madigan. My mom's going to be the first Secretary of Art of the United States. And, boy, does she deserve it!'

'Wait a minute, Taggart. I wouldn't be too sure about that. Not everyone is as liberal-minded about fascinating women like Cheyney Fox as you and I are.'

'It's going to happen, Mr Madigan. She's going to win. My mom is going to knock them dead in the art world, just as she did with Andy Warhol, her galleries, the museums she created. My mom's a winner, Mr Madigan, and she is not going to lose this one.'

'I'd like to think you're right, boy.'

'She's OK isn't she? The pressure isn't getting to her?'

'About the nomination? No, I don't think so.'

'Then about what?'

The boy was quick, Grant would give him that. One of the things he liked most about Taggart. 'How much do you know, Taggart? Level with me.'

The boy suddenly flushed pink. And then, unusually for him, was tongue tied. That told Grant what he wanted to know. He walked to the drinks tray on a table in a dark corner of the room and poured a glass of water. Taggart drank it down and placed the glass back on the silver tray. 'Shall I pour you a whisky, Mr Madigan? This is a celebration, I hope?'

'How long have you known, Taggart?'

'Since I was a little boy. Six, maybe seven years old, something like that. I don't remember. I seem to have known you were my father all my life, Mr Madigan.'

'I've known a few days. And only by guesswork. Your mom hasn't found a way to tell me yet.'

'You don't think I was deceitful do you, Mr Madigan? I mean not telling you that I knew you were my dad? I wanted to tell you, really wanted to tell you, but I was afraid to.'

'Afraid I'd run away?'

'I don't know. Maybe. I think it was more that I wanted you to love me, really like me, before I told you. I just wanted it to be the right moment when we all came together and knew each other. I didn't want it to go wrong.'

The boy was clearly flustered. Grant tried to ease things. 'How about that drink you offered me? It is, after all, a great moment meeting your son for the first time, and having him turn out to be a lad you already like.'

The boy beamed. A light came into his face that reflected both pride and an adolescent enthusiasm. He rushed to pour his father a much-too-large shot of whisky.

'It's not going to go wrong, Taggart,' said Grant, accepting it. 'Look, Tagg, I want to marry your mom. I'm very much in love with her. Deeply in love with her. And though I never expected ever to have a son, there is no boy in the world I would rather have for my own than you. I can't pretend to be a father to you the way that Kurt Walbrook has been. You've told me enough about your life with that dad for me to understand he was all the father I have never been to you, and probably never will be. Maybe I can be something else to you. Taggart, I am very proud that you are mine. But it's going to take a lot of getting used – to having an almost grown-up son. A great deal of getting used to for all of us, this getting together as a family.'

'Are you sure you want to take us on?'

Grant took a large swallow of whisky, then said with a smile, 'Yes, Taggart, that I do. And I think we can manage it. More than manage it, Taggart, make a great, rich, wonderful life together. I think we should give it a go. What about you?'

'I think I'm one of the luckiest guys in this school, maybe even alive. I had a wonderful papa. He was one of the most interesting and exciting fathers any guy could have. He never minded talking to me about you, though we did that mostly in private. And then one day he was gone. And that was the most terrible day of my life. The worst thing that had ever happened. The only thing that made it bearable was that I knew I had another dad and it was Grant Madigan, another very special kind of man, as interesting and special as my papa. Everything I had been told about you, had read about you for all those years, told me that.'

The boy's sincerity, the adoration in his eyes for both Kurt Walbrook and Grant Madigan, was touching. It reached down into that core of love within Grant that had until then only known Cheyney Fox. He reached out and placed a hand on Taggart's shoulder. The words would not come. For the moment he was unable to express what he felt for this most remarkable boy. A lump stuck fast in his throat. All he could manage was, 'And when we met?'

'I kept thinking how different a dad you would be to Papa. A completely different kind of man. So American. Much bigger, an adventurer, a rough and tough, sort of hard-bitten kind of a man. Another father to be close to, to look up to for the second time around. Boy, you have no idea how relieved I am that you know I'm your son! I feel very emotional about it.'

With an awkwardness that was touching, Grant Madigan reached out and grabbed Taggart, crushing the boy to him in a huge bear-hug.

He felt the boy hug him back. A moment father and son were never to forget. They fought back tears when they stepped apart and touched each other's cheek affectionately, and smiles crept across their lips.

'How about calling me Grant? I think we could start from there, Taggart. I want to marry Cheyney, as soon as possible, and I want you to be there with us. But, before I can do that, we have one great problem to solve, and that's the reason I'm here. Not because I wanted to find you and know you – although I do, of course, want that very much – but more because your mom has not found the courage to tell me we have a son.

'I think she never expected any more than I did that we might meet and fall in love again. Or that we might have loved each other always but put that out of our hearts while we let the circumstances of our lives sweep us along. I think she's riddled with guilt for not having shared you with me. Guilt is a negative, destructive emotion that she could do without at the best of times. Now, with all this pressure, her life's work laid bare for all the world to judge, and the possibility of losing the art world's plum job, this guilt our love has fostered in her is the last thing she needs.

'I can't convince her of that, but I cannot stand around and watch her suffer trying to find a way to tell me about you. That's really why I am here. To meet you and take you back to your mom, so that we can confront her with the fact that whatever she did has been right for all of us. She's had it hard enough. Let's make it easy for her.'

'You're right, Grant. Guilt sucks.'

Grant began to laugh. Threw back his head and lifted the heaviness from their conversation. The boy laughed too. 'That says it all, Taggart. Let's cut out of here and go tell your mom just that.'

It wasn't easy. But, at last, they were able to get back to America and present themselves to Cheyney. 'Our son and me together, better than words and explanations,' said Madigan.

They who were three could now await as one the world's poor verdict upon the life of Cheyney Fox.